. . . The Fame People . . .

She had to lunch with the Greek in Juan-les-Pins. How she hated his love of ships. Didn't he have enough? Did he have to love them as well? He was the richest man in the world according to the press, but her banker had his doubts. It was rumoured that he'd marry Margery. How many noses that would put out of joint! Especially the Japanese pianist who loved him to distraction. Of course, he wanted Margery because he couldn't have her.

She fingered the strings of pearls that she never took off. They were the second most valuable set of their kind, and their milky glow was famous. They were a challenge in their way because she always had to outshine them. The day people said 'Your pearls are so beautiful,' instead of 'You look beautiful,' was the day she was old.

She prepared to dress for the shipowner. She was Margery Caversham, superstar. She had all the money and power she could ever want.

All she wanted was to die.

Also by Patrice Chaplin

A Lonely Diet
Harriet Hunter
Cry Wolf
By Flower and Dean Street
Having It Away
The Siesta
The Unforgotten
Albany Park
Don Salino's Wife
Another City

Patrice Chaplin

THE FAME PEOPLE

Heinemann · Mandarin

A Mandarin Paperback

THE FAME PEOPLE

First published in Great Britain 1988
by William Heinemann Ltd
This edition published 1989
by Heinemann · Mandarin
Michelin House, 81 Fulham Road, London SW3 6RB

Mandarin is an imprint of the Octopus Publishing Group

British Library Cataloguing in Publication Data

Chaplin, Patrice
The fame people
I. Title
823'.914[F]

ISBN 0 7493 0063 9

This novel is a work of fiction.
Any resemblance to actual events or persons,
living or dead, is entirely coincidental.

Printed in Great Britain
by Cox & Wyman Ltd, Reading

. . . The Fame People . . .

. . . Chapter 1 . . .

Every day she woke up and felt his dying. No shrink had so far been able to relieve her of this morbid ritual. Consciousness came for Margery Caversham with the sound of the first shot and she'd feel the gaping wound tearing apart her breast. The second filled her head with a watery blood and the world with all its trivial catastrophes receded. There were two more shots. The liver exploded. Dino's dying was part of her body; some days she felt it was her payment for still living. She told nobody, because she disliked the fanciful.

The maid from Dover brought in the breakfast. The staff shortage was now acute in France. Because of some law against the wealthy, work permits for foreigners had been withdrawn and there were not enough staff. That's why everyone went to funerals these days. As you paid your last respects you bid for the corpse's staff over the open grave: a deft financial gesture secured a butler, a chauffeur. The trouble was the other families bid openly against you. The clergy weren't keen on these fancy hand signs – was it some new religion practised only by the wealthy? So although Margery would never, in the old days, have chosen this fresh-faced dullish girl, even for menial duties, it was she who now stood in the bedroom. The maid from Dover had moved from château to palace and now to Margery. Because of death she was never out of work.

'Bring me the *Herald Tribune*, the *New York Times* and *Newsweek*. And bring me a bottle of Vichy water. Always keep the refrigerator in my dressing room filled with Perrier, Vichy and Henniez.'

Margery looked after herself. She drank two litres of mineral water daily, didn't smoke, rarely drank, walked a lot. After a good breakfast of fresh yogurt, fruit and muesli, she got to work on her face and body with Laszlo's products, especially prepared for her. He would give her a million dollars down every year if she would endorse the new beauty range, but Margery didn't need a million dollars. She worked out in her private gym behind the bathroom. She did all her self-improvement secretly. After a needle-point icy shower to close her pores and tone up her circulation, she dressed in a formal black silk gown and lay back on the bed. She looked at the sky, the woods, the fields, the vines, the river – all hers. Even in winter it was pretty: December and hardly a leaf had turned.

The Château, a country residence in the hills above Cannes, had been built in the early nineteenth century. It still retained its original touches – the shutters, huge fireplaces, oil lamps, raftered ceilings, courtyards, a well. It had always been a family house and Margery tried to keep it that way. Dino had always said he wanted a home, not a stage set. There was nothing forbidding about the Château, except the security exits at the edge of the grounds, and the white carpets downstairs.

The heavy gold metallic wallpaper printed with Beardsley peacocks gave the bedroom a warm glow. Silk Persian carpets in black and gold rested delicately on the black lacquered wooden floor like pedigree pets. Beside the bed stood a Japanese silk screen patterned with ornate dragons and ornamental trees in gold and silver with scarlet berries. She'd spent her wedding night in the large, French-style Napoleonic bed made of cherry wood, and she'd never part with it. The starched linen sheets, hand-stitched by nuns, had been purchased from an obscure shop near Lake Como. Ormolu clocks chimed, each with a distinctive, pleasing voice. The rare, highly prized antique occasional tables stood haughtily on spindly legs like blue-blooded relatives. They held a Louis XVI casket, a Persian second-century necklace, a Ming bowl. Nothing as common as a teacup was ever placed on these tables. The tables amused Margery. They reminded her of her snobbish mother, long since dead. Eau-de-nil muslin drapes sweetened grey daylight and softened glare. Margery's rooms were always well lit and full of country flowers. The doors were tall – the doors of French apartments painted ivory, edged with gold motifs. The shutters painted in matching ivory were stencilled with a glorious gold from Siena.

The maid from Dover brought *Time* instead of *Newsweek* and seemed to think Margery would want her list of the morning's messages. Without reading any, Margery handed it back, saying, 'Only when I ask for them.' The girl seemed reluctant to leave. Some kind of excitement was getting the better of professional deportment.

'Maybe you should read the list, ma'am. I was told–' She couldn't continue.

Margery had forgotten the maid's name. She called them all 'ma petite', which got round the problem. So this girl had seen a celebrity's name on the list and got overexcited. Margery told her to concentrate on the tasks she was meant to do and get those right.

At ten-fifteen Julian, her business manager, made his entrance. Some days he tried a forthright entrance, even a touch of bravado. Today he crept in. Whatever he did displeased Margery. He sat near the bed on Dino's favourite chair, a present from Dali, and murmured the slight rise and fall of the stock market like an incantation. He wore a pale grey linen suit bought off the peg in Cannes and a black roll-necked cotton sweater and conservative black shoes. He played down his body; it was fleshy and soft and he soothed loneliness and sexual frustration with constant secret eating. His hair was black and plentiful, his eyes dark and sombre. He could have been good looking. Margery disliked his aftershave: something in his skin chemistry turned the perfume sickly and cheap. Cheap was never allowed near Margery. She'd always thought, but could never prove, that he had been in love with her husband.

'And now Nestorin will be all over the place,' he said.

Nestorin, the famous baby milk, was good solid stock. 'What do you mean, all over the place?' she asked.

'Last night a factory exploded in Africa. Illegal staff made the milk cheaply, and the safety procedures weren't up to standard. The fumes from the explosion have killed three hundred workers and there are townspeople burned or dead. There'll be a major scandal, madam–'

'Of course there will.' Margery knew the stuff of scandal.

'The stock will go right down. Everybody's selling as a protest–'

Margery was used to hearing bad news. She cut it short with 'My children are all Nestorin. A quarter of a million each. Except Alex.'

'It's a most unpopular holding. Disgrace has put the price down to–' He looked on his list. 'Everybody's selling.'

'Then it's just the time to buy.' She waited but he didn't see the joke. 'A joke, Julian. Get rid of it – I don't want dirty stock. Send some money to whatever fund you think' she said. Julian reacted to tragedy like a woman. 'Next.'

Her four children had a vast network of investments. Dino had always felt safe with gold but she had diversified after his death. Unless the actual planet blew up, her children, whatever happened, would always be rich. Julian murmured the progress of the German mark. Margery told him to call London. She wanted a prominent member of the aristocracy to bid for the Modigliani at Sotheby's the following week.

'I'll go to a million five but let them think a million two. And tell him to let the Sotheby's people know he's bidding on my behalf.'

Julian knew all about that.

'And the maid from Dover. She knows the rules, doesn't she, Julian? She knows she can never sell titbits of my life story to the press?'

Julian was appalled. 'Madam, she has signed the usual agreement, as have all the staff.'

'But it doesn't apply if she leaves this country.'

'Yes, but she doesn't know that, madam.'

'She could go to Venezuela, Julian, and discover she has a literary bent.' South America was the one area of the world where Margery had no control.

'Not the sort,' he said.

'Just the sort,' she replied. 'The dull sort who suddenly think they've missed out on living.'

As Julian crept from the room like a disgraced dog, he could feel her dislike. He closed the door softly, as though on the dying. Margery called him back.

'I want that picture.'

Then she lay back, and the lights on her answering machine flicked on, off. Secretaries took care of all that. She wondered why she disliked Julian. He'd spent his life working for her and the family. Perhaps that was why. Julian's every gesture was a reminder of long service. His smooth financial murmurings were really a cry of 'What about me?'

A pile of scripts waited to tempt her back to the cinema. For no reason, she suddenly thought of Jane Kirkland. She was blonde, apparently, some kind of entertainer, and was running around with Alex, Margery's adored elder son. Jane Kirkland. It was merely a suggestion of a bad thought, no more. But that's the way the terrible things come: a thought, dismissed, then returning. She pressed a buzzer and said, 'Check out this London girl running around with Alex.' She released the buzzer before the secretary could answer.

She had to lunch with the Greek in Juan-les-Pins. How she hated his love of ships. Didn't he have enough? Did he have to love them as well? He was the richest man in the world according to the press, but her banker had his doubts. It was rumoured that he'd marry Margery. How many noses that would put out of joint! Especially the Japanese pianist who loved him to distraction. Of course, he wanted Margery because he couldn't have her.

She fingered the strings of pearls that she never took off. They were the second most valuable set of their kind, and their milky glow was famous. They were a challenge in their way because she always had to outshine them. The day people said 'Your pearls are so beautiful,' instead of 'You look beautiful,' was the day she was old.

She prepared to dress for the shipowner. She was Margery Caversham, superstar. She had all the money and power she could ever want.

All she wanted was to die.

. . . Chapter 2 . . .

Jennifer, the English secretary, tried to catch her as she slid into the back of the silver Rolls. 'What about your messages, ma'am?'

'Not now, Jennifer.' There was no one in the world who couldn't wait. And the silver car purred along the cypress-lined drive to the security gate and then down towards Cannes.

That assumption cost Margery a great deal. When she returned in the evening the deed had been done. Nineteen-year-old Alex had run away to Gretna Green and married Jane Kirkland. It was in every newspaper, on every TV programme, in the world.

Margery was stunned, a rare experience for her. She poured herself an immense drink, not even looking at what it was. 'Why the fuck didn't someone tell me?'

Jennifer, white with terror, said, 'But we tried. I sent the English maid in with the message list first thing. I tried to stop you as you left the house.'

'The English maid!' Margery was aghast. 'To tell me news like that!'

Kay, Margery's eldest child, snatched the list of messages from the secretary. 'It's rumoured that Alex has left London,' she read. 'May be heading for Scotland. He's too young to marry without consent. The London agency telexed it this morning.'

'If only I could call Clifford,' Margery said.

Kay looked worried. 'Clifford?'

'Odets. He'd understand.'

'But, Mummy, he's dead,' said Kay.

'That's what I mean. All the best ones are.'

Kay couldn't see why the American playwright should understand her brother's shotgun wedding especially. Margery had always adored his work: after Dino died, she watched *The Sweet Smell of Success* every night of the week. Kay thought turning to a deceased playwright for help was a sign of shock.

Margery sat close to the log fire with its faintly perfumed smoke and thought of her beloved son. He had such sweetness. 'It's always the ones you love that give you shit,' she said softly.

'There is an upside,' said Kay. 'The girl might be nice.'

'Not a chance,' said Margery.

She looked absently at a painting by Manet. Across from the two small Picassos hung a huge Gauguin. The paintings were so full of life – more, genius. Sometimes she worried that their blaze of energy put the mere mortals in the room at a disadvantage. She'd once stood beside the Gauguin and asked Dino if it put her in the shade. He'd replied, 'Gauguin would have loved you, babe. You're a highly wise, primitive being. You were just born into the wrong background.' He had loathed her aristocratic past.

The room was comfortable and luxurious. Enormous white sofas formed a semicircle around the fire. The Steinway grand piano was closed, its top crowded with framed photographs of family and of special friends from the movie world. The white carpets, indisputably pure as freshly fallen snow, the white walls, heavy white silk drapes, the silver-framed mirrors, all gave the room a special quality. This was real luxury, fragile but forever unblemished – a white world in which the only blackness was Margery. She wore black at all times. Tonight she was still clad in her Courrèges tunic with its short skirt. Even her Courrèges boots were black. The news of her son's elopement had eclipsed the evening beauty ritual after which she usually changed into one of the long flowing deep-black gowns by Chanel. She always pinned a white gardenia at her throat when wearing the otherwise unrelieved black as she had foresworn jewellery, apart from the pearls, in the early days of her widowhood.

The house and terraces were full of white gardenias. There were gardenia bushes all round the house, with creamy-white waxy flowers and glossy dark green leaves. And she, the bereaved goddess, wafted around in a cloud of unique gardenia perfume made to a secret formula in nearby Grasse – the exquisite scent of the flowers was very difficult to capture.

Her daughter Kay wore Joy. The secretary, Jennifer, wore no perfume: it caused an allergic reaction which in that house she kept to herself.

Kay fluffed out her long gleaming hair, black with auburn streaks. She was darker than Margery, olive-skinned with black slanting eyes and lashes so long they almost touched her cheeks, and a firm sensuous body. Margery didn't know much about panthers but her elder daughter sure looked like one – lithe, graceful and cruel.

'I don't want to sound selfish, Mummy, but a million hours ago before the Alex thing I agreed to go down with Guido to hear Callas.'

'Down?'

'He's flying his plane to Milan. I start filming on the 20th. I told them I could ride.'

'You will,' said Margery absently. Four-legged beasts couldn't come in the way of stardom. 'Just make sure they tranquillise whatever you're on.'

Kay put on the brightest lipstick in the world. 'Can I borrow your diamond earrings? The pear-shaped ones. After all, you never wear them.'

At least Kay had fun. Margery's other daughter, Charlotte, looked after tramps in the Bronx, for God's sake! A beautiful kid like her picking up drunks, feeling guilty because she was rich. Thank God Dino didn't have to see that act. His little girl. 'Your sister hasn't phoned?'

'No,' said Kay carefully. 'I wouldn't worry about her as well. This is Alex's night.'

'Are you worried about money?' Margery asked.

'Why? Are we in trouble suddenly?'

'About having it.'

'Of course not, Mummy. I enjoy it. It'll bring every sap to the door, but I know when I'm looking at a sap. Lucky for me I like to go hunting and find my own meat.'

'Someone has to have the juice,' said Margery. 'So why not us?' She got up to ring for the maid to find the earrings Kay wanted and saw Jennifer, white and stiff with misery. 'Go and get the 1965 photograph album. The one with pictures of Alex. It's in the Japanese room.' This room, a little-used salon adjoining the main hallway, was so named because of the Japanese works of art it contained. These had recently been loaned to the Metropolitan Museum of Art in New York, and Margery had made up for their absence by bringing over a mixture of paintings from the London house: a Landseer, a Turner, two Klees.

'Why do you want to look at pictures of Alex at a time like this?' asked Kay. 'It'll only hurt you.'

'Because I want to take them out,' said Margery calmly.

'Why?'

'Because he's out!'

Kay experienced a spasm of unusual pleasure. Alex, the favourite – out of the album, out of the house, out of Mummy's mind? She swirled and swished in front of the fire, the scarlet silk of her Chanel dress feeling good on her body, its long jewelled sash hanging like a lash. Scarlet made her feel wonderful. She'd have liked to wear black occasionally, but that was forbidden at the Château: only Margery wore black.

Jennifer was allowed black skirts – always knee length, never higher. Her Fair Isle sweaters came from the Scotch House in London, her silk shirts from Turnbull and Asser, and shoes by Elliott encased her long English feet. For social evenings Jennifer wore lace dresses, off the peg, by Mary Quant or Ossie Clark. Jennifer wept discreetly as she gave Margery the photograph album. Like a Greek chorus, she expressed the emotion of the Château. Tonight it was anguish. Margery kicked off her boots and made herself at ease by the fire. It was essential to be friends with your body, whatever the circumstances. The maid from Dover came in with the earrings for Kay – diamonds, vulgar things, which were kept in an unlocked drawer in the dressing room.

Margery had to will herself to open the album. The beauty of Alex's face hurt her. She could not tear out the photographs. She closed the book.

To get her attention Kay said, 'By the way, Mummy, they're planting a cherry tree in the place where Daddy died. The President called while you were out and suggested we might like to go to the ceremony.'

Margery sighed. 'He certainly takes his time. Dino's been dead three years. What does he want? Votes or something?' Upstairs she could hear Shane, her youngest boy, singing along with Mick Jagger full-blast on the stereo. She must make sure no one ever told him Alex took drugs. The agency said it was only some grass, but Margery knew you didn't see just one cockroach. It had occurred to her that Alex, if he needed such chemical input, should get it by prescription from a doctor. That way he avoided the low-life connections. But didn't she know that was part of the attraction? He walked those city streets like an angel, his light put out by darkness.

Kay was stroking her mother's hand. 'Come on, darling. She's a nobody.'

'What d'you mean, she's a nobody?' screamed Margery. 'She's the woman who's taken my son!'

. . . Chapter 3 . . .

Jane Kirkland had first seen Alex doing a drug deal in the car park below her flat two months earlier. He wore bikeboy gear, and his hair was long and slick and black, the hair of a Red Indian. He wore enormous shades with yellow rims that flared up at the sides and made him look like a fragile flying insect. Even for the mid-sixties he looked definitely weird. She'd seen his pushers in the disco across the Finchley Road; they said they were businessmen from Iraq. She did not know the bikeboy was Margery Caversham's son.

Jane went back to the gas stove and stirred the huge pan of Sainsbury's beans. The gas came and went in smelly puffs.

One of the hippies just back from India had rigged the pipe to turn it back on. He said he'd come by again and fix the electric meter so it went into reverse. The Doors were blaring out from the living room and giving the straights in the flat below a bad start to their day.

Jane sang and danced barefoot as she cooked and the strings of bells around her ankles clinked and jingled. She wore a bright orange mini-skirt and a shimmering, apple-green twenties blouse, loosely woven in silk thread that she'd found in a second-hand shop in the King's Road. The blouse got a lot of attention. It had cost five and six, but she kept that to herself. Part of her long fair hair was pinned up at the top of her head and she wore long silver earrings. Sometimes, when she modelled, the photographers said she had a French Impressionist look.

She tried not to tread on Lucy's rabbit, which hopped about on the stained lino. Lucy was lying in the living room having a nervous breakdown which Jane couldn't fully comprehend as she'd never had one. Lucy's boyfriend, a Hell's Angel, was trying to talk her into sanity. Jane reckoned Lucy had been pushed into being what she wasn't. She'd done all this overachievement at Oxford to please Dad, and Dad was still the same cold rat's arse he'd been since she was born a girl.

A knock on the front door, an officious kind that should be avoided. Electricity, rent, bailiff, rates – there was such an abundance of things not paid for. On went Dylan and they all sang along to that one. Jane told Lucy's boyfriend to forget about answering the door. No one with good intentions knocked like that.

'I'll have to ring the mental hospital.' The Hell's Angel had an educated accent. He'd taken Lucy's route: finished school, university, a good degree, then fuck-all. For a year he'd followed the poet Allen Ginsberg. 'Lucy will have to go in. They'll need to send an ambulance.'

'You can't ring anyone. The phone's cut off.'

Jane spooned some beans on to a dish and added slices of German sausage. 'Give her this. She's got to eat. The bread's over there.' It was perched on top of a pile of makeup, plays and photographs. The biker looked at the top photograph, turning it round so he could see it properly.

'You've got to get photographed like that to get parts,' Jane

had been placed in a slender silver vase on the grand piano. The rose, a fresh one daily, assured his wife that he loved her.

'Kid, you've got something more than the average actress. You've got an edge because you have sex appeal,' he told Jane.

Jane said she didn't reckon the British cinema stars were a turn-on. Certainly not the girls. They were tough English and snapped away like bulldogs or were cute. Some of the men were sexy.

'It's this country of yours, kid. All the chances go to the fellas. They get the attention. They have the promotion and they're encouraged to be sexy. The girls, well, they're covered up in shawls with grey wigs playing grandmothers. Or if they are sexy it's tongue-in-cheek, like, I've got big breasts but don't take me seriously.'

'The women don't have passion,' she said thoughtfully.

'No they don't. And the men are scared of it.'

Al came from working-class Chicago where they took sex very seriously. He knew about women, loved them – that's why he could turn them into stars. He poured Jane another gin and asked how she saw herself. Jane reckoned she belonged in Europe. She was definitely a European type, like Margery Caversham.

Al laughed. 'No one's like Margery. God broke the mould when she was born. I'd have done the same if I'd been her agent. She made a lot of people rich, four-Oscar Margery. But she's a mystery, hard to copy. She never declares herself. You're left with a wonderful performance but only a suggestion of the lady.'

'She's English, yet she's sexy,' said Jane. 'Breathtaking.'

'Not English any more. International. And she only did one movie in England before Della Prima, the great Italian director, took her off to Rome. Italy made her sexy.'

Jane asked if he knew her.

'Years ago in Hollywood. Dino, her husband, would ask me up for tennis. I saw some of their action – not much.' Al believed in being truthful, but discretion came first with the Cavershams. And there were things to be discreet about.

He topped up her gin. She didn't like drink much but wanted the interview to go his way. She needed to eat, somewhere to sleep, some money, but right now she held all that away, all the boring little survival needs, and her eyes lit up as he told her about Hollywood: that one day her name would be up in lights.

Al Streep sometimes had trouble with England. He loved it – so much more civilised than America, especially where he'd grown up. But the English didn't have their heads screwed on. He sat a young girl like Jane Kirkland in front of commercial TV's top director and the guy went cold and stiff and said, 'She's not my cup of tea. Sorry, Al,' in his public school voice. And he went for a young puppy type that Al's wife had been training. Al blamed it on the public school system. English men seemed scared of sexy women. And Jane had done a piece out of Tennessee Williams, the rebel girl played by Joanne Woodward in the movie. She even got the accent right. Her dress was skin tight and she had a body that could do justice to that sort of frock, and the guy didn't even get a hard-on.

'I think,' said Al, 'you're going to have to go to Hollywood. Because that's where you belong. You don't fit here. And I'm not sure how long Italy's gonna last. Where do you come from?'

'South London.' She said it too quickly and he knew it was a lie. He gave her the professional eye.

She was young, yet not puppy young. She had a sophistication and she was streetwise, but she wasn't rough. She was hard to define. Maybe she hadn't found her identity yet. But Al knew she was a star. His assistant looked at her photographs and said, 'She can't play juve leads, Al, because she looks as though she's been around. Those aren't young eyes.'

Al's wife, Dinah, said Jane should have a thorough training – drama school, rep; she needed the basic groundwork. What his wife really needed was Jane out of his hair.

Jane was very good about not getting the part, and even showed Al how to skate. She kissed him goodbye and asked for a few bob to get her bag out of the locker at Leicester Square. He started to put his hand into his pocket and she said a couple of notes would really set the day up. 'I'll pay you back.' So Al got out some notes, but Dinah, who'd been listening around the door, came in and said, 'This agency has a policy, darling. No loans. It's for your own good, darling. Because you'll go out there and work even harder.'

'But I'm broke,' said Jane.

'Exactly. And that's what will make you a great actress – because you'll have come up from nothing.'

As Jane left she thought she probably had. A seaside boarding house. How more nothing could you get?

Mrs Streep shut the door. She was thirty years younger than Al but that didn't mean she wasn't jealous. She decided to be careful and play it all down, but the words that came out were, 'I hope you're not fooling around there.'

'I just want one director. That's all. Just one to say, Yes, I'll use her. Not thirty saying she's great.'

'She's odd, Al. Off-key. And she's got a street kid's eyes.'

'Of course she has. That's what'll make her.'

. . . Chapter 4 . . .

Jane's mother kept a boarding house on the seafront at Hastings. She loved going to dances at the end of the pier. She made even a trip to the corner fish and chip shop a happy occasion, and her house was always full of people and entertainments. She loved the sea, but then she loved life. She gave Jane some advice: 'You'll never be happy all the time you want to be better than you are.'

But Jane hadn't belonged in a run-down seaside resort. She'd wanted Hollywood. Ever since she was a child she'd wanted to be a star. She'd joined the amateur dramatic group but the people were too staid, so then she'd been a backup singer in a local pop group. She'd left school early and had graduated from selling rock on the pier to hosting her own show on local radio. Her voice had not been responsible for the promotion: the producer was interested in her visual assets. She had bright hair and light caressing eyes, and the sea air had made her complexion velvety and full of lovely colour like a peach. She had everything going for her, as Harry, a local taxi driver, kept saying, but how did she get from Hastings to Hollywood? Although she had the pick of the local men Jane was infatuated to the point of obsession with American superstar Jay Stone. She watched his films endlessly. Jay was sexual dynamite but he had about him an air of mystery unusual in that business. He was almost unbelievably good-looking. Her mother said, 'No one looks that good. You have to pay for looks like those.'

'Meaning?'

'For one thing he'd be vain, self-centred. No good for you.' Her mother said she was better off going with a normal good-looking guy like the taxi driver, but every time Jane made it with Harry she saw the superstar's face. She could visualise it in the most crucial moments of passion. The fact that he was the fantasy lover of millions made her feel desperate.

For days on end, she would drift across the well-worn shiny squared lino to the open front door, then back through the homely kitchen to the scullery and the outhouse, trying to think of a way to get him. The narrow two-storey terraced house was early Victorian and hadn't been redecorated since the early fifties. The wallpaper had a faded pink floral pattern; the scullery walls were a deep shiny green like gleaming, freshly boiled Brussels sprouts. Rag rugs were laid in the best rooms. Everything was polished. There were several brown chiming clocks, and a glass bookcase full of romances and Edgar Wallace detective stories. An old Aga in the kitchen was used for boiling water and drying towels and tea cloths. The hens out back cackled dramatically at a bored passing cat. The gleaming red oilcloth on the scullery table as always held a pot of freshly brewed tea. Each downstairs room had an open fireplace and an old-fashioned fender with coal boxes at each end. Bette, Jane's mother, had been behind the times due to lack of money, but now some of her antiques were beginning to be worth something. She wouldn't, however, part with a thing: Bette disliked change.

The house had a cheerful lived-in atmosphere that made everyone welcome. Bette had filled the upstairs cupboards and drawers with dried flowers and lavender bags and there were bunches of wild flowers on top of the wardrobe. It was an old custom and it made the house smell sweet. It also gave it a personality hard to forget, and former boarders invariably remembered Bette and Hastings when they smelt those particular country flowers. The sound of chickens was another distinctive feature. She had a dozen in a coop at the end of the yard: she liked the breakfast eggs she served to be fresh.

Jane couldn't get Jay Stone's face out of her mind. She decided it was his expression that aroused her yearning. He looked out of the screen and every woman in the audience thought he was looking at her alone. It wasn't just to do with good looks: he was also charming and very eloquent, and he had a totally unique voice. It was caressing, seductive, sarcastic on occasion. He made words come alive and people listened to him. His voice was easy to imitate and many actors were now trying. After all, they were copying the best. It was rumoured that he could make a woman aroused and give her satisfaction just with words. Jane read all the gossip magazines and scandal sheets, avid for rumours. His most famous scene was with the American sex bomb Cynthia Jago. He seduced her during a poker game. The sixties hadn't seen anything hotter than that. Yet it wasn't explicit; he just implied what he had to give. The buildup between them was almost torturous.

It was during one of her mother's card games – she had open house Tuesdays and Fridays – that Jay Stone appeared on television. He was making a rare visit outside the US to star in a film in England. Jane's friends, drawn from all social classes, gathered round the set. They pretended not to like him.

'Watch it, Jane. He's unstable.'

'Definitely into bondage. I've always thought so.'

Her mother, considered an expert on age, said, 'He's never forty. More like sixty.' But Jay's face from whatever angle gave nothing away. Jane conceded that he might have had facial tucks but kept it to herself. She didn't say anything either about her plan to get him on her radio show.

Her friends went back to the card game. She knew they really came round to see her mother, even the sophisticated ones, because just being with her mother made people feel good. It had become the practice to be married from Jane's mother's. The local kids wanted a sendoff from a happy house.

Jane began the pursuit of the superstar. It was a short one. He had a tough PR team guarding his life, and an unshakeable wife. He would never do radio even for the BBC, let alone Hastings – that sort of thing belonged to the Stone Age. So Jane tried the fans' route. Disguised as a journalist she got into his London press conference. Her looks, not her made-up credentials, got her in, but she couldn't get near Jay. The big-time press gathered around him like wolves and then it was all over. In the crowd in the corridor, she thought she saw him, but it was only one of his lookalike fans. At the last minute she hid in a lavatory. What could she do – follow him to his hotel? Many of his fans did some crazy stuff. She couldn't go back to Hastings, not when she hadn't even seen him.

The last of the day's sun moved to the side of the building and streamed through the lavatory window. Security men started checking the building for stubborn groupies. Something flickered against the window's frosted glass and a voice she'd have known anywhere said, 'I can't wait.'

Jane lifted the window and saw, on the dusty bit of roof outside, Jay Stone stripping hurriedly to his minuscule underpants. Then he held up his arms, embracing the mild heat, drawing it into his deeply bronzed body. The sun moved and he moved, wanting to catch every last ray. He shielded his face and she remembered that sun was ageing. Then he stroked his body and turned to see his reflection in the window – time for a private moment of narcissistic pleasure – and there was the girl, her mouth open, ruining everything. Jay was immediately charming. How often had his PR people reminded him about being nice? He told Jane he'd escaped the crowds to get the last of the sun. 'I couldn't wait.' He loved sun and there was never enough in England. One of his special requirements was the use of several balconies at the London hotel; the film company had hired several suites at great expense. In this interview building he'd had to climb through a men's john as it was the only place on which the sun still shone. Who knew? Tomorrow could be dull.

Jane was amazed. She'd never in a million years imagined Jay Stone could be self-absorbed, let alone a narcissist.

Jay looked at the girl in the window. Her skin was divine. What he wouldn't do for a transplant of that! He discovered that she came from a bracing seaside resort. Did that explain the exquisite colouring and freshness? Security guys arrived beside her in the lavatory, prepared to treat her as a fanatical groupie. Jay waved them away. He was fascinated by the girl but not in the way they thought. As a child he'd been sickly, and unknown to his public he'd come from a poor family in the Midwest. No sea there. The doctor kept saying that if they could get him to the sea he'd be well, but there'd never been enough money. He'd conjured up a seaside, filled drawing books with its yellow sand and people. But now he was a celebrity, the coastal areas he frequented were all exotic, over-colourful, and could never match the purity of his childhood fantasy. He liked the way this fresh young girl described Hastings. And when she mentioned a new commercial attraction, rejuvenating seaweed treatments, Jay was sold. He'd let her know the time and day of his visit, on one condition: absolutely no publicity.

He did visit Hastings. Jane was eighteen, and he was whatever age he was passing as. What happened in Hastings during his visit changed her life. She ran away to London and it gave her a rebirth, a shelter. Its anonymity soothed her. She just about survived. Over the past four years she'd gone from photographic sessions to acting group to nightclub to dance class to auditions – always towards stardom.

About her father she knew nothing. She reckoned he'd been one of her mother's lodgers passing through.

She remembered her mother's advice, 'You'll never be happy all the time you want to be better than you are,' as she left Al Streep's amazing apartment without even tube fare. She believed her mother was one of God's chosen ones, born full of sun. What person could put that out?

. . . Chapter 5 . . .

Jack Goddard was holding forth at the bar of the actors' pub in St Martin's Lane. He said he was a movie director, but he was mostly doing commercials. He liked the look of the roller skater in yellow and wanted to be introduced. He got an Irish extra to do it. He told Jane she had star quality. 'The way you came in. Instant reaction. Everyone knew you'd arrived. A star changes the chemistry of the surroundings.'

She liked Jack's indisputably clean look. The trousers were pale blue, immaculate, no creases, no sag; the shirt white, a true white that would not be challenged. He had a pleasant, unmemorable face. He'd been to a minor public school and had nice manners. He was on the up escalator, big films were mentioned, but then he'd had five beers. He could in fact be a great director, because this was the sixties and you could be anything. Right now he was going to get drunk. He told Jane getting work was dependent on being in the right place at the right time with the right photographs. He knew exactly how to get the best out of her face and body. He bought two bottles of red wine and took her in a taxi to his flat in Earls Court. He loaded a camera. Then he tried to kiss her. She didn't want it. He said he'd try again when he was sober. Then he tried to take her photograph but was too drunk to get it right.

'Why don't we just give the afternoon up to drink?' he said, opening the second bottle of wine. He put on the latest Stones LP and spilt wine on his shirt. He spent a good half-hour getting rid of the stain: he had to meet a producer about directing the next Bond movie. Wearing vulnerable colours like bright white gave a sense of control over the world, a suggestion of perfection. It was a lovely autumn afternoon and Jane lay on the small balcony like a cat. She felt free, all her life in front of her. From that moment on the balcony she could go anywhere, any place, do anything. It was all inside her. Fate didn't even come into it.

Originally Jack had fancied Jane but drink had made him remember his missing wife. 'She's mad about Laurence Harvey. A lot of women are. Some mates of mine wanted to go and smash him up but I don't need mates for that.'

'Where is she?'

'Living with another actress so she's always available for him. He doesn't have a very good effect on women.' Jack named some of the casualties. 'Why do you all go for shits?'

Jane thought women went for attractive charismatic men, and often such men were shits as well. She genuinely liked listening to Jack Goddard because she was interested in other people's lives.

She soon saw that Jack wasn't a director in the real sense of having done it, any more than she was an actress. They both reckoned the Royal Court was a good place to be. George Devine the director would like both of them. All they had to do was get to meet him. Jack made some instant coffee while Jane did what she could with the food the wife had actually left in the cupboard.

'She took the curtains, the spoons, even six eggs. She took tins of baked beans. What was I supposed to eat?'

She hadn't, however, taken her clothes, which she'd called rags from the past. She was intent on making a new start for Laurence.

Jane cooked spaghetti, to which she added oil and herbs. She found a tin of anchovies that the wife had missed because it was flat and dark. Jane had learned to go without eating and not think about it. For five months the previous year she'd lived in Chelsea and slept on a pile of newspapers on a painter's floor. She had less than sixpence a day for food and spent it on two rolls and two ounces of spam from Waitrose in the Fulham Road. But she'd gone to ballet classes and acting groups every morning, and washed dishes in a fashionable café at night to pay for them. It was not uncommon in the dancing class to find beautiful girls pirouetting away on six cups of coffee and an apple a day. Jane had been a nightclub performer and an artist's model. She'd had a patron, one of the deb beauties of the early sixties, who gave her five shillings a day to pose. But nothing stayed. It all changed – life, her, everyone in it; that's what she loved about it. Sometimes out of sheer exuberance she danced in the underground or with the buskers in Leicester Square. Other times she danced because she needed money.

Jack asked where she lived.

'I'm just moving on.' Now her stay in the Finchley Road flat had been brought to an abrupt end, she thought she might move back to Chelsea. It was easier. The rich liked artists and were inclined to be generous. You might be given a spare room or be asked to look after a flat. You could always doss down on a floor. She thought she might get work as a waitress in the Café des Artistes.

Jack's ex-wife had left behind a rail of Biba clothes and he told Jane to choose something and they'd go to a party. The wife was small, size eight, but Jane tugged on a mauve cotton dress and wrapped a pale pink feather boa round her neck. She put on her high-heeled Italian leather shoes. Jack said she could pick up her yellow coat and skates any time. He combed and brushed his thin fair hair, trying to cover the bald spot, and chose two film scripts with covers, pale blue as baby blankets. 'I'm going to introduce you to the Bond film producer,' he said. 'I don't want you to get excited, but they're always looking for a new Bond girl. They test enough.'

She thought that went for the directors as well. Jack would be making the next Bond film and she'd be clamped in Sean Connery's arms about the time films were shown on the moon.

They stopped off in the King's Road at the Diner to look among the artists and art students. Jack wanted his painter friend Bruce Proudfoot to see Jane. He reckoned Bruce would want her to model. 'You've got to be seen in these cafés, Jane. Make an impression. Come in every day. They're all scruffy and mad-looking in here, but some of them have made it.'

Jane knew all about the café. You could get a three-course

meal for one and nine, and whenever her hand-to-mouth way of life led her to Chelsea she always called in at the Diner, even if she only had fourpence for a tea. A tramp used to get in there and eat the leftovers. He wasn't thrown out, because the owner wasn't sure if he was an artist. Some of the big names dressed and behaved like him and worse. The tramp had thought Jane and he were on about the same rung of life. And because of that he'd introduced her to someone who would help her. The man, about thirty-five, had been very good-looking but it was all starting to go. Once he'd been an extra, now he was a bum. He listened to Jane's tale and said, 'Every morning you wake up and say a hundred times "I am a star." That's what I do.' He had an educated voice.

'And are you?'

'Of course. They just don't see it yet.'

She asked the tramp why the guy hadn't made it – he'd obviously had a lot going for him. The tramp said, 'You can have everything and not have luck so you go nowhere. Or you can have nothing but you're lucky so you go a long way. Then there's a certain kind who can make luck happen – and that is art.' As she was going out, the tramp added, 'Anyway, Jane, it's bad taste to be famous when you're still alive.'

On the way to Jack's party they crossed Lots Road at the World's End and Jane saw a houseboat, lit up like a firework display, its deck full of elegant guests. These were people having a really good time.

'That's John Whiteman's boat. He's a millionaire,' said Jack. 'Made it out of washing machines in less than a year. Now he's into dry-cleaning machines. It can't get clean enough for Whiteman.'

Jane decided to forgo Jack's party and the meeting with the Bond producer. Somehow she thought Jack's party was one party he wouldn't be at.

She started up the gangplank.

'You can't go up there,' said Jack, aghast.

Jane laughed. 'Let's see if I come up clean.'

He didn't follow her. He didn't have the confidence in himself that she had in herself. He could call the shots in the actors' pub, but in the fast lane you had to be real, and if you went on that boat and put failure near those people, they'd drown you. He waited for her to be put ashore.

Jane didn't let the bodyguards stop her. 'Have I got an invitation? John just gave me one, by phone. Perhaps he wants us to tumble-dry together.' They let her by but had the guest list out. They wanted her name, 'Don't worry about it. As long as John knows my name.' And she walked towards the 'in' group on her high-heeled Italian shoes. She thought, 'What the hell am I doing in this yard? This lot are celebrities.' She saw a pop star, a top model, the top photographer. Pink Floyd's latest LP floated out across the Thames. She walked into the group looking at one man after another as though expecting someone. She walked right past the host. He was just someone with a beard talking about diversifying. To John Whiteman, money was like cockroaches. Get two to fuck and you had twenty. He was going out of white goods into pyramid selling.

The bodyguards weren't asleep on their feet. They came after her: no gatecrashers at Whiteman's gig. But the racing driver Del Grainger said, 'Hi, Toots. Looking for me?' He was loaded to the hairline but could still see straight. He left the American film starlet in the dazzling white dress and put his arm round Jane's shoulders. 'What's your poison, Starry Eyes? Just one. Then we're off. You should have found me earlier. I've been down the hatch too often.'

She'd never met him in her life. Obviously he'd mistaken her for some intimate acquaintance. She didn't know how to play it, so kept her mouth shut and let her eyes do the smiling. At least if he looked as though he knew her it would keep her on the boat. He lifted his glass and toasted her arrival in his life. 'We'll go for a spin, Toots. But you'll have to drive.' His voice had a soft Irish lilt.

John Whiteman arrived beside them eager to throw her out. Del slung his free arm over the financier's narrow shoulders. 'I love this guy because we're going to get rich together. It's all advertising from now on. That's the future. And futures. Coffee beans, John?'

John decided not to speak to Jane. He knew she'd crashed his party, but he couldn't do a thing about it because Del Grainger had picked her up. And there was Del's wife downstairs talking to Marianne Faithful about the transition from pop music to acting.

Del pulled Jane close and danced with her to 'Itchicoo Park'. 'You should have bells in your hair and rings on your fingers.

You're unadorned. Let's go to our boat and change some of that. Do they call you Starry Eyes? I wish I had them.'

He walked unsteadily, his arm round her shoulders, and she led him past the curious guests, past the bodyguards, down the gangplank. She assumed 'our boat' was a neighbouring one, but he stopped at an enormous pale Mercedes.

'Look I don't drive and you don't know me,' she told him.

'Get in.' He opened the passenger door. Once behind the wheel he sobered up. He drove fast, leaving London by the first motorway.

She was relieved to be leaving Jack Goddard behind. This guy, although drunk and silent, was still powerful and single-minded. But then he was a star.

After a while she said, 'We've never met. You don't know me.'

'Oh, but I do, Toots. You're the girl who wants in. There's a thousand of you outside any party door. Walking on to Whiteman's boat wasn't such a smart idea. He's vulnerable because he sometimes mixes with dubious people. In that situation trouble usually starts.'

'Meaning?'

'A pushy stranger could want in for a dozen reasons. His bodyguards are not the brainiest guys.'

Del looked like a moviestar: dark curly hair, blue eyes, a strong sensual face. He had all the charm he needed, and he was number one, worldwide.

'So I saved your arse, Toots.'

'Not Toots. Jane.'

'That's nice.'

'Are you sure you didn't get me muddled up with someone else?'

'I like small waists, slim bodies with energy and high tits. No, you don't look like anyone else.'

He drove to some dark spot on the Thames where a boat was moored. She knew about his Hampstead mansion recently purchased for his new wife. The boat was the place his wife didn't get. It was functional, masculine, meant for real sailing. He turned on some lamps and got busy with the drink. 'I didn't know the first thing about wine,' he said. 'Then I got invited to a famous wine family in France. First surprise – although he bottles it he doesn't drink it. The second, quality doesn't mean you leave out a hangover. I drank gallons of it because I thought, "It's the best there is, so no additives. Its safe." On my third day I didn't know whether to go to the airport by taxi or ambulance. I've never been so ill.'

He showed Jane how to tell good wine from the rest. He held a full glass over a white napkin and explained about the reflected tint. But she was more interested in looking at him. Now he was on the boat he seemed a serious person, not even drunk. She told him about her career, making nothing seem like a lot. She'd had two small parts in rep, a role on TV. She told him about Al Streep and how much she wanted to go to Hollywood. He liked listening to Jane because it had nothing to do with him. It didn't harass him. It wasn't demanding like the stuff his wife came out with.

Jane felt very attracted to him but the fact of the wife bothered her.

'Do something for me,' he said. He meant an acting piece. She thought he meant something sexual.

'Oh, I couldn't,' she said.

'Well, you won't get far in that business.'

'I'm sure you're right, but I've got to do it by talent or forget it.'

He laughed. 'I think we're at cross-purposes. Come here.' And he pulled her to him. 'You give me ideas.'

She loved the way he kissed. He ran his hands over and over her breasts and she got very turned on. He was a man who liked sex but he didn't want to hang around for it. He took what he wanted and she liked that. But when his hands got under her skirt, into her knickers, she backed off. Did he have a virgin on his hands? Or a set-up? He looked round hastily for the guy with the camera. It was known to happen. She told him she couldn't do it without knowing the person. He gave her two seconds, then started to take her dress off. It was tight, it didn't even slide up over her buttocks and there seemed to be no zip. As it didn't belong to her she didn't know how to get out of it either. Everything she had that night was someone else's, including the racing driver. He gave the dress one fast tug, almost decapitating her. She screamed and he said, 'Let's do it with it on.' By then she'd cooled down. She wanted him but she also wanted it real, and she knew she had to wait for that. Real only happened when you made people wait.

'It doesn't matter,' he said and got going on the wine. 'But don't prick-tease.' He put Marvin Gaye on the stereo. 'That dress of yours is a chastity garment. I liked those big dirndl skirts in the fifties – with lots of petticoats underneath. D'you remember them, or are you too young?'

She could imagine him, a sultry-eyed smoocher, sought after in the Irish dance halls.

'What does it feel like to be world champion?' she asked.

World champion was such a transitory thing. He was only interested in the next challenge, how to coax out a bit more speed.

She knew she'd not see him again. Even if she slept with him that wouldn't change. She loved the way his hands held things, the way they'd caressed her. But she wasn't part of Del's world. Tomorrow reality came with the wife and the French circuit and the jet set world. She was just a phase on the pleasure moon, chosen because of a supple waist. She knew about these things because she always knew where she fitted. It was the best armour she had.

She said he looked just like an Irish film actor – same eyes.

'No, he looks like me.' He got the car keys and turned the lights off. As he helped her up the steps to the deck he told her how he used to go to the Irish dances and said that was his best time. He wanted everything, had nothing, except hope. Before they got in the car he said, 'I'm bored.'

She said she was sorry.

'No, it's not you. Sometimes I don't know how I'll get through the next five minutes.'

'Are you anxious?'

'Of course not. It's all so predictable. That's why I race. To leave the predictability and the boredom.'

On the way back to London he swigged at a bottle of vodka and let her drive. It didn't matter that she couldn't – he'd teach her. This was fun and he was no longer bored. She got behind the wheel of the huge car – enough drinking had gone on for her to do anything. The driving bit was OK until it came to stopping: she didn't know how to.

'The brake pedal,' he said. She hit the wrong one and they shot jumpily across red lights. He was beginning to enjoy himself. 'I'd love to have slept with you, Toots. We really would have had a very good time. I can tell that. Our bodies – well, they were saying yes hours ago,' he said seductively.

'I can't stop. Please take this wheel.'

'We could have fucked all night and not run out of juice.'

'Del, I'm fucked right here. Please tell me what to do.' She took her hands off the wheel in desperation to get his attention then clamped them back on. A car was coming towards them. She was no longer sure which side of the road she was on: the other car's lights were blinding and she couldn't tell how close they were.

Del was enjoying some adventure off the track so let her handle it herself. 'Come on, kid. You're an actress. Improvise.'

She got a foot on another pedal, went even faster, then turned the wheel sharply sideways. The car careered across a well-tended front garden and came to rest against a shed. Del was still laughing and the engine was still running when the house owner in pyjamas shone a flashlight through the window. He saw Del's arm around the girl. 'Come here to do your necking, have you?' he asked.

Del thought that was hysterical.

'Ruined my borders. You'll have to pay.' Then the owner recognised the ace racing driver. Here he was, drunk, with a blonde at the wheel, and his wife was a brunette.

Jane made it into the newspapers, but not quite in the way she'd intended.

. . . Chapter 6 . . .

Alex Caversham appeared on the front page of the same newspaper. He'd been caught in the zoo at night in an empty cage, closed in. Because of his clothing and odd appearance, the park police at first thought they had a rare animal intruder on their hands. Alex had taken red leb, grass and a liquid medicine intended for schizophrenics, and on the resulting high had got round to worrying about wild animals and how sad it was that they were kept locked up. So he went to try it for himself and spent the night in the next cage to a rather elegant slim creature that looked like a bird – he wasn't sure, for by this time he was hallucinating. He talked soothingly to this creature, who responded by staring unblinkingly for hours with huge caressing eyes. The eyes, Alex decided, contained all the wisdom that had been and was to come, and there was nowhere he'd rather be.

In court he left out the drug angle and said he was making a protest for wildlife. It was his first tangle with the law and he hated any kind of publicity. The Caversham lawyer then had his turn and got the story into better shape. The magistrate let Alex off with a fine. He couldn't really touch him: he was Margery Caversham's son.

They met, the two infamous tabloid characters, at Peter Woolf's party in West Hampstead. Peter's father was a government minister – that was all Jane knew about him. She'd been asked along because Peter desperately wanted to get into the racing set, and in the street life circles she frequented she'd now been upgraded as a racing champion's mistress. It didn't matter that she didn't know him and had spent less than three hours in his company, most of it drunk. Del Grainger was popular and the press loved everything he did; they were prepared to love Jane. She said nothing at all, which implied that she'd done everything.

Peter Woolf said Del was hard to meet.

'Not for everybody,' said Jane.

The story had got into the tabloids because the house owner wanted a little notoriety. First he demanded a colossal sum for his damaged shed. Del said it wasn't even scratched and gave him half of what he wanted. The house owner, not satisfied, said Del was drunk and called the police. Then the press arrived and the house owner did a lot of talking. He wanted to sue. Del said, 'You've been paid,' and left in disgust.

Jane had been driven home by a reporter who wanted a scoop. What worried her was that actually she had no home, unless she went back to Jack Goddard's flat. She thought she should get out at the Café des Artistes in Redcliffe Gardens. It was one of her safe places. Instead she got out at her onetime patron's smart house in Chelsea, which added spice to the story: 'Kept girl in Tite Street. Del's racy life.' Although Jane had said absolutely nothing, the press gave her a persona.

Alex dropped into Peter Woolf's party because the door was open and he liked the sounds. He loved Neville Brand's music. He was on his way to see Brando, who was in England making a movie. His mother had told him to call, though he couldn't remember if he'd met him before. He wondered if he'd be like the guy in *Viva Zapata*. Whatever he was, he was part of that world, Margery's world. So Alex stayed on at Peter's because he could smell some good spliff. He also stayed because Jane was in the room. Slim, with an innate elegance, she reminded him of the birdlike creature in the next cage at the zoo.

Peter Woolf asked Jane to get him in at Del's next race meeting and started talking about Formula One and circuits, about which she knew nothing. People were looking at her – was it star quality or the fact that she was Del Grainger's secret sin? It was funny how many things she could remember, having known him such a short time. The wine he preferred, how normal life bored him, how alcohol seemed to fade in his body, leaving him sober and sharp. A mere hour before he'd been a party drunk. She was sure he was thinking about her too. She would have loved to see him again, but only chance could provide that meeting – he wouldn't.

Jane's eyes kept straying to the weird boy in the shades. His skin was pale, bone structure beautiful, stunning. He wore a battered leather jacket, Indian moccasins and dark cords. He looked as though he travelled. As her mother would say, 'That one's got sand in his shoes.'

'That's Margery Caversham's son Alex,' said Peter Woolf. Jane noticed that, although a lot of people gathered around him, Alex always seemed alone. He had a natural aloofness which made approaching him difficult.

What did he do? Peter didn't know. He was the movie goddess's son. What else? The zoo incident was definitely down to hash and other gear. It certainly wasn't public defiance of his mother. He could do better than sit in a cage, said Peter. Alex was the kind who took a dive off a high board. Peter made it sound like a compliment.

Twice Jane passed close by Alex to get a drink. If she'd caught his eye she didn't know it. His shades were huge, almost aggressive. He was agile, sinuous, beautifully made. She knew him – before she even approached him she knew all about him. Cool didn't come into it, he was glacial: his was a cold in which you perished. You needed good survival equipment to tangle with him. But his charm hid the ice, and once they'd spoken she forgot what she'd intuitively known. She went up to him and said, 'I've seen you around.'

'I expect so.' His voice was deep, mid-Atlantic. She filled in a silence with, 'We were in the same newspaper. We're the sin people.'

'Oh, yeah. You're the racing driver's friend. How come he didn't teach you to drive?'

'We never had time.'

'Oh, I see.' He'd interpreted her remark as a sexual boast.

'I mean we didn't spend much time together.' The music changed to Marvin Gaye. She asked if he wanted to dance.

'No, I don't dance.'

She was in the company of the son of the greatest superstar in the world. And she couldn't think of anything to say. She wanted to say hundreds of things, ask questions. Instead she said, 'D'you want a drink?'

Alex said he'd get it. She watched as he went to the table, terrified someone would lure him away. Again people were looking at her. She'd spent several minutes alone with the focal point of the party; twice as long as the other people who'd approached him. When he brought her a glass of wine she asked if he liked London.

'Sure.'

'Why?'

'It's not France.'

She loved the way he brushed his long hair back off his face. How beautiful he was. She was dying for him to take off the glasses.

'How was the zoo?'

'Quiet.'

'You like quiet?'

'I only like it quiet.'

She asked what he was doing at the party.

'I can find quiet in the loudest room.'

She told him about the Maharishi, how she'd done meditation, how it made her feel. 'I heard him talk at the Hilton. The Beatles were there.'

'Yeah, but in India he's not such a big thing. He's like average, compared with some of the gurus they've got. Hundreds have reached higher attainment than him.' Alex had just come back from India. 'Apparently he can levitate.'

Jane didn't know what that was.

'Lie on the floor and go up to the ceiling like he was on a magic carpet. I'd love to do that.'

Alex had a strong physical presence. His body was slight yet somehow he seemed big and vibrant. He took off his shades and his eyes were tawny yellow and curving at the corners. Then he smiled, the tantalising, marvellous Caversham smile, and at that moment she fell in love with him. Her heart registered the fact with a strong, threatening drumming. She saw him as a captive bird, his song dying inside him. He didn't belong in that room, that town, but soaring above the Himalayas. He would feel at home in vast distances.

She asked him if he knew the Café des Artistes. Why didn't they go there? She wanted to get him on his own.

'Yes, well, I would, but I have to go and visit a guy.' He remembered Brando and the promise to his mother. He put down his glass without bothering to finish his drink – he didn't like alcohol – and they started towards the door. He found his torn and battered leather jacket and looked in the pocket for the movie star's address. 'You must like speed,' he said.

'Speed?'

'I mean generally. He's the greatest racing driver in the world ever.'

'How about the drug?' she asked.

'Yes, how about it?' he replied.

'Do you like it?'

Now they were entering his kind of territory. He wasn't sure of her so he gestured nonchalantly. 'I could. Yeah, I reckon I could.' He'd had so much speed he reckoned it came out of his arse. Some days he could do Del Grainger's circuits in his head and even beat the real thing.

As they left the party a girl said shrilly, 'There goes Del's mistress. She's just picked up the teenage wonderboy. What's she got – a magnet in her pants?'

Jane started giggling and that's when he started to like her.

'What's your name?' he asked.

She told him. They stood close together. She had the impression he was going to embrace her: she was sure he wanted to. Then he turned and started off towards the tube. 'Well, I'll see you around, Jane. So you go to the Café des Artistes? I'll drop by one of these nights. Or we'll meet at the Marquee. I'm always there.'

She knew that wasn't true because *she* was always there.

Life was suddenly urgent and could get upsetting. She did not want him to go. He'd go up the street and visit a guy and she'd never see him again. Most people she met she didn't see again but Alex's going would be an actual loss. She felt – she knew – that already there was something between them, something that wasn't at all unfamiliar. It wasn't a question of getting to know him or of love growing. It was all there. Did he want it, or even recognise it?

'Let's go to the sea,' she said.

'What, just like that?'

She wanted to take him to the sea because she wanted to give him a present for being in her life. And she loved the sea and could bring out the best in it as it did in her. The sea could enchant.

'You look like someone who should be by the sea,' she said. 'Or somewhere wild.'

'You don't want to be taken in by the zoo gig. The press exaggerate anything. I'm not wild. I don't like it that way.'

'I bet the sea would make you feel great. We could get someone to give us a lift.'

He considered it – the sea with the girl who'd become inseparable in his mind from the zoo creature, companionable in the next cage. 'I'll maybe pass by the café. I don't think I could handle all that water just now.' And he went off to the movie star's party and she went to the sea.

He thought about her during the night and wished that after all he'd gone with her. He felt he'd missed out on something.

The next day Al Streep called Jane into his office to meet Ed Dworkin from LA. He was casting a movie that required a certain kind of individual girl. Al said Jane was it. In exchange Ed would make her name. But Jane was not the type Ed was looking for, and he chose instead Al Streep's top English girl, Gracie, with the sweet smile, all girlie and secure.

Then Al's wife got involved. 'You've got to do something with Jane,' she told her husband. 'She's got to be properly trained – I've already said so, Al.' She turned to Jane, who was trying not to look like a failure. 'You're to go to drama school. I won't hear no.' Dinah got out a huge book. 'You'll do Juliet, darling, for your audition, and you'll get in because I'm going to train you. And you've got to tone it all down.' She meant Jane's image. 'You're going to wear normal clothes. Get rid of the eye makeup. That style. It frightens people. And darling, you should have told us you were having a relationship with Del Grainger.'

'What difference does that make?' said Al. 'It wouldn't make Jane more saleable. They just want to know what he's like in the sack.' He turned to Jane. 'What *is* he like?'

'I don't know.'

'Very sensible,' said Dinah. 'Keep saying that, because he has a wife, and wives don't like that sort of thing. They get divorces.' She threw a Polly Peck dress to Jane. 'Put that on and get your hair off your face. Look young.'

Jane held the frock between a thumb and forefinger as though it was contaminated. 'I'm very sorry, Mrs Streep, but I can't,' she said.

'Look darling, it's a present. You've got no money.'

'No, I can't wear it.' It had a large spray of wild flowers over the left breast. 'You see, it just isn't me. And I can't go to drama school. I can't do it that route. I just have to be me.'

Al's wife looked at her with interest. She didn't have a child. She felt stirrings of an unfamiliar emotion: could it be maternal? 'But the me doesn't get any work, my love. I do. So do it my way.' She threw the dress back to Jane. 'You don't have to wear it out there. Just when you're working with me. So do it.' Dinah was definitely effective. She was all courtesy and civilised control on the outside, but her patience level was that of a raging tiger.

Sighing, Jane took off her street gear. It was like stripping away her identity. She put on the dress with the floral bouquet over the left tit and felt she'd betrayed herself. This dress put her back in Hastings.

Al's wife said, 'Now you look lovely.'

Al knew it was all wrong. Dinah would just turn her into another Gracie.

'Now we'll do Juliet. And I want good clear enunciation. I want projection. Forget you've ever seen Marlon Brando.' Al's wife thumped the Shakespeare book. 'He's been around for hundreds of years. He's beyond fashion.'

Jane sighed. 'All I want is to make my name.'

Later Al said to his wife, 'She's not an all-round actress. She's a personality. And she'll come into her own. It's just not the time for her yet.'

'Al, she'll go to RADA, then into rep. And we'll build her slowly: a small part in a long West End run, then television.'

She could see it was far from what he wanted.

'There's no overnight stardom Al. That's over. And how do you know she can take the strain? All she gets out of this agency is rejection. You don't know where she comes from or even where she lives.'

'I can always get hold of her.'

'A phone number in a dry cleaner's isn't exactly a fixed address.'

. . . Chapter 7 . . .

Del Grainger was killed when he unaccountably skidded off the track as he was coming round the last lap in the Grand Prix. He seemed to lose his concentration. The disaster, splashed across every newspaper placard in town, saddened Jane. He was reckless – that she'd seen on their drunken drive from the boat to London, and in the garden shed episode. It was as though he wanted to escape boredom, which led to the unexpected. In this case, death.

Jack Goddard came running towards her waving a newspaper as she came out of the Pheasantry Club, on the King's Road. She'd been trying to fix up a place to live.

'I've been looking for you everywhere. We'll do it – three parts,' he gasped.

'It?'

'It's a goldmine.' His eyes narrowed and his face became all sharp like a playing card. He stroked the newspaper gently like a flat pet. 'You're going to write it and I'm going to sell it. We'll have every newspaper in town bidding for it.'

Jane asked what 'it' was.

'Your affair with Del Grainger. Well your dalliance. No, we'll tell lies and call it an affair. Who knows? He's dead. We'll spin it out. Three Sundays. The *News of the World* gets first sight, of course.' Jane was shaking her head defiantly so he said, 'You're going to have to defend yourself.'

'Why?'

'Because you've been labelled a scarlet woman. Fight. That wife will.'

'But there's been no affair. I didn't even know him.'

'So? Who's going to believe it? They'll tar and feather you now he's dead. Get in first. Just tell it how it happened. Go on.'

Each event he managed to enlarge so three hours became thirty. It ended up as a love affair: true love, passion and sacrifice because they decided Jane must believe in the sanctity of marriage. For Jane, Del's wife came first.

'But I hardly knew him, Jack.'

'Don't even think it. You did. Better than you know. Together we write it, improve it, sell it.' He asked for fourpence from a stranger to make a phone call. 'Hang around, because when I come out of the call box I'll be a rich man.'

Jack wrote the story of the affair. He kept telling Jane it was for her own good – defence of her integrity. She finally saw the point of that when the 'exclusive' of the bereaved wife hit the late editions. She called Jane a lot of names that meant tart. An amazing amount of people corroborated the 'affair'. John Whiteman told the truth.

'She came on to my boat as though she was looking for someone. I was giving a small party, just a few friends. Del spoke to her immediately, called her "Starry Eyes". He'd certainly not mentioned her before, but he wouldn't would he?'

A nightclub owner in St Tropez said Del and Jane used to dance the night away. 'That's great,' said Jack. 'We now sue for defamation.'

Jane was nervous. All she could remember was the racing driver saying, 'I'm bored. That's why I race.'

'Great,' said Jack. 'We say he wanted to die.'

'What's in it for you, Jack?' She thought it was money, but it was a chance at fame. He was fed up with commercials and trying for the big breaks. If he got rich and famous and wore white suits by Mr Fish he might get his wife back. Jack told Jane she should bless the colour scarlet because scarlet would make her name. Del's scarlet woman. There was even talk of a movie.

With the first instalment from the tabloid sale Jane got back her flat on the Finchley Road. She paid the six week's back rent and cleaned up the mess left by Lucy's rabbit. Lucy was in the local mental hospital trying to find out what it was all about. Jane went to Dinah's daily Shakespeare class and also wondered what it was all about. Dinah told her that hundreds tried to get into London drama schools, and some had real talent and originality yet didn't get spotted. Jane could go on as herself and get asked to leave the stage before she'd finished the speech; or she could go on as a copycat version of Dinah and get in just like that.

'Al's pulled strings, darling,' said Dinah. 'You audition just before Christmas. Write it in your diary. My life begins now.'

Jane went to a call box and phoned Bette in Hastings. 'Mum, there's some stuff coming out in the Sunday paper. About me. I just want you to know it isn't true.' She could hear the clocks chiming, the hens, the serial on the radio, the chatter of visiting neighbours. It all sounded so homely and safe but she knew it wasn't for her. She sighed deeply and wished she could have been satisfied with what she'd been given. Her mother had such a sunny life. 'Also, Mum, my photo's in, so it may get all that other thing started again.'

'That's silly, duck – you shouldn't have let them know what you look like. But they won't put you together with a boarding house in Hastings. After all, you've changed your name.'

Jane laughed. She hadn't thought of that. Her mother had sense.

'No one's been asking? Because something came out in the London papers. About a racing driver.'

'No one's asking anything. You just forget all that and enjoy yourself. Look on the bright side. You must be someone if you're in the papers.'

'But, Mum, I've told lies in the article. About this racing driver.'

'Well, that's what show business is, a lot of lies. I wouldn't worry about it.' Bette sounded light-hearted as usual. Nothing got her down. She told Jane the latest gossip. The girl next door was having a baby, and Bette reckoned Harry the taxi driver was the father. Jane wanted desperately to ask her mother if she'd done the right thing: lying about a married man, now deceased; causing pain to his wife. But what looked like one thing in London was quite another in Hastings, and Bette had never understood her daughter's desire for a thing called fame.

'They'd have slammed into me, Mum, if I hadn't got in first. That wife would.'

'I told you, girl – it's dog eat dog in that business.'

Jane's money ran out. She stood in the call box, her eyes

filled with tears, and wished she could go home. But she had no home and there was no going back.

Back at the flat Jane washed the kitchen walls trying to erase Lucy's messages. It seemed that when people went mad they were compelled to write things on walls. The messages all made sense until the last line. Jane went out to empty the bucket down the drain on the fire escape. She was wearing a minuscule white denim skirt and a floral transparent top that she'd tied beneath her breasts making them jut out. It had flounced sleeves and was very feminine. Her naked midriff and waist were firm and brown. Her white boots with their huge cutouts were imitation Courrèges. The whole outfit cost less than ten pounds and she looked like a million dollars.

As she emptied the bucket she saw the pushers from Iraq in the car park below with Alex Caversham squatting by the side of a car. She didn't want to see him: he hadn't turned up at the Café des Artistes, she wasn't wearing any makeup, also the first instalment of her love story was coming out the following Sunday and she was anxious. The late autumn sun glinted on Alex's shades. She slid back into the kitchen and shut the back door softly. The fire escape creaked as he climbed the stairs. He knocked on the glass pane.

'Hey, Jane, I've got something for you.'

Hidden behind an open cupboard door she swiftly applied makeup. He knocked again.

'I really want you to have this.'

She smoothed on some lipgloss. Was she so up she could afford to turn her back on the one person who'd made her happy? 'Just you, Alex. It's no to the pushers.'

He came in softly and leaned against the sink. He wore the same battered jacket. 'Maurie's a friend of mine. He's clean.'

'They're pushers, Alex, and the police have always got their eye out. I don't want to get busted on top of everything else.'

He flipped out a photograph. 'Go on, have a look. She's my best friend.'

Jane took the photograph: a very thin girl made up to look like a tropical bird?

'She was next to me in the zoo. I went back and got her photograph. She's completely silent, doesn't even sing. I said

I'd pay for her to be returned to her natural habitat but the zoo said that was a bad idea. She'd go back and the other birds would kill her instantly because she'd smell differently. She'd smell of captivity.'

She handed back the photograph.

'No, it's for you. She reminds me of you. I think I fell in love with her.'

Jane laughed. She thought it was a joke – then.

'You don't look – well, you're down. It's funny I never thought you could be,' he said.

So she told him about Dinah making her act like Dinah and it all feeling wrong. She was losing herself. Then she told him about the 'Del's scarlet woman' revelations written by Jack Goddard.

'Let's go to . . .' He paused. 'Morocco.'

'I can't. The article's coming out this Sunday.'

'Then I think it's the very best time to go to Morocco.'

'You do?' She was surprised.

'You should keep your eyes open round about now, or you'll trip in some serious shit.'

'Who says? He's dead.'

'Yeah, but his lawyers aren't. What if they ask you about him in bed – an anatomical question like a measurement, for example? What are you gonna say? If the wife brings an action for defamation you're in trouble.'

'You know a lot about it.'

'Sure I do. My family's always up against this sort of thing.'

He helped her carry the rubbish bag down to the bins, then took her across the road for a six-shilling curry lunch. She was surprised how sensible he was – but then he wanted to save her.

'Let's go to Morocco. Now.' When she didn't answer he said, 'I thought you were into the "let's do it now" game. I chickened out last time about the sea so you're winning.'

'Let's go and visit your mother,' she said.

He laughed drily. 'Let's visit yours.'

'Absolutely.' She stood up, ready for Hastings.

'Let's get married,' he said, over-casually. 'Then the press will really have something to get worked up about.'

. . . Chapter 8 . . .

Kay's apartment on the second floor of the Château was like something out of a silent movie. It was all black and white tiles and mosaic floors and arches and low understated sofas and pale columns. It was never allowed to be cluttered. The few objects on display were essential for the effect and of the highest value. Kay loathed muddle and bric-à-brac and believed one object, if chosen correctly, could have the effect of a dozen. In the entrance a fountain splashed into a shallow pond lit by ever-changing colours. Her bed was huge, silky and perfumed and a gilt harp from a 1920 movie stood in one corner. The rooms were lent secrecy by lacquered screens and gossamer drapes. There were photographs of her father everywhere, of her and her father. No lovers. She had had so many she hardly remembered their names. Physical endowment she did remember, but she was only interested in the chase and the seduction. The harder the guy was to get, the more excited Kay became. The minute she'd had him it was over. And then they quite often did terrible things like getting on their knees and pleading to stay or crying. One even left his wife.

The apartment was designed like a silent movie set because that was the one slice of celluloid her mother hadn't excelled in.

Elle finished photographing Kay in the bedroom, then suggested they take some outside shots. But Kay had seen Mummy pacing the grounds. It looked like walking if you didn't know her. Kay gave the journalists her sweetest smile and said that was all she could do. The Italian superstar Lucia was coming for lunch and bringing the legendary director Della Prima, who'd discovered Margery. The journalists asked if he was offering Kay the lead in his next movie. Kay smiled obliquely and her maid showed them out.

She'd lied during the interview. Did she spend time or thought on clothes? Never! She implied she tumbled out of bed into the nearest thing. She had no beauty secrets, she said. She had dozens, but they remained secrets. Assembling the clothes took up a large part of her life. Like Margery's her shoes were made by Ferragamo, simple black pumps, low-heeled or stilettos. The shoes were built on her last by Mr Ferragamo and the last, a wooden block copy of her foot, had cost over £600. Like Margery, she ordered a dozen pairs at a time. Kay loved antique dresses. She loved them before collecting became fashionable. She made special visits to London to the Kensington Antique Market and two second-hand shops in the King's Road. Here, for next to nothing, she bought twenties originals with labels, Patou, Poiret, Vionnet, Molyneux. She bought dozens of soft, lustrous robes in silk and satin, and heavily beaded dresses. She found a Molyneux 1930s original in a London market and took it to a Paris fashion house and had it copied in scarlet silk. Floor-length, with long sleeves, it was all cut on the bias so that it clung to every curve, and her midriff was naked. It was impossible to wear anything underneath. The dress was much admired. Other women tried to copy it, but they didn't have Kay's body. Since jeans had become popular she wouldn't touch them, and chose instead tailored three-piece suits in white leather or lace. In London she also bought Mary Quant, Foale and Tuffin, Courrèges, Paco Rabanne. She bought her jewellery from Tiffany or again found it in markets. She was partial to lockets and watches on chains. She loved real amber from the twenties or long jade necklaces. However often she visited Hollywood she would never shop there: everything was too vulgar.

She had a Japanese masseuse who worked on her body daily. The masseuse, like her hairdresser, travelled with her, except that they went tourist class. She got the best from whatever country she happened to be in. She arranged for the best movement teachers to give her private lessons daily. She took saunas, went swimming, had facials and acupuncture. It was an obligation to be at one's best – better than best.

She sat on her bed and looked at the photos of her father. She didn't remember him spending one second on his personal appearance. He shaved, brushed his teeth, took showers, splashed on cologne, treated looking after himself as daily chores to be hurried through. Unlike most Southern Italians, he didn't take pride in his appearance – and yet he looked wonderful, a god. He had it all for nothing. Kay thought of the way his smile had lit up his face when he saw her, his little girl.

He would pick her up and throw her squealing up into the air, and his embrace when he caught her was the nearest thing she knew to total belonging. The smell of him, how she remembered it – that smell meant love. He would carry her into the garden and teach her the names of flowers – but that was before his other little girl had come along.

Kay took off the necklace she always wore when being photographed. Dino had given it to her when she got her Baccalauréat. It symbolised victory and she liked to be seen wearing it in public and in the press. The string of alternating sapphire and ruby stars, engraved on the clasp, 'To my darling daughter Kay. Dino', always attracted attention: no one had ever seen anything like it.

People said that when Dino came into the room he brought sunshine. He always spoke Italian to those he loved, his voice husky and expressive. His eyes were pale blue and mesmerising. He had a hooked nose, smooth brown skin and thick black curly hair. He had a strong face with a cleft chin and a mouth well-shaped to the point of perfection. It was a very expressive mouth, and he would run his thumbnail along his bottom lip when he was preoccupied. She only remembered the years when he was in politics, and at work he never stopped moving. At home he was still, and gave himself to the family; he loved just being with his children and wife. Often, of course Margery wasn't there: she was away making movies. In a sense Dino brought them up. He was mother and father. He had a feminine side in that he was caressing and tactile, and how he could soothe. Kay remembered having a fever – they were in the house in LA – and Dino sat up all night holding her so that Margery could sleep and look her best on the set the next day. He chose to sit up – not through weakness, Kay knew he was a very strong man; he decided to do it because he was tougher than Margery and he didn't have to look like a million bucks. And he talked to her and bathed her head and held her and got her through the burning and the shivering, the chills and the nausea. He even dealt with the fever nightmares. 'Tell me. Just tell me,' he said softly, 'and I'll take it away from you.'

'Daddy, I'm scared.'

'You're all right, I promise you. You're over it. I know these things.'

And because he was confident she felt much better about

feeling ill. That's the quality Dino de Stefano had: people told him their problems, and then they felt better.

He wasn't impressed with grand people, he treated everyone the same. But when the family was due to meet a celebrity, he always pretended to be terrified. He'd pull faces and mime the imminent meeting and the kids would laugh. The thought that he was gone still made Kay's throat ache. His death had broken her but she never talked about it. It had made her distrust life. And the family? Well, that had never been the same. When Dino was alive it was all sunshine, but now he was dead it was all black and they – Mummy, she and the loyal secretary, Jennifer – staggered about in the darkness pretending they could see. The others Alex, and Charlotte, had had the sense to get out. And Shane was too young. It seemed inconceivable to Kay that someone so amazingly gifted, so special, such a poet of life as her father should no longer exist.

She refused to cry, and lifted from her travel bag the latest script. Her mind travelled quickly away from the banality of it, off to her favourite subject, Princess Miranda Cecile's daughter, Jacey. The story that this wayward girl went into restaurants and made bets with her friends that within one hour she'd fuck every guy in the place, excited her. She hadn't been able to get it out of her mind since the reporter mentioned it earlier. Kay imagined what it would be like to have thirty guys, one after the other. Did some of them watch? All of them? Or did they wait in line? Or she could have two at once. She'd heard of a woman who had two guys fucking her in the cunt at the same time. Did both cocks go in and stay in? Or did each have a thrust? Burning with an unusually intense excitement, Kay lay down and did it to herself and came, and then again, until her body felt relieved at last. She ended up on her back at the side of the bed looking up into the eyes of her father. 'Shit!' She shut her eyes immediately. She wondered if Mummy had heard what she'd got up to with Guido during the night. It would be much easier to have men in her Paris flat, but around Mummy there was more action. That's where the power was.

Downstairs Guido told his driver, 'She's a fantastic lay but she doesn't come.'

The driver said he was sorry.

'She'll do anything but she doesn't get near an orgasm.'

'Well, as long as you do,' said the driver. 'That's all that matters.'

'No it isn't,' said Guido. 'Because she kind of holds it over you, the fact you've given in and come and she hasn't. They're all into games, those Caversham kids. Even the young boy, Shane. If I'd rolled double sixes he'd have given me his racing bike. If he'd rolled fives I was to give him my Porsche.'

'If you've got that much money all you can do is play,' said the driver.

'But they don't play. It's a challenge.'

As Guido left the Château grounds he saw Margery walking alone. You could be too rich: it was a terrifying thought.

Kay sat beside her mother on Dino's favourite bench. It was engraved 'Con tanto tanto amore. You are everything for always. Margery '64.' Kay asked if her mother wanted to talk about it, the thing that worried her.

'Someone outbid me on the Modigliani. There was a sale at Sotheby's.' She couldn't go on. What did her daughter care about it?

Margery was wearing a classic camelhair coat with a tie belt at the waist. Her long black suede boots were decorated with a silver and blue art nouveau pattern up the outer sides. Her black hair, shoulder length, was cut superbly, flowing and immaculate at the same time – not a hair out of place. In London she let Leonard look after it – he did everybody. But in Cannes she liked Jules to fly down from Paris.

Kay said she was sorry about the Modigliani. 'Perhaps somebody wanted it more, Mummy.'

'No, Kay. Someone outbid me. I know when that's happening.'

Kay said she was sorry again. Then she asked if there was any news about Alex and the girl.

'All I know about her is what the London office tells me. Jane Kirkland. She's said to be very alive.'

'Perhaps she'll be good for Alex, Mummy.'

'Kay, I'm talking about the person I love most in the world.' Her tone was sharp and hurtful; she was very angry.

Kay's eyes closed in pain. She realised that, whatever he did, Alex would always be her mother's favourite. So she swiftly talked of the movie offers she'd received, of her fiancé, Guido, whose father owned La Scala and several textile factories. The best photographers in the world wanted to come to Cannes to photograph her. Margery didn't answer.

'Isn't it fun?' Kay insisted.

'Is it?' said Margery, refusing to be challenged. She sighed deeply. 'If he'd only come to me, shared it with me. What have I ever done except given him everything? He was the one child that belonged to me. As I carried him, during the pregnancy, I felt he was a love child. I didn't feel any real bonding with the others.' Then she realised she was talking to one of them. 'Oh, Kay, it's always a mistake to talk from the heart. That all ended for me when Daddy died.'

Kay's throat had gone into an involuntary spasm. She couldn't stop swallowing, as earlier she couldn't stop coming. Her whole body was like an express train of sensation, out of control.

'Well, Mummy, you can always pray.' Kay decided that was the most spiteful thing she could say to an aetheist in trouble.

'Kay, if God's so wonderful let him show himself.' Margery got up and called the German shepherd. It was a stupid idle dog. So many pedigrees were a mess – she'd always been told that mongrels were better. And that made her think of Jane Kirkland. She'd have all the energy of a street bitch on heat, never ill, strong, common and nice. The 'very alive' hurt her. Then she noticed Kay's face. 'You look exhausted.'

Kay shrugged. 'I don't have to ride the horse in the movie, Mummy. They'll get me a stand-in. The insurance is too high. For them.'

'I guess I shouldn't blame Alex. As Andy Warhol said to your sister, Alex is a boy of his time.'

Margery could almost hear Dino say, 'Not ride the horse, huh? You ride everything else.' It was conceivable that Kay was a nymphomaniac. What worried Margery more was that Kay always had to take the dominant position.

Even before Kay returned to the house Margery had slipped back into the past, to when everything was real and vivid. She could see Dino so clearly as he came down the hill towards her. From that angle he seemed tall but like many small men he always held himself well. He seemed full of the joy, the very essence of life. Even now she could see his body, dressed in black with a red scarf around his neck, well tied, and his head, so beautiful against the piercing blue sky. It seemed that he was all that existed in the world against that sky. And seeing her, he smiled, the very special smile meant for her that her beauty provoked in him. And as he came nearer, her body surged with happiness, ready for the onslaught of passion. With him she fused into an ecstasy she could never have imagined: it was beyond lovemaking, it was too good. So many women loved him, wanted him. He was so easy to love. He always said that if Margery hadn't come into his life he could so easily have been bad. He'd have taken advantage of his attractiveness, had everything on offer. But Margery was the one woman who could really love him deeply, and he was the one partner who could satisfy her needs and create more. She never got tired of Dino. She remembered the way he grasped her, quickly kissing her face, her neck, her breasts, and she so eager to take him into her body.

She loved him at all times – when he was shaving, working, on the telephone, asleep, making a speech in the Senate. He was her God, her father, her lover, her friend, her soulmate. Remembering the sexual ecstasy made the present-day reality nothing but a thin, transparent membrane. Margery sat in anguish, her hands locked together in her lap. She remembered New York '58, meeting the President. She wore pale pink, a great big skirt emphasising her tiny waist, and the girls wore ruffled dresses, soft, in sugared almond colours. Alex wore a dark suit like his father. And then she remembered Dino at the sink washing his hands with scented soap. He wore a pink shirt and dark trousers; he hated wearing jackets. She watched his broad back as he scrubbed his hands. How attractive he was. How she longed to go and put her arms around his chest and press her body into his back. But someone was in the room waiting, wanting his attention. There was always someone in every room. The trouble was he loved everybody.

In the spring they went to Paris, just the two of them. In Montmartre in the Place du Tertre, where nineteenth-century painters had starved and turned out masterpieces, they'd stood by the famous cherry tree painted by Utrillo. Dino said, 'Does genius extract payment? Does it demand great suffering?' She asked why he wanted to know. 'I think they have to be exiles to produce what they do,' he said. 'And to do the great works you've got to pay a price. And maybe it's never even recognised until you're dead. The deliverers of greatness go through this life with terrible labour pains. Their reward is at most an occasional ecstasy. To create what was not there before is perhaps blasphemous. They have to starve. Maybe that's the only way to do it. Do they have a choice?' And that's when he started to take an interest in the paintings she'd collected as an investment. That day she wore a soft gold dress, very feminine, and her long hair was loose. The cherry tree was made more exquisite by the spring sunshine, and the wind had blown some blossom into her hair. He said, 'Always remember this moment. It's ours.' And he broke a spray of blossom from the tree and gave it to her.

But there were always other people needing him. That was the problem with great men: other people wanted them too. But then she was a movie star, and he'd accepted that. He had Washington, she had LA. He didn't feel apart from her even when they were in separate continents; she felt uneasy – she was deeply possessive and jealous of any rival. But she was always full of him – his thoughts, his love, his semen, his children, his words, his wisdom. When she gave birth, he was there from the first contraction till she finally slept exhausted after producing the baby. And then it was her he cherished, not the new child. He was proud, not of himself, but of her.

And now she felt cut in half. Part of her was with Dino – wherever he was, in whatever form, rotting in a grave or gracing some higher realm. Beautiful summer days brought him back. Their beauty reminded her of the passion, their splendour was pierced by her loss. A summer day could never be the same again. She dressed what was left of her in black. She had to go on. Dino had always said, 'Life is for living.'

. . . Chapter 9 . . .

'Let's just go.'

'Where to?' asked Jane.

'Morocco,' said Alex.

'What, now?'

'Sure.'

Jack Goddard, wearing a new white suit from Mr Fish, was at the wheel. 'I'm not sure, Alex, but I don't think they do shotgun weddings in Morocco. I think you'll come up against a bit of religion. What's wrong with here?'

'He's nineteen – that's what's wrong with here,' said Jane.

'Nineteen-year-olds marry,' said Jack. 'I was one of them.'

'Not without permission from your parents or guardian,' said Alex. 'And I know what the answer would be.'

Jack turned the car north. 'Then it's Gretna Green.'

Jack said he'd be part of it because they'd need to keep out of sight. After Sunday's episode in the popular tabloid Jane was a legend: 'Del's girl. Del's true love'. Journalists from all over Europe had gathered around her Finchley Road flat, waiting. When she didn't show up they got stories from the neighbours. Their accounts weren't exactly the stuff of legends.

Jack was accompanying them because Alex Caversham had come into his life like Santa Claus. Jack would take this young, innocent, beautiful boy and turn him into the biggest star since his mother. Alex had money. OK, it wasn't sitting in his pocket, but at twenty-one the bank door opened in earnest. Also anyone doing good for someone's son got appreciated. Jack was sure that Margery would not let his efforts go unrewarded. He'd move Alex ever so slowly towards his film. First he'd put the idea in his head, get him hungry, let him see that's what his looks were for, for God's sake. Then he'd lead him to the deal. It was like having a virgin. Jack was so excited his driving was extraordinary: far from being discreet, he drew every eye on the motorway.

The real reason Jack was there was that Alex Caversham decided he wanted him along. He needed someone to deal. Jack wasn't smart enough to see that Alex only looked fragile. He was hard, obstinate and mercurial, and when people tried to use him he'd turn it so he used them. Within a day he'd turned Jack Goddard, director and impresario, into his pusher.

At first Jack didn't spot it because he thought he was in the driving seat. He was cruising along thinking about the script he'd write for Alex. Suddenly Alex said, 'Stop the car, Jack. There's a guy around Manchester or somewhere that does drugs. I need some grass and whatever else he's got.' He gave Jack two five-pound notes. 'You go in for me in case I'm recognised.'

Jack, appalled, said, 'I'm not into that, man.' Then, to placate his star, he added hastily, 'Not that I think it's wrong. But it is against the law.'

Alex said, 'Fine, but I just don't know if I'll be in the mood to hear all these movie ideas of yours, Jack. I have to get a little high.'

'Why?' asked Jane.

'Because otherwise I get a little low.'

Jack did the drugs deal. Then he started keeping the stuff on him in case Alex was recognised. The only thing he didn't actually do was roll it. Alex liked to do that for himself.

Jane was on to Jack instantly and thought he should be watched. It was ironic. When he was doing his commercials life was flat but harmless, unless you called his wife running off after a movie actor harm. But the minute he tried to touch the big stuff – immortalising Alex Caversham – he got screwy and unlucky.

They ate at motorway cafés with the truckdrivers. Jane wore Alex's shades and leather jacket. Winter was early and the weather had turned icy. Jack kept telling Alex to keep his head low. Who knew what the Cavershams would do once they knew he'd split?

Jane couldn't wait to sleep with Alex. On one occasion he got hold of her hand and the way he held it was more sexual, more exciting, than any erotic touch. He looked at her as though he knew all about how to please a woman. His shyness was just something he put on for the outside world. She didn't believe in the getting married part of the trip, but how she wanted it – not just to be a Caversham, but to be married to this unique, beautiful boy. She wasn't sure, absolutely, that for him it wasn't some rave-up up the motorway with a bit of suspense thrown in. She felt she'd known him always, for ever, but what did he feel? She'd learned a long time ago that guys didn't like a lot of questions, so she kept her mouth shut and tried to be companionable.

Jack was excited enough for the bride and groom put together. Alex responded to him with sarcasm alternating with gentleness. Secretly to Jane he said he thought Jack had sold out, had lost his dream, and now he'd never be at peace. A hundred Mr Fish suits and exploitive tabloid deals wouldn't do it.

To impress Alex, Jane talked about the parts she'd played in rep. And because he hadn't seen the TV series in which she'd been an extra she gave herself a lead part. She quoted Al Streep and promised she'd get to the top.

He smiled very sweetly and gently as he agreed with her. He knew she was no star and everything she'd done had failed. He knew because he was used to stars. Her failure touched him; her brightness and love of life pleased him. He felt much older than her, more responsible, and when she said, 'Are you sure you want to do this? I am three years older than you,' he said, 'Compared with me you're still in your pram.' And he did seem wise, even ageless. She'd never met anyone like him.

At Kendal, just before the Scottish border, Jack said it was all right to get a night's sleep. He chose a small bed-and-breakfast place. It was dark, so no one was going to be seeing too much. Jane and Alex went straight up to the room while Jack chatted to the landlady. She was suspicious because there was no luggage.

'We've got the luggage in the car but we're only staying a night. We're going to tour Scotland.'

'Wrong time of the year. Too cold.'

She made three cups of tea and Jack took them upstairs. He was horrified to find Alex rolling a spliff. 'In this clear air it'll travel all over Kendal.'

'Tell her it's for my asthma. You buy herbal cigarettes in health food stores, after all.'

Jack knew he had to take control. He said, 'Look, Alex, I don't know how the bread scene is with you, but I don't believe your mother's going to be – well, she could be hostile. Mothers like to go to their sons' weddings. She might cut you off.'

Alex laughed, a dry scathing laugh.

'So you may need all the loose cash you've got. I mean, it happens. And there's all that Ward of Court stuff they can pull. So I'll pay for this trip and your getting married. But you do it my way. No grass, no speed. Don't wear shades and hide your hair. And, Jane, you wear shades and dye your hair.'

Jane and Alex were laughing aloud.

'OK,' said Jack. 'But I think it's the only way you're going to get married. I'm not at all sure you just walk in and they do it. Remember Dominic Elwes and Tessa Kennedy.'

Alex said not to worry: he'd put his head in a paper bag and smoke. 'No, really, I'll keep it to myself. I've learned a few things from guys who've been inside.' And he urged Jack out of the room. Then he turned on his portable cassette machine. Jane was intrigued – she'd never seen one before. The Doors' LP – Alex had heard them at the Roundhouse. He lit the spliff and then he got hold of her. He was powerful and sensual, an amazing lover.

Jane had had a lot of experience, most of it from the local taxi driver in Hastings. She had a strong sexual appetite and knew when she was getting a hungry person or an anxious guy. She also knew a lot about getting pleasure, the ways to change it about and prolong it. She liked to be told she was good in bed. She didn't have to worry on that score, but this boy was better. Usually he seemed so spaced out and remote, yet with a hard-on he was wild.

Afterwards he lit up another spliff and she said, 'What about Jack?'

'Why? D'you want him too?'

'I mean what he said about the dope.'

'They don't know about spliff up here. And if they do, they shouldn't be living here. This is a one-sheep town.' He lay beside her and fondled her breasts. 'You've got a beautiful body.' She'd heard it many times, but it never palled. She told him he was marvellous in bed.

'Yeah. Well, I like you.'

'But you're a very good lover. Have you–'

'Had lots of partners?' He laughed, the Caversham laugh, full of gold.

'Well, have you?'

'No.'

Alex had been seduced by a thirty-five-year-old society friend of his mother's when he was thirteen. Since then he'd had over two hundred girls and women.

'Why d'you want to marry me?' she asked.

'I like being with you and I want to go on being with you.' He also liked her because she was not a star.

'We don't have to marry to be together,' she said.

'No, that's true. But I feel I want to take care of you. You're my friend. My true friend. We're going to find we're on the same side.'

The next morning their departure was delayed because she wanted Alex again. She was mad, completely wild, about him. His mysterious isolated quality made him more exciting, and for the first time in her life she had what she supposed was a multiple orgasm. He held her gently, lovingly. Jack waited downstairs and heard her final orgasmic cry. He told the landlady they were fooling around, pillow-fight stuff. Kendal might not have heard about pot but it knew about orgasms.

The landlady said later, 'The sheets! You've never seen anything like them. Honeymoon sheets? More like a brothel.'

At Gretna Green Alex spotted Mo, the big one who used to be his sister Kay's bodyguard. Then by the registry office there were two more guys from the agency. He slithered down in the seat.

'Turn left,' said Jane.

'No, right,' said Alex.

Jack dithered and the engine stalled. They were outside a big inn, which was now, courtesy of the weather, a frothy snow palace. The sun came out bleakly and turned the walls orange.

'You can't stay here, man,' said Alex. 'They'll notice all London numberplates. Drive on.'

'But what about the marriage,' said Jane.

'We'll come back. Go north.'

'Did you tell anyone?' she asked Alex.

'Of course not.'

'I couldn't,' said Jack. 'I had no idea where we were going.'

'It's the agency,' said Alex. 'Ever since my father was killed we have special surveillance.'

'What's that for the average person?' asked Jane.

Alex looked at her with his hazel eyes. How they disturbed her, made her ache for him. 'They just hang about and make sure I stay alive.'

'CIA?' asked Jack.

'That sort of thing. They must have spotted Jane and me and caught the action north and put two and two together.'

'What can they do?' She was quite frightened.

'Only what my mother tells them. Drive on, Jack.'

'Why don't you call your mother?' asked Jane suddenly.

'Don't be crazy. They'll get me back and I'll never see you again. This is the only way. Trust me.'

At Dumfries Jane's face was on the newspaper placards so they couldn't stay there. At a village further on Jane went with Jack to the registrar's office. Jack was now convinced Gretna was no good: it was the first place reporters would look. The office was shut. Jack banged on the door.

'Where's the fire?' The registrar opened the door. He'd just left the comfort of his bed and wasn't pleased to see them. The freezing air turned every bit of his exposed flesh scarlet. He wouldn't open his office today if their lives depended on it. Looking at them again, he thought, he could have left out the 'if'. They were southerners judging by their lack of clothes.

'It's urgent,' said Jack.

The registrar didn't care. He had a mop of orange hair and a face like a splotched carrot.

'Can marriage take place anywhere in Scotland apart from Gretna Green?' asked Jack.

A long look at Jack and Jane told the registrar they were both obviously over twenty-one and he wondered what the fuss was about. He said, 'You can marry anywhere in Scotland as long as you abide by the law which says you reside fifteen clear days in one place and then your Notice of Marriage is hung for eight days. After that you can be married.'

'What do you mean, hung?' asked Jane.

'Hung. Displayed. So anybody who has any objections can make them.'

Several names came to mind without any effort.

'Have faith,' said Jack. 'You've come this far. We'll go further into Scotland. No one will know you or him there.'

At Hawick they split up. Jane and Alex would go by train to Edinburgh and Jack would drive around for a day so they had a chance at least to get the marriage ritual started. But at Hawick station Jane was recognised and now they had trouble. The reporters, unlike the agency men, were not discreet.

Jane and Alex got off the train at the next stop. 'We'll find an inn,' he said. 'Something right in the country. Edinburgh's out of the question.'

Jane was certain the agency men would find them. Alex said sure, but they couldn't infringe on his life, they could only save it, and report to Margery.

Shivering, they crossed a rink of iced grit that had in warmer days been a lawn. The sun came out, stayed long enough to melt a top layer of ground, then disappeared and the cold turned everything back to ice. Jane banged on the side door of a church while Alex hid around the corner. 'No names. Don't forget,' he said. He had no faith in churches but he had been brought up a Catholic.

The parson had a rigid face like a tightly laced shoe. He knew all the answers, or if he didn't the questions shouldn't be asked anyway. He looked as though the only person he got on with was God.

'I want to marry someone,' she said.

'Yes?'

'A boy of nineteen.'

'Sorry!' He shut the door. He wouldn't have that sort of thing in his church. He opened the door only to say, 'Go back where you came from, miss, and marry the boy there.'

Alex waited, his black hair hanging down his neck. His clothes rose blackly up to meet it. He seemed to have renounced all physical existence except the sucking in and out of cigarette smoke. His face was translucent, pale and beautiful. Like a tide taking the sea far out, the beauty of his face took away all her frustration.

Now it looked as though they couldn't get married, it became a matter of urgency. The obstacles gave it a reality it didn't have on the joyride north. Alex hated authority, petty officials controlling his freedom; he'd marry a sheep on the hillside to get back at them. But he didn't want to be parted from this strange girl. And now he'd shown his hand, he had to win – or else Margery would. On some legal pretext she'd get him back to Cannes, and the girl would go off on her own road and if they met again later it wouldn't mean much. It had to happen now. He took her hand and tried to warm it by putting it in his pocket. Her summer boots were stuffed with snow, and her long, uneven fringed gypsy skirt was damp round the hem, but she didn't complain. She wasn't moaning about the cold or even asking for a hot drink. She had endurance and he respected that.

Over the next hill was a village, almost hidden by the steep slope. Alex liked it. It had a registrar and the office was open. 'The only question is have they seen the newspapers?' he said.

The registrar was a middle-aged woman, small, bright and kind. 'Come in. Come in,' she said. 'You're Margery Caversham's son. I recognised you immediately. I saw that article about you and the zoo. My, you've got her eyes. She's my favourite.'

'I don't want to be hasty,' whispered Alex to Jane. 'but I think we just got lucky.'

The woman treated their request for marriage with respect.

Alex explained that they'd been residing in the area for over twenty-one days – more like twenty-eight.

She looked as though she'd like to believe it – but how could he be in Scotland and in a cage at the zoo at the same time?

'On and off, you understand. But my fiancée's been here non-stop.'

She accepted that, but she still had to hang the Notice of Marriage for eight days.

'Do you have to?' Alex jiggled some money.

'It's the law of the land, but it's so cold now the glass is iced over most of the time. No one could read it if they wanted to.'

'You couldn't put it up at night and take it down in the morning?' said Jane.

She laughed and said to Alex, 'I think people should have privacy. I bet you haven't had much. The famous should be allowed to live their lives – that's what I say.'

Alex warned her about the press, and she said she'd say nothing.

'Have you asked your mother for permission?'

Alex was stuck. Was this part of the law? He said, 'Yeah.' Then he said, 'She's possessive.'

'Has she got anything against Jane?'

'Nothing. Except she doesn't like girls who get involved with me. She won't give permission. That's it.'

'You could wait till you're twenty-one,' the woman suggested.

'I could,' he said, 'but life is so precarious. I think when you want to do something very much you should do it. Otherwise everything changes around you and the chance is gone.'

'D'you want to be married morning or afternoon?'

'Earliest morning,' said Alex. 'Now all we've got to do is keep out of sight.'

The woman said they should stay at the farm at the top of the hill. It was quiet, and was run by people like her, who liked to live and let live.

. . . Chapter 10 . . .

'So your mother's possessive,' said Jane.

It was their second day on the farm and they were lying in bed. Alex didn't want to talk about his mother. He was having a great time and it was real. Here he was, with a beautiful girl trying to do something against the odds. It was much better than an ordinary wedding because they really had to try for it. They couldn't even go out now because the reporters had sniffed out the story. It was in the papers, on TV.

Jane couldn't get over how good-looking he was. And how hotly sensual. She'd never known anyone that good, who could do it for that long. Her body throbbed for him all the time. She kept telling him that, and he'd get a hard-on and do it another way. She'd say, 'Go on. Put it up me,' and pull her knickers to one side. And he would look at her, aroused but always in control, dominating her. And then she'd get really turned on. Why was it so good? Because he was strong, not indulgent, erotic? The truth was that she loved him.

On the third day he was moody. 'It seems I've been shut in here so long I know every cow on the mountain,' he said lifting away the awful yellow of yet another egg. 'Shall I tell them about fish? Have they heard of it? When we're married we're going to have steaks and champagne.'

Reading seemed the best form of oblivion. They sat against the fireplace, covered in blankets, and read Mickey Spillane. 'Shall we play cards again?' asked Jane.

'We daren't. It might get boring and then what would we do?'

Eleven hours more until bedtime.

Lunch: mashed potatoes and something containing the old enemy egg. They'd told the farmer's wife they were from the French tourist office, but as they never went out she probably didn't believe them. And the registrar had no doubt said her piece.

'Of course,' said Alex, 'these people could make plenty if they talk to the press. It probably doesn't occur to them. You don't come across nice people often.'

'You are,' she said.

'Oh no, honey, I'm not.' She thought he was joking.

'You're charming and sweet and gentle. Things I'll never be,' she insisted.

'Yeah, I can be all of those. But I'm also not nice. But even not-nice people need someone.' And he lifted out his foot and lifted her skirt, right up. 'Pull those down and come and sit on me. We'll never have it this good again. We've got hours and hours to do it.'

By the fourth day their relationship was worked out. He was boss and she his sex object, always ready to be aroused. She'd do anything for him, die for him. Living for him was of course quite another matter.

Jack found them on the fourth day. 'I got to the next town after Hawick and there was this great flock of reporters and people and police. And you and Jane were supposed to be on that train. Was I pleased you weren't! So I just drove around trying every registry office. When I got to this one I had to tell her my whole life story before she said she might have seen you.' He was carrying a huge movie camera. 'I'm going to get the exclusive on the wedding, and sell it. OK? We'll split three ways.'

Alex didn't answer. Jane said no. Jack had his usual answer: 'If I don't others will. May as well look nice.'

'You keep it on ice,' said Alex. 'If the others find us you can have an exclusive. If not it's just our home movie, our wedding present. Let's get out for some air. I've been locked up so long I'm beginning to feel insecure. Especially as I've read every Mickey Spillane book in the house. Twice. And I could do with some really strong blow.'

'What's that?' asked Jack.

'Gear. Dope.'

'But I got you all that in Manchester.'

Alex looked at him as though he was out of his mind. He was from another planet, a space cadet. 'You don't put it in the bank to accrue interest, Jack. You smoke it. And now I've smoked it.' He was obviously restless, almost irritable, and wanted a walk. He ignored Jack's entreaties to stay hidden and started off across the snow. Jane ran after him and took his hand. Jack hurriedly took pictures of the elopers walking up the hill.

It occurred to Jane that her fiancé could be an addict. She said, 'I don't do drugs. I think it's a really bad thing to get into.'

'If you feel like that, Jane, you're right not to touch it.'

'How does it make you feel?'

'A real buzz. I go through the door between life and afterlife. Purgatory maybe, or the other place. It's sure different. Other drugs give me belonging. I'm part of the sky, a frog, a bit of dirt, God. And there are combinations that take you whizzing out of your body off to other galaxies. And the colours are so fabulous.

Indescribable.' He went on going down the menu of his chemical pleasures and she felt uneasy. She knew him in one way, very well – but in others? She had cold feet from the snow, but even more from the idea of marriage.

'Do you take hard stuff?'

'What, shoot up? You know my body by now. See any tracks?'

'Why don't you? Shoot up?'

'I don't need it.'

He walked fast and they were out of sight of Jack and the intrusive camera.

'But today you seem edgy,' she persisted.

'Jane, I'm not an addict. I just can't be shut up day and night.'

'We don't have to get married.'

His eyes slid sideways and watched her secretly.

'We can live together,' she said. 'I've never thought of marriage before.'

'Nor have I,' he said. 'I was obviously waiting for you.'

So she said she wasn't sure she believed in it.

'I do,' he said.

'I've never seen a happy one, Alex, and I bet you haven't.'

He shrugged attractively.

'Name one.'

'My parents. My father was very happy.'

'Did you get on with him?'

'Yeah. Yeah, I did.' He lapsed into silence.

'What's your family like?'

'What, now? Unbalanced. Because he's not there. He was like the centre. He was very alive and, well, you always noticed his eyes. The first thing you saw when you came into the room: was he in a good mood, happy? He was very spontaneous. I still remember his voice. It was kind of musical. Had a range, lows, highs, I've never heard a voice like it. And I always wanted to get close to him because with him I felt safe. We were an ill-assorted lot, my family, we didn't belong together. My mother is English, classy, and he was from a Naples slum. My sisters were space cadets, and I, well, I don't know who I was, quite. Except he loved me. He held us together. And now he's gone. I think we all miss him very much but can't talk about it. It's too upsetting.' He took her hand and squeezed it. 'It's funny, I've never told anyone so much about my family. Except Lucien.'

'Who's Lucien?' She felt happy again, part of him.

'He's a guy I love. He's very smart. He taught me everything I know.'

For a moment she wondered if he was saying Lucien was gay. 'What sort of person is he?'

'Not like Jack Goddard. He's got a mind like a whip.'

'Perhaps we should have brought him along too.'

Alex laughed, a rare genuine laugh. 'Toss for the bride.'

'He's gay?' she asked sharply.

'I'm having you on.'

Once again she said they didn't have to marry. He turned and kissed her and felt for her breasts. He said, 'I'm not an addict.' That meant they should get married.

Alex liked to run rings round people. For him, stardom was like treading in dogshit. You cleaned your shoes and tried not to do it again. He said he'd take care of Jane and show her Morocco, the desert, then they'd go east and keep going until they ended up round the globe at Warhol's factory. He explained to her that she thought she wanted to be a star because it was her way of making where she'd come from bearable. She thought he might have a point, but she hadn't told him where she'd come from – not in any detail.

'Stardom is a structure you've built up because you think it's one that works,' he said. 'All you've got to do is climb it. Don't look down, don't feel depressed, don't admit the past, look like the ones who've made it, keep climbing and then it's twinkle, twinkle, Oscar night.'

Intuitively she knew not to ask questions about Margery Caversham. Alex was sick to the heart of people wanting to know about his mother.

Jack driving a car was suicide. Crossroads were the crucial test of his personality as a driver. What would the other car do? Jane kept throwing in her nickel's worth of advice from the back seat. There was a near-collision with a truck. She screamed.

'It's OK,' said Alex. 'He's the kind of driver who is more dangerous to other cars than himself. He'll never have an accident.'

'He's got me fooled.'

'Analytically it's not in his nature. There's a world of difference between the guy who is always nearly having an accident and the guy that actually does.'

'Have you been to an analyst?'

He smiled. 'Of course not.' He'd been to eleven – Margery's attempt to get him off drugs. When he was fifteen he didn't speak for six months. They said it was because he was in shock – his father's murder. Actually, he had nothing to say to any living being. His trouble was that he had it all – the looks, the graces; the gods had smiled and he himself had nothing to do. He could, with the help of drugs, chemically change reality for a while.

Jack coaxed the car up a deserted lane covered with thick ice. He got out. 'Come on – photograph.'

To the left, a parapet of sheer ice and a generous view of Scotland. He wanted them side by side on the parapet. 'Come on, kiss Jane.'

'On this? You're mad.' Alex tried to keep his body as balanced as his mind. Jane skidded.

'Jane, stand still,' said Jack.

She was shivering violently. Suddenly over the top of a hill two dozen cows came racing towards them. Alex and Jane, with graceless haste, broke up the romantic embrace and ran for the car.

'Sound the horn!' yelled Jack.

Alex made faces at the cows. 'They can't hurt you, man. They're only cows – just inquisitive.'

Jane flapped her arms. Jack kept throwing rolls of film and leaflets at the cows. Noises like *shoo* kept the animals amused, and then suddenly they'd had enough. They turned and moved slowly back over the hill.

All of a sudden Jane was upset. 'Your mother is bound to be looking for you. You'll be made a Ward of Court and all this will be for nothing. Or the press will find us.'

A farmhand clanked by with a bucket and said, 'Nice day.'

'Keep out of sight,' Jack growled. 'He's probably a *News of the World* reporter.'

'Where's his camera,' laughed Alex. 'In the bucket?'

Jane was still upset. 'And I ought to phone Al Streep, I'm supposed to do an audition for drama school.'

'They'll sell you out,' said Alex. 'Before you even finish the call.'

'Al's my agent, and he's been very kind to me.' And then she knew why she was upset. This elopement took her further and further away from what she'd always wanted: fame.

The police knocked on the registrar's door and asked if Jane Kirkland was trying to get married.

'Jane?' The registrar was surprised. She hesitated.

'You'll have to tell us. Her father's very ill. We've had a phone call.'

'But I haven't got a father!' Jane exclaimed when she got back to the farm.

The registrar was standing breathless in the kitchen, having run up the hill. 'He was definitely a policeman. I know him, he's local.'

'My husband says there's press all over,' said the farmer's wife. 'It's terrible the way they poke their noses into people's lives.'

'It's a trick!' shouted Jack.

The back door was shoved open and a huge bouquet of flowers seemed to come in all by itself. There must have been three dozen large blooms. Behind it, two men. 'Hello, Alex. How's it going?' one of them said. 'Ah the bride to be. Thought you'd like some of these. You don't see many this time of year.' And he pushed the bouquet towards Jane's hands.

Alex flew to the door yelling 'Get out!'

'Come on, Alex. Let's have the story. There are one or two things we want to clear up. Did Del Grainger know about you and Jane–'

'Get out!' said Alex again, his voice sharp and ruthless.

'Don't spoil your chance of marriage. Let us take over the action for you. Our paper–'

'Out!' And Alex, now completely immersed in the world of Mickey Spillane, took the first reporter's collar and threw him into the snow.

'Be reasonable,' said the second, 'and we'll be reasonable with you. Otherwise there'll be no wedding. Your mother–'

'That's blackmail,' and Alex slammed the door.

It was opened again and the reporter said, 'It's a pity you let someone like this' – pointing at Jack – 'spoil things.'

The farmer's wife was in the stable giving a bottle to an

undernourished pig. The reporters asked her questions. She said, 'They're in love – can't you respect that? You don't respect anything. I do – so get off my land.'

In the kitchen, Jane was already on the phone to the policeman who'd started the trouble. He was pleased to hear from her and she got a Scots blast of welcome. Suddenly she was sick and tired of people interfering in her and Alex's lives. She asked the policeman who'd phoned him.

'A relative.'

'Saying?'

'Your father's very ill.'

'I don't have a father.'

'I didn't know that. We have to follow up all enquiries.'

'You also have to take all the names and phone numbers of the enquirers.' She remembered that from her radio chatshow days. 'What was this relative's name and number?'

'The woman said she'd ring back. I'm still waiting.'

'I suggest it was one of the national newspapers and you get a generous backhander.'

'No! I wouldn't do that to anyone, miss.'

'Alex and I have spent a lot of time and other people's time protecting our privacy, which we have every right to protect. We're not criminals, are we?'

He said they weren't. He liked the sound of her – forthright, no southern smarm. He said, 'The Sheriff can give you permission to marry quickly. Get a solicitor at this number and you might get hitched today.'

Jack's car roared into action and he gave the inhabitants of the village an exhibition of driving that would long be remembered. He bounced left then right, ploughing through a pile of stones that had up till then been a wall. Outside the court there was no action. Not without gratitude they crept into the building and followed the solicitor up the stairs. Alex took a twenty-five-milligram inhibition-breaker packed in a pink and blue capsule. No saliva, alas, and it stuck to his throat like a miser to a twenty-dollar bill. 'I'll do my best,' said the solicitor, 'but it's up to the Sheriff now.'

Two men in kilts stood in front of the Sheriff's desk. Alex and Jane had to hold a Bible and take an oath. The tranquilliser turned Alex's words into a choke. The Sheriff listened to the solicitor's dramatic plea while his eyes took in every detail of the unkempt couple before him – an affront to his conservatism. He listened, and said there wasn't reason sufficient to grant a special licence; he would not have his country used for quick marriages. He got that off his chest and turned his fierce gaze on the solicitor. The solicitor said, 'It will be impossible for them to be married, sir. They've been hounded and harried by the press. The newspapers will cause embarrassment to Mr Caversham's mother.'

'I have great sympathy for people hounded by the press,' said the Sheriff.

'His mother has ideas against marriage, sir. These have been well coloured in the popular press. But she is a lady who perhaps considers herself above the law and feels people should live together as they will, free of legal obligation–'

Alex's eyes opened in amazement. This guy lied good.

The Sheriff's face darkened. Then he pronounced, 'Marriage is an acceptable part of our society and a necessary one. Mrs Caversham, although a great actress, is not above the law. Also people must be allowed to lead their own lives. In this circumstance, as these young people want to follow the law, I will grant a special licence.'

The Sheriff allowed a few seconds of extreme gratitude, then said, 'What I've always wanted to know, Mr Caversham, is why your father, Vice-President of the United States when he was shot, was called Dino de Stefano, yet you children are called Caversham.'

'De Stefano is Italian, sir.'

'So?'

'Caversham is an old English name going back to Charles II. My mother thought we'd do better with Caversham.'

'Why was your father shot?'

'Because someone didn't like an Italian being Vice-President,' replied Alex coolly. 'So maybe my mother has a point.'

The Sheriff could see Alex was no fool. He'd had the best education, he had good manners, yet the Sheriff didn't like him. 'Did you see much of your father?' he asked.

'No, sir,' Alex lied. 'I was always away at school.'

They got to the main door and saw the street full of people and cameramen. 'Put coats over your heads,' said Jack. 'They mustn't get one picture.'

'We can't, man,' said Alex. 'That's only for criminals.'

The path to Jack's car was long and difficult. They were besieged by questions and well-wishers, and covered in confetti. 'It's Margery Caversham's son,' people murmured.

Jack nearly slaughtered the engine starting it up, and then drove crazily to the registrar in the village. 'It's a trap,' he hissed. The car bounced from side to side against thick snow, skidded on ice. 'That solicitor – where is he? He's not driving behind us. Yet he's the one with the licence.'

Seeing what was ahead of him in the way of driving skill who could blame him, thought Jane. So this was fame. She hadn't realised she was still wearing her colourful gypsy skirt, now torn and crumpled. The farmer's wife had lent her a thick roll-neck sweater. Her shoes were mere whisps of soaked leather, one sole flapping. In comparison Alex looked cool, even elegant, in his torn leather jacket and cords that never seemed to get dirty.

Reporters had flocked to the registrar's house and were already surrounding the door when Jack's car stopped. The flashbulbs blinded Jane. The men stared inquisitively at her stomach. Pregnant? Was that the reason for all the fuss? She took the huge sweater off. No bulge. They'd have to be content with a simple romance of a superstar's son and a deceased racing driver's mistress three years older.

A photographer on bended knee begged Alex to uncover his face. 'If you don't give him one soon,' said his colleague, 'he'll never be able to get up. He's got arthritis'.

Amused, Alex took his arm away from his face and smiled, genuinely. This became the famous wedding photograph and that smile nearly broke Margery's heart.

'Get in the house. They'll get nothing,' shouted Jack, ignoring the cameras clicking endlessly.

Jane felt completely overwhelmed amongst the shoving, purposeful men. It was all too chaotic, on the verge of violence. 'Doesn't it worry you?' she asked Alex.

'No, I'm used to this.' He'd recognised two agency men in the crowd. He made a gesture indicating 'I'm all right. I can handle this.'

One said to the other, 'Toss for who tells Margery.'

Inside, Jack shut the curtains as a few agile journalists scrambled over the vegetable patch. The marriage took time because Jack kept taking flash photos, making the registrar nervous. She kept losing the place in the book and her voice shook. Alex gestured for Jack to cut it out, but this was Jack's moment too – he owned the wedding. And then Jane realised they didn't have a ring. Her eyes shut in horror. She'd forgotten all about it, possibly because she never believed it would happen. But Alex produced one, a simple thin gold band.

The minute it was over Jane sat down, dazed, almost faint, and the registrar kissed her. The woman was very emotional – after all, she'd just conducted the wedding ceremony for Margery Caversham's son. She got out the sherry. The farmer and his family pushed their way by brute force through the throng of reporters and into the house carrying champagne and an iced cake. The farmer turned and with one huge foot slammed the door sufficiently hard to send flying several would-be intruders. Jack opened the champagne. The farmer and his wife liked Alex because, although he was the son of a celebrity, he had no side. He didn't come on all airs and graces. And the girl was lower-class, like one of them.

Suddenly the room was peaceful and Alex sat down beside Jane and said quietly, 'Now you're my wife.'

She felt a surge of intense happiness unlike anything she'd known before. And she sent out a prayer, a gesture of gratitude to God and the universe for allowing her such joy.

'Where did you get the ring?' she asked.

'In London. Just before we left.' He showed her the box. 'You see I knew we'd go through with it.'

Jack was saying, 'The good things, they come out of nowhere too.'

And Alex thought, looking at his wife, My father would like her.

. . . Chapter 11 . . .

Alex and Jane moved into Jack Goddard's flat in Earls Court because the press couldn't find them there. In return Jack took her flat on the Finchley Road, and because he was feeling optimistic about directing Alex on film he turned the living room into an office. With his second half-share of the racing driver exposé he bought blow-up silver plastic furniture which gave Alex plenty to laugh about. 'But the guy does try,' he admitted, and went to look for his friend Lucien, who had taste.

The Earls Court flat contained just a bed, a clothes cupboard and a stove. Alex liked it because he hated possessions. He moved in his stereo sound system from Lucien's and a book in French by Céline. He agreed that Jane should get some large floor cushions – he hated chairs. 'But that's it. Don't get carried away.'

She spent a week scrubbing the floors, the cupboards, even the walls. Alex didn't join in, because surroundings didn't bother him. He went out a great deal because he had to placate Lucien. Lucien, a banker's son, had French Swiss nationality. At thirteen he had been the junior ski champion of Switzerland and from that pinnacle of fame had gone downhill fast. Lucien had an unlimited allowance and an unlimited drug supply, and he was Alex's best friend. Now that Alex had suddenly got married, Lucien felt jealous and left out.

Dino had taught Alex to keep people in compartments. 'Don't let A know C and D. Then you're safe and more effective. You have the power.' Alex had asked why. 'Because A and C and D can get together and they're all in and you're suddenly out. And they know everything about you and they go behind your back.' Alex said that was paranoia. 'Don't give me fancy textbook words, Alex. I'm talking about life.'

Alex had had to admit that his father played the game of politics beautifully: no one knew who he knew.

So, influenced by his father's thinking, Alex kept Lucien away from Jane. Lucien loved him and he would resent Jane – and Alex never knew when he might need Lucien again. Another rule of Dino's had been, 'Don't throw away what's valuable even if you think it's outworn. Fashions change. The old comes back.'

Alex said his friend was possibly a genius because he could arrive at a conclusion instantly without going through the process of rational thought. Also he was capable of encompassing all facets at once and could argue from six different points. Lucien had a mind that could see around corners – he could have done anything; he chose to do absolutely nothing.

So Alex told Lucien that his wife was not an integral part of his life and that nothing need change between them. They'd gone to school together and later had shared women, rooms, flats, boats, hotels. Lucien's love for Alex was total but had never been physically consummated. Lucien was sensitive enough to know that Alex had no bisexual potential.

Jane intuitively felt that men didn't like too many questions. The girls she knew who had been pushy and demanding had come unstuck. She believed that if someone wanted to tell you something it would come out in the end. She felt quite wrong asking about Margery Caversham or Kay: she was worried in case Alex might think that was why she'd married him – in order to be part of that dynasty, and to promote herself as an actress. But his frequent absences from the Earls Court flat worried her, so some questions did begin.

Alex was evasive. 'Lucien and I shared a place.'

She wanted to know what it was like. He hoped a shrug would take care of that. It didn't. 'Just a place,' he said.

'Where?'

'In Eaton Square.'

'But it's incredibly expensive around there.'

He didn't disagree. Jane wanted to know what their life was like.

'We'd get up around eight and go to parties or clubs–'

'They don't open in the morning, Alex.'

'Eight at night, Jane. We'd stay up all night. We'd go to bed at daybreak.'

'Like vampires.'

'If you like.'

Did they eat together? Who cooked? Who were their friends? She needed to know more about it.

He sighed. 'We just sat in the dark and talked and smoked. Then we'd go and see some people and listen to some sounds or take in a movie. Then we'd go back to the dark and talk. He's got the most intricate mind. He's taught me everything I know.'

'Did he look after you, or – who cleaned the place?'

'No, Jane. No one cleaned anything.'

'Did you have a cleaner?'

'No, baby, we just lived there. Then when it got too squalid we just shut the door on it and moved to another place. Then that one got too filthy so we went somewhere else.'

'Didn't you even wash up?'

'Jane, do you have a cleanliness fetish?'

'Around you, yes, I think I do.'

'We didn't wash up or wash the walls or anything. We just moved on. There's no mystery, nothing for you to worry about.'

'So who paid for all these flats?'

'He did. He's got a lot of bread. Flats are not important to Lucien.' Alex wanted her to like Lucien even though she was not going to meet him. 'He taught me how to defend myself. He's given me the greatest gift I could have had: detachment, non-reaction. We did that in India. Because, believe it or not, although they're dying or starving they've still heard of Margery Caversham. Hers is the second most famous name in the world – they did a poll.'

Jane wondered what else they'd done in this dark dusty life. She was desperate to know if they'd slept together. She sensed that Lucien loved her husband and was therefore a threat.

'When can I meet him?'

Another shrug – Alex did a lot of those. 'I'm just going to take a walk. I think the place looks great. It sort of sparkles.' And he ran sure-footed down the stairs like a Red Indian. From the window she watched him walk swiftly to the corner of the Earls Court Road. She strained out and saw him bend and get into a low flat car.

She phoned Al Streep then and said she'd do the drama school audition. Dinah took away the phone and said she was very upset. Why hadn't Jane told her she and Alex Caversham were going to marry? They'd befriended her. What a repayment.

Jane said, 'Alex doesn't trust anyone, Dinah, so I couldn't phone.'

Dinah said coldly, 'That's wonderful. I trust you enough to devote hours of my time to giving you a career. That you say you want.' She felt betrayed and was near to tears. 'The audition is off as far as I'm concerned.' She hung up.

Jane phoned the drama school and said she wanted to audition as arranged.

When Alex came in he said, 'So that's what you want to be like – Al Streep's wife. D'you want to speak with that horrible upper-class English voice? Because if you do I don't want to hear it.' And he imitated Dinah exactly.

'So you know her?'

'I've seen her on television in that Shakespeare series. Lucien and I used to get high and she'd make us higher, believe me – hysterical.'

'But, Alex, I want to be a film star.'

'There's nothing wrong with that – I wanted to be a jazz musician – as long as it stays as want.' He put his arm round her and the bad moment was over. 'Come on. It's only life. Don't take it so seriously. After all, no one's ever got out of it alive.'

She laughed and he threw her backwards on to the bed. 'Let's go to Morocco.'

Forgetting that it was only a kind of game, she said, 'I can't. I must do the audition. Just to see.'

'Loser. Let's do it.'

She started to take her clothes off.

'No, let's do it and get high.' He indicated the envelope of dope by the bed. 'Roll one.'

She got out the papers, the block of leb, the roller, the knife. He watched her make the joint. She did it too quickly. It was a delicate ritual for him, rolling the stuff. The anticipation should be beautiful. 'Do it again, slower,' he said.

He put on his new Django Reinhardt LP and suddenly she realised that he didn't have any possessions in the flat. She had her clothes, books, photographs, makeup, skates. She'd bought new cooking pots and crockery, but he was happier eating out of a paper bag or in a restaurant. She asked when he'd move his things in.

'I don't have any.'

'What, nothing from the past?'

'My childhood things are in Cannes. I've got clothes and stuff all over the place. I always carry my passport in case I want to travel.'

So she asked if he'd ever wanted to do anything – she meant a job.

'I'm always doing things.'

'Like be someone.'

'Jane, I have enough of that back home.'

'But you got into the zoo because you wanted to know what a wild animal feels.'

He shook his head. 'No, I didn't find out what wild animals feel, but I sure know how it feels.'

'Meaning?'

'To be free. Because that cage was the one place my mother couldn't get at me.' He changed the record and lay back on the bed.

'What's she like?' Jane hardly dared ask the question.

'She's a very remote person.'

'Then why does she want to be involved with you?'

'Because I'm her, and she's me.'

Jane assumed that some dope had gone wrong. She hoped that's what it was: there was a hint of Lucy in that last remark. She knew little about his childhood. Alex had told her his mother didn't like too many possessions around – she said the children should rely on their own qualities and inner resources. He and his two sisters used to play the 'Let's' game. It was a dare, and was something to stimulate them, because they knew, in spite of the sparse toy cupboard, that they could go anywhere, do anything, and sooner or later they'd have everything.

Alex couldn't bear his mother. For as long as he could remember she'd poisoned his existence. He could still hear her heartbeat as he'd heard it in her womb, beating through his body, tom-toms warning of disaster. She still enveloped him – with her arms, her thoughts, her desire for him to be great. Her need of him was almost indecent. He'd been forced to put a geographical distance between them. Nevertheless, he refused to blame life and the world for this state of affairs. He felt proud that his hatred of his mother had not turned him against women in general and made him mean.

Jack pushed into the room with armfuls of newspapers. 'Part two of "Del's Scarlet Life". I'm handling translation rights. Now an offer from two papers for the wedding. Did Del know about Alex, they're asking. Well, did he?'

'Of course not,' said Jane.

'Maybe he should. It's just a thought.' He wanted to see how Alex would react: he didn't. 'An American film company wants the rights of Del's love story. That's you, Jane. Now we're getting exciting. Visconti, Alex – he wants to see you. It's a big, big part. I've also heard that Della Prima, your mother's Svengali, would like to see you. You're a natural – you know that?'

Jane felt a stab of pain. Was it jealousy? She pointed to a magazine under Jack's arm. 'Who's that?'

'This is Kay Caversham. Three-page profile. She's on the front of all the mags. Making *Baby Blue* in LA – her first film.'

Jane grabbed the magazine. 'She's not as beautiful as you, Alex.'

'No,' said Jack. 'She hasn't got his eyes. She hasn't got his sex appeal. And that's why everyone wants Alex.'

'Don't tell *her.*' Alex rolled another spliff.

'So what do you think?' asked Jack.

'I think,' said Alex, 'that you should go to the tube station and buy me an ounce off the Moroccan.'

Jack didn't speak, but his face reddened. Alex went on making the spliff.

Jane said sharply, 'I think Jack's come in with some incredible news, Alex. This is really exciting. Don't you see? We could be stars.'

Alex looked up, one scathing glance, then he returned to reality. He lit and smoked it and let the two punters get on with fantasy.

For the first time Jane was angry with him. She desperately wanted to meet Visconti, and here he sat, this spoilt boy, denying her that right. Jack started to speak but Jane shook her head. She asked, 'Will you see Visconti, Alex?' No answer. 'We could go and meet him – at least we could do that. I would like to do that.' When he still didn't answer she said, 'I want to do that!'

Alex smiled at them both. 'I married Jane because I wanted to be with her – to live with her, spend time, do things. I didn't get married to be obsessed with myself or ambitious or out to put the next guy down. There's no way I'm ever going to be there, Oscar night. I've seen my mother collect four. I know what that costs.'

Neither Jack nor Jane knew what to say. He was so far removed from their own experience.

Finally Jack said, 'Look, man, I'm handling a lot of stuff for you. The press are all over me because you're a Caversham and Jane's had this blown-up romance with a dead racing ace. I'm stuck up at Jane's flat with a disturbed girl and a white rabbit and five hundred press guys at the front door, at the back door, and Lucy doesn't even know if she's having hallucinations or they're real.'

'You can walk away from it.'

Jane had never heard Alex sound so cold.

Jack said, 'All those opportunities! That money! Are you mad?'

'Get a stand-in then,' Alex got up. 'Get a guy like me and put a pair of shades on him. Be his agent. Put him in a pop group. Be hip. Get rid of that grammar school accent and talk like Jagger. Be a little better than an agent. A touch of wise man. Gurus are in. Buy a sunlamp and sit under it. It's smart to say you've just come back from India.'

'Find someone like you?' said Jack, taking it all seriously.

The thing is, there is no one like Alex, thought Jane.

'And in the meantime go and see the Moroccan before he gets busted or something.' He threw Jack a ten-pound note – Jane didn't think she'd ever seen one before. 'And get a few tabs. Say they're for me so you don't come back with sugar pills. And, Jack, have a drag. Come on now.' He encouraged Jack towards the spliff. Jack didn't want it. 'Take one deep drag and you'll know what it's really all about.'

Jane wanted to say 'Don't do it', but she kept out of it, walked to the window and looked out. The place reeked with dope fumes. Jack must have taken a drag because Alex said, 'Take it down. Easy. Don't let it go too soon. Come on. Again. Nice and deep. I liked what you said about her banging a dead racing ace. Go for broke – say she's having it with his ghost. What's one more lie? You've told a thousand and been paid for them. But don't worry, I won't say anything. Just get off my back.'

He sounded just like his father when he was dealing with bad guys. They'd always show up with a proposition and a Brooks Brothers suit. Dino would whisper, 'Shut the fuck up!' and the men were as silent as a tomb. No one hassled Dino – because he was clean. Alex realised the one image they all retained of his father was the same: Dino washing his hands. Kay mentioned it; his mother kept going on about how energetically he washed and how good he'd looked doing it. Charlotte said, 'Daddy told me he'd be the Vice-President when he was washing his hands in the White House.' Dino washing his hands – was it a symbol of another kind of clean-up? Dino always said he could handle bad guys because they came from the same street as him.

Jack breathed nice and deep and threw up violently over Alex's feet. Alex, amused, cleaned it up. Jack was embarrassed.

'Listen, it happens,' said Alex. 'Your first blow? You have to get used to it.'

'Don't get used to it,' Jane whispered urgently.

'I'll go and get your stuff.' Jack got up shakily. 'I prefer drink, that's mother's milk to me. And can I say you'll talk about a film, Alex? I've been offered five hundred if you'll just say yes.'

'Say what you want,' said Alex. 'It's a free world.'

Jane thought a lot about Jack. He had energy and he could pitch an idea, but the passivity inside him, like a stinging jellyfish, would win. He'd become a crook.

Alex said it wasn't passivity but a delirious, almost sexual desire to fail. And inventing a story and making money out of it wasn't being a crook, it was called public relations.

. . . Chapter 12 . . .

The US Government wanted to plant the cherry tree to commemorate Dino de Stefano's death just north of the spot where he was gunned down in September 1964. Margery had the same laugh as Alex for the unfunny moments. 'Jamaica Avenue. D'you know where that is?' she asked Shane. 'It's the road to the airport in New York. And it's full of traffic all the time – lanes full of cars, lorries, taxis, and on either side dilapidated houses. Sad people live there. And Dino used to hate that ride to the airport. He'd say, "You know, I wouldn't be caught dead here."' She sighed. 'Well, he was.' She sat too still, too silent.

Shane didn't feel that it was right to speak just then, and he was glad when Julian came in and gave him a huge wink, saying, 'Mick Jagger's on TV. Hurry up, it's starting.'

Shane almost rushed from the room, then looked at his mother. 'If Daddy hated that street so much why not plant the cherry tree somewhere else?'

'Isn't that just what I was thinking?' said Margery.

'Somewhere he did like.'

She nodded at Julian and said in French, 'This boy's got sense. Not like his fucking brother.'

'He speaks several languages too,' said Julian in English. He'd spent the day trying to placate her, keep Kay calm, keep the press away. His jaws were aching from all the smiling he'd had to do.

'We'll plant the cherry tree right here in his favourite spot by the river. Let the President come here. Dino did enough for that lot. Anyway I'm not going there. I wouldn't set foot in America ever again.'

Julian muttered something about the healing effects of time, and Margery looked at him as though he was out of his mind. He'd seen that look before and the person got fired. 'Julian, my husband was murdered, five bullets. Because he wanted to improve the lot of those poor black bastards and others like them in the States. What time is going to make me forget that? Clock time? Old age? Perhaps my memory will go? Then I might fucking forget my husband was shot five times in the fucking rain.'

Julian indicated Shane still standing by the door.

She wanted to ring Julian's neck, roast him and eat him, like a big fat piece of pork.

Shane said, 'President Kennedy got shot. I remember going to that funeral. But I don't remember Daddy's funeral.' He looked upset and Julian put his arms round the boy's thin shoulders. Someone had to give him affection.

'I really want to go hang-gliding, Mummy.'

Margery shook her head.

'You say I can do anything, yet when I ask, you always so no. All I want is to go hang-gliding.' Shane pulled away from Julian. 'Why not?' He stamped his foot.

'Because it's dangerous,' said Margery.

'Is it true my brother got married? Kay wouldn't tell me. It's in all the newspapers, even the German ones.'

'No, he didn't get married,' said Margery. 'He just thought he did. He's a Catholic. They marry in a church.'

Julian blinked in astonishment. Was she now believing in God?

As though reading his mind, Margery said, 'Dino was a Catholic. He believed in God. Let's hope there is one for his sake.'

'May I watch Mick Jagger now? I don't feel very cheerful,' said Shane.

She nodded and the boy sped away.

'Everyone comes to the ceremony. Except that girl,' Margery said.

The phone rang while Alex was making love to her. With one hand he reached out, lifted the receiver and pressed the receiver rest, disconnecting the caller. Then he let it go, so that the line was engaged.

There were two kinds of women, he thought. There were the passive, receptive creatures whose only wish in life was to adore him and give him pleasure and so get quite a lot themselves in the process. He knew with every thrust which sent them shuddering off to an even more piercing orgasm that he could say, 'Die with me,' and they would. And he could say, 'You'll do anything I say,' and they would. It would increase their pleasure, the thought of sexual suffering. Sometimes he became cruel, hurting them, and they yielded to that and cried out and begged him to stop while their entire bodies begged him to go on. Alex took sex into a whole new sphere. Within one fuck he could put on a three-act Greek tragedy, the players passing through ecstasy, suffering, near-death, then back to ecstasy. And he'd use the room and the furniture, even the street if he had to. He fucked them enough to pierce their souls and there they were – all revealed to him, all his.

That was the first kind of woman. And the second? All other women. Some said he was the best lover, unforgettable. It was in his blood – he'd got it from his father.

Alex had to admit it was the one thing that had come naturally – no effort, nothing to learn. Everything else had to be learned, and he wasn't so good at that.

As she came Jane pulled his hair and clawed his back. 'Go on,' he whispered. 'Go on.'

Afterwards she was ashamed of her savagery. 'You're just staking your claim on me, leaving your mark,' he said 'It's kind of primitive, but understandable.'

'Why? Why should I do that?'

'So other women know I'm yours.'

'Are there any?'

'Of course not.'

Once again she brought up the subject of other women in the past, and once again he said he'd never had any. He felt obliged to lie. His father had said, 'If you're serious about a woman give her a kid but don't let her get into your world. She doesn't choose your friends. And whoever you sleep with, tell her she's the best. Why not make someone happy? You get so little chance of that.'

Had his father had mistresses? A lot of people wanted to

know that. But Alex instinctively knew he had not. He'd found the woman he wanted, who gave him total pleasure. Why waste his energy and opportunity on something less good? That was dumb. Alex knew his father's thinking. So instead of a business meeting two afternoons a week that took place naked in anonymous hotel rooms, he took his daughters shopping or ice skating. He even sat in the room while Kay had her piano lessons. Dino had always touched the kids. Alex realised that his mother never had, except later when she tried to kiss him. She'd say, 'Alex hold me,' in a dark, broken voice, and he'd leave the room stealthily. That was after his father's death.

Dino was short, much shorter than Margery. He was stocky, fast moving, no more than five seven. Alex was his son, his special kid, whom he always included in whatever he was doing. They'd take trips into the Sicilian mountains and make camp. Dino taught him to lay a fire and how to make the twigs catch. They'd cook fish on the seashore and sleep in the shelter of the dunes. Dino taught him about boats, cars, men. Alex knew his father was a great man, not because of the public acclaim but because he did justice to life: he used it well.

Alex got up and made Jane a coffee. She was still laid out, burning, wanting more but too exhausted. How could sex be that good? He said, 'Making love truly does put us together. I really feel that's what we do. Make it. Make love. Like making pastry.'

'What do you know about making pastry?'

'I used to watch our cook.'

'I bet your mother didn't cook.'

'Actually she did, because my father insisted she make pasta. Sophia Loren made pasta.'

'Did she look after you?'

'Sophia Loren?' His eyes were loving and gentle again.

'Your mother.'

'Of course she didn't. My nanny took care of me. Or Julian, the estate manager. I hardly saw my mother. They sent me to all those schools – the American school, Swiss schools, the Lycée – so I did absolutely nothing, I was so miserable. That's the secret when you're pushed: do nothing. I wanted to study with Sartre. Existentialism, that's what I wanted to know about. But it had to be the Prince Charming route. They were training me, preparing me to take over my father's empire.'

'Then what did you do?'

'Finishing school.'

She laughed.

'Sure. In New York at Andy Warhol's factory. I was part of his pop group for a while. I was in the underground movies. He did a film, *The Chelsea Girls*, I watched it being made. Some of the stuff Andy does or allows to be done is as far out as you can get. I love that guy because he let me just go in there and be me. I didn't have to be anyone's son. He said if someone wants to be in movies you control their lives. What he doesn't realise is he's so desperate to be famous I could buy his.'

He dragged on an ordinary cigarette for a change, and looked at his watch.

'So you're into power,' she said.

'No. But I like to know where I stand. My father taught me that. Are you a buyer or a seller? You go in a room. What do you want in there? I usually just want to get out.'

'So you're not like him,' she said.

'I hope not. He's dead.' He looked at his watch again. 'I've just seen the date. I'm twenty today.'

She squealed and grabbed him. 'I've got to get you a present.'

'That's right,' he said. 'I'll have it right now.' And he pushed her under him and made love to her again. It was one o'clock when he turned on the main light and looked down at the street. He loved an anonymous lively place with transient people. 'Let's go to the diner,' he said. 'I'll buy you the best they've got. Five shillings for two.

'Why don't you take me to Alvaro's?' she asked. 'That's more your patch.'

He disliked 'in' places. He threw her her dress and sweater. 'Come on, let's eat. That Jack's a real son of a bitch. He's got my dope and my pills. I bet he sold them for double before he even left the tube station. He learns bad habits fast.'

'Do you like him?'

'Oh yes. He has the exact right face for a pusher. You never remember it.'

'Look, Alex, don't joke. He's got me in the press. He got us married.'

'That's what I said. He's a pusher.' He saw that the phone was still off the hook. It rang the minute he replaced the receiver. He said 'Hello' and his face changed, became remote. He hung up and said, 'They've arrested the Moroccan. They're holding him in Brixton. I'll have to go down there and bail him out.'

'What about Jack?'

'Yeah, he's down there too.'

Jane could see that the birthday dinner was out the window. He'd forgotten he was twenty by the time he'd hailed the cab. She went with him because she wanted to stay close. Jane was so much in love with Alex Caversham that she'd have accompanied him down a mine shaft.

She was amazed at the love and sweetness he gave the Moroccan, who was all hyped up being in jail.

'Look, man, I suffer from claustrophobia. I can't stand it. Get me out of here. You've got to,' he babbled.

Alex talked to him gently, soothing him. 'Just do a meditation. Still your mind. This place is a good test for you, that's all. You can win. You don't have to suffer.'

The Moroccan said, 'Look, I've got your gear. When they got me I stuck it in my mouth up in my cheek.' He showed Alex his bulging cheek. 'If I swallow it I'll be high as shit and claustrophobic. What shall I do?'

Alex looked casually at the two policemen on duty. 'I think your present arrangement is the best.'

'But I'm absorbing it all the time, Alex. It's this big.' He indicated something the size of an egg.

Alex shook his head. 'I'm going to get you out now. I'm putting up some bail this minute. And I'll take you home.'

'I can't stand this small space.' The Moroccan started to jump and shout. 'I'm used to the desert.'

With Jack Alex wasn't loving. He listened to the story of how a plain-clothes cop had pushed in on the deal and caught him red-handed. 'My father is a magistrate in Salisbury. He's not going to like this,' Jack said.

'It's OK,' said Alex. 'It's your first offence.'

'If the press get it–'

'Look,' said Alex, 'you're not in the press. You just write the stuff.'

Even though he was a Caversham and called his own lawyer he couldn't get them out. He would have to wait until ten that morning, then attend the magistrate's court and put up bail. He tried unsuccessfully to see the Moroccan again. He tried to send in a doctor to tranquillise him. He spent the night pacing up and down the Earls Court room. 'Poor little guy. He never got a chance in this fucking world,' he said.

. . . Chapter 13 . . .

After the jail and the court and the drug hysteria, Jane needed to get back to herself, to what she was. The sea – how she longed for it – so she made Alex get up early and she took him to Cromer on the Norfolk coast. It was bitterly cold but they had one sweet beautiful day, a day she would remember for a long time. He said, 'The sea really changes you, you become another person. I've never seen such a change in anyone. I can see why you like it.'

She crouched down at the water's edge and listened to the different rhythms of the sea and felt cleansed. She watched it buffeted in by a strong tide, all grey and green and full of ferocity; it came in to its fullest extent, then reluctantly slid back, pulling with it all the stones and small rocks in a triumphant rattling. She knew its moods, its songs; she loved its wildness. And for the first time in a long while she felt truly herself.

Alex told her his father had felt good by the sea. She asked what sort – there were many different kinds of ocean.

'My father had no taste but he knew what he liked. He liked the big Atlantic rollers.'

'How d'you mean, he didn't have taste?'

'How could he? He came from poverty – crucifix on the wall, a tin pail to wash in. If you did make any real bread you moved into a house that was extremely vulgar. That was Italy. My mother taught him about taste.'

The sea made Jane's face clear and translucent. She looked younger and more beautiful than he'd ever seen her. He thought maybe they should live at the coast – an unselfish consideration, because he loved cities.

When he said he was cold, she didn't move, but sat hypnotised by the sound and movement of the breakers. Out there somewhere in that expanse was what she really wanted and belonged to. Perhaps the sea brought her a new person?

She used to think it would bring her father. She told Alex to go and get a hot drink and something to eat, but he didn't want to leave her, partly because she was so curiously changed but also because he was suddenly afraid she might not be there when he returned.

'I wanted to take you to the sea,' she said, 'because I wanted to give you a present for being in my life.' He caught her hair as the wind tugged through it. That day Alex didn't take any drugs. She made him feel calm.

On the train back to London he asked why she'd ever left Hastings. Why live in a city if you could live by the sea?

'How could I go to Hollywood from Hastings?' She thought of her childhood in the boarding house. The sea, when it was rough, kept her awake at night. She could hear the waves crashing on the beach and breaking over the promenade. Like a pulse it went through her. Then she stood right at the farthest end of the pier, selling rock. Through the slats she could see the waves. It felt as though she was on a boat. Sometimes they let her work the pleasure boats, collecting tickets from the day trippers – but it wasn't Hollywood.

Alex asked her again about her mother. It was obvious she loved her. Why didn't she go and see her?

'Oh, I can't,' she said automatically. She was getting back into the Jay Stone time again. She had to shut that out fast. She could hear fairground music and it was all tumbling around in her thoughts. 'I did a radio show.' She was trying to get control. The fairground music came into her dreams often, loud and mocking, and she heard Jay Stone saying, 'People heat up too much and they have to pay a price.' In her dream Jay Stone looked old and matter-of-fact like a gardener. He was telling her something in a brusque way but she couldn't look in case his face was not right.

'A radio show?' Alex was enthralled.' 'What a great thing to do. I'd love to do a radio show. No one would know who I was. I could say what I wanted and no one would ever see me. I'd have relationships by word and thought, night-time conversations with the same caller. Let's go and see your mother.'

She tried to smile as she shook her head. 'Hastings just gives me the horrors.'

Looking at her he saw she still had them. 'What kind of trouble did you get into there?' he asked.

She was thinking, I'm vulnerable. And reckless. I changed my name but I didn't even change the colour of my hair. The truth is I forget the bad stuff so easily. Sometimes I meet someone I haven't seen for ages and I'm not quite sure who they are. So I'm pleased to see them and then when I'm halfway through inviting them back and giving them lunch I realise they're my worst fucking enemy. And my photograph's been in every paper in the world. He'll have seen it by now.

Alex said, 'You have nightmares, Jane – I've been meaning to tell you. You get into quite a bad place when you're asleep.'

Because he seemed wise she decided to ask him for some advice. 'If something bad has happened to you and you decide your way of dealing with it is to forget it and go on as though it never happened, yet occasionally it starts edging into your thoughts, do you make a real effort to get it out of your mind by thinking of something else, or do you just let it all come in and face it at the risk of going mad?'

'I think you should tell me about it.'

She said she couldn't.

'Then I'd keep it out until you're strong enough to let it in and confront it. When you're ready just let it float up into your mind, into your consciousness, and be detached. Like watching a movie. Just remember, the more you keep it pressed down, the more it'll want up. You're entitled to your privacy, Jane. I won't ask you about it.'

They held hands and sat very close, in total harmony, and she knew that nothing could ever break them up. Then she saw Jay Stone's face and the fairground music started, and it was worse than any horror film. She said, 'Alex I will tell you when I can.'

Every time Alex went out Jane rehearsed the Juliet speech and the Tennessee Williams modern piece. She wanted to get rid of Dinah's influence and do Juliet her way, but the actress had had too much power. Whatever Jane did it always ended up like Dinah.

Just before Christmas she went for the audition fully intending to be herself even if she had to make Juliet unconventional. But when she got on the stage, in front of the panel, she was so nervous she couldn't think, let alone improvise. In the end she simply copied Dinah. Conformity paid. The panel were sufficiently pleased to take the unusual step of telling her that on the strength of her Juliet she'd be offered a place the following term. They didn't say anything about the Tennessee Williams piece, which Dinah had not had a chance to change. Jane put on her roller skates and whizzed through the city. She was now on her way to stardom.

These days the flat was full. The Moroccan was sleeping in the kitchen; members of pop groups were always dropping round; Jack was there doing deals which Alex was never going to honour; and then there were the famous pop stars and their hangers-on, and various society beauties who'd known Alex in Cannes. They were all having a look at Jane. After a visit Lucy said to her biker lover, 'Now she's a Caversham I thought she'd be flash, but she's just the same: she hasn't changed a bit.'

Alex watched Jane from the balcony as she skated along the Earls Court Road, and he called to her. She looked up and saw that she was loved. She took him into the only unoccupied place, the clothes cupboard, and told him she'd been accepted for drama school. He didn't speak. She began to feel less thrilled. 'I couldn't tell you I was going in case I flopped,' she explained.

'No, Jane, that's not it. Was it you they accepted, or Al Streep's wife? All you did was copy her.'

He went back to his group. She pulled the phone into the lavatory and told Al Streep. He was genuinely pleased for her.

'Tell Dinah thank you.'

'She's here.' He put Dinah on the line, but when she knew it was Jane she hung up. Al said that was a lousy thing to do.

'Not to louses. She's a taker, Al. She took that innocent boy. Can you imagine the revenge Margery Caversham will extract? Thank God you're not part of it any more.'

Jack, wearing a huge second-hand beaver lamb coat from the Kensington Hypermarket, pushed aside the group around the bed. Alex was lying watching 'Top of the Pops' on TV. The hangers-on admired the fur coat and Jack admitted it had only cost seven pounds. Underneath he wore serious stuff: a patterned floral shirt from Liberty, and Mr Fish trousers tucked into long leather boots from Toledo.

'I've made it,' he told Alex. Alex paid no attention, so Jack said, 'All the money you'll ever need.' He tossed a contract on to the bed. As Alex still failed to react Jack was forced to say, 'The Del Grainger story starring Jane Kirkland and Alex Caversham as Del, for crissake!'

When the group stopped shouting and yelling with excitement Alex turned down the sound and asked what had happened. Jack told him yet again. All Alex saw was his wife's face: how she wanted it.

'So where do we celebrate?' asked Jack.

'Before anyone goes apeshit celebrating, I've got to confess, Jack, that I'm no actor and nor is my wife.'

'D'you think they care about that?' said Jack. 'They want you, Alex, because you're Margery's son. You're photogenic, you're mysterious. They'll do anything to get you on screen. The guy's standing on his head just to meet you.

'You won't get penny one,' said Alex. 'Because I don't act.'

Jane said sharply, 'You did with Warhol.'

'I appeared, Jane. Appeared. I did not act.'

Jack cut in with, 'They want you, Alex, because you're altogether more stimulating than Kay. Your mother's refusing everything, so they want you. Read the contract. We're way past penny one.'

Jane noticed she wasn't mentioned. She was just bait to get Alex Caversham on screen.

'Maybe Alex doesn't like playing in his wife's torrid love story?' suggested a groupie.

'No, I don't mind playing fiction,' said Alex sarcastically.

Jane was almost in despair. She couldn't believe he was turning it down.

For once her life was filled with fame, and she couldn't touch it. It was like blowing bubbles: touch them and they burst.

Jack was saying, 'You're a major attraction, Alex. Your wedding's given you a lot of media attention. People want to know about your life. And your looks don't hurt any. Let's go and eat and sign the damn thing.'

Alex wouldn't even look at the contract. It was something he would never sign, even on his deathbed. He remembered his father walking away from a colossal cut in the trade union takeover racket. He could have had a piece of America in his pocket, but he just got up from the table and said, 'It's not for me. I'm out.' He'd been wearing a pink shirt, a silk tie, dark trousers and a thin, plain leather belt – very Italian. Alex felt they were in Italy because he knew the men around the table were all childhood friends of his father's, even relatives, but it had happened in New York. Dino had told Alex to say goodbye to Uncle Sandro; then they left, and Dino said they wouldn't be seeing these people again.

'Why?'

'It only confuses the issue. Your "no" must mean something. Don't go for half measures – leave that to the women. Their "no" means "Seduce me into saying yes."' He took Alex's hand – he could still feel the impression of his father's gold signet ring hard against his fingers.

Jack was winking at Jane reassuringly, as if to say, 'He's a prima donna but he'll come round to reason.' She thought it best not to speak: if she'd opened her mouth once, she'd have screamed the place down. Then Alex would become more stubborn and the groupies would get a free laugh. Jack threw the contract into the air nonchalantly and put it back in his pocket. 'I think this deserves the Terrazza. The White Elephant? The Troc?'

Jane said, 'Alvaro's.'

For Alex it was dinner time, nothing else, but he didn't want to upset Jane any more – he'd talk to her privately later. He said he preferred the Greek restaurant in Camden Town.

Jack went, as he said, 'apeshit' over that. Who'd notice them in there? So they went to Alvaro's, which was packed, jammed with celebrities: Brando, the Stones, the Greek shipping magnate's daughter Sophia, who couldn't keep her eyes off Alex.

'It's better than the Diner,' said Jack. He'd been completely turned around by fame – the desire for it, its taste. He couldn't get enough of the movie stars in the restaurant. He didn't have a gesture in him that did justice to his greed. And then Lucia came in, the most gorgeous Italian of them all, and the whole restaurant got up and applauded. 'That's not English,' said Jack.

Lucia's beauty was so amazing that Jane couldn't work out if it was makeup, surgery or if she'd been conceived on another planet. She wore a pale blue loose dress trimmed with gold, and a turban to match with a gold stud in the centre that brought out the tints in the blue. It wasn't an ordinary blue, it had a hint of turquoise, and it was ravishing. Perhaps on Lucia even colours became superlatives. She was brown, serene, cherished and fêted. Her shoes were backless gold stilettos dotted with scarlet studs and she carried a stiff scarlet bag with an art nouveau design on the back. The bag stood upright on the table and contained only a modest pressed-powder compact. Also an assortment of health aids: vitamin pills, ginseng, royal jelly ampoules, a powerful vitamin C sustained-release tablet for fatigue, a hunk of real yeast for nerves – she was taking no chances.

Around her fluttered a pretty fair girl in a flimsy yellow dress and a young man in a scarlet jacket with embroidered lapels. Brando's companion, wearing a sari, waved a greeting. A pop star in a tunic with a steering wheel on the back felt starry enough to cross the room and kiss her. She had gold bangles up one arm, a dozen in different sizes and designs so very little flesh showed.

'Smack?' said Jack. 'She's hiding the tracks?'

Alex sat silently toying with the Italian hors d'oeuvres without any real appetite.

Jane was wearing her best outfit, a Bill Gibb long knitted coat of many colours, over a short rose velvet skirt. She had strings of bells around her ankles and although it was winter wore flat gold shoes.

Jack gave up trying to include Alex in the conversation and turned to Jane.

'I used to know O'Toole,' he said, 'before he had his nose done. That was at the Oxford Playhouse and I was doing some directing. It was before his desert movie. Something happened to him in the desert. They do strange things to people. He wasn't the same afterwards.

'What's that got to do with now?' snapped Jane.

'Quite a lot. Because I think he should play Del Grainger.' He indicated Alex. 'Because I don't think our alternative star will.'

Suddenly Lucia screamed, 'My God, it's Alex!' and Brando leaned across and smiled at Alex, and the Stones waved hello, and Lucia's friend in the scarlet blazer pulled Alex across to their table. Then an actress joined them, pop stars, the shipping magnate's daughter Sophia – they all gathered around. Jack watched, without seeming to, by looking in a mirror. 'You know something? He's the biggest star of the lot,' he said.

Jane could hear Brando saying something soothing and nice to Alex, something about a dinner. The new transvestite model had his arms over Alex's shoulders. Sophia was smiling into his face. Alex did not introduce Jane. She had never felt so excluded in her life. You could feel more anonymous amongst the famous than amongst the anonymous. She saw him look at her, and it wasn't the greatest look in the world. She wanted it, he had it, she'd never get it, the look said.

Good manners returned Alex to his seat and he spent the rest of the evening with his wife and host. When they got outside Jane said, 'At least you had a good evening.'

'Yeah. I'd have preferred to be listening to some sounds with the Moroccan.'

Just then Brando leaned out of a long expensive car and beckoned to Alex. 'Don't forget Tuesday. Bring your wife.'

When Tuesday came, however, Alex said he'd rather go to Camden Town and eat Greek. Jane thought she was actually going to die, but she kept it to herself.

Jack said, 'I don't know what it is. Three film directors after him. A movie ready to go. Every chat show in America wants him. Yet he doesn't say yes and he doesn't say no. Does he know how much we want to do this, because I wonder.'

'He knows,' said Jane.

. . . Chapter 14 . . .

Kay flew back from Hollywood ten days before Christmas to be with Mummy. She knew Charlotte wouldn't go – she was too busy doing good in New York – and Alex wouldn't be asked. She wanted Mummy to know that at least one of her children was doing right by her. Also it presented an excellent opportunity to have Mummy to herself and win her over. For as long as she could remember she got her mother's matter-of-fact side whereas Alex got something altogether warmer: when Margery looked at him her eyes filled with happiness. So Kay had done everything she could to be looked at like that. She'd tried to get Margery's attention: 'Look at my dress, my hair. I came top in class. I got my Bac. Guido Cortese wants me to go to Milan for the new season's opening at La Scala.' And Mummy would seem very pleased but the eyes didn't change. Over the years Kay had come to the conclusion that it was because Alex was a boy.

The press flocked around Kay at Nice airport and she gave them the big Caversham smile, lots of teeth. It meant nothing but photographed well. She was wearing a Paco Rabanne dress made of silver discs linked together like chain mail with a matching helmet and silver boots. She'd applied silver body makeup and lipstick. Her hairdresser carried Kay's blue mink and silver fox stole and waited discreetly in the crowd for the Château chauffeur to collect the luggage. The press asked Kay about her first film, *Baby Blue*. Sure she was riding a horse, bareback too – no problem. They asked discreetly about her much-publicised 'friendship' with her leading man. Nothing doing there. So they tried Guido Cortese, the son of the Italian industrialist. Wedding bells in the air? She didn't answer, because she'd just seen her father. She didn't go pale, because she was already made up pale. Quite distinctly, in the airport lounge, he was bending over a rather battered suitcase, his black curly hair quite long at the front, flopping over his forehead as it did when he was young. Of course it wasn't Dino, it was just some young man who had the good fortune to look like him. She remembered her mother describing the early days of their love affair. After meeting him, quite by chance, in Rome while filming with Della Prima, she'd accepted his invitation to go dancing. He was in his mid-twenties and very sure of himself in a quiet way. Also very dangerous. He made you want him, which had always been her role. He allowed her to get the impression that he was a lawyer in Rome. In fact he was the junior member of a legal firm in Naples and had only recently taken his exams. He was a marvellous dancer and she loved the way he moved and how he made her feel high. They'd spent a few days together and then she'd returned to London. He'd written to her, always from a Rome address, articulate, passionate letters. Margery decided she couldn't live without him and went back to Rome; also Della Prima had offered her a second film.

She arrived earlier than she'd intended and went straight to the address Dino had given in the letters. There at his friend's apartment she found out that Dino did not live and work as a lawyer in Rome but in Naples. He was one of many kids from a poor background. She also found out what train he'd be arriving on. Instead of waiting at the hotel as arranged she went to the station. She couldn't wait to see him, she loved him so much. And there he was, getting off a third-class train packed with peasants from the south, wearing not the usual elegant suit but peasant trousers and a white vest. His hair was long and unruly and hung over his forehead. His cheap shoes flapped and he carried a battered suitcase which contained the suit he was going to wear to meet her: he'd planned to change at the station. It was very hot and around his neck he wore a cheap red scarf and a gold cross and chain. Margery was acutely aware of people's style. She rejoiced in the beautiful, needed elegance. And here was this poor youth, no different from dozens of others coming to Rome looking for the big break. At first she'd thought, Oh no. Can this be what I left London for? I longed for this; fantasised about this? Then as he got closer she saw his eyes, and that's all she saw. They were proud, hot, far-seeing eyes and they glowed when he saw her. And he smiled, not too much. Then he put down his case and held out his arms and she came to him – running. He smelled of fresh sweat, and from that moment she was crazy about the smell of his sweat. And from that moment, as he cradled her against him, she wanted to be in his life. So far every man she'd met had had to be in hers. Then he took her hand and walked with her to a taxi, showing no sign of embarrassment that he was dressed so poorly and she so well. Margery said years later, 'I've never seen your father ashamed. That has to be unusual.'

Again the reporters asked Kay about Guido. Guido's father was dressed in Gucci from the moment he was born. He was one of the most powerful men in Italy, choosing politicians and police chiefs and grooming them for his needs. He owned a chain of factories across the country, a right-wing newspaper, a bank. He entertained visiting royalty, gave money to hospitals as long as he was photographed at least a dozen times doing it. He spoke several languages, was well educated, had beautiful manners, hated the Left. Instead of a heart he had a control tower. People did what he wanted. He was used to it that way. His temper was legendary. Oddly enough, though, Kay did not dislike him. Old age had neutered him, and in her company he kept his right-wing views to himself, out of deference to her father. When he wanted to thwart a dream he wasn't subtle: he simply bought the dream and threw out the dreamer. When Guido, his eldest son and heir, showed a disinclination to go into factory management he gave him sixty seconds to explain why. Guido said he'd prefer a life in music. His dream was to become a musical director at La Scala, Milan. The father promptly bought up the shares until he had a controlling interest, and promptly barred his son from the theatre: he could make and break tough politicians so he could surely remotivate a sensitive, misguided son. Men worked and made money. Women listened to music. It was fine for men to accompany them in the evening. Guido had better familiarise himself with factory management speedily or he'd be singing on the streets of Naples. Naples to Old Man Cortese was Alcatraz. Kay had been angry about what he'd done to Guido, but why didn't Guido retaliate? Kay hadn't seen the old man's threatening, bullying manner. Other, bolder men than Guido had been stopped in their tracks. The old man's anger was ferocious. Guido described it as Wagnerian. During such a display he terminated contracts, broke careers. It was pointless going against him unless you could win; otherwise withdraw and wait until he was in a good mood.

Kay was aware that he could do many favours for her in Italy. Who knew what she might require in the future? She might choose to direct films, even own a studio. The Cortese connection ensured success at least in one country.

'Yes, I expect to see Guido Cortese this visit,' she said. 'After all, he is a friend of the family.' And she thought how good-looking he was, good company, an excellent driver, a pilot. He knew everybody. He only appeared at a disadvantage when in the company of his father.

Then the reporters switched to the real news, her brother Alex. Her smile dropped and she got into the Rolls. As the driver sped up into the hills he said, 'It's all Alex these days, Miss Kay. No one talks of anything else.'

'And I came all this way for a bad time,' she hissed.

Once again Margery read aloud the two excerpts from 'Del's Scarlet Woman'. It made sense to Kay. Where was the mystery? Del Grainger was divine and this girl had gone after him. Who wouldn't! Then she'd simply picked up Alex in some low-life hovel and married him on the rebound. Death did funny things to people. It had made her mother unrecognisable. Margery without Dino had become a recluse.

'Why do you keep wearing black, Mummy?' Kay asked.

Margery sighed. 'Because it's the only colour bearable.'

'But it's over three years.'

'Kay, don't keep bringing time into it!' she snapped. 'Now it says here quite distinctly that this girl has been sleeping with this racing driver for over a year. Well, all I can say is she didn't do it very well, because according to my people this girl lived in near-poverty.'

What could Kay say? The racing driver was mean? He liked poverty? It turned him on?

'Kay, for my daughter you're sometimes a disappointment. I'm showing you a piece of lousy PR and you don't see it. All your life you've been steeped in PR. Don't you find it odd that the only locations mentioned in the exposé are two boats and one front garden? Now that isn't a lot for a year. She never went to his home, nor he to hers. A house in Tite Street is implied, but I've taken the implication out of that because I've found out who lives there.'

Kay sighed. 'So they did it in cars, Mummy.'

'They never did it, Kay. She was never seen at race meetings. A girl like that would push herself in there.'

'She's discreet.'

'Kay, why keep defending her? And the wife apparently got his action every night.' Sometimes Margery sounded like Dino.

'So he does it in the day as well. That can happen.' Didn't Kay know!

Margery thought she'd scream. 'This, Kay, was a girl who met a famous man at most once and got a lot of mileage out of it. She's a liar. It's been ghost-written. And it's full of crap.'

Kay could see that Margery had a new interest in life: hating 'the girl'. 'Why don't you get someone to ring her up and ask what he was like in bed? And then you'll know.'

'Know?' Margery was impatient.

'Mummy, I can find five girls who slept with Del Grainger.'

'And you make six.' She sounded almost bitter.

'I wish I did. He was divine.'

Margery took off her reading glasses and lay back on the

sofa. Kay looked at the photos of Del and Jane, Jane alone, Jane and Alex. 'They're even bringing in a subplot: jealousy over my son made Del Grainger careless and want to die.'

Kay saw how photogenic her brother was. Three faces and you only saw one.

'Mummy, do you think Alex is more photogenic than me?'

'Sometimes, darling,' said Margery diplomatically.

'Tell me the truth. Is he better-looking?'

'Oh, Kay, do stop competing with the boys all the time. You're supposed to attract them not take their place.'

'You haven't answered me.'

'Of course he's not better-looking, Kay. You're the one who gets all the movie offers. I don't know how this girl trapped him. She obviously likes to hang around the famous.'

'She married him for his name,' said Kay.

'*My* name!' Margery's tone was sinister.

'Then why don't you just buy her off? Give her enough money.'

Margery laughed. 'I think I already have.' She snapped her fingers and Jennifer hurried in and set up the projector and screen. 'Remember our trip to London just before Daddy died, summer '64?' The newsreel movie flickered on to the screen and became steady. It showed Dino, Margery and the children walking around Leicester Square. Police held back the crowds of fans. 'Make it lighter, Jennifer.' Margery pointed to the entrance to Leicester Square tube station. 'Put the sound on, Jennifer.' The commentator said that the royal family of the entertainment world even had time for buskers, especially the little blonde waif. 'There! There she is!' And Kay saw a thin girl with golden hair dancing and singing in the gloomy entrance to the tube station. Her eyes were black-rimmed, the lids painted silver; her mascara so thick, the lashes were like spiders' legs. She came through the gloom like a ray of light and the dance got faster, wilder.

The commentator said, 'And Dino is taken with her. And in true showbiz spirit the blonde waif is appreciated.' Dino threw her some money. Shane, who was holding Margery's hand, wanted to give her some too. 'Look at her face,' said Margery. Shane went forward and gave the girl some coins. She stopped dancing and smiled. 'Close-up on her face, Jennifer.' The picture pulled in. 'Hold it.'

Kay could see the girl clearly now.

'I never forget a face,' said Margery.

Kay wasn't sure. The makeup was so different.

'It's ironic because Alex wasn't even looking at her. He was looking at some birds hopping about. Roll it back, Jennifer.'

Kay couldn't even remember the incident – there'd been so many. The girl was fabulous, though: ragged, barefoot, with proud beggar's eyes. She looked at the photos in the newspaper.

'That was my Christmas surprise, Kay.'

'Oh, I don't know, Mummy – you can read so much into a photograph. You could cut him off. If the attraction is financial, stop his allowance. He's still under age, so that'll bring him running. And she can go on doing that dancing she does so well.'

Margery thought her daughter had a cruel streak. She knew for a fact that Kay had gone and doubled her Nestorin stock. Right behind Julian's back she'd purchased $100,000's worth of falling shares, used her film money to do it. If that got out! Margery couldn't bear the pictures of the children burnt in the factory explosion. She sent $50,000 anonymously to the African hospital and didn't even tell her family.

'What does Shane want for Christmas?' Kay asked.

'Mick Jagger.'

'But he's got all the albums.'

'No. He wants Mick Jagger.'

Kay looked upset. 'I thought it was my chance to shine.' She snuggled close against her mother, and Margery patted her and wished she was Alex.

Margery watched the staff hoist up the Christmas tree as Shane ran round and round, childishly excited. She kept seeing Dino bringing her the small citrus tree in Rome. It was their first Christmas and they had no money: he couldn't afford a fir tree. She watched him stand the young tree, it was hardly more than a plant, bearing oranges of different sizes, on the hotel window ledge. And then he turned and smiled. 'Happy Christmas, cara.' It was the last time they were poor, for Dino got lucky the next year and he couldn't go up the ladder fast enough. She'd never seen anyone work as hard. She remembered the poor time, and that Christmas was the happiest, ever. Her eyes filled with tears, and she quickly put on dark glasses so Shane wouldn't see.

The orange-tree flourished on the window sill in the winter sun: it was so lovely and gay, and after that came only good things. Those times could only be mourned. What surprised her was that they were still there. Life with Dino was in Technicolor, and the rest black and white. And then she panicked. It occurred to her that she might never get over her loss. Panic sent her running to her private phone.

Alex answered and she asked if he was alone. He said he was although Jane was doing some voice exercises in the lavatory.

'I just wanted to know how you were?' She tried to keep her voice steady. She really wanted to say, 'Alex, I need to talk about Dino. You're the only one I can say this to.'

'I'm fine. And you?'

Margery had never had a hostile audience so she didn't have any technique handy. This conversation seemed worse to her than confronting a thousand disappointed fans.

'Well, obviously, I'm not fine.' Her voice shook uncontrollably and the prepared speech flew from her mind. 'Of course you've done this deliberately. You've done this to break open the wounds caused by your father's death.'

'Mom, I love her.'

'How much more are you going to hurt me? You blame me for Daddy's death. You always have. I know you do. Dr Erikson said you did. Why don't you tell me to your face – I mean my face –'

'Mom, I think you've gone crazy.' Alex had never heard her like this.

'You're the one person in this universe I love. So what do you do? Something so evil even your sister couldn't have thought of it.'

'Mom, Charlotte's doing very good things in the Bronx.'

'I meant Kay. Do you realise what I have to go through? Your father dying. I've never got over that. Your leaving. Your drug addiction. And now this – this girl.'

'Mom, I love her.' His voice was icy.

Margery breathed in, a long deep breath, then another one, and the panic eased off. 'Now, Alex, the President is coming for Daddy's ceremony. The cherry tree is being placed by the river

D'Or. You remember Daddy's favourite spot. Of course this is a private occasion. Just family. You have to be here, Alex. You must show your respects.'

'Sure. I'll bring my family.'

'Alex, that girl is not acceptable.'

'Then I won't come.'

'Then you're cut off.'

'That's OK. I can earn my own living.'

'I mean cut off from me.' Her voice was savage. 'And your money stops too. By the way,' she continued crazily, 'your sister's in a movie. They say she'll be very good. Truffaut wants her. And, Alex, you can come home for Christmas.'

'Mom, I think we need some space from each other.'

'You've just got it. You're cut off!' she screamed, and slammed down the phone.

Jane was no longer doing her rehearsal. She was listening at the door. Nonchalantly she came into the bedroom. 'Who was it?'

He looked like a fox sensing a trap. His eyes were large, nostrils flared. 'No one important. Let's go to Morocco for Christmas.'

'But they don't celebrate Christmas.'

'Exactly.'

'Let's just get on a train and go,' she said.

They spent Christmas in Marseilles. It was the best one either of them had ever had.

. . . Chapter 15 . . .

Julian crept into Kay's apartment as she was packing. 'Visconti is coming here,' he said.

'Oh, really?' She was the daughter of a legend but it didn't mean she was tired of the famous. 'How marvellous.'

'He's coming to see you.' Julian delayed the good news because he didn't like her, or rather, he thought she didn't like him. 'But he can't get here until tomorrow.'

'But I have to be in LA tomorrow.'

'Kay, that's what I told him but tomorrow is the earliest.'

'All right, all right. Phone LA and say I'm delayed.' She sat on the bed, elated.

'The word of mouth on your film must be pretty fantastic,' said Julian. 'He must have seen the rushes.'

'But how could he? In Italy? Tell LA I'm delayed because Visconti is coming to see me.'

'There's nothing like the truth,' said Julian, 'look at your mother.'

Margery's father was an equerry to King George V and was descended from the Tudors. Her mother could trace her line back to Charles II. Margery loathed English snobbery and fair looks. Before Dino de Stefano in Rome there'd been many men, a lot of sex, a lot of mistakes. She'd had a particularly vile abortion in the 1940s. Over the years before she met Dino she'd hung a discreet veil. Her mother soothed loneliness by gluttony. Margery opposed her at all times. Because the family was Tory, Margery found plenty to admire in the Labour Party and openly supported them. Because she was the most beautiful girl in London she was given a small part in a wartime movie. Immediately after the war she appeared in the famous English film *After the Dark*, and although her role was secondary to the male actors she became a star overnight. Even today her performance hadn't dated. That was a curious aspect of Margery Caversham – she never seemed out of fashion.

Immediately the film was released the Italian superstar director Della Prima took over. He simply appeared at her mother's Chelsea house and asked Margery to come with him to Italy. Now Italy was a place Margery had always longed to visit. Against her mother's wishes she gave up the blue-blooded life and the chance of a smart marriage and signed with Deluxe Studios in Rome. She'd always had a classless voice, well-modulated and attractive but not particularly English. She felt much more herself speaking Italian. And then, after America, she acquired a transatlantic accent.

Margery had one quality that made her a star above all others. You couldn't stop watching her, you couldn't get enough of her. Apart from this she had a gaiety, and a laughing wickedness. As for her beauty, it was said that every camera fell in love with her. She burned with a sexuality that made men queue up to see her films. Margery was all grown up, witty, elegant. She liked to win, had to win, on screen and off.

They wrote the scripts to fit the woman: *femme fatale*, bitch, sex goddess, empress, queen, witty elegant female detective, and at least two versions of *Camille*. They tried twenty ways to get her to play Odette from Proust's *Swann's Way* but she said the scripts were never right. In the end she said it was never meant to be filmed: it was something to be read; everyone had their 'Odette'.

She had an infallible instinct in picking a role, and nobody and no amount of money could sway her: no victims unless they became winners, nothing domestic or homely; absolutely no theatre or television. She'd found her metier and in over fifteen years she'd never had a flop. She made thirty films and collected four Oscars, as well as dozens of other prizes and awards. The professional recognition was very important to Margery and she had to have those awards. If another actress outdid her, it was an injustice – the movie industry had gone mad. If she stepped in she expected the other woman to step aside. She'd use anything to win, and her rivalry at Oscar time was famous. She'd even use the once-hated English snobbery.

Towards the end of her career Margery chose never to make more than one movie a year so the public was always in a state of need. Never let them leave the table with a full stomach. After she turned thirty-five she concentrated more on dry comedy. She liked the bright actors with the quick repartee, and chose them as her co-stars: quick-delivered, sophisticated lines you could hear. Dick Powell had been one of her all-time favourites. And Bogart.

Margery had her own interpretation of why she was a star. She said it was because she had a never-ending injection of Latin love from Dino. He was in her thoughts, her voice, her body. Her performances were sometimes an attempt to portray him, as though she was trying to be him. The mixture of Naples and cool Englishness was dynamite. No other star had her chemistry.

She nearly made an error of judgement when the celebrated Swedish director Venn wanted her for *Hurricane*. Two hours into rehearsal and she saw that Venn was stronger than her. He would suck out her juice and leave her, an old grapeskin to be plumped up again with his intellectual ideas. She'd be forever ruined. She ran for her life. She was never ever challenged. Really she didn't have to act, because she was already an enchantress.

Her films played in every major city in the world non-stop from 1950 until the mid-sixties. She grossed more than any other star ever. All she had to do was defend what she was and not let some half-smart creative director try and change it. She was what the public wanted.

When the press asked her what made her such a star she said, 'I was born that way.' And it was true. She'd never had to learn it, just uncover what was there. When Kay asked, 'What do I have to do, Mummy?' she answered, 'Nothing. Just enchant.' Then she realised that of course Kay was different from her.

Other stars deferred to Margery, not because of her box office triumph but because she was intelligent and shrewd. She could sense a film going into trouble like a car going out of control. She knew how to put the brakes on. Some participants fell out but they could be replaced. The film always survived.

And now at the beginning of '68 scripts, dozens of them, still arrived weekly and were not read. She'd never go back. Her 'no', like Dino's, was absolute.

She'd recently found a new outlet for her power drive: investment in the industry. That way she could still dictate, up to a point, what appeared on the screen.

Margery kept other guests away so Kay could have the great director's fullest attention. Dinner was nice, almost like the old days when Dino would bring a pal over from Italy. Margery loved to speak Italian more than any language in the world. After dinner she left them alone as so far Visconti had not made any kind of proposition to Kay. She went upstairs and played Monopoly with Shane and Jennifer. She wished Shane had more friends. Come to think of it he didn't have any.

'Don't you like people, Shane?' she asked.

'Only in films.'

'Why's that?'

'Because they're safe. Otherwise you never know what they're going to do.'

Margery stroked his glossy hair, so like Alex's.

'I figure I could have friends if I went hang-gliding.'

'Yes, angels,' said Margery.

Downstairs the great Italian director said, 'Kay I want you to do something for me.'

'Anything. Just ask.'

'I have seen your brother's photograph in the press. I never guessed he looked like that. I want you to speak to him. I must have him for my next film. I am hungry for him.'

When Guido Cortese arrived Kay was still wearing the famous scarlet evening dress, slim and slinky, and the long diamond earrings. She smiled and he knew she was dangerous. It was exciting, much more so than with a vulnerable girl. He caressed her and said her eyes were full of sins.

'Always keep it plural, Guido.'

'I hope it stays that way. How was it with Visconti? A movie?'

'Some people are born lucky.'

He didn't notice the bitterness in her voice. 'Of course you are.' He kissed her bright red lips.

'Let's play games.' And she put her hand into his pants and was stroking him so eagerly that he nearly came before she'd even got it out.

'Hold it,' he said breathlessly. 'Let me have a turn here.' And he stroked his burning prick against the cool silk of her dress. 'I've got to cool it off then it'll be good for you.'

She let him do all the usual stuff, then she bent him forward over the bed and tied his wrists to the bedposts and his ankles to the bed legs. She got his belt and beat his buttocks.

'Not so hard,' he moaned, unsure whether he liked it. She lashed him hard.

'Lift your arse up.'

The next lash nearly got his balls. He shouted at her to stop.

'If you want to have me, have this!' she retorted.

He kept his arse pinched in to try and avoid some of the pain, but it couldn't be avoided. She'd done a good job tying his wrists. He tried to pull them away from the bedposts. 'Kay, this is not a game.' She stopped. 'That's enough now. Untie the cords,' he begged.

She disappeared from the bed. Was she just going to leave him there? For one terrible moment he thought she was going to take a photograph. She came back and stood over him with a riding whip. Her face was so beautiful. As she lashed him she thought, That's for my brother. And that's for the directors that prefer him. And another for my brother. And that's because he's got Mummy.

Guido's cries had woken Shane, and Nanny was at Kay's door. Kay became conscious of the banging and she stopped, her arm aching. Guido's buttocks were scarlet and were bleeding in two places. The blood wasn't as bright as her dress. Was he unconscious? He didn't speak. In her frenzy she thought she might have blacked out. 'Guido?' His eyes were open, unseeing. She was appalled. Had she killed him? She went to the door and told Nanny to stop making a row and go to bed. There was nothing wrong. An over-loud television – what else? She sped back to Guido and tried to find a pulse. He was breathing and that cheered her up considerably. She bathed his face with cold water, put cold cloths on his buttocks and thighs. She couldn't untie the knots. She got a pair of nail scissors but his hands were bound too tightly. She managed to free his feet. 'Guido, for God's sake talk to me.' Then she was angry. He was a man. He was twenty-six. Surely he could take some control over what happened? Why had he allowed her to tie him up? His buttocks were now coming up in huge weals. His skin was moist and cold. Frightened, she telephoned her mother's bedroom.

The first thing Margery said was, 'Lock the door.' Quickly, efficiently, she turned Guido on to his back and lifted his legs so the blood went to his head. She told Kay to prop cushions under his knees. She covered him with two blankets. 'Go and make some hot sweet tea. Put honey in it.'

'What about brandy, Mummy?'

'No alcohol. He's in shock.' Then she got to work on the cords. It meant two snips in the flesh of his hands, but after what he'd been through she didn't think he'd mind. She rubbed his hands and got the circulation going.

When Guido came round they spoke Italian so Kay didn't understand the intricacies. Guido said he'd never dreamed a girl could do such a thing. Margery was actually appalled but kept it to herself. Surreptitiously she'd assessed her daughter's eyes: they didn't look mad. Margery went on soothing the swollen buttocks with cool cloths soaked in witch hazel. She gave him homeopathic pills for the shock. Then she dressed the bad cuts.

'You shouldn't do this sort of thing,' she told him.

'But I didn't!' He was outraged.

Margery had to stay in control or several bad situations could arise – even a legal one. In Italian she said, 'Guido, I am a woman of the world. A man usually gets on top and does it to the woman. If you want to be staked out on a bed and beaten that's your business, but don't use my daughter.'

Guido was furious. 'I did not choose it to happen.'

'Then it's time for a psychiatrist,' said Margery swiftly.

'For her!' He got to his feet. 'She needs a lot of things. She's vicious.'

'Be careful, Guido.' Margery's voice was still gentle. 'It's my daughter you're talking about. Don't get in that position again unless you know what you're doing. It's dangerous.' She had turned it around completely so that it was the Italian's fault.

The next morning Guido was very pale and said little. He didn't want to take Kay to the airport, or indeed see her again. Kay said, 'OK, you're worried about me. But, Guido, I'm more worried about you. You just let me do it, docile as a lamb. And I don't want to mention it now but you had a hard-on. I mean, Mummy saw it. Put it this way – there's some good in everything. Perhaps I've uncovered a desire for masochism in you. Isn't it lucky it happened with me? You watch it, Guido. Because anything could happen. Next time you could be killed.'

'You Cavershams say anything to change the truth. Is it your money, power, pride, or what?'

'Our blood.' Kay smiled. 'Well, that's what Daddy said as he lay dying. We have dark blood and he cursed us all.'

Guido blamed what had happened on his relationship with his father. He allowed too much to go by unchallenged. He was becoming soft. First he visited La Scala and watched the rehearsal. How he loved that place! Marcello Tallaforos wearing a long black coat strode on to the podium. How elegant, how supreme the man was, like an eagle. He came down from a great height to give human beings the exquisite, the divine. Then Guido made an appointment to see his father. The old man spoke first. When was his son going to marry the Caversham girl? The family needed the alliance. Guido said when he started work as musical director of La Scala.

'But that place is taken,' said his father. 'Some Southern Italian got the job. It's all they're good for. Wine and song. We Northerners are world-class and you should be more proud of yourself. You're a man of business not a troubador.'

Guido blamed his father for the Southern Italian getting the job and would never forgive him. His father said opera house decisions were not up to him, he just supplied the money. What was one more lie? He'd crushed so many dreams.

Guido refused to do any work at his father's head office. He made an occasional appearance so he could pick up his salary. The old man didn't mind as long as he married the Caversham girl. Guido now described himself as a playboy and devoted himself to his new occupation. What better way to get back at his father?

When Kay got to the airport the press swarmed about her in droves. She was confident and smiling outside, but inside she was very shaken up. She hadn't expected anything like that to happen. To tie a man to the bed and beat him until he screamed – this time yesterday the thought had never crossed her mind. She was scared because she didn't know what she'd do next. She had power and strength, and, now hate, which made her dangerous. Life for the first time was frightening.

She talked charmingly about her new film, *Baby Blue*. Of course she was modest and praised Lucia, the main star. Then a journalist said, 'What about your brother? Now he's very special. Does it bother you that people say he's the good-looking one in the family? D'you think you might get him into movies too?'

She felt that it said a lot for her as an actress that she didn't collapse. All she could think of was the dancing waif. It was she who'd sensationalised her brother. If it wasn't for her greed to be someone, Alex would have remained unseen, unheard of, drugging himself to death in some hole with Lucien.

'What do you think of the marriage?'

She spoke in anger, not thinking straight. 'I think my brother is far too young. I don't think this was a thoughtful decision. After all, he hardly knows her.'

'Is this the opinion of the family?'

'Absolutely. We hope for his sake he's done the right thing. Thank you.' And she walked away to the waiting plane.

Halfway across the Atlantic she cheered up. The first-class treatment including non-stop drinks helped. She thought about whipping Guido. Of course it was sexual. The sight of his arse rising up and down against the strap. It had gone wrong because she hadn't played around with him in between the strokes. And she imagined what she'd do next time, because there'd surely be a next time. He'd liked it – no, needed it.

. . . Chapter 16 . . .

Alex said, 'So what that my sister said those things about you? She doesn't know you.'

'She had no right. Do something about it!' Jane was furious.

'I don't speak to my sister. Just ignore her. That'll really get her mad.'

'What does she know about me?'

'What does it matter?' He was trying to cook a pan of spaghetti. The money thing was a drag. He thought he should economise and start eating at home. Lucien, of course, would give him anything, but not for Jane. Lucien, who could approve of anything the universe had to offer, would not accept the runaway marriage: he was cut out and felt it.

'She's got everything – a movie, Guido Cortese, the jet set, the fabulous life. I bet she knows Robert Frey. Why get at me?'

'Jane, my sister is a nymphomaniac. She's got nothing.'

It took Jane's mind off the insults which had made headlines in several papers. Jane wanted to know exactly what a nymphomaniac was.

'I think it's a chemical thing.' He got the spaghetti on to the table. 'It's an excess of something in your metabolism so you keep needing stimulation then you get overstimulated. You can't come and you can't get satisfied. You start going crazy and doing all kinds of things. I'm sure if she took the right sedative she wouldn't have this problem. But who am I to help her?' He ate his spaghetti neatly, swiftly.

'It's not psychological then,' said Jane. Alex didn't think so. He got the Italian sweet out of the oven.

'Thoughts could cause the chemicals to shoot up or chemicals start the thoughts – I don't know.'

'Does she look – odd?'

'I only saw it once. She got a kind of wolfish look. Eyes very bright and slanting, which they're not usually. A bit demonic. And a wolf smile as though she wanted to gnaw on flesh. She was in her bedroom, and I knew she read quite sophisticated pornography because I'd been through her stuff. It was about two years ago after my father died. I think that's when it started. And I think she was reading some of that when I came to the door and it was locked. I had to make her open it because the King of – someone royal – had arrived and she wasn't there. My mother was getting angry. Anyway she must have got it off herself or with the butler, Carlo, because when she came down she was tired-looking but definitely not excitable. And Julian told me she gets guys to fuck her for hours. He doesn't know for sure but he certainly hears the action. He says it's hours. Then that guy goes and another arrives. Off we go again. So obviously being fucked isn't doing it for her.'

Jane didn't understand.

'Ideally she'd just want one guy and a good bang. Obviously she doesn't come. Except on her own. I think she's very goody-goody to please my mother, but all that's going to fall apart now she's in movies. I think she's the next Clara Bow. She'll do whole football teams. So don't worry about what she said. People will be saying much worse about her.'

Jane said it was really nice of him to cook for her.

'I'll be doing a lot of this.'

'What, you like domestic life?'

'Not especially. But I'm cut off. Nothing doing until I'm twenty-one and that's nearly a year away. Then my mother has no say.'

Jane said she'd get a job. 'I'm sure Al Streep will help me. Well, *he* would but Dinah won't.' Then she had a good idea. 'Look, I'll go to drama school and get a grant. We'll live off that.'

'Go if you want to speak in that prissy English way –' He imitated Dinah.

'I'd rather speak like you. I love your voice.'

He took her hand and caressed it and looked at her so warmly that her eyes closed in pleasure. She'd never been so happy.

Jack Goddard said she should make a statement to the press. They were waiting at the door, dozens of them, at the Finchley

Road flat. What was Jane going to do about Kay Caversham's attack on her marriage? She told Jack she was to say nothing: Alex wanted it that way.

'I need money, Jane. We've all done a lot of spending in the last couple of months. I've got to pay the rent on your flat and frankly Alex isn't saying yes to much, in fact anything.'

She told Jack they were cut off.

'Then that's crazy. He's got to make a movie. Push him.'

Jane was undecided. The relationship was so good she did not want it to change. 'If he made a movie he'd become well-known and he'd change and then our scene would change. Maybe he wouldn't love me any more. What if I make a movie?' Alex wouldn't like that either but at least it was safe: she'd have the control.

'Yes,' sighed Jack. 'But they're not asking for you.'

That one hurt. She crossed to the cupboard and looked through the rail of freshly purchased clothes. If she'd known about the cut-off she'd never have gone so crazy in the boutiques. But it was the first time in her life she'd had real money and she went wild. Alex said it was normal and good for her. 'You've always been without. You've got a lot of hunger there. So eat and fill yourself up.' Clothes, shoes, makeup, books, records. She put on an amazing white leather suit with white fur, slit up one side, and high-heeled scarlet film star shoes. She loved those shoes, couldn't stop looking at them. She looked soft, with her newly dyed white hair, Baby Doll style. She painted her mouth pink then outlined her lips in a slightly darker colour. She looked too damn good not to be in movies. It was madness to coop up all that glamour. In the mirror she could see the jumble of Alex's daily possessions by the bed: he never picked up anything – he was so used to servants doing it. She saw an envelope bulging open with powder; she noticed it because the powder was whiter than her suit. She couldn't imagine what it was. Beside it was a looking glass. That was a surprise. Alex didn't spend time looking in mirrors. Then she went to see Al Streep. She wanted some advice.

Al met her at the Savoy. He said he had business there, but really he had to keep her away from his wife. She looked incredible, he thought. The expensive superglamorous, super-white look, with her curves – it was pure sex. Every man in the place had an eye out. The white brought out the loveliness of her skin. How the directors of the forties and fifties would have loved her! She'd been born too late. She was in the wrong place. 'Hollywood's your pitch,' he told her admiringly.

'Would going to drama school help?'

'No. You're not going to be a theatre actress. You'd learn to talk in the English classical way then you'd have to unlearn it. You'd have to get an approximation of American to fit in. Classless is better, Jane. Go to LA because that's where the movies are made.'

Jane said she'd always believed it was her real home.

'Can't you get the boy to take you? He must know everyone.'

Jane explained that he wasn't as Al imagined, sensitive and dreamy. He was a tough number who didn't like the movie business. Then she told him about being cut-off.

Al said make it up with Margery Caversham. She, Jane Kirkland, should go of her own accord. For crissake, who couldn't like Jane?

John Whiteman came into the Savoy bar and approached Jane like an old friend. He invited her and Alex to his boat the following night. He asked where she was living. She kept it vague. He said she looked like a million dollars and took his time saying goodbye.

Al didn't look impressed, so she said, 'That's John Whiteman. He's a millionaire.'

'Yeah,' said Al. 'But you're worth more than him because you'll keep it.'

'Meaning?'

'Give him a year.'

Al got some more drinks up and toasted her. 'To my unsung star.'

'If you don't approve of me in drama school why did you agree to it, Al?' she asked.

He shrugged. 'Dinah wanted you to go that route. I had to agree because I wasn't getting you any parts, only rejection. But my instinct says go west.'

The press were waiting as she left the Savoy.

'What do you think of Kay Caversham's remarks? She is your sister-in-law.'

'I don't think,' she said. 'Except about how happy I am.'
'So it's OK for Kay to slag you off in Cannes?'
That got to her. 'No, it's not OK.'
'Careful,' said Al. 'The answer is always "No comment".' And he stopped her saying anything more and got her into a taxi.

She made headlines the next morning. '"Kay is not OK," says new Caversham girl. "She should not have slagged me off like that".'

Alex came in as she was waking up, and tossed the paper on to the bed. 'Nice photograph. Un-nice day.'

She asked where he'd been.

'To see my bird, where else?' He meant the one in the zoo. Frequently he drove up there with Lucien and took its photograph and talked to it. He loved its long slender legs and amazing extraterrestrial eyes.

Jane screamed when she saw the headlines. She wanted a lawyer.

'It's OK,' said Alex gently. 'They twist everything you say. Don't worry. They ask you a question and if you say yes they manipulate that reply into their question and write it as though you'd made a statement. Do you like Marlon Brando? Yes. Headline: 'Del's racy mistress now says she likes Marlon Brando'. The only answer is 'No comment'. Keep saying it.'

She told him she would like to see his mother. He looked really surprised. 'I want to sort out the problems between us,' she explained.

'Babe, you're married to me, not my mother!'

The envelope of white powder by the bed had gone but there were plenty of butts on the floor. 'Alex, how much drugs do you use?'

He sat on the table, swinging his legs nonchalantly. 'Hard to say. Depends if I'm in company. Alone I reckon three joints a day. Maybe five. Yeah, five. You can count the roaches. They're by the bed.'

'Nothing else?'

'Of course not.'

'But on the way to Scotland you asked Jack to get pills.'

'Come on, Jane, I was getting married.'

'You don't take them normally?'

He shook his head.

'Yesterday there was some powder just here, in an envelope.'
'Yes, well, that was insulin. You know my friend the Moroccan. He's got diabetes.'

She thought the Moroccan friend was sure unlucky: bad health as well. She wasn't medically informed but she'd have been surprised if insulin was carried loose in powder form. The trouble was Alex never seemed high. She asked again to see his mother. He wouldn't hear of it.

Jane painted her nails scarlet and when the varnish was dry decorated each nail with a gold and black flower. She was wearing a new soft lilac pyjama suit. She looked at the rail of wondrous new clothes, but who would see them? Jane, with money, had a good time. She'd bought embroidered silk and satin dresses from Ossie Clark, and fantasy medieval princess dresses. Plenty of Bill Gibb intricate knitted coats and sweaters, all colours of the rainbow, muted shades, subtle and beautiful, blending one into the other. She had long snakeskin boots and a scarlet bag like Lucia's. A silver all-in-one playsuit, backless with a high halter-neck. The suit made a noise when she walked – she liked noisy clothes. Her favourite coat was made of white ostrich feathers. It was very short and underneath she wore minuscule paillettes of iridescent silver like the scales of a mermaid's tail. Sometimes she scooped up her hair into a bouquet of curls on top of her head, allowing a few loose wisps to cascade down the sides of her face. She painted her lips white. She wore Je Reviens perfume or Ma Griffe or Cabochard. She looked stunning when she went to the shops in the Earls Court Road or the Diner for a coffee – but she got no nearer stardom.

. . . Chapter 17 . . .

Margery sat in her office wearing tinted glasses with black frames decorated with pearls. She wore a simple black Yves Saint Laurent suit which showed how much weight she'd lost. A Lanvin black silk scarf was arranged around her neck – to perfection. Today the solitary gardenia was pinned at her waist. She'd just ordered a whole new beauty range from Estée Lauder, luggage from Fendi and some lingerie from the White House in Bond Street. She was concerned with looking as young as possible. She'd lied so much about her age that she'd forgotten it herself. In fact she was over forty. She'd decided to go back into life and marry the Greek. The decision had been provoked by fear. Her life was out of control for the first time. She could not get over Dino, perhaps because she'd allowed him to take precedence over everything else. By embracing another human being she'd at last start to forget.

Jennifer came in wearing her Aquascutum mac and carrying an umbrella. She always wore her mother's engagement ring on her third finger and the pearls her father had given her on her twenty-first birthday. Her fair complexion never tanned. Suddenly Margery felt sorry for her.

'Oh, Jennifer. Why don't you go and have some –' she couldn't think what Jennifer could have – 'fun.'

Jennifer didn't know what fun was but pretended she did. She said working for Margery gave her all the fun she needed. Margery sincerely hoped not. That's not what Jennifer was paid for.

'Seriously, ma'am, being with you is fun.'

Margery laughed. 'I never thought you were a liar.'

Jennifer's face fell.

'Oh, go on, silly. Can't you tell I'm kidding?'

Jennifer asked for a weekend off to go shopping in London. She wanted to buy some cashmere sweaters and suits from Simpson and Jaeger, and more Fair Isle sweaters from the Scotch House. In the summer she always wore Liberty print dresses in English pastels, blues and pinks, which looked pale and washed out in the fierce Mediterranean sun. She always had her hair cut by Vidal Sassoon. Margery said, 'Get Julian to fix you theatre tickets. And Jennifer – have fun.'

Somehow they got through Christmas. That was always a miracle. Only Shane enjoyed it.

Julian brought her the *Wall Street Journal*. It relaxed her. She liked to move her shares around. Suddenly a company would catch her eye. It was like picking a horse. She was rich enough to make mistakes but she never did. If she hadn't been the legendary superstar she'd have been a business advisor.

Her best friend Marion had left her lover, Mo Cohen, head of two Hollywood studios, and was staying in one of the guest suites at the Château. She'd spent half the night recounting her sexual affairs. She'd had one with Frankie – who hadn't? Then Jack – well, did one brag about that any more? All this talk meant she was insecure about being alone. There came a point, no matter how beautiful you were, when age took over and your hormones took a dive. You started worrying about being alone.

Julian gave her some cheques to sign. She told him the house was cold. 'Turn everything up.'

'D'you think so?' He was surprised. 'It's really quite hot. Everything's full on.'

'Then get maintenance to check the system. I'm cold.'

But it wasn't a cold, more a chill. In her, not the house.

'Did you find out who got the Modigliani?'

'No,' said Julian flatly.

'I want that picture.' Her voice was savage. 'Modigliani had such a terrible life. He reminds me of my son.'

'Is he French?' asked Julian.

'Italian. He went to Paris as a young man and drank and drugged himself to death. As he said he would. And when he died his mistress, a young girl who'd been obsessed by him, went to the top of the house. She was nine months pregnant with his second child. She jumped to her death.'

'And you want the picture!'

'It's of her. The girl. He had a cursed life. He said so himself. The French call Modigliani "the cursed one". I've found out who the girl's agent is.'

'The girl?' For a minute Julian thought she meant Modigliani's deceased mistress. But there was only one 'the girl'.

'Al Streep. Remember him? He used to come up to the LA house and make up a four for tennis. Get him on the phone. And Julian, don't tell anyone I'm calling Streep. Especially not Jennifer. There's too many soft hearts about.'

Julian went back to his office thinking, That's one girl who's not going to be famous. He reread the two Sunday instalments of Jane's love affair with Del Grainger. Margery had underlined the parts that did not make sense to her. Julian laughed in spite of himself. Margery Caversham could see through anything.

After Dino's death in front of her in the gutter in Jamaica Avenue, Margery didn't think she had anything left to lose. But life always had a custard pie up its sleeve. She found she'd lost her son.

To Al Streep she said, 'I hear you've got a nice young girl. Gracie. Well, I want to see her in something substantial. I told Mo Cohen last night to sign her up. Columbia should be the best studio.'

Al couldn't believe it. Then she said, 'And Jane Kirkland. You must remember her. She eloped with my son. I think now she's a wife she should spend her time looking after Alex and not gadding around show business.'

Al said, 'She's very special, Margery.'

'Yes, I know how special she is. I just want to feel she's giving Alex the special part.'

'Shouldn't you discuss that with Alex? He must have known he was marrying an actress.' Al was too old for blackmail.

'Put it this way,' said Margery. 'Why don't you telephone me if something comes up for her and we'll talk about it. And I'll phone Mo Cohen now and say we've talked about Gracie.'

Al didn't like it, but Dinah had been listening in and loved it. Gracie had made it. One call from Margery Caversham. And after all it wasn't as though Jane Kirkland was besieged with work.

Margery occasionally ate out, especially if Kay was home or a guest was staying. She particularly liked the Italian restaurant between Grasse and Mougins. For one thing it was discreet. It was friendly, with red checked table cloths, earthenware jugs filled with the new wine, freshly baked rolls. The pasta was homemade, so was the banana or mint icecream. Margery liked it because Dino had liked it. It reminded him of the taverns of his youth. He hated anything pretentious. The owner and his wife had adored Dino, and on his death had closed the restaurant for a month. There were photographs of him in each dining room and they had their own collection upstairs. Margery had made sure they'd been invited to the cherry tree ceremony on February 6th.

She took Marion there for lunch. Since Dino's death Margery had eaten a lot. Marion said it was a substitute for sex and Margery didn't disagree, but she liked food and didn't mind if she put on weight. Marrying the Greek meant she'd be back in the public eye. She hadn't expected to want a man in that way again and she still didn't. She was marrying for other reasons. She needed to get her life moving again.

'I realised last night listening to you that I don't want to end up alone,' she said.

'Oh God!' cried Marion. 'Is that the effect I have on people?'

'Alone in that house, getting old.'

'You could go back to the movies,' said Marion cautiously.

'That's out, so I'm marrying Big Boy.' That was Kay's nickname for the Greek. 'It'll put some noses out of joint.'

'You're telling me,' said Marion. She could think of two world-famous figures. 'That Japanese pianist.'

'Have you seen her? Poor ugly thing. She so adores him. I almost wish I could feel like that for someone, something, even a cat. She's so gifted. At the piano that is. It's a pity the Greek isn't musical. He just likes fame.'

'What is his background exactly?'

'Ordinary. His father owned a fishing boat. It built up from there. His mother didn't quite take in the washing, but that sort of thing. He married a Greek girl and had, I think it's four children. She died. He's actually kind and likes a simple life. He just got too rich.'

Surprisingly Marion was wearing very young clothes. Having passed through London she'd made the obligatory visit to Biba. She wore a short chiffon slip with ostrich feathers around the hem and a chiffon hood with more ostrich feathers. Her coat was dazzling orange and pink, all psychedelic: you could see a hundred of them on the Portobello Road. Margery thought that for forty-two passing as thirty-five this was a mistake.

'I went to Robert Frey's house outside Paris,' said Marion. Robert Frey was France's top star and had been for five years.

'What, a party?'

'He doesn't give parties,' said Marion. 'It's the most modern house I've ever been in. Chrome and glass and black ebony, hard brittle surfaces, everything electronic. Surveillance everywhere. He's paranoid. Also he can dim his house lights or turn them on from a switch in his car. He's got bugs everywhere, so whatever you say he knows about it. Before he comes into the room to greet you he watches you secretly for ten minutes. He gets to know a person that way. He didn't sleep with me.' Marion sounded surprised.

'In those clothes I'm not surprised.' Margery gave a wild burst of laughter.

Marion looked taken aback.

'Go back to Mo Cohen, Marion, and grow old gracefully.'

Marion refused to be hurt. The clothes were the new her, ageless. This new her did meditation and didn't worry about age and possessiveness. 'I also met the pop star Rick de Palma in London. He's got a tango record collection – you know, the old 78's. We danced most of the night.'

'And?'

'I refuse to give you sexual pleasure by proxy,' snapped Marion. 'He's into deserts and oneness and Timothy Leary and Ginsberg.'

Margery now saw the point of the psychedelic clothes.

'You're not eating,' said Marion. 'A slither of Parma ham? A salad?'

'I'll lose another three pounds by the beginning of the week. I function best at nine and a half. By the way, Marion, I think we should both consider hormone replacement therapy. That way you leave out middle age. You can have an implant in your butt.'

'No matter how much weight you lose, Margery, you never lose those breasts. They're always incredible. You're so lucky. I leave out a hundred calories and it's instant sag.'

'The Greek keeps telling me how Dino promised him an entrée.' Margery laughed. 'Sounds like something on the menu. It means he wants to meet people. He wants to be in at the White House.'

Marion laughed. 'He's just a little boy.'

'Just in that department. Otherwise it's all not so little.'

Marion laughed, a sexual laugh this time. 'Is that why you're marrying him? I wouldn't blame you.'

'I told you why. I can't be lonely.' Also her children needed a father. All the stuff Kay was pulling would never have happened if Dino had been there. And Alex and the drugs – if Dino had caught him he'd have broken both his arms. Margery did love her children although she had trouble showing it. The Greek was warm and he'd be good for Shane. She was bringing them something – a father.

Marion said, 'Mo and I were talking just before I left. He was saying Dino didn't care what he wore and I said he did. I remember he wore those thick, heavy, smooth wool sweaters, cool to the touch.'

'I bought his clothes,' said Margery. 'He hated suits. Liked to be in his shirt sleeves. He didn't care about his appearance. He'd put on anything as long as it was natural. He dressed down: a sweater and a pink shirt, dark corduroy trousers. He liked wearing scarves. And ties. He did buy those himself, dark patterned silk. Conventional. Nothing flash. I got him his shirts from Brooks Brothers, two dozen at a time.' She sighed deeply.

'Everyone loved him,' said Marion suddenly. 'He warmed people.'

Margery sat in silence, unable to dwell on that subject any more. She'd made the mistake of thinking that time healed.

Marion said, 'I think you didn't have time to mourn. You were looking after the kids.' Her eyes filled with tears and she started crying. 'I'll never get over him, so God knows how you feel.' Shakily she poured some wine. Margery put her hand over Marion's.

To change the subject Marion asked, 'Has the Alex thing died down?'

'Only in the press. Not in my mind.'

'It's been front page in the States. I bet Nestorin's happy. It sure came at the right time for them.' Marion wiped her eyes.

It happened on the same day, thought Margery. The baby milk factory blowing up and Alex eloping to Scotland. Where was the third thing?

. . . Chapter 18 . . .

With the money from the sale of the foreign rights in the Del Grainger story Jane bought jazz records for Alex and tickets to see Rick de Palma at Wembley. She bought herself a stunning pink and orange psychedelic outfit from Biba with ostrich feathers around the hems of the short slip and coat and around the matching hood. The Kensington Market was full of second-hand fur coats but she refused to wear dead animals and chose instead a military coat, long, navy, with a belted waist and collar you could push up high, for three pounds. The material was excellent and the coat didn't seem to have been worn. Then she went to her secret second-hand shop on the

King's Road and realised that it was there that she'd seen Kay Caversham. She remembered this incredible girl with a marvellous figure buying practically a whole rail of evening dresses from the thirties. They'd both got their hands on the apple-green silk-knit thirties top at the same time. Their eyes had met. Kay's were black and without mercy, but then she had smiled and her voice was low and musical. 'No, you have it. Please.' And she let go of the desired object. Jane could tell she was someone.

Jane had decided to go to drama school and would apply for a grant. After all, she was in England, not California. She might belong there but she wasn't there, and Alex would never agree to her going. Term started on January 10th. She would have to tell Alex and didn't look forward to his reaction. But when she got back to the flat she had other news. She'd been to the doctor: she was having a baby.

He was listening to an African band on the stereo and she waited for the track to end before asking him to turn down the volume. The Morrocan was making a couscous so she asked Alex to join her in the bathroom. All of a sudden she wasn't sure he'd be pleased. They'd never even mentioned children – it had just never occurred to either of them.

'Alex, I've got news,' she began.

'Oh, God. Not another million-dollar film. Who's it about this time? The Alex Caversham story starring Jane Kirkland as sister Kay?'

'How about mother-to-be.'

He got it at once. Very gently he laid his hands on her stomach. His eyes were full of light and he was very tender. She imagined his father then. That's how he'd have been when Margery told him the same news.

'Oh, Jane, I just never thought this would happen. That I'd have a kid. That I'd have a woman to love. Oh, for God's sake, I've never been so happy in my life. I'm going to church to light a candle. I'm going to take the very best care of you. I've got to call Lucien.' He kept thinking of ways to express his joy.

She was happy too. She was now truly his wife. That was drama school out of the window.

'There's just one thing, Alex.'

He couldn't think what that could be.

'I won't be able to get a grant so we've got no money.'

That made him thoughtful. 'I guess I'll get a job. It's time I sorted out what I want to do.' He embraced her. 'It's such a lovely time for a child to be born.' And she agreed the sixties were almost too good.

Margery screamed and Kay leapt down the stairs, colliding with Julian, who was also running, and the maid from Dover. The dog barked mournfully. Kay threw open her mother's door. There was no intruder and her mother seemed uninjured. There was just a picture – yes, a Modigliani – propped up in front of her. Margery still held the note.

'You'll never guess who got the Modigliani? The Greek outbid me so he could give it to me as a present. Now that's wonderful timing. It arrives the very morning I hear that my son has made that girl pregnant. That's the end of the Greek.'

'Oh, Mummy,' said Kay. 'How could he know? He's just being kind.' She stopped, intrigued. 'Did Alex ring you?'

'Of course not.'

'So how do you know?' She was now jealous. Didn't she want to be the first to give her mother a grandchild? What the fuck was Alex doing?

'I've got my spy, don't you worry,' said Margery.

Kay waved Julian and the staff out and shut the door. Her mother was still looking at the picture.

'What does that mean, that she's having a baby? I mean in real terms.'

'I've cut him off, Kay. You can't get more real than that.'

'But his trust surely makes provision for children.' Kay was suddenly filled with rage. 'How dare she! How could she be so –so – babies grow into people. They go on. That marriage won't last a year.'

Margery was glad that Kay was being angry for her. She was seething with such a mixture of emotions – all bad. She felt almost ill. Her sanity had fled minutes ago when she got the spy's phone call.

Kay said Jane must have an abortion. 'Make her see this marriage is nothing but a lull between Alex's drug excursions. He's probably OD'd on acid and having a little rest. Get Marion to go over and talk her out of it. It's no fun bringing up a kid alone. It'll all go wrong, Mummy, and it is your grandchild.'

Margery's mouth tightened. She felt her face age irrevocably. Misery did that quicker than anything. 'You can't persuade people to have abortions, Kay. But you can assure her I'll have nothing to do with it, this child. And I have certain controls over the trust so she's not going to be lucky there. She'd have more chance of winning the football pools.'

'But when he leaves her won't he be liable for support?'

'Sure,' said Margery. 'But he has to have something to support her with.' She sat down, badly shaken. Her gardenia had come loose and been trampled on the floor. It hadn't occurred to Margery that Alex might have sex with anyone. For some reason the thought was unbearable.

'Daddy would buy her off,' said Kay. 'He'd charm the shit out of her and give her a few thousand and make her sign a waiver on the trust.'

They sat in silence imagining the baby, the pram, the attention, the press. And then perhaps, worst of all horrors, another baby.

Kay said, 'D'you remember Daddy dealing with the Riocco brothers? He said if you do a fair deal you never see me again, but stitch me up and you've got me for eternity.'

Margery shivered slightly and her voice was almost frightened. 'Why d'you think of that, Kay?'

'I think Daddy, for all his humanity, was ruthless.'

Margery tried to be nonchalant. 'What's that got to do with your brother's mistakes?'

'Well, he did curse us as he lay dying. And I never understood why he did that.'

Her mother had nothing to say.

Kay concluded, 'Maybe curses work.'

One hour later Margery had got control of herself. She decided to do nothing about the girl. Marion would not be despatched with bad news to London. They would simply ignore the girl and that would hurt her more than anything; after all, she'd married into the Caversham dynasty to better herself. Margery's silence at the news of her pregnancy would be a foretaste of the greater silence to come. Jane Kirkland would get nowhere, ever.

Kay found her standing again in front of the Modigliani

painting of his last mistress. 'The Greek phoned twice, Mummy.' Margery didn't answer. 'He wants to know what you think of the painting.'

'I buy my own art works. I'm not used to little seducer's presents.'

'It's hardly a box of Milk Tray. It cost a million five.'

'I don't like to be patronised, Kay.'

'He's a very, very attractive man,' said Kay. 'I can't tell you how many women want him, just for one night. He's supposed to be incredible. And Jacey – you know Jacey, Princess Miranda's daughter – well, she wanted him. She has to have everyone but he is not one she could add to her list. She got invited with her mother onto one of his cruises, and she just walked into his bedroom and took off all her clothes – she has a pretty good body apparently – and made a few suggestions. And he just lay there and with one gesture indicated that she put it all back on and leave.'

Margery laughed roguishly. 'He sounds old.'

'He's a big man, Mummy. He says something and it reverberates. He's a man who doesn't have to use expletives.'

'Why don't *you* marry him, Kay?'

Kay squealed with laughter. 'Because he's crazy about you. He's chosen you out of all the women in the world. It's fabulous.'

'It's not women that type of man is after,' said Margery. 'He just wants the chance to outdo a great man. He's marrying me because of your father, Kay. He wants to be reassured that he's a greater man.' She looked closely at the picture. 'How many people get a chance to see this close up? He was like your brother – out for destruction. A morbid, cursed, terrible life, yet one of his pictures goes for a million five.'

Kay felt warm and included and part of her mother's thoughts and decisions. She wanted to share her life too. 'I'm not absolutely sure, Mummy, that I'm that good in the movie. I saw a rough cut.' That got Margery's attention off the painting. 'I seem to smile a lot. All the time, in fact. I met an actor out in LA, something Nicholson, he's done some horror movies. We've got the same smile. Look, I'm not as good as Lucia. It's her movie. D'you think I smile because I'm nervous? I wanted to ask the actor that. Why he kept smiling.'

'Never mind his problems. I'm going to phone Mo Cohen,

Marion's ex, and get him to run the movie. I think he should get a really good editor involved –'

'You can't cut Lucia's part down.'

'No, darling. But I can cut some of the smiling. In fact I'd like to see a print here. We'll go through it frame by frame. Then I'll choose an editor, and we'll have a really big première.'

Kay said, 'I didn't realise you cared so much.' And she burst into tears.

'Kay, you are my daughter.'

Big Boy sat at the Château dinner table and looked as though he'd finally made it into heaven. The volatile French politician Jaspard sat on his right – it was tipped he'd head the Socialist Party at the next election. Marion looked wonderful in a Worth satin gown. Margery felt almost sad that this beauty would have to change, become old. Marion's baby-fine hair lifted like a blonde cloud around her face, but Big Boy didn't even look at her. She was a mere senator's daughter. His eyes stayed on the jewel: Margery Caversham, descended from an English King; wealthy in her own right; well-connected; accepted anywhere; and desirable. The daughter Kay worried him. She fussed over her mother like a troublesome lawyer – it wasn't protection, but possessiveness. His excitement increased wildly as Margery talked about her parents, the old house, the last king. She tried to explain to him why a house was called a seat. She had authority – he liked that. So far he had not laid one hand on her, but he knew exactly how he'd handle her. She'd been in dock a long time: she needed careful steering. His daughter Sophia had told him the Caversham's called him Big Boy. Were they referring to his penis? It couldn't be his height.

He had a strong sensual face and distinguished grey hair. His teeth were white and strong and all his own. For a man of fifty-five he was in fantastic shape. He didn't exercise fashionably or go jogging but simply lived well. He loved sailing, walking, dancing. He ate well but healthily, drank little. He liked sex and plenty of it, sometimes five different woman a day. His hands were solid and capable and he really got hold of things. He liked being real. He'd met a million flakes in his time and knew what to avoid. He wore a grey three-piece Cardin suit and pale blue shirt with starched collar and cuffs. His gold cufflinks and watch were from Cartier. On his dark blue silk tie he wore a ruby pin. His shoes were hand-made by Ferragamo of leather so soft it was like having his feet encased in kid gloves. He hated the stiff leather of so many men's shoes. His feet were important to him and he looked after them. In return he moved swiftly, never had accidents and was at peak form when sailing on his marathon solo journeys. His grandmother always said look after your feet and your back and God will do the rest.

Because he lacked the formal education received by the people his money brought him into contact with, he compensated by always keeping ahead of the times. He liked to be *au courant*. He read every major newspaper in the world and got well-informed opinions from friendly politicians. He had very definite views and hated the paranoia of governments and the way they didn't look after their own. He found it abhorrent that politicans were hung out to dry for doing what many other men did anyway, sleeping with an attractive woman whose profession was sex.

The Profumo/Christine Keeler case was in his view a good example of state hypocrisy and press hysteria. Its tragic ending was all the more a condemnation of political double standards and he was glad he was beyond the vagaries of governments. He spoke four languages fluently and knew the customs of the people he was dealing with. He tried very hard to be fully aware of the times he lived in, and by understanding the sixties he ended up liking the young. At least they weren't hypocritical.

After dinner Kay played the piano. The right person had trained her so it came out pleasant enough and not too long. Marion rather surprisingly made a tactful early exit, but the daughter stayed. She kept talking about Hollywood, her film, her next film, her modelling for *Vogue*, and the fee.

When he first saw her he knew what she needed – a good spanking.

Finally he got Margery to himself when Guido Cortese called Kay. Margery insisted that she take the call in another room. Margery was actually nervous of Guido. She thought he might turn the unfortunate sexual experiment into a legal matter.

'You've got a problem,' the Greek said as soon as they were alone. He was thinking about Kay.

'So you know too? Well, she's over two months pregnant and Alex seems to want it. I've had good health all my life. It took Alex to send my blood pressure up. I had to take Librium for a week.'

'That's not long. I've known women take it for years. The young are selfish, Margery. What are you going to do?'

'I've done it. I've cut him off.'

The Greek shook his head. 'Give him an allowance – not too much, but enough. Otherwise she will go to the press now she's pregnant.'

'So?' said Margery coldly. 'She can't make up too much about me. I'm not dead. Yet!'

'The press like her.'

'Do they? Why?'

The Greek thought about it. 'She's the sort things happen to. Also she's warm, sympathetic.' He couldn't translate the Greek word he wanted.

Margery couldn't believe she was hearing this. This was what happened when she mixed with people outside her circle.

'I think, if you don't mind, I'll handle it my way. I know my children.'

He took her hand between both of his. 'I want to help you. Look, I have five children. My eldest boy spends his life in a car going a hundred miles an hour. Even the police can't usually catch him. And if they do he's my son so they let him go. Maybe they should hold him. Otherwise he'll die. Sophia always liked your son Alex.'

Margery remembered that Sophia was his daughter.

'Maybe when this other business finishes there could be a little something between them,' he went on.

'I didn't know they'd even met.'

'These sixties kids have a good time, Margery. They go to these restaurants in Chelsea where the movie stars and pop stars go, the discotheques. They hire planes. Party. Acid. Sex. They are not afraid to let themselves go.'

She thought he'd bore her to death if he went on. She said, 'I want to make one thing clear for when we're married – no kids.'

The Greek spent nearly a week negotiating the marriage settlement. Margery made it as difficult as possible, like a movie contract. Lucien's banker father gave her some provocative advice. She always turned to him for the special stuff. As he was a speculative banker she kept their discussions secret. She was never sure if he'd end up the second richest man in the world or in jail. She appreciated his cool, sophisticated approach to the burning problem of her son Alex.

'Let them get on with it, Margery. We only put them in the world. We don't have to answer for their actions too. They have choice and free will. Alex knows what he wants, even if it isn't what you want. You offered him the best as you saw it. He walked away.'

'You sound very calm about it.' She knew Lucien was no stranger to drugs.

'Lucien asks and I give. I don't want to make the decision how much he should have. Let him do that. I don't try and live his life or punish his sins. He's free.'

Margery said, 'Freedom is a very dangerous thing. Your son told me that. He knows more than you.'

The banker sighed. 'I hope so. They tell me he's psychic.'

On the Greek's last night in Cannes she invited a few local celebrities to meet him. That part of the evening he enjoyed. He wanted them to cruise with him during March – all of them, and their friends – he'd make sure they had a good time.

The second part of the evening he did not enjoy. Kay showed *Baby Blue* and Margery sat wearing tinted glasses, making notes. The Greek felt he no longer existed. Kay kept nudging her mother, whispering suggestions. When at last the lights went on, Kay wanted to see a film that would be entered at the Cannes Film Festival. She'd been asked to be one of the judges. The Greek found the film incomprehensible. The lights went on again and it was after one. He said, 'I'd like to spend some time with your mother now, Kay. I have to leave early tomorrow.'

Kay simply ignored him. 'Let's have one of Mummy's films on. Oh, go on, please!'

'But Mom never shows her films,' said Shane.

'Please, please!' and Kay pulled Margery's hands. 'If you're pleased with what I've done let me see *Mambo*.' She looked like an excited little girl.

'All right, Kay,' sighed Margery. 'But only half an hour, because we've still got guests.'

The Greek realised he was a guest. The other, a member of the English House of Lords, was asleep in his chair. As they watched the film Kay kept reminding Margery of what happened when she was making this scene, that scene. 'D'you remember when Daddy came and told you you were nominated and Grace Kelly came in and –'

Margery gave her a look. Cut-off. Guests were present.

For 'guest' read 'outsider', thought the Greek.

He knew what he'd have to do – get them on his territory. He'd get a ship organised for the following week. He wanted to get to know them and decided it was easier one at a time. So he took Shane upstairs with the nanny to see him to bed.

'What d'you want to do when you grow up, Shane?'

'I want to be like Rick de Palma.'

'Oh, the pop star.' The boy's room, he noticed, was not lavish. There were few toys, nothing special at all. 'So you want to perform, Shane?'

'Not particularly. I just want to be famous.'

'But you are. You're a Caversham.'

'More famous than Kay or Mom.'

'D'you remember your father?'

'Not really. I was always away at school. It took five bullets to kill him. Most people just need one or two.'

'It depends where they're hit,' said the Greek.

'He was hit everywhere and he was still alive, because he cursed people.'

'People?'

'Us.' Shane laughed. The Greek thought his jokes were in poor taste.

'I expect you've got lots of friends?' He knew the boy hadn't.

'No.'

'Don't you like people?'

'No. Only pop stars. Kay said she'd bring Rick de Palma here. She goes out with everyone.'

The Greek wanted to like the boy. He'd really try with this one. He told him about boats and ships and how he'd take him on a cruise the following week.

The boy said, 'I don't think Mummy will come, because she has to arrange the opening for Kay's film. You have to send out all the invitations at least six weeks ahead, so people are free to come.' And with that information the boy fell asleep.

The Greek's suite was in the guest wing on the second floor adjoining Kay's apartment. As he was going down the stairs from Shane's room he heard a surprising conversation. He didn't like eavesdropping particularly, but it wasn't the sort of thing he could easily interrupt.

Kay was wearing a scarlet dress as though ready to go out. A man in a leather jacket stood in the shadows swinging his car keys. The Greek couldn't see his face.

She'd said, 'So you did show up. Why hide up here?'

'I'm not hiding,' said the man, an Italian. 'I've just arrived. I drove from Milan and the road over the border was terrible.'

'So for all your protestations you come back, Guido. I ought to whip your arse off. You're impertinent.'

'I am here, Kay, because your mother invited me to meet her future husband. I would not dishonour your mother.'

'Dishonour? What dishonour? Such an old-fashioned word.' And Kay moved up to the Italian and kissed him and took off his belt. Then she undid his trousers, pulled them down and got hold of his cock. She got to work on him so thoroughly that the Italian had a hard-on in seconds.

'I don't want to,' he said.

'I'm going to beat you because you love it and that's why you're back here. It's got nothing to do with dishonour. At least not to my mother. But this time you'll pass out with ecstasy because I've thought of other little things to do to you. I love your cock, but don't come now or it'll be no fun.' And she started to pull him into her room by his cock.

The Italian said, 'You shouldn't behave like this, Kay.'

She pushed him the rest of the way by his buttocks.

'You treat me like a woman,' he said.

She slammed the door, then the Greek heard the sound of the belt and the Italian cried out.

The next day the Greek proposed the cruise the following week but Margery said she had to arrange the gala for Kay. He said Kay was a pain in the arse and meant it.

'Be careful,' said Margery. 'You're talking about my family. There's no cruise, no anything – not until the President has been here for the cherry tree planting.'

. . . Chapter 19 . . .

Alex lay with his hands on her stomach, where he could feel new life if only his fingers were sensitive enough. 'I never thought I'd love anyone,' he said. 'And now I do. I've always wanted someone of my own to love.'

Alex remembered his mother years ago, lying on the lawn in Los Angeles. He must have been lying beside her, cradled in her arm, because he saw quite clearly his father's face bending over her, his eyes so full of love. And Kay shouted, 'Mummy is so beautiful she can have anything.'

And his father said, 'That's right. Anything.' And he sprinkled petals on to Margery's hair. From that position Alex could see the side of her stomach. It looked like the side of a hill. His sister Charlotte was in there, about to be born. When they were alone his mother would put his hands on her stomach and say, 'Go on, Alex. Feel the baby kick. It's Alex's baby. Our secret. OK?'

That was another broken promise, because the baby was whisked away upstairs to the nursery, out of sight. He knew betrayal even at two and a half.

Jane said, 'But I won't be a famous actress now.'

'Thank God!' he said.

'But it's what I always wanted.'

'Well, I like you because you're not famous.'

'Why?' she said.

'Because, Jane, I've had it all my life. I've had enough.'

'But your mother's the greatest star ever.'

'You know, Jane, I live in this decaying body in this place of sin but I must look out with the eyes of an angel. I'm very aware that this is just a stopping-off place. And now I'm bringing into it another spirit, imprisoning it in flesh and blood because of my desire. I have to redeem that by giving love, all my love, to the child, to you. And that's what I'm going to do. And in comparison with that, Cannes and its merry-go-round is just sin, a place of bad illusion.'

'So that's how you see life,' she said. 'Are you a philosopher?'

'I told you. They never gave me a chance to be what I was. I just worked out myself and then I worked out the rest of it from there. The answers are in me. Lucien knew them anyway. He just pointed the direction and let me work it out.'

Lucien again. She didn't want to ruin a happy time by asking about him and why she couldn't meet him. She thought once or twice he'd phoned because when she answered the caller hung up. She wasn't used to people keeping other people in compartments. She found it hurtful. She liked everyone to be together, getting on, around a warm fire. She was like her mother in that.

When Jane was a teenager at home in Hastings she used to watch TV to see Jay Stone. Sometimes there'd be a report from Hollywood or he'd be a guest on a chat show. While she was obsessively watching for him she quite often saw Margery and Dino and their family on the TV news. They always looked so glamorous and enviable. She remembered the public mourning when Dino de Stefano was murdered, and her mother said, 'Now he was a good man. He'd have been President and changed the world.' A lot of people said that. 'Now de Stefano's gone who knows? He had the power to stop wars.' Five bullets, and a secure time shattered. The royal family of the entertainment world – she'd never dreamed she'd get near them, and here she was at twenty-two having their child.

Alex took her to breakfast at the Diner to celebrate. The old friends were pleased to see her. She'd not changed. So she'd made it big with the Cavershams? But she still had time for everybody. Alex didn't have much to say to strangers unless he had a specific purpose in mind, so he sat in the corner and ate the dish of the day. When she finally joined him her face was glowing.

'I haven't told anyone,' she said. 'I just want it to stay inside me. The happiness. D'you know what I mean? If you tell, it kind of goes flat.'

'Let's play truth,' he said. 'Let's hear what screws you up about your past.'

She took a shaky breath.

'You are the mother of my child. I've got a right to know.'

'Let's hear the truth about Lucien.'

'What is there to tell? He's a guy who saved my life. I didn't speak for six months because I hadn't anything to say to anyone. Then Lucien came by and told me about the astral body inside the physical body and how it can travel anywhere in the universe. And how after this earthly death it goes on its journey in another realm, depending upon your state of evolvement. He said we could travel out of ourselves here and now and go to the destination of our choice. I said, "Let's go" and broke six month's silence. He's worked you out. I said you want to be a star but you're not like the ones I know. They're all pushy and self-absorbed and Lucien said no, she's an escaper. Now that had never occurred to me. So what are you escaping from?'

She couldn't remember how much she'd told him on the train coming back from the seaside. 'There was a problem. I dealt with it. I left.'

'You had an abortion?'

'Of course not.'

He was pleased to hear that.

The story was too horrific to tell. She said, 'A friend of mine had a tragedy. I'm going to leave it like that, Alex.'

After the meal he took her to the chemist's and bought vitamins and perfume. He wanted her to wear flat shoes. He was going to get a job. Then he said, 'We're going to see your mother in Hastings.'

She was appalled.

'You've got to be connected to your family at a time like this. You need your own people around you, Jane. You live amongst my people.'

'I've got Jack.'

'Jack's anybody's. After a few drinks, everybody's. And Lucy's a little disturbed. And the street people – they're all transitory. There's no reason why you don't want to see your mother, is there? I'd like to meet her.'

'Let's meet her when I've met yours.'

She knew he was going to get his own way. She quite believed that Lucien had been to Hastings and read some back issues of the papers, checking her out. But it never made the papers. The only bad thing about Hastings was the time the big wheel caught fire at the fair. But then she was a kid. She couldn't forget it, but she didn't want to think about it now in case the resulting fear flowed into the new world growing inside her. Only good things would get in there.

Kay imitated Big Boy on his boat. She walked up and down the dining room with a rolling gait. She stuck a cushion under her sweater to give her a slight paunch. She did the sharp flicking to and fro of the Greek's mournful eyes and got his voice to perfection. Shane, overcome with laughter, punched the cushions. Then Kay started singing and doing a Greek dance. She tossed imaginary plates into the corners of the room, smashing them. Shane cried, 'Oh, stop, I'll bust a gut.'

Margery, watching them from around the half-open door, thought Kay's performance in the drawing room was a lot better than the one on the screen. Maybe she should have the Greek along for her next movie.

'And d'you know what he said to Mummy? "Your boy doesn't have too many toys." So watch it, Shane. He knows he hasn't got Mummy, so he'll get you. You'll get the toyshop treatment.'

Margery came into the room and her children, pleased to see her, hugged her.

'We've got a lot of guests coming for the ceremony next week. So be helpful please. Make them feel at home. And Shane, you're going back to the Lycée.'

'Oh no,' said Shane. 'Absolutely not. I can't.'

Kay started to intervene on his behalf, then thought better of it.

'When I marry I'll be travelling a lot. You go to school. That's it.'

'I hate that man!' shouted Shane. Margery sent him from the room.

She turned to Kay. 'Now try and get Charlotte into some decent clothes while she's here. Take her shopping. She looks like a bum.' Margery looked out at the garden. A dozen men were preparing the grounds.

'Will you be sorry to leave this house, Mummy?'

Margery didn't answer. She was thinking that the only real thing she and the Greek had in common was a deep passion for money. The games you could play with it. This week, with his help, she'd soared on the stock market. It was better than sex – at least she thought it was. She hadn't had anybody since Dino. Occasionally in her sleep she felt Dino was there with her, satisfying her. She supposed it was a dream caused by frustration.

'I've decided to show my breasts in the film,' said Kay. She was referring to her second film, due to start early spring.

Margery said, 'I read the script. I didn't see any reason to take off your clothes.'

'Well, make a reason. I'd love to do a blue film, a perfect erotic turn-on. Everyone watching me, getting off on me, hundreds of men. I guess I'd have to change my name.'

'Why?' said Margery coolly. 'If that's what you want to do. There's hundreds of porno actresses.'

'Oh God, Mummy that was a joke. If Alex said that there'd be a drama, a crisis, but I say it and it's like I asked what I should wear to dinner. You don't care about me.'

'Oh, Kay.' Margery so longed to be alone.

'You're not even shocked by what happened with Guido.'

'Kay, you have your independence. You're twenty-three. It's your life.'

'But I don't want independence. I want your love.' And she started to look as though she'd get seriously upset.

Margery said very firmly, 'It's always "want". I want, want, want! What about give, help, love, aid? Try these out and you might be more lovable.'

Margery started to leave the room. Kay said, sharp as a knife, 'So you're going to be a grandmother? Well, I'd think about that. How d'you know it's Alex's? I mean, that marriage was very quick.'

'Oh shit!' Margery stopped suddenly. 'The racing driver had dark eyes, didn't he?'

. . . Chapter 20 . . .

'Well you can't have it both ways, Mom,' said Alex. He lay back on the disordered bed, a spliff in his mouth, the phone at his ear. 'She either lied about the racing driver because she wants to be noticed and the baby's mine, or she did have a scene with the racing driver and the baby could be his. Which is it?'

'Well, as long as you know,' said Margery. 'She got your name pretty quick.'

'And how are you, Mom? Being the Merry Widow, so I hear.'

'Be at the ceremony on the 6th and we'll have a talk. Just you.' And she hung up.

Alex didn't know what to do, so he went to look for Lucien. He wasn't in any of his usual afternoon haunts; he was finally run to earth not far from Jane's old flat, in the Purple Pussycat disco. Lucien reckoned you should experience every kind of life possibility, murder, passion, envy, joy, sacrifice, so you understood it, could detach yourself from it and come out clean as a whistle. It wasn't therefore surprising to find him in the company of a recently released murderer and two hookers. As Lucien would never take life he had to get the flavour of that experience by proxy. One of the hookers had visited the murderer in jail, felt sorry for him and they'd had a jail wedding.

Lucien was amused by that. 'At least you always knew where your husband was,' he chuckled. 'Luckier than most wives.' He turned to Alex. 'You should tell your mother she doesn't know when she's well off. Just think what you could have done seeing how you like things in captivity.' Lucien still believed absolutely that his friend had married to get even with his mother for having power over him. Lucien indicated the girls and asked if Alex wanted some action. They could all snort some coke and get into some dancing back at the murderer's pad.

Alex said no. 'I'm going to have to clean up my act because of the baby.'

Lucien took his hands and pulled him up and started dancing. The music was African enough to get them going, and when Lucien and Alex got going they were sensational.

At the beginning all the flower kids in kaftans with strings of daisies in their hair joined in, but the music speeded up and Lucien and Alex were the only ones who could handle it. They danced to a near-frenzy, some primitive pulse in their bodies taking over, providing the energy.

Jane stepped into the disco by chance, looking for Lucy. The place seemed more exciting than usual. The very young hip kids and flower children were all watching two fantastic dancers. The music was throbbing and almost unbearably loud and these guys gave it everything. Were they good! Then she saw that one of them was her husband.

'High, higher! Higher, higher!' chanted the crowd.

Then Alex broke away to wipe the sweat out of his eyes and Jane called to him. For a moment he seemed confused. The rhythm had almost hypnotised him. Jane pushed through the fans and reached him. He wasn't displeased to see her.

'Who's your partner?' she asked.

'He? He's Lucien.' And he started pushing her away to the exit to avoid introductions.

'But you didn't tell me he was black.'

As Alex persuaded her out through the neon winking door she looked back at his dance partner. Was he a rival? Was there something wrong with him? With her?

Lucien certainly knew how to dress. He wore tight black leather trousers with gold chains slung across the hips, a black silk shirt tied at the waist, and a long, intricately patterned sash from Hindustan. His soft boots were made up of patches of velvet in many colours, lined with lime-green silk. A gold ring from Cartier on every finger, and when he went out on to the street he slung a long black leather coat over his shoulders. His ears were pierced and today he wore one simple gold heart.

On the way back to Earls Court Jane didn't speak. The tube made her feel sick, but even more she was sick of being lied to. When they got on to the street she said, 'Once, a long time ago, when I asked you to dance you said you never danced.' She imitated him refusing her. 'At Peter Woolf's party.'

'That's not a lie. I never dance in places like that. I don't party dance. I like getting going to a rhythm.'

'D'you get going to a rhythm with Lucien in bed too?'

'I've shared a girl with him on occasion.'

'You're amazing. You're either both up the same girl at once or in my case you can't both see me together. I'm no clairvoyant but that guy's going to break us up.'

'You're paranoid. Lucien can't meet paranoid people,' he said, glad to have found an excuse for not introducing them.

'I don't even know him and I feel his eyes on me. Green, aren't they? Green eyes wanting me dead.'

Alex tried to cool her down. He'd been caught out and didn't like it. Emotionally he was back in Cannes when nanny told

Margery he'd been jerking off on Kay's porn stuff. Margery had handled it OK for her. She said, 'We all shit. We all have sex. What's new?'

'I find it insulting that I'm not allowed to meet him. Is he insulted too?'

'Oh, look, Jane, I'm not used to dealing with more than one person at a time.'

'Dealing!' She was even more insulted.

Alex stared at the littered street. Of course Jane couldn't be part of him and Lucien. It would disrupt the very subtle relationship they had. They could make one word mean a dozen things – they had their own language. If she joined them, all that would be disrupted. Also, of course, she would see that Lucien loved him and he wasn't altogether sure she would like that. Keeping them apart was essential. A threesome was never on the cards, but now he had to make a decision. Jane and the baby, or his life the way it used to be. That included, apart from Lucien, his family and money. He reckoned Jane was a better deal any day. 'I've got a job as a house cleaner. I can make ten and six an hour. I'll never see Lucien again.'

Jane's pregnancy was the happiest time of her life. She felt ripe and luxuriant and very loved. The jealousy over Lucien was snuffed out. Alex did six hours of house-cleaning a day, and an external philosophy and Eastern religions course three times a week. He didn't have time for nightlife. He liked an early high-vitamin supper, some television, and bed by ten. That way the baby had the best chance. Every day he made sure they walked through Holland Park for an hour. 'That's what my mother did.' He laughed. 'And look what she got.' He often held Jane close and said how happy he was. 'You're a beautiful person and so warm. I want lots of kids, OK?'

'You can have whatever you want and do whatever you want.' She was happy enough to feel generous.

Jane's mother wrote a letter.

> I read in the papers you'd got married. I can't tell you how proud I am of you. Everyone in Hastings is talking about it. Dolly who runs the fish and chippie

on the corner has given me a pair of sheets for your wedding present. If you want to bring your husband down here I'd love to see him and you know I'll make you both welcome. I've got your friend Betty from the radio station staying permanent. And a honeymoon couple from London. And the regulars. Eight breakfasts in all. Not like the old days, eh? Well, you choose love. If you don't want to come you know I'll understand. I trust you, Janey, and I love you whatever you do.

Mum

Alex said it was one of the nicest letters he'd ever read. He wanted to meet her now. A warm mother! How did Jane ever leave home?

Jane said she had serious doubts. Alex got emotional about it. 'A woman like that will be an asset to a grandchild.' Jane could see there was a good side: her mother was great with kids. She phoned her and said she'd bring Alex, but just for the day. No neighbours. No old friends. Whatever she did, her mother must not mention Jay Stone. And she should take down the poster and all his photographs out of Jane's old bedroom if she hadn't already. And she wasn't to mention a thing.

'D'you think I'm a fool?' said her mother.

Jane signed up for a painless childbirth course and Alex said he wanted to come with her. She realised the baby meant everything to him. Then he started doing karate, three evening classes a week. 'It's the best present I can give my child because I mean to stay alive. My father died because they knew he couldn't defend himself. Now if he'd learned self-defence he'd have given out a signal and they couldn't have gone near him. What happened to my father could happen to me or our child.'

'Alex, who did kill your father?'

He didn't answer.

'It's none of my business but you make it sound sort of ongoing. They never really got to the bottom of it, did they?'

'Well, there's your answer.'

'It was political, wasn't it?'

'Yes, Jane.' He sighed.

'So how –'

'So?' He spoke coldly now.

'What good would learning karate have done? They shoot from a long way off, don't they, political killers?'

'Not this time. They weren't taking any chances. Right up, face to face.'

'You saw it?'

'I was there.'

She felt quite disturbed. It was nothing like they'd said on the news. Alex carried on kicking his legs out making a swooshing noise. He had very good reflexes and balance.

'My teacher showed me his belt and said, "This tells you I can kill you." Then he showed me the grades on the side of the belt. "These say you can no longer kill me." He is beyond measure. Isn't that a marvellous thing?'

'That's not what they said on the news. That the killer came right up face to face.'

He sat on the bed and held her close. 'Jane, my father was a popular man. Can you imagine the shit that would have hit the fan if the public knew – knew that a guy could get that close and get away? The government had to write its own script and cover itself. There's no mystery.'

Later she asked, 'Who does your mother love best?'

'All of us the same.'

'Oh, come on. She must have a favourite.'

'No. My mother is democratic.'

Not about everything, Jane thought.

The cherry tree ceremony filled the papers for days. She asked Alex why he hadn't gone. 'Was it because of me?'

'Of course not. I'd rather remember my father in private.'

And she was so happy she felt good enough to face Hastings.

. . . Chapter 21 . . .

Charlotte was small and curvaceous, with masses of jubilant red hair like a Pre-Raphaelite model. She still wore the black mourning dress from the cherry tree ceremony, and the Greek noticed her nails were black too. She maybe took a shower but she didn't bathe – she certainly wasn't how he'd imagined a Caversham woman to be.

Margery was laughing privately with Marion. The Greek asked what was funny.

'If Dino could have seen that speech. When the priest got it wrong and the President said "We'll blossom now" instead of "this blessed vow". How he'd have laughed. Especially at that one with his knees in the earth. He always said if that one gets in, to go to Russia immediately.'

Marion laughed.

'But leave your money behind.'

Marion said, 'You know there's a Mexican woman who polarises you. No, truly. It's the latest thing. Gallo's gone there and it works. Let's do it.'

'Polarises you?' said Margery.

'So you point in the right direction.'

Margery laughed, then said softly, 'Well, mine would be right away from Greece. I don't want to give up this house.'

'I didn't think marrying him meant you gave things up. I thought the other way round,' Marion said.

The Greek was talking to Charlotte about her job in the Bronx. She helped the homeless, druggies and drunks and got them shelter or on to a programme. She was saying how bad the shelters smelt sometimes. Vomit and –

'Charlotte, this is a dinner table. Have you forgotten what one's like?' Margery was appalled.

Kay said, 'Mummy, you're going to have to cut her money off. She just gives it to drunks.'

'Is that true?'

'Of course it is,' said Charlotte. 'I can't spend one buck as long as there's one starving person in the world.'

'You sure say the wrong thing at the wrong time.' And Marion laughed at the Greek.

'I think it's touching,' he said. 'But why hurt yourself through this harming life, Charlotte? It doesn't help.' And he explained the basics of economy, how it worked, so that if a rich man like himself gave his fortune away over a wide area, no one actually benefited.

Margery said, 'I heard today that Dino was responsible for stopping –' she paused. 'No, I shouldn't talk about it. He was solely responsible for stopping an Eastern Bloc reprisal and it turned out he was right. A lot of the good stuff will never surface, because they don't want to make him a martyr.'

No one spoke.

She went on softly, 'I think he'd agree with that. As Bogart said, "Life is for the living."'

'So live and be happy,' said Marion. 'No one deserves it more than you.'

After dinner, movie time again. Margery was monopolised by her family and the Greek again felt left out. They watched film after film and basically Margery was trying to teach Kay how to get on the right side of the camera and upstage her co-stars without them knowing. They gossiped a lot, names he'd heard of.

'Whatever happened to Jay?' said Margery. 'Jay Stone. I did two movies with him.'

'What a sexy man,' said Marion.

'A beautiful face,' said Margery, 'I used to tease him about it. I said you look better than me – they're gonna switch the parts.'

'He must have been gay,' said Kay.

'No, he had a wife and –'

'What does that prove?' said Kay.

'He was narcissistic. What happened to him? I must find out. Women disappear at the so-called height of fame – but never a man. What was his last movie?'

They couldn't remember.

'You'll have to get back with Mo Cohen,' Margery told Marion. 'Otherwise we'll never hear any gossip.'

The Greek accompanied Margery on a short walk with the dog. He asked what had happened to Kay's Italian friend.

'Oh, Guido – she sees him. She's trying to have a baby by him. That's just crazy if she wants to be a movie actress. It'll take her away from the screen and she doesn't really love Guido.'

'No, I don't think so,' said the Greek.

'But he's perfectly nice and he might settle her. I don't know.'

The Greek did. The only settling would be the sort in de Sade. Did Margery know what went on? He thought he'd deal with that himself when he was head of the family. He'd leave Margery out of it. She had enough pressure.

'The boy doesn't have too many things. I'd like to give him some presents.'

'No,' said Margery. 'He has enough. That's how they've all been brought up. I don't want them to be reliant on things. When they're twenty-one they can do what they want. Alex had just one teddy bear and a few bricks – he learned to use his imagination. And don't get at Kay.'

'You spend so much time on her.'

'I'll soon be leaving her, to be with you, so don't begrudge her that. My family has had a tragic experience. We all need time to heal.'

He put his thick arms around her. 'You'll heal with me. I promise you that.'

Then he kissed her, getting his tongue between her unwilling lips. All at once she started to respond. She was very good – a slow fire to begin with but a good blaze at the end. It was like riding a bicycle, she thought. Once learned you never forgot.

Alex was sitting with his back to the wall outside Earls Court tube station, reading a newspaper. 'My mother's marrying the Greek,' he said. 'Jesus!'

'What's wrong with him?' asked Jane. 'Everyone else wants to marry him.'

'It's wrong. All wrong.' He was very angry.

'I thought he was quite a man.'

'I don't mean him – he is a nice guy – but my mother's not so nice. And I have to read it in a newspaper. A million people know before I do. It's my mother's first mistake.'

'Why?'

'Because she's not got over my father. And any man who gets netted in by her is a poor son of a bitch. He's gonna come out of there feeling two inches tall. All she's gonna do is make comparisons. The Greek will throw himself over the side of one of his ships and be glad to do so.'

'Why don't you talk to her?'

'Because it's her life.'

'I expect she feels the same way about you marrying me.'

'No, you make me feel two feet taller.' He stood up and linked arms with her. 'What do you want? Anything. Say it.'

'You.'

'A movie?'

'Fine.'

He started towards the little cinema off the Boltons. She stopped. 'Oh, look, I'm not into horror films. I really don't like them.' And she shivered and thought of Jay Stone.

Kay rode Guido as hard as she could and her breasts leapt up and down and he reached up and held them.

'You like doing that, don't you? Being on top?'

'Get it right up me,' she said. 'Guido, I want to have a baby. Do it to me.'

'You'll have to come.'

She rode him even harder. 'I can't.'

'Then stroke yourself.'

As she did so she could see herself in the mirror, his prick inside her, his hands fondling her breasts. She rubbed her clitoris but she needed a lot more. She closed her eyes and thought of Jacey. She'd be straddled over two guys, one on top of the other, and another in her mouth. She thought about all the things they said she did, like covering a guy's prick with whipped cream and licking it off – in a restaurant.

'Tell me what you'd do to Jacey,' she whispered.

'Kick her out.' The very mention of Jacey was enough to make Guido lose his erection. The tramp didn't get kennel space at his home. But Kay was off in her own erotic world, a multiple orgy, an orgasm beginning. She hoped he'd shut up so she could get there, but Guido said, 'I love you,' and the orgasm dwindled away.

'Just come in me, Guido.'

She had to have the baby, the first Caversham grandchild. As soon as he'd impregnated her she'd marry him. Mummy would never accept Alex's child.

Margery stayed in bed late. The Greek's eau de Cologne, made especially for him, marked his place beside her. It was like a dog marking his territory. Quite out of place having a man in Dino's bed. She got up and removed the sheets and pillow cases. As she bent over the bed she had an overwhelming feeling that Dino was behind her. She stayed bending, unable to move, terrified to look round. She said, 'I'm sorry, I won't do it again.'

He was waiting for her, the other side of death. All she had to do was be faithful to his love, for her remaining earthly days. Was that such a lot to ask? Dino had always been possessive in life. She didn't think death changed much. The romp with the Greek had been satisfying, but sex was just an appetite which she could control.

'You know it didn't mean anything.' She turned round. A ghost would have been just too much, on top of all her other troubles but Kay was there, sitting on the dishevelled bed. Kay had heard her mother talking to herself and felt worried. She said, 'I went to the doctor and got the times of my ovulation and I concentrate on sex with Guido during those three days.'

Margery laughed. She loved 'concentrate'.

'But he's got all these peasant ideas. He says I won't conceive if I don't have an orgasm with him at the same time. Is that true?'

Margery had no idea and couldn't care less. 'So you're going ahead and marrying him?'

'Only if I get pregnant.'

'But you'll have to stop filming.'

'So? I'll stay here with you.'

'Kay, I'm about to get married. I won't be here.'

'You can't just shove off and leave Shane.' She wanted to add 'and me'.

Margery knew that her daughter needed love and approval and that she really had to give it. If she failed, the girl would go – as Dino used to say – to the bad. Margery stroked Kay's hair and said how good she was looking, and that other people thought so too. They'd make her film première a gala to remember. Kay grabbed her mother and put her head on her breasts.

Margery, taken by surprise, did nothing for a moment. She did not like the sensation at all. Then she tried gently to extricate herself, but Kay got more emotional. Feeling imprisoned Margery pushed too hard. 'Don't do that, Kay.'

Kay sat mute, head bowed, eyes filled with tears.

'For crissake, you're not a kid!' Margery sat beside her and put her arm round her. 'I've got the right editor, by the way. Mo Cohen had him flown in from Australia. He was doing a film there but we've taken him off that. He's started work immediately on yours so it'll be a pretty damn good opening night.'

Kay believed her mother would love her if she got pregnant.

'I suppose we'll have to invite that tyrant Cortese. Dino used to fight with him. He said Cortese didn't believe in the poor: he couldn't see the point of them, so they shouldn't exist. But then your father got more worldly and political and knew you had to deal with what was actually there behind the throne. But not too much. Mix with shit and shit rubs off on you.'

'You can't leave here and just go off with the Greek, Mummy. What about –' She paused.

'Yes?' Margery's voice was cold.

'What about my father?'

. . . Chapter 22 . . .

For the visit to Jane's mother, Alex put on a suit made of fine grey cashmere, a legacy from the Cannes days. He added a dark green knitted tie. Most of his stuff was stored at Lucien's last place: as Alex still had a key he didn't have to confront his friend.

'Look, she's just an ordinary person, my Mum. She won't mind what you wear.'

People's parents. I'd better watch it, he thought. He bought her a selection of jams from Fortnum and Mason.

'You don't have to be nervous seeing my Mum.'

'Well, I'm nervous seeing mine,' he said.

Jane's mother's small terraced house was just off the sea front. A key hung on a string behind the letterbox so anyone could let themselves in. Jane was wearing dark glasses. She didn't want anyone to recognise her. The house, with its highly polished lino, smelt the same. Two dogs leapt up as she came in. A cat sat on the stairs.

'Hello, Mum. Me,' she called, but her mother was in the betting shop. One of the lodgers put the kettle on, then a neighbour popped in with some tips for the 3.30. Jane kept her face averted but the woman recognised her and exclaimed, 'Janey Jones! Oh, what a treat! And your young man!'

Jane knew coming home was a mistake.

The neighbour shook Alex's hand. 'Well, she always did like movie stars.'

Oh shit, thought Jane. She'll mention Jay Stone next.

'Joan Crawford – now she was your mother's favourite. Her mother and me spent our lives in the pictures. I've got a present for you, and I want to wish you all the luck in the world. I look after your mother's extras, you know. I let my spare room.'

Jane's mother came in off the street with a young boy who'd hurt his knee. She was still lively and energetic, with bright eyes, but she had aged in the four years since Jane had last seen her.

Bette wore a green and white striped cotton button-through dress from C & A and a young-style blue demin jacket. Her shoes were flat ballerina-type things scuffed from walking on the beach with the dogs. She had good shapely brown legs and never bothered with stockings. Her permed hair was bleached by the seaside sun. Her skin was brown, her cheekbones high. And the eyes, slanting and fiery, didn't miss a thing. She wore a cheap bright rose lipstick.

'It's lovely to see you, duck.' She gave Jane a kiss. 'I'm really pleased to meet you,' and she shook Alex's hand. 'It's an ordinary sort of house but you're welcome.' Then she took the crying boy into the scullery and bathed his knee.

'You remember the Joan Crawford movies?' said the neighbour to Jane's mother.

'Never out of them.' She turned to Alex. 'And your mother, Margery Caversham, we all loved her. She never went off. You know Janey was conceived in the movies. Well, as good as.'

'Oh God!' muttered Jane. What was her mother going to say next?

'That's where I met Jane's father. In the cinema. Then he lodged here. It was after a Veronica Lake and Alan Ladd film that I got involved with him. He was a sailor, Royal Navy. Then he went overseas.'

'Well, you did a good job bringing Jane up,' said Alex.

Jane was hot with embarrassment. It wasn't a good job, a bad job – just no job. Her mother got on with life and Jane joined in. If she didn't want to go to school, that was fine – her mother wrote a note. It was all up to Jane, and in retrospect it was all too lax.

'I've made your special,' said her mother, taking a fish stew out of the oven. She gave the boy a toffee and told him to go on home, but he wanted to stay with Auntie. As Jane helped her mother lay the table she whispered, 'Don't say anything.'

Her mother shook her head.

'And you've taken those posters down?'

She nodded once.

'And I'm pregnant, Mum.'

Bette kissed her warmly. 'You'll make a good mum.'

Alex couldn't understand a lot of what Jane's mother said,

because she had what he supposed was a seaside accent, but he liked her. Trouble began when he wanted to stay on. Jane said they couldn't because her Mum was full up. She kicked Alex hard.

Her mother said, 'I think you should go back with Jane, duck. You can come and spend your holidays here.'

Alex loved everything about this woman. She was made for him: the way she set the tea table, her quick smile, her deft movements. Watching her made him feel creative and he yearned to draw her. It was obvious she didn't depend on other people. She liked them to have a good time and do what they wanted. The only odd thing was that after lunch, which she called dinner, she brushed and washed the floors barefoot.

The neighbour said, 'She's got gypsy blood, our Bette. You want to ask her to read your tea leaves.'

The house was full of chatter and laughter, the radio playing. He never wanted to leave.

Before they left, Jane's mother took them for a walk along the front and Alex picked out special stones and shells from the beach. Jane didn't want to be out at all and kept her head down.

'If it's a girl we're going to call her after your mother.' Jane looked uneasy and hostile – he'd never seen her like that before.

'What did happen here?' he said to both of them. 'I know it's nothing that bad because around your mother bad things don't happen.'

Bette said, 'It was just the ferris wheel caught fire when she was little and it gave her a funny feeling.'

'What, sort of delayed?' said Alex. 'I mean, she didn't leave here till she was eighteen.'

Jane's mother didn't know what to say, so she just nodded her head.

Jane said, 'Look, it's just something that's not really resolved.'

'Yeah, I can see that.'

They had fish and chips and played pinball. For once Jane did not enjoy the sea and it did not enhance her. He'd never seen anyone get out of a town so fast. As they left she said to her mother, 'Has anyone been asking – you know?'

'Well, there was a bit of talk, like. Some reckon they saw him. I'm not going to lie to you. I'd just stay away for now.'

'If they do come asking, what do you say?'

'Janey, what you told me. But it's four years. Go and live your life.'

At the station Alex kissed Jane's mother as though saying goodbye to a much-loved friend. On the train he said, 'I'm going back to see her and spend time there, even if you won't. Tell me the truth – did *you* set fire to the big wheel?'

Jane burst out laughing and thought how simple that would be.

'What's your real name?'

'Kirkland,' she answered almost arrogantly.

'Jones. Janey Jones.'

She shrugged, feigning nonchalance.

Alex didn't like being kept out of her life.

When she got home she wrote a letter to Alex and put it inside the cover of her childhood Bible. That was one place he'd never look. On the envelope she put, 'In case of accident or death please open'. She phoned her mother and said she'd written it all down and where Alex should look, if anything happened to her.

'At least you got that off your chest.' Bette didn't want to talk about it. She didn't dwell on the unpleasant things in life, and in the past Jane had kept a great deal from her. Why give someone bad news if they couldn't do anything about it? Jane thought her mother was brave and admirable, the way she'd got by without a man: she didn't even see it as being left. She was one of life's truly happy people.

The letter began:

> Dear Alex,
>
> This concerns Jay Stone.
>
> I was mad about him for years then he came to England to make a film. I was working on the radio show so I tried to interview him. Of course I got nowhere near him, but I did sneak into his London press conference. I got nowhere near him there either. I was hiding in the lavatory and he, obviously a narcissist or sun worshipper, suddenly appeared on the bit of roof outside the window. He stripped off to get the last of the sun. So I talked to him and he was very interested in Hastings when I mentioned a new

opportunity we'd started there for keeping your youth. It was based on seaweed. He said he'd come and meet me as long as it was incognito . . .

. . . As Jane left the lavatory she was stopped by one of Jay Stone's bodyguards, who took her name and address. She saw a table piled with opened fan letters, some adoring, others demanding, some with suggestive photographs.

'They'll do anything to get to Jay,' said the bodyguard, looking at a photograph of a woman in an erotic pose with the caption 'This could all be yours'.

'Does he read all that?' Jane asked.

'Sure. He loves all that.'

After the second week of waiting, Jane, pining, had caressed his face in a movie magazine. How could it be so perfect? Her mother kept saying. 'He's too good-looking. You pay for looks like that. He'll be no good to you – too self-centred.'

During his second week into the film Jay Stone learned that he was no longer perfect. The director said his legs gave away his age. 'They look old, Jay.' Jay recoiled as though he'd been told he had bad breath. Then he made an immediate, inconspicuous visit to Hastings. He had to keep his youth: his survival depended on it. He didn't entirely believe in the magic seaweed but the girl in the lavatory had looked sensational. If Hastings could do it for her, why not him? He would do just about anything to be young.

The resort was not as he'd imagined it or as she'd described it. She took him around the seaweed cure clinic. Dark glasses hid his famous eyes as he sampled the products. He ordered what looked like a ton of seaweed for his hotel baths. But would it restore ageing legs? He doubted it.

It was when she talked about her mother that Jay Stone decided to enjoy the day. He wanted it ordinary – he got little enough of that. They took an open bus along the front, had fish and chips, played pinball on the pier. He sunned his body but kept his face in the shade. Jane was surprised because he'd virtually smothered it with protective cream. At the rock pool he stared so intently into the water she thought he'd discovered some strange fish, but he was only looking at his reflection. She told him how much she loved films. They had the same favourite: *Les Enfants du Paradis*.

'Remember the leading actress?' he said. 'How beautiful her eyes were? D'you know why? She put belladonna drops in to dilate the pupils and make her eyes look more luminous. But she put in too much and after the film she went blind and never recovered her sight.'

Jane was appalled and said it wasn't worth it. Jay Stone said an immortal film was worth any sacrifice.

He kept sniffing around the fairground looking for excitement. It was the afternoon and things were flat. To keep him entertained Jane told him about the big wheel catching fire when she was a kid. Amidst the smoke and flames she'd seen plastic figures which decorated the wheel twisting and melting. Horrified, she'd thought they were real people. A fireman told the owner of the wheel, 'You've gone too far – it's overheated. To get this excitement costs lives.'

Jane's mother kept assuring her the melting figures were plastic but she couldn't rid herself of the memory.

Jay shivered. 'To get that excitement costs lives. Well, everything has a price – doesn't it just?'

He bought a stick of rock and was ready for home. Jane used her best tactic, seduction, but he captured her enticing hands and said, 'Let's keep it friendly.' He promised to meet her again – she could visit the set. But her dream was real in front of her and she wouldn't let go. She suggested pleasures way beyond his wife's range. He didn't go in for sexual release except with his wife, and that was functional low-key and rare. His energy went into his image. Again he rejected her, saying he must leave. But he also liked people having to try hard to get him: it increased his power. She heated up in a way that was out of place in public. Decidedly aroused, he went with her to the privacy of a backstreet room. Jane held him and said how much she'd longed, ached, to sleep with him. She was explicit about the details of her fantasies. How varied they were. He liked it all far too much. 'I should not be doing this,' he said. He wiped a handkerchief over his face and for a moment looked odd, disquieting. She supposed he wanted to stay faithful to his wife.

'Don't you go with other people, then?' she asked.

'Rarely.'

He would much rather cool down and talk, he said. He sat her beside him and asked more about her mother. How he wished he'd had one so happy. A sickly, lonely child from a poor family, Jay had wanted to be something more than he was. He knew all about dreams. Jane said how much she wanted to be in films herself. Her little dreams came out in hot bursts. How well he understood. Where she was, he'd been. A kid who wants the moon – only a star could understand that. He prepared to leave her as he would a friend. A kiss on the cheek, a promise to phone. She cut through all that with a direct suggestion that aroused him so much that he even forgot himself. There was too much professional sex about, and here was a real person with a wonderful erotic imagination and insatiable cravings, all centred on him. He did try to tell her he was no good for her. He compared himself to Dorian Gray. Jane had never heard of him, and just lay back invitingly on the bed.

'Let's say I've given up personal gratification for public acceptance. I cannot love,' he said.

Jane didn't want a lot of chatty rejection; she pulled him down on top of her. 'Just do it. There's no hangups.' She sensed, quite correctly, that he was frustrated. His wife had values and he liked them, but you couldn't get hot about values. Jane promised it would be good for him, to let himself go and really do what he wanted for once.

'I shouldn't,' he said. But he did. Against the sound of the sea coming in, he finally gave her what she'd wanted so much. He was a star in the bed and in her mind, and it produced in him more intense excitement than he'd felt for years. How did she know that he liked to be told in detail just how good he was, how good it felt? She stopped talking, closed her eyes, near ecstasy. Liquid drops were splashing on her face. She supposed it was his sweat. He moaned, a gasp, the drops got bigger, splashier. She opened her eyes. Above her, the perfect face did not have the expression of high arousal she'd imagined so often. It wasn't sweat that was falling, but great-sized drops of hot flesh and skin. The face was melting. He was trying to cry out, as his face began to slide and bulge, the beauty melting away, becoming gristle, bone, two misshapen eyes. As she screamed she heard distinctly the fairground music and the fireman saying, 'They went too far. Too much excitement and now someone has to pay.' And for a moment she wasn't sure where she was.

When Jay Stone had had his ageing face remodelled it was a medical triumph, but they told him not to let it get too hot, too suddenly, or the facial structure could become unstable. Burning sun on the face was out. No leaning over a log fire or kitchen stove. A sudden rise in temperature caused by anger or lust should be avoided. Playtime with his wife was cool, and he let his staff lose their temper for him. It hadn't occurred to him that someone could heat him up so much in bed, that he'd find inflammatory fantasies in a real person. But as Jane's mother had said, 'You have to pay.' The price of passion with the seaside girl was high.

Jane remembered the naked movie star crouched in the corner of the temporary room, while police and ambulance men climbed over the bed to get to him. Jane couldn't look. She'd got her clothes on and just become part of the group in the house – a witness, no more. But the landlady knew it was her who'd called the ambulance. Jane quickly slunk off round the back streets as soon as the ambulance had gone. She'd been seen, for sure – the landlady, people on the pier, assistants in the seaweed establishment. Luckily for her, the hospital couldn't make an identification of the man. Jane ran to the station and got the train for London. She phoned her mother, told her what had happened. She didn't know if Jay Stone was dead.

'They'll say it's my fault, Mum. So don't tell them anything. You haven't seen me. You don't even know if I'm alive.' She felt instinctively that Jay Stone would have a tough group around him: bodyguards, lawyers, private police, not to mention his wife.

Jane's mother went to the hospital but the unknown man had been transferred to a hospital specialising in burns. They didn't know if he was still alive . . .

. . . Chapter 23 . . .

Lucien called on Jane one day when he knew Alex was out house-cleaning. He brought a huge bunch of flowers and a hamper of fresh fruit. She wouldn't let him in, so he stood on the stairs. He looked as though he could adapt to most places. He wore a beautifully cut blue silk suit, as neat and clean-lined as a good envelope. His pale grey shirt was buttoned high. No earrings today. No gold chains over the hips. He looked like a B-movie star's lawyer. He didn't look so black in daylight. In fact he had a white person's face with black skin and green eyes. His hair was crinkly and there was plenty of it. He had a resonant, well-educated, quite seductive voice. His father was Swiss French and his mother came from Zimbabwe.

He again extended the gifts. 'Please take these, Jane. Don't worry, I won't come in. I just want to say I'm very sorry I caused you pain. I would so gladly have met you and been your friend, but Alex didn't want that. Anyway I'll be going now.'

'Why didn't he? Want that?'

'Because he's frightened I'll take you away or you'll take me and we'll like each other more than him. You see, his sister Kay always tried to take everything away from him.'

Jane, being an only child, had no experience of this kind of rivalry.

'Please take the flowers.'

She took the flowers. He seemed so mature, and there was something hypnotic about his eyes. 'I'll do it Alex's way if you don't mind, so I won't ask you in. And I'll tell him you called.' She was starting to get some things right in life.

'Please do,' said Lucien. 'And take the fruit. Give it to Alex if you like.'

'I'd rather not.'

He started down the stairs with the basket, then turned and smiled, a nice smile. 'I'm sorry it had to be this way. Incidentally, how is he?'

So that was the point of his visit. 'I'll tell him you called.' She started to close the door. He came back up a few steps. 'Jane, if you ever need anything please ask me.' He sounded serious. 'Money, anything. I think it's wrong Alex is cleaning people's lavatories at a time like this. You need him here.'

She wanted to say, 'So do I but what can I do?' But then he'd come back up the stairs and become part of her life.

Lucien got into his Italian car that the locals were eyeing with envy. Smart, he thought, and liked her for that. He remembered the beggars in Spain that came up from the South, the fearless ones the rich Northerners dreaded. She had those eyes – hungry. She'd take your wallet, your suit and live in your house. He thought Margery Caversham should be worried.

A man stood beside the bed in the dark, crying. Jane wasn't sure she was even awake – after all, she wasn't so happy she couldn't have a nightmare. She pushed her head under the pillows. Alex said, 'What is it, man?'

Then the lights were on and Jack Goddard, sobbing, said, 'My wife. She killed herself.'

Alex put on his pants and got Jack into a chair. It was a nightmare but Jane wasn't asleep. Alex was good at dealing with disasters. He made Jack some hot sweet tea, wrapped him in a blanket, kept talking to him, holding him. 'You've gotta believe, Jack, that we all go on, like it or not. She hasn't gone anywhere you're not going.'

Laurence Harvey had stopped seeing her months ago. She'd got depressed and just gone to bed and stopped eating. Her flatmate was away on tour. When she came back Jack's wife had been dead several days. Neatly piled beside the bed were letters to Laurence Harvey telling him how much she loved him, how she was dying slowly, giving him a chance to reach out for her. If he had he wouldn't have succeeded. The phone was cut off, so was the gas. It made starving to death easier.

Jack said he was going to kill Laurence Harvey. He'd identify her body then kill him.

'There's no future in that,' said Alex.

Jack wasn't too concerned about the future.

'If you want to get even, squeeze him out of his patch. That'll hurt. Be bigger than him. You're a producer, aren't you?' Alex wasn't entirely sure. He knew Jack claimed to be just about everything else. He just wanted to keep talking to get Jack listening. 'So let's get the show on. I'll be your star.'

Jack stopped sobbing. He couldn't believe what he'd heard. Nor could Jane.

'If it's so important to you, man, I'll do it. I'll do anything to help you. Now let's go and identify your old lady then we'll see some people.'

Alex came in as it was getting light and made some coffee. He was cold and kept flapping his arms like a bird.

'She looked a sight,' he said. 'Jack said she'd aged twenty years. Then we had to tell her mother. What a night!'

'So why did you say you'll make films? It won't bring her back.'

'To stop him killing Laurence Harvey. It's nothing to do with Laurence Harvey. It was her fantasy. I read the letters. I'd love Lucien to see them. Fantasies are incredibly strong. They are in a certain dimension and are fuelled by a lot of energy.' He opened the cupboard and behind a stack of records was hidden a painting of a bird. He gave it to Jane. It was in blue and gold and very strong. 'It's my bird. It's the only thing I will ever create. I'm going to give it to our kids.'

'Why is it the only thing?'

'Because I hate action. It leads to reaction.'

She was angry. 'But you deprive yourself of so much joy.'

'Joy! I'm only interested in moving on. To the next place. Joy in the next place is peanuts. If you're detached, you go easier. That's why I don't have luggage.'

She realised he was talking about somewhere a little further than Morocco.

'Well, for myself I just want to have a good time. Eat well, sleep, enjoy life, wear fantastic clothes, have sex.'

'You can't take this body with you, Jane. Better figure out what you do take and get it in good shape. I never liked this world much. I like it better now I know it's all suffering.'

'Not for the famous,' she said.

'I'll let you know. I'm on the market tomorrow. He's such a poor hustler, Jack. I feel sorry for him. I just couldn't see him killing a guy.'

April, and the flat was full of people. The windows were open letting in the city air and spring light. Lots of directors were mad about Alex because he looked like his mother. They came from every country in the West, together with the press and TV. Jane felt so left out. All she was was someone having a baby. Even famous people came to see him – old friends of his father's, pop stars. She remembered especially an English writer who'd lived with Scott Fitzgerald. Everyone seemed impressed by Alex: he had quiet authority. Jane was already jealous of him.

Jack spent all day on the phone, juggling the offers. It seemed that Alex would have to go to the States. The Johnny Carson show wanted him. And others.

Finally one night Alex came in and said, 'Visconti wants me for a part.'

'Jesus,' said Jack.

'That's the part. He's doing a film about the Bible.'

Jane followed Alex around the nightspots with the pop stars. She sat on the mattresses in the Arts Lab while he talked about transcendental states. She went up the King's Road while *Paris-Match* photographed him choosing gear. She hated it, because it wasn't her. How she wanted to go back to the days when it was just him, her and the baby.

She blamed Jack but couldn't talk about it openly. Of course he was still upset about his wife. At least Alex's decision to be a star kept Laurence Harvey alive and Jack out of jail. When anyone challenged his right to promote Alex Caversham Jack said, 'I'm a child of the sixties. So I can do anything. Or nothing. I can hang around with the rich or get by or make a real art-house movie or be a follower of the Maharishi.'

Filming was due to start in September. About the time she'd have the baby.

Everywhere Kay went they talked about her brother – and she got asked to a lot of places. He was the true Caversham heir; his stardom was measured in superlatives. After Visconti there was a line-up of directors wanting to work with him. That's what got her – directors wanting to work with him while she got offered films. He, Alex, had a say in what was made. She held herself together beautifully. 'Of course I'm pleased. He's my little brother.' And what was worse, *Baby Blue*, her debut film, was now released. Although the gala opening, courtesy of Margery Caversham, had been the sensation of the winter, her performance had not matched it. She was promising. Margery had done everything she could but Lucia, the lead, got all the acclaim. The critics, perhaps because they owed it to Margery, used safe words when referring to Kay.

Friends in the industry asked Margery what she'd thought. Margery said, 'All she does is goddam smile.'

It was while Kay was playing croquet at the de Luces', in England that she suddenly had the urge actually to see Alex: after all, for once they were in the same country. It coincided with the arrival of yet another period just when she was certain that this time she'd succeeded in getting pregnant. Her breasts had swollen, her stomach was bloated but the doctor told her these were phantom symptoms quite common in women desperate to conceive.

She wanted to see Alex in the flesh and check for herself if he was that sensational. She'd also terrify him, as she had as a child, by telling him about public occasions where he would have to speak, his voice trembling with nerves; gala dinners where he'd be filmed making a bad entrance; not to mention the society soirées he'd be obliged to grace, and the host would expect him to be clever like Dino. Then she'd wish him luck with his movie career. She might be miserable but she'd leave him sweating.

She phoned Lucien to get her brother's number. 'I just want to congratulate him. He's so in demand.'

'Kay, cut the crap. Instead of embarrassing yourself quarrelling with Alex why don't you think a minute? He had no money so he had to clean people's houses. He's having a kid, he needs money. Suddenly film directors are after him. Let's face it, it's a better deal than cleaning the john, even though he's an introvert.' He paused. 'Introvert. Get it?'

'Oh, Lucien, you're an angel.'

Of course her brother didn't want to be a frontrunner. Hadn't he always hopped out of the limelight? Charlotte was the same. What a waste.

She phoned Margery, who was holidaying in Greece, and told her Alex didn't want to be a star – what a sweat for him. 'Let's help him, Mummy. Put him back on the payroll. I'll put in half.'

Margery saw through that one and phoned Alex herself.

They got off to a bad start when he said, 'Ah, the Merry Widow.' She asked him how he liked the fast lane.

He didn't like it or dislike it. It was something he already knew about. He'd do it for a while.

'Wouldn't you rather do something else?'

'Well, yes. I would rather have studied philosophy and Eastern religions, but as I remember, that wasn't on. I was being groomed for more worldly stuff.'

'I too progress a little, Alex. Of course I shouldn't have tried to push you into politics. I admit that interfering in people's lives is a mistake. I should have let you go your own way, given you freedom. But Dino always said freedom is a very hard thing for people to handle. It's as bad as fame. Failure, now – they can be quite dignified and remarkable handling that.'

He knew the Greek was in earshot because she'd said Dino, not Dad. That was one son of a bitch who was gonna wish he'd had a little more failure, a little less fame.

'Why don't you go and study?' she said.

He paused. An offer was in the air. 'I am not coming to your wedding,' he said. 'I'm not coming anyway after the things you let Kay say about my wife.'

'If you want to be a movie star go ahead, Alex,' Margery said coldly. 'Either way there'll be a cheque in your bank. So start studying. And sometimes Kay is on your side.'

Jane was so relieved she'd got him back. How she'd dreaded the separation when he went to America, and his being Jesus in Italy while she was giving birth in London. He said Jack was pissed off but then he was weak. 'I can't do his living for him. He was just out for the main chance.'

She suspected most people were, given half a chance.

'He'll make out. He'll find someone else to exploit. Anyway, I saved his life and maybe Laurence Harvey's life.'

She didn't see Jack Goddard again for years. She didn't remember him a year later. As he'd said himself, he was a product of the sixties. But the seventies were on the way, and they were an altogether tougher time.

. . . Chapter 24 . . .

Wasn't life ironic? thought Margery. Of course, it should never be trusted. It was at her engagement party to the Greek that she met the pop star Rick de Palma. Kay brought him in, no doubt to stir up Guido. Margery first saw him standing amongst her oldest friends – agent Sue Graham from Hollywood, socialite Jessica Leland, the cult writer Nolan, the US Vice-President, Marion and the de Luces. Rick looked like a bitter angel with his floppy golden hair, and his wise eyes that had seen splendours and hells. Margery thought he'd seen far more than anyone else in that super-sophisticated group, and he was only twenty-six. When he spoke, she noticed he had a broken front tooth, and she hoped he'd never mend it. He turned and looked at her, really saw her, going beyond the beauty and the allure that dazzled the average onlookers and kept them out. His eyes made her feel a little dizzy and giggly. He knew that too, and he widened them. It was a sexual look.

And she turned around and went upstairs and for the first time took off her black.

When she reappeared at her engagement party she was wearing a soft, sensuous, flowing Chanel gown in pink silk with a delicate apricot lace overskirt and stole to match. The couture house had always reckoned that dress signalled reciprocal love. She'd pinned a short veil of apricot lace to her hair, studded with hard pearls like drops of ice. Her slippers had slim French heels and rhinestone buckles.

Every member of the party was amazed by the transformation. She looked less severe, younger. She looked, said Marion later, as though something had happened to her.

The chamber orchestra played Schubert. Not the Greek's choice – he'd wanted something lively. Dino's portrait filled one wall. He seemed to fill the whole room: wherever you stood you were aware of him. Charlotte said, 'It's as though Daddy's here.'

'But does he approve?' said Kay.

'Oh, you know Daddy,' said Charlotte. 'Keep going. Don't cry over spilt milk.'

'That was your English grandmother, stupid.' And Kay walked away. Charlotte was too outrageous, she thought. She was all worn out from picking up drunks and putting them together and dealing with their fixes and medical problems. She never had any sex or any fun. Her face had thickened. Above the nose it was too wide. And she was smoking a cigar. Kay had heard lots of stuff about her sister from friends in New York. Like she didn't use Tampax but old rags. And Mummy's New York apartment was full of dossers who put ash and butts in the Ming vases, and Charlotte didn't pull the lavatory chain. The servants couldn't stand it and locked everything away. Kay thought the girl should go into therapy but Margery said she was distracted, a dreamer. Also she was short and almost dumpy. Kay didn't want even to associate with her. And here she was at Mummy's big occasion wearing a Stirling Cooper dress that was meant for a tall agile girl.

Marion got Margery's attention for half a second and said, 'What do you think?'

'About what?'

Marion indicated Rick de Palma. He was wearing rich hippy clothes – rose-coloured suede trousers, an embroidered kaftan and a Zandra Rhodes beaded shirt. He had rings on his fingers and gold clip-on Cartier earrings. His leather choker was a mere strip enhancing his neck. The leather bands around his wrists were thicker, suggesting bondage. It was just gear, Margery could see that, stage stuff. Take it all off, and was he beautiful? She was sure he wore makeup, definitely eyeliner. No one was lucky enough to be born with that kind of optical emphasis.

Marion was after him, then, and so was Kay. It could turn into a complicated evening.

'He doesn't eat food,' said Marion. 'Just olives. So I asked the cook to make it interesting for him. Stuffed olives, black olives, with stones, huge Greek olives covered in garlic. What else can you do with olives? He hasn't eaten food for two months.'

The Greek took Margery's hand and said he felt happy. 'I'm glad you changed your clothes for me. It's a sign. An omen.'

She agreed with that.

'From now on, Margery, I don't want you to think. Just lie against me. I'm strong for both of us.'

As she squeezed his hand she saw Rick watching her. He turned his attention to the Giacometti sculpture. As he stood beside it she realised what he looked like: a work of art.

Lucia arrived late – her plane had been delayed. Her dress was stark black silk with long sleeves and a skirt that was slit up to her thighs. Huge white flowers were painted above the hem and on each side of the slit. Jennifer, shocked, appeared beside her. Didn't she know only Madam wore black? Lucia was despatched speedily upstairs and allowed to choose a colourful gown from the guest suite. Kay found her crying.

'I am so ashamed,' Lucia wailed.

'Don't be.' Kay was appalled to see her upset. 'It's ludicrous of that secretary. It's just a little flourish of power on her part, one of the few she's allowed. My mother doesn't give a damn who wears black.' Kay encouraged her back into her own gown, and holding her hand took her downstairs. 'You're with me, so don't worry.'

Lucia was surprised Kay Caversham could be so nice.

At one point before dinner every guest had a chance to admire Margery's ring: a large blue sapphire in a bed of yellow diamonds. The band was silver and exquisitely engraved.

She'd moved Dino's rings to the third finger of her right hand, and as she'd done so she had felt as though an electric shock was passing through her.

For an engagement present the Greek had not been lavish. He'd simply towed a sailing craft into the nearest harbour with a full staff at Margery's disposal day and night all year round. In her cabin he'd filled one drawer with boxes of jewels. Everyone had reckoned she'd get a Manhattan skyscraper at least.

She gave him a movie projector and screen. She could see it was going to be a selfish marriage. For a start he knew she disliked boats.

That evening for a few short hours Margery reminded everyone of what had made her a star. Her charisma was on full blast, and the guests were awed, silenced by her beauty. No one could stop looking at her. It was as though she held all the light in the room.

At the dinner the Greek noticed Guido and Kay literally fighting over who got the chair next to Margery. After the toasts Margery said, 'It would have been perfect if Alex was here. But maybe God doesn't like too much perfection, so we're pleasing him tonight. Anyway, I want to toast my son wherever he is. And I know that Dino de Stefano would be the first to welcome my next husband to this house.'

The Greek was in fact far from happy. He was supposed to welcome her to his home, that's what he'd understood, but she'd insisted on the party being held in Cannes. She said it was nearer than Greece, nearer for the American guests. He'd loved the guest list and he didn't want to lose a single one. For that reason only, he agreed to Cannes. Forty people sat around the table, most of them superstars in their own right. All the men with the exception of the pop star wore formal evening clothes. Shane wore a dark green velvet smoking jacket and bow tie.

Shane asked the Greek, 'Do you break plates in Greece?'

The Greek laughed. 'Only in celebration.'

'Well, let's do it now,' said Shane.

'It wouldn't be right now.' He ruffled the boy's silky hair. 'I'll explain our customs to you and teach you our dances.'

'And we'll throw plates? I've never seen Mom looking so beautiful. Something's made her happy.'

'But of course,' said the Greek. 'We are engaged. That's why.'

Shane didn't think so. He said, 'Do you chuck plates anyhow, all over the place?'

'Oh, come on,' said Kay. 'There's more to Greece than that.' She turned to the Greek. 'I adore Melina Mercouri. Have you met her? I'm sure you have. I loved that film, *Never on Sunday*.' For once Kay was being very nice to him, but then Kay, for the first time in her life, thought she might be in love. The beauty of Rick de Palma had made her half crazed with passion. She'd spent days, nights, yearning for him. He was hard to get to see, even for her, but he wouldn't pass up a chance to attend Margery Caversham's engagement party.

Kay had planned the sleeping arrangements. Guido was in the guest wing in the Greek's old bedroom, and Rick would be in hers. Margery looked across at her daughters and smiled. Then she felt Rick de Palma's eyes on her and felt fluttery and sharply happy. When finally Margery looked his way, his eyes were still on her, bright and challenging. Their eyes met and held and there was an acknowledgement between them. Was it a meeting of souls? Whatever it was it was deep.

The de Luces didn't like the Greek, nor did Margery's aristocratic friends from England. He was considered vulgar: some people could have too much money. If he put a foot wrong these were the people who would let him know it with a cruel glance, a private joke amongst themselves that could nonetheless be overheard.

The marriage would take place in Greece on July 23rd and they'd honeymoon on his island in the south. If it got too hot they'd go on to Switzerland because Margery liked good air.

The attention turned to Rick de Palma. He was, discounting Margery, the biggest star present. The straights at the table had already been reassured that he was very intelligent. The girls asked about his life. They were dying to know his past. Rick said he'd done everything: drink, drugs, acid, fame, existentialism, sex, India, transcendental meditation, abstinence, money, luxury, power, gurus. He'd spent some time with Timothy Leary, and had crossed China when it was impossible to get in. He'd been one of the top pop stars in the world for five years, always in the charts. Now he was going to do something new.

'What, go into the solar energy programmes?' said Kay. 'So many Hollywood people are doing that.'

Margery doubted that was what he had in mind.

Rick said, 'Maybe I'll try a relationship – I've had everything else.'

Margery had turned her back on her fiancé. He was deep in conversation with the French President: the fact that it was his engagement party didn't stop him from selling ships. Kay told her mother that Rick was bisexual.

'Yes, I'll lay money on that.'

Kay said, 'I hope it was alright to bring him, Mummy.'

'So do I.'

After dinner they moved through to the famous art nouveau salon resplendent with original Gaudí sculptures and friezes. A Gaudí staircase in one corner led to the small, intimate parlour above. The decor was black, white and gold, a celebration of the organic, with carved plants, flowers and fruits everywhere. There were Gustav Klimt paintings, and theatrical posters by Mucha showing women with hair alive and brilliant and like foliage. The room created the impression of a forest. A black and white sofa was embellished with stylised carved plants, its appliqué fabric patterned with flowers and foliage. William Morris wallpaper, pale mauve with dark fronds and leaves, and Lalique lampshades and vases in frosted and clear glass, took the visitor back to the early 1900s. The mirror was engraved with birds and trees. Two Gaudí clocks stood opposite the doorway like the host and hostess waiting for guests to approach. Margery was one of the few stars who never allowed pictures or photographs of herself to be present in her rooms. Even the Oscars were not on display.

Marion had a vested interest in the Cavershams. She'd slept with Alex during an Easter holiday two years before, six times in all, and she'd been infatuated with him ever since. He was the best lover she'd ever had: the right mixture of detachment and sensuality, eroticism and control. The mere thought of his body inflamed her imagination. And he didn't seem young. She had nothing against young men, but he was more like thirty-eight than eighteen. She hadn't told Margery, because she wasn't sure how modern she was on that subject. She was in fact very modern, but not when it came to Alex. She'd have torn out Marion's baby-blonde hair in tufts if she'd known her son had been seduced. Of course Marion knew she wasn't the first and didn't believe what he said about an occasional serving girl and one of Warhol's ex-stars. She'd heard rumours about the eccentric Manhattan shoe heiress who was supposed to have had him when he was twelve. Marion looked at Shane, who was nearly fourteen. There was no comparison: Shane was still just a child.

But it was Rick de Palma who brought up the subject of Alex when he asked Kay about her sister-in-law.

'Who?' She couldn't think what he meant.

'The racing driver's ex who married your brother.'

'Why d'you want to know.' She sounded hostile.

'Because I come from South London too.'

'I don't think that's her spot on the dial,' said Kay.

'Well it's in her love story with Del Grainger. I come from Peckham Rye. Ask her if she knows Peckham.'

'I doubt I'll get the chance.' Kay couldn't sound scathing enough.

'Don't sound so snooty. We Londoners go a long way when we put our minds to it. Ask her if she knows Peckham and then you'll know if she knows South London.' He grinned at her and chucked her under the chin.

Marion wanted to ask about Alex – did he love Jane Kirkland? But Margery was lying back against the Mackintosh sofa talking to Capote on the telephone and who knew when that would finish? Bringing Jane Kirkland into the evening would be like presenting Margery with a sack of horse shit. Marion would get Kay on one side later.

Margery replaced the receiver and said Capote sent love to everyone. Then she closed her eyes. There was a sudden electric feeling on the top of her left hand. She turned quickly. Only Rick de Palma's fingers. She looked up into his face, taking her time about it; she felt a little breathless. Sexuality was a stranger to her body. His face was lived-in and used like the face of a battered tiger, and yet it was beautiful.

'I've got something for you,' he said, and gave her a white rose.

She held it and thanked him. It was a serious occasion.

'I know you're going to be happy at last.'

Margery smiled a young smile, and her face softened and all

the vestiges of her tragedy were gone. And then she remembered Dino, and how he'd pulled her into the hotel room in Rome the first time they'd made love. He'd put his hand round the back of her head and lifted up her hair saying, 'Wear it up. Go on.' He was desperate to have her, but there was time – time to play around. It was going to be that good. Without thinking Margery lifted her blue-black hair on to the top of her head.

Rick said, 'Don't do that. Don't wear your hair up like that.'

'Why not?' She was intrigued.

'Because it makes you look as though you belong to someone else.'

Shocked, she let her hair fall. 'But I do.' And she looked at her fiancé.

Rick shook his head. 'Not him.'

The mood was broken by the arrival of the helicopter for the politicians returning to Washington and Paris. Margery waved goodbye as the machine lifted into the night sky. She still held her white rose. It was more valuable than all the jewels and presents put together. The following day she would press it in her book of favourite French poems.

The evening ended early. All Margery's social events fitted in with her desire for good health and continuing beauty. The guests never had enough of her, so they never got bored.

'I'm going down to Andalusia to live with the gypsies for a while,' Rick told Kay. 'I love their customs, their music and their passion. And their poverty.'

'Poverty?' Kay was surprised.

'Some people are desperately poor, yet they never seem it. They're so rich in other ways that the material pinch doesn't seem to matter. Those people are glorious.'

Kay was bold. 'I'd love to come with you and we could take a movie camera.'

'That would be very nice, Kay, but I always travel alone.'

'Do you?' Margery had been listening. Their eyes met; she smiled at him, and in that instant, to her astonishment, she fell in love. It was like a sunrise coming up in a sky that had been dark for too long.

No one slept that night. Kay couldn't find Rick. Nor could Marion, who when she met Kay in the corridor for the tenth time said she was too emotional to sleep.

'About Mummy getting married, you mean?'

Marion agreed that that was what it was. At least the pop star wasn't with Kay Caversham. Individually they'd realised he could not be with Charlotte. That left the guys. They made tea then everyone joined them in the kitchen, except Margery and Rick. It was the end of an era. The Château would never be the same again.

The following day Kay noticed three things. Her mother asked Rick to sing. Frankie hadn't got asked that. She didn't look at him once, even when he spoke to her – was she shy suddenly? And when she did finally look, her eyes blazed like the sun coming up. Kay couldn't believe it. Panicking, she turned to the Greek, who was teaching Shane a card trick.

'Do something!'

'I am.'

'Well, I'd do a little more or you'll end up as just someone who opens the door.'

He thought she'd flipped, and got to his feet. 'D'you want something?' He meant a drink.

'Take Mummy on a cruise now and make it a long one.'

Then his daughter Sophia said, 'She's awfully fond of the singer.'

'Show business people are always like that,' he replied and went back to Shane. They got on well together and the Greek believed he'd save him. 'Save' was a big word but the boy's needs were that great.

'I mean your fiancée,' said Sophia.

'No, it's Kay who likes the singer.' But the Greek wasn't looking or even interested.

Kay moved in on Rick and asked where he'd spent the night.

'Outdoors. I just walked in the woods. It was lovely.'

Kay pulled him to her and let him feel her much-admired full breasts. 'You'll like me in Malaga. I'm passionate too.'

Margery answered the thirtieth congratulatory phone call and said that was it. She automatically looked for Rick, her eyes seeking him out. Kay had her arms around him and was kissing his face. But Rick's eyes, as though sensing Margery's desire, turned in her direction. He kissed Kay's hand but his eyes were on Margery. They told her, this one's for you.

Kay took the kiss on the hand as submission and pulled him with her to an upstairs room. He wasn't exactly busy in bed and didn't mind her doing it all. Most of the time he lay back and smoked a cigarette while she sucked him off. Then she got on top of him; she wanted this man but still couldn't get satisfaction. In the end she faked an orgasm. He knew all about those: he'd done enough in his time.

As Margery dressed for dinner she said to the Greek, 'I bet that pop star stood on a lot of street corners before Don Mink Inc. discovered him.'

'What, you think he's a gay whore?' asked the Greek.

'I think he's every kind of whore.' She didn't want to love him. She'd say anything to talk herself out of it. 'He even slept with Marion, who's now all dizzy about him. And Kay. And I guess Lucia gets a turn.'

She must talk herself out of it. But she was Margery Caversham and she could have what she wanted. And sooner or later she would have him.

A month before her wedding Margery said she couldn't marry after all. The Greek just couldn't believe it. 'Is it Dino?' he asked.

So easily she could have blamed it on him. 'No it isn't. I have my own reasons.'

He tried to ask questions, but she wouldn't listen.

'Your boy needs a father,' he pleaded.

'Oh, don't we all? Mine wasn't that good if you must know.' She peeled off the ring and gave it to him.

'You keep it.'

He wasn't hurt, because it hadn't been an emotional thing. He was puzzled and rather amazed that he'd not understood these people. But they were too famous, too powerful. He was only rich. He could only leave them to their kind, to fate and God.

The next day Margery Caversham married Rick de Palma in a chapel in Spain. Not even the village locals knew it had happened.

. . . Chapter 25 . . .

'Mummy got married in a village in Spain,' said Kay.

Shane didn't look surprised. He just concentrated on the little things in life that he could control. 'But why didn't we go?'

Kay shrugged.

'Maybe Big Boy thought he'd be kidnapped or something. Or shot like Daddy.'

'Not the Greek, dumbo – Rick de Palma.'

'Gee, Kay, that's not very nice of Mom. He was with you.'

Kay laughed shakily. 'I guess she feels life is short suddenly. And after all she is, well, years older than him. You know Mummy's forty-five this year.'

'It's not fair. Someone comes into the house and you get to know him and you like him and then he's gone.'

Kay told her brother not to whine. The Greek had his own kids to occupy him.

'Why didn't Mom tell me?' asked Shane.

'She wouldn't have told me, let alone you,' said Kay. 'But I've got to look after everything if she dies. I'm the next in line. It's like royalty. We can't even travel on the same plane. It's the money thing, Shane. Anyway, forget about the Greek. You get some friends. Boys of your own age.'

Shane knew what he'd do. On his fourteenth birthday he'd leave the Lycée and run away like Alex had done. The house was very lonely without Margery.

Kay had a four weeks' shoot on her French movie, *Day of the Wolf*. She had some explicit love scenes with the star, Robert Frey, who was known to get very real in that department in front of the camera. He was one of France's top actors, powerful, heading towards politics. His turn-on was to have sex on screen and then see it in his private projection room in the evening. Kay made it clear contractually that she'd only do a partial strip. Her drawers stayed on.

Kay sat alone in her apartment off the Champs Elysées. Although elegant in the extreme it seemed musty and unwholesome. She opened the shutters and pulled up the blinds. The afternoon street was full of formal semi-rich people she would never meet. The sun shone directly on to her greàtest treasure, the Matisse given to her by Margery on her twenty-first birthday. She closed the blinds again to protect the painting.

The carpet was pale green, soft and nice to lie on. She had a collection of Eileen Gray furniture and several Bauhaus chairs. The doors were chrome and black glass, and behind the settee stood a large Chinese screen made of red lacquer. What Kay liked about the apartment was that no one came into it. It was normal practice for Margery to allow friends and relatives to stay at her various houses and apartments. Kay refused visitors, even her closest friends. Lovers got in but were encouraged to leave after the sexual act. She did not look to men for companionship. She thought Robert Frey might visit, just to say he'd invaded her privacy. He wouldn't touch her – he didn't fancy her, she could see that.

The French actor was extremely good-looking in a glittery way. Apart from his mesmerising blue eyes women went mad for his power and catlike ruthlessness. He was always photographed wearing Valentino or Balmain three-piece suits. His shirts were impeccable with starched cuffs and silver cuff links by Georg Jensen; he liked white suits and snakeskin trousers and black fedoras with black bands. Kay had seen him in the evenings at the smart places wearing a black silk suit and a long cream scarf with its ends fringed in gold. He still wore Porsche sunglasses but was afraid they were becoming too popular.

Frey was an image-setter for the French. He looked after himself and one way of doing it was to have no competition. He would not be pleased if Kay arrived on the set dressed to kill – no French actress would dare. But Kay was a Caversham and she decided that next day she would wear an Yves Saint Laurent blazer with nothing underneath and tailored culottes. Tomorrow was snapshot day and the press were allowed to get all the photos they pleased. Frey on the set always wore blue jeans and Marlon Brando T-shirts with the sleeves rolled up to reveal tanned biceps. A leather jacket was always draped over his shoulders. Tomorrow Kay would get the photographers' attention. Her mother had taught her all about getting that.

Suddenly she felt worthless, utterly lost. Was life just a sordid competition with overdressed men? She had a good mind and an ability to concentrate and she longed for the worthwhile. If she hadn't been born a Caversham she would have applied herself to a rewarding occupation that would have absorbed her restlessness. She'd always enjoyed science at school. She could see herself at a space station directing things. She wanted power and discovery and the satisfaction of hard work.

She phoned her mother, who was now on the first step of her honeymoon journey to the East. Margery sounded concerned as she asked, 'What's wrong, Kay?'

'Oh, Mummy, I'm tired of the merry-go-round.'

'What's wrong!' Margery was nervous. Was there another man tied to the bed who couldn't be revived? Did it never stop?

'I would like to study physics and chemistry and –'

'Oh, Jesus Christ, Kay.'

'And get a worthwhile career and –'

'And I thought something was wrong. Kay, you interrupt my honeymoon to tell me you want to play with Bunsen burners!'

'But there just isn't time to do anything worthwhile because you have lunch guests and then you can't settle to anything because you know dinner is at seven-fifteen and there are more guests. So I don't do anything and I should.'

'What's gone wrong with Frey? Is he taking too much of the frame? Is he in every frame?'

'And I can't marry Guido because he doesn't want it. It's the old man who wants it, but I can't marry into that family. I can't do that to Daddy.'

'Daddy's dead!' Margery's voice was merciless.

'Not to me.' And Kay hung up, her eyes full of tears. She kept kicking at the lacquered screen hoping to damage it. Then she remembered it was hers not Mummy's. No one had ever understood her; she didn't understand herself. She'd had hundreds of men yet had been unable to get on with a sexual partner, to get near the remotest pleasure. Was it because she had a dirty mind that she couldn't share her sexual thoughts with another person? Who would love her? It was right that Rick went to her mother. She sat and waited for darkness to come. Nobody rang. Nobody knew where she was. She couldn't even drag herself out to eat. Then she decided she was too famous to feel so bad. Famous people didn't suffer from loneliness. Immediately she phoned Guido at his house in Milan, then at his other house on the coast outside Rome. The servants believed he was out of the country.

So he wasn't going to see her again, he was sticking to that decision. She'd change it. She'd simply get in her Ferrari and drive to Italy and get him back. Rage at his insolence took away her gloom. Then she remembered the photo call on the film set. Frey, unlike most French actors, liked an early start. If she was going to look better than him she'd need a good night's sleep.

Guido was in fact watching Giulini conduct at La Scala. He was so moved he cried openly.

He was a man of twenty-seven with a desire to be happy and have a good life. He decided, as he listened to the music, to stop seeing Kay Caversham. She was taking him away from the person he wanted to be, warping him. The pain play and the way she made him ejaculate made him feel used, like a whore. He was a man who got up a woman, for crissake. How had she got control? Because he'd wanted to give her pleasure. Instead she gave him humiliation. Her skin had a smell when she was excited and it stayed on his body for days, however much he bathed. He was beginning to dislike that smell. It reminded him of his endlessly repeated failure.

He went to the house of the Countess Gitti after the concert. He made love to her and was relieved he could still do it without trimmings. He wished he loved her. Afterwards he went to see his father, who never went to bed until three or four in the morning. Again he asked for a job on the administrative side of La Scala. He wanted, needed, to be involved with music. His father said he understood but the real money was with the textile factories. Music was just a night out or for the ladies. Guido argued – and lost. His father said, 'While I'm alive you do a man's work. If you're that keen on music learn the flute.'

The next night Kay phoned Guido in Milan and said she needed to see him. The truth was she felt lonely but she'd never admit it. He sounded distant and said he had his own problems. So she was worried about a movie? Couldn't she talk to her mother? Of course the world didn't know about Margery's secret new life. Quite distinctly Guido said he would not come to Paris. Her hand longed for the feel of a whip.

'Get here, Guido!' Her voice was raw.

'Goodbye, Kay.' His tone was final.

This time she did get into the Ferrari and head south. She'd left a message with the production office: 'Margery ill.' They'd hold up any film for that.

Guido wasn't at home so she went straight to his father's house. The old man was immensely pleased to see her. This was a match he'd give an eye for. The staff excelled themselves with the lunch but Guido didn't come. His father talked about Dino as though he'd known him well: easy once someone was dead. She doubted whether her father would have known a man like Cortese intimately, for she was sure he'd been a Fascist. She could tell people's political inclinations even if they couldn't themselves. It was almost a physical thing.

She excused herself early to go shopping and paid a surprise visit to Guido's office. As it was siesta time the office was empty. She walked through to Guido's private suite and there in the shuttered room saw him with a large blonde woman. They were straddled over a leather sofa, and the blonde's huge breasts swung out at the sides as his rhythm increased. She clutched him around the buttocks, pulling him deeper into her. It had obviously been a sudden decision, this sexual act, because they were both partially dressed and the door was unlocked. The blonde sighed and seemed to give herself up to it, to him; then she came, with loud shrieks, pummelling his back, beating him on the buttocks with her heels.

God, thought Kay. Why couldn't he make me feel like that?

She went into the street, shaky as hell, needing a pill, a drink. She desperately wanted somewhere quiet. No people, absolutely no people. She fumbled for her Yves Saint Laurent sunglasses and realised she'd left them in Guido's suite. She went into the nearest chemist's and bought a cheap pair. The customers stirred up like a flock of birds, whispering, 'That girl – she's Kay Caversham.'

She got out of there, panic rising, and tried to get a cab. Nothing doing. Everybody looked at her because she was now a mixture of famous and mad. It must have been an indication of her state of mind that the one person she chose to see was her brother Alex. He had always seemed so wise; also he was family.

Kay got to his Earls Court flat in the early evening. The girl wasn't there, unless she was hiding in the bathroom.

'I had to see you – I took the first plane out of Milan. Alex, I'm in trouble,' she said.

'Yeah, well, I can't help you, Kay. I try helping people and they usually end up worse off and hating me.' He thought of Jack Goddard, who now talked of suing him. He'd read it in the papers – something about a breach of contract.

'Is your wife here?'

'She's doing her childbirth class. She'll be back any minute. You can't be here, Kay.'

Kay licked her lips; she was nervous and pale. He'd never seen her like that. Clothes were Kay's thing, but her leather trousers didn't do anything for her, and her Zandra Rhodes beaded shirt looked kind of lost as though it would be better on a hanger.

'I've got to do a movie with the big one, Robert Frey. I've lost my sexual confidence.' She wrung her hands.

Alex was cold. 'Well, I shouldn't worry. He's all tied up with Romy Schneider.'

'That's what it says in the magazines. Don't believe what you read.'

'So he'll leave you alone.' Alex agreed that Frey was a big star and trouble and that even other stars were terrified of him.

'I can't seem to get it right, Alex. You know – in bed.'

'I know my mother ran off with your boyfriend. I agree it's a problem, because you need my mother.'

'She is *my* mother as well – although you'd never think it. How did you know? About Rick?'

'Because she rang me and told me, and she rang Charlotte in New York. I always said she'd flip.'

Kay asked sweetly if she could stay with him, just for the evening. She couldn't be alone. He didn't trust her, the way her eyes were already taking in the details of the flat. He was sure she was spying for his mother.

'I want you out of here, Kay, before my wife gets back.'

She stood up shakily and said something that could have been 'please'.

'I love my wife. She's having a kid any minute. I'm going to give her all the protection I can. Kay, you're out.'

Kay ran down the stairs. He called after her, 'Unlike you, Kay, I don't care about the money. If you wanna know – it's got blood on it. I know!' And he slammed the door.

Kay went to Lucien and said she was doing a costume fitting in London. Then she said nothing and smiled a lot. He took her to Alvaro's – they gave him a table anytime. She smiled even more and didn't eat. Lucien said, 'You don't know who you are, Kay. I can tune in to people.'

'Oh, come on! That's Charlotte's problem.'

'You don't want to face the truth, because you're on the gravy train.'

She didn't understand.

'If you did what you really wanted, it would be all-fall-down time with Mummy.'

'I'm an actress.'

'Yes,' said Lucien. 'You sure are.'

It was so obvious what she was.

. . . Chapter 26 . . .

For a month Margery tried it Rick's way. He took her to all his places – the Gobi Desert, Baghdad, Marrakesh, then the smaller places that hadn't changed for hundreds of years and were full of the essence of the peoples that had lived there. He asked her, 'Why do you want me?'

Margery replied, 'Because you're everything I'm not. And you're very good at it.' She couldn't look at his face enough. The expressions were so compelling they changed her whole chemistry. She felt like a young girl in the first flush of love. Then Dino would come into her mind and she'd think she was being unfaithful. She tried to blank him out by deliberately thinking of other things. He'd become an intrusion. Next, he'd be an enemy.

They dined in the most exciting places in the world. Her choice, then his.

'You are a star, Rick. And you're more female than I'll ever be. You're like a cat. I'm mad about cats.'

He felt her gorgeous breasts. 'Not more female than you.'

'I'm a manipulator.'

'All the best women are.' He loved to feel her.

She said she couldn't bear it if he went off with a guy. He said the desire for that was so rare and he could take care of it. He had a choice about going with men. With powerful women he got carried away. That's the way he was.

She liked life on all levels with Rick, but her honeymoon wasn't perfect. She knew Alex's child would be born any day. 'Oh God, life isn't what you think it's going to be. At one time it was so perfect. We were blessed.' She'd get her spy to check the baby. Miracles did happen. It could be Del Grainger's.

Rick kept saying, 'Come on, lady, I'll cool you out.' He was known for his cool, but there were areas of her life that even he couldn't reach. She told him nothing about Dino, and next to nothing about the real passion of her life, Alex.

When Kay arrived back her Paris flat was full of flowers. Truffaut? Her new director? Robert Frey? Guido had sent them. How lonely she felt. How she wished he was with her. Even the phone was silent – and she was supposed to be a movie star. Margery Caversham's phones were never silent. Somewhere she'd been had. She thought everything was OK at three and a half, then they'd put a son into the world whom Margery preferred, and Daddy took him everywhere. She'd spent her life worrying that her brothers and sister might get ahead of her, get better treatment, inherit Margery's magic. She was so lonely she wished she'd kept the maid on. They could have played cards. She tried watching television – nothing doing, mind not there. A couple of drinks and she went down into the street. She walked down the Champs Elysées and picked up the first man that thought he was picking her up. He was going to say, 'Let me fuck you, gorgeous.' She said, 'Yes, let me.'

They went to a hotel because she didn't trust any stranger on home ground. Rule one after Dino's death. This guy – no killer, but how could you tell? – was probably a thief and would come back and strip the apartment. Also he might blackmail her if he found out her identity.

She went into the hotel room determined to make it work. She'd be just like the blonde being screwed by Guido. She'd just be there, passive, and let the guy do it all. This was just an anonymous guy with a prick, and she could do what she liked with it.

Things went wrong as soon as she took her clothes off. For a start the guy couldn't believe what he was looking at. She was so beautiful – what the fuck was she doing with him? She must be someone famous, he thought – he did know her face. Yes, she was a model. Those tits!

'Jesus,' said Kay. 'Next time I pick up someone blind.'

She lay back on the bed and opened her legs. 'Just do it. I want it.'

At first he couldn't even get it up because he was so overcome. She was too classy. So Kay turned out the light and got some dirty talk going and he got excited. The moment she escaped into her fantasies about Jacey she got hot. Just close her eyes and be there with her getting it from five guys. She just wanted the guy to lie still with it up hard and shut the hell up while she got on with it. But he spoke. He was too real, and he was starting to distract her. Then he came.

She threw him out. When he'd gone she stayed in the room. She must get to Jacey. Princess Miranda's daughter was hard to meet apparently, but not if you were an anonymous man in a restaurant.

A difficult day on the set and she felt terrible without her mother around. Frey was polite but devastating. Everything revolved around him whenever he appeared – on screen and off. His bodyguards surrounded the set and got in the way of the technicians. She was surprised Frey was so civil and well-mannered: he came from a slum in Marseilles. The director was just someone who did what the star wanted. Frey had incredible eyes and she could see why he was number one. Margery said he'd stay there for years because the French, unlike the English and the Americans, were loyal to their idols.

Kay was all right as long as she did everything his way and didn't have ideas of her own. Her agent said it was looking promising. 'Just do it, Kay. His way. It'll be fast. He'll cut you during the editing but you'll have a good credit – co-star with Frey. Your next film – that's the one that will matter.'

Guido was waiting outside the studio. She was relieved. 'Why didn't you come on the set?'

'He, Frey, won't allow visitors.' He gave her the sunglasses she'd left in his office. 'I'm sorry you had to see that.'

She asked what if felt like having that woman. What did the woman feel? She wanted to know every detail.

'We neither of us have easy lives, Kay. I can't have what I want. My father won't let me near La Scala. I can't even get a job on the administration. What shall I do?'

'You could be an impresario,' she said. 'You'd be big in music then.'

'About the time you're a passive loving woman.'

'What about a rich wife?'

He said he'd think about it.

'Oh, shit, Guido, what's your next excuse? A headache when we get our clothes off?'

'Why not? You treat me like a girl.'

'I'm pushy, I can't help it. Be a bit more challenging and I'll be less pushy.'

'I really do love music,' he said. 'I'm going to be part of that world. So I lose the factories. They'll go to my brothers. I'm going to go to the administrator and get a job. And if my father makes it impossible I'll go to the Metropolitan in New York.'

'Marry me, Guido, and you have your own opera house.'

'Why?' He didn't like it.

'Because I'm lonely and I'm scared of what's inside me. I need looking after. Not fucking – looking after. Take care of me and I'll repay you.'

He was touched by her honesty, he felt sorry for her, and he remembered he'd once loved her. He said yes for all the right reasons, but 'no' would have been a better answer.

... Chapter 27 ...

Alex did the breathing with Jane to get her over the pain. It was 1968 and the hospital staff weren't exactly keen on natural childbirth. They would have preferred the usual medical procedure – an injection, gas and air, delivery on her back. They accepted that giving birth wasn't being ill and that women had a right to do it the way they wanted, but they would still have preferred her to take the injection.

Alex told them 'You push that to make it easier for you.'

It was obvious that he would be there at the birth. As it was a first child the midwife reckoned Jane would be in labour for several hours, so she went for dinner leaving a staff nurse on duty. But Jane, whether because of all the correct breathing or the lack of drugs, passed through into the transition stage within minutes. Then she gave a huge push and started to scream. The baby was coming out.

'Pant,' said Alex. 'Just pant and let the baby turn. The head has to turn.' He pressed bells for doctors and nurses. Her screams brought the staff nurse running.

'Don't make such a noise, Mrs Caversham. You're a long way yet. I told you to have an injection. You'll upset the other mothers.'

Jane let out one huge scream and the nurse saw the baby's head. The nurse and Alex delivered the boy. Alex held him so lovingly, the nurse said afterwards – it was like the eighth wonder of the world. Then he went away to the phone and Jane could hear him telling Lucien, 'I've had a boy!' No one took any notice of Jane. She felt a little shaky and shocked. She was desperate for a cup of sweet tea. But it was so muddly, all of it. They had to get the doctor to stitch her up and she had gas and air for that. Then they got her to the ward. By the time she got the tea she was too shocked to hold the cup. Eventually Alex was beside her but she didn't feel good. 'It's OK,' he said. 'All you've done is have a baby. Next time we'll have it at home.'

She'd felt very alone after the birth, a stranger in a strange place, not loved or even noticed. It felt more like a death than a birth. She didn't ever want to feel that isolated again.

And as she held the baby she felt – well, that does it. Later she said to herself, why did I feel that? Because you're a mother now. The movie star business is a thing of the past.

She hated the hospital because she didn't know where Alex was at night. Was he with Lucien? Even though she was going through postnatal blues she could still feel jealous. On day four – she was supposed to stay for eight – she discharged herself. Alex had got a pram and baby blankets. She'd been sent more flowers than she'd ever imagined, a lot from the press. The photographers were there on the steps as she got out of the taxi with the baby.

'Just take it easy,' said Alex. 'Don't get too high then you won't get too low.' She thought he must be talking to himself.

Margery's reaction to the news was, 'Well, he's made his

bed. Let him lie on it.' She called Julian and said, 'Someone will have to take a look at the baby.'

'I thought you had a spy, madam.'

'You go, Julian. Take some time off in London and see some theatre. And check that baby. Get its photographs. And get the racing driver's photographs.'

'So you think it's not one of ours?' said Shane overhearing.

'It is certainly not one of ours. And don't listen at doors.'

Kay's reaction was to be sick. But Marion, who was visiting Paris to do some shopping, said, 'Why be like that, Kay? She's not getting anything from you. She didn't even have a private room, she had the child in a public ward. And Margery won't acknowledge it.'

'She will. She likes babies.'

Marion wasn't too sure. They were OK when they were inside Margery's womb, but the minute they were liberated into the world they were shoved very fast up to the nannies in the attic.

'She didn't breastfeed,' said Marion. 'She said it would spoil her nipples. She wanted her body to be used exclusively for your father.'

Kay felt cold, and even sicker. But at least Mummy was giving her a huge wedding because she'd done things right.

. . . Chapter 28 . . .

The first day Jane went alone to the park with the baby a woman stopped her and said, 'I'm Del Grainger's widow.' She was slim, dark-haired and conventionally dressed. Jane waited nervously. 'Can I see the baby?'

'You can,' said Jane coldly. 'But it's not Del Grainger's if that's what you're worried about.'

The woman peered into the pram and Jane said, 'Don't get too close.'

'Well, you're lucky. It's more than I've got. I want to know the truth – it would help me. Please tell me.' The woman was almost crying.

'How did you find me?'

'Through Lucien Millineux, the banker's son. He said you were a compassionate person. Did you sleep with Del? I must know. You see, I don't believe it, because I thought we were happy. How could you say he was bored? Did he say that?'

'There are some things you can only say to strangers. I can't help you, I'm sorry.' Jane pushed the pram towards the chemist's and didn't look back. Later she would gladly have reassured the woman, later she was compassionate; but in those days she was vain, ignorant and young.

Jane's mother had sent a parcel of handknitted baby clothes. In her letter she said she'd be glad to see them when they could make it down to Hastings. 'It's funny,' said Alex, 'she doesn't ask to see the baby.'

Jane laughed darkly. 'Nor does your mother.'

'No, but your mother is the kind that would want to see him. I'm going to get someone to drive us down and show her the baby.'

'I'm not up to it,' she said hastily.

'Then we'll ask her here.'

'Don't be silly. She runs a boarding house. She can't leave, she works. My mum has never had a holiday – well, I've never known her have one.'

Jane wasn't too ill when asked to pose for the newspapers and magazines, he noticed: 'Margery Caversham's first grandchild.'

Jane wore something that would become the super-fashion of the following season: a calf-length, tight button-through skirt with the buttons undone to her thigh. Somehow it looked sexier than all the very short stuff. She'd got it staight from the designer for nothing; in return she must try and make it famous. A year later, even Kay Caversham was wearing a midi-skirt. Jane wore a canary-yellow T-shirt with a personal message stencilled over her breasts – another fashion first. Exercise had got her figure back in a week.

When the press asked Margery what she felt about her grandchild she replied, 'Absolutely no comment.'

Charlotte found the photograph of Jane in a New York newspaper blowing along the gutter, which was where she found most things. She'd just turned eighteen and she'd never had a man, a date, even a night out. Since she was sixteen she'd worked in the run-down areas of New York. She spent hours picking drunks out of doorways, persuading them out of gutters, getting them on the programme, and the next day they didn't even remember her. One was really nice. He'd been an accountant before he hit Skid Row. Cleaned up, sobered up, he was a nice guy to talk to. He was a special case because Charlotte had helped him day and night to stay off the stuff and regain his confidence. She got him back to work. Sometimes she felt she had given him a transfusion of her very life. He got a job in the shoe district of New York, then he got a girlfriend. He stayed off drink and pills. Charlotte felt a personal feeling of achievement. Six months later she ran into him on Fifth Avenue, and he didn't even remember her. He was a guy doing a job, about to get married – what was this blood-smeared near bum on about?

So Charlotte asked herself what she was. They called her Angel of the Gutter, but why was she doing it? Who cared? She quit – just like that. She said to her group leader, 'I'm getting out for the wrong reasons. An ex-client didn't recognise me and it hurt.'

'No one can stand the job long, Charlotte. You're feeling guilty. Everyone who quits feels they've lost. The reason is never right, but like them you've had enough, so get out – do your own living.'

But Charlotte felt that was living – helping people that no one else would touch. It was the nearest you came to the divine. Nothing after that, however high, would make her feel as valuable; no Oscar could give her that. How often she'd tried to explain it to her mother.

Because she liked the look of Jane and the baby, Charlotte went straight to London to see Alex. She brought a bag of presents from the States: Real Indian moccasins for Jane, toys for the baby, an Indian pipe for Alex.

Jane thought Charlotte was the runt of the litter. She had none of the Caversham elegance. She wasn't even good-looking, wore second-hand ill-matched clothes, and talked a lot about politics. She was extreme left-wing. She spoke with a strong American accent.

Alex asked if she would go to Cannes.

'What, with the pop star in residence?'

'At least he didn't marry Margery for what she could do for him. He's already done it for himself,' said Alex. 'And Kay doesn't have to go red-alert, because he's got his own money and won't take ours. He's even got his own chauffeur.'

'Do you like him then?' Charlotte asked.

'How do I know? I never met him. Jane and I saw him at Wembley. I like his songs. He's strong, weird.' Alex sat as he always did with his arms around Jane as she breastfed the baby. He loved them both so much.

Charlotte said, 'Margery is a short-sighted bitch. If that's super-living I like it better in the Bronx.'

'Don't be stupid, Charlotte. Get in there and get your share,' said Alex. 'You left New York all of a sudden, I think alarm bells have gone off in your head. So get back to the Château and guard what is yours. Don't forget Margery hasn't made a will. We have our trust fund but that's peanuts compared with what Margery's worth.'

'But you just got through telling me how Rick de Palma isn't a taker,' said Charlotte.

'What if they had a kid! So you get in there and look after your own. Or the new kid will get it.'

Jane shivered. She'd never seen Alex so hard, almost vicious. There was a hatred in him that all the hippy meditations and macrobiotic diets couldn't do anything about.

Charlotte flew to Cannes the next day and told Margery the baby was lovely and so was Jane.

'It won't last,' said Margery.

Charlotte shouted, 'But, Margery, they're happy!'

The Dover maid secretly sent some baby clothes for Alex's child. She thought it was outrageous the way the baby was left out and she knew what that felt like, working in the Château. Alex told Jane not to mention it to Julian when he came round. 'It all gets back to my mother. That's why he's coming here, to look around. Treat him like the press guys: no comment.'

Julian cooed and smiled at the baby who was lying on a blanket on the floor. 'I must take some photos. He's so cute,' he said.

Alex handed him a package. 'There you are, and there's my blood type, my baby's and Jane's.'

Julian chuckled. 'Alex, you haven't changed. Does that dope make you paranoid?'

'Just my mother.'

Julian sat beside Jane on the bed. 'Don't you think you should live in a better place? I mean, this is so ordinary. You haven't even got a proper living room.'

'We're fine,' said Alex. 'This is what we want.'

'I think you should have some money, Jane, and get a nice place. You need a garden and an extra room for the baby. This is the best time of your life, after all. Don't you want to move?'

She didn't answer.

Alex said, 'I've just taken the lease off the guy who lived here before. This is our place.'

'I think your mother could do something,' said Julian. 'It's not right. And what job are you going to do, Alex?'

'He's studying,' said Jane quickly.

'He's always studying. He's the longest-running student around. Wasn't that what the Warhol experience was called – study?'

'Warhol let me be myself,' said Alex. 'When I went into the Factory I wasn't Margery Caversham's son. He didn't care who I was.'

'I doubt it,' said Julian. 'He's a star-fucker, don't you worry. And because you're a star he gave you your greatest wish – anonymity.'

'I'm no star,' said Alex.

'You must be, because your mother and sister are frightened of you.'

When Julian went to the lavatory, Alex said, 'Say nothing, Jane. Let him say it all. Doesn't mean a thing. He's working for my mother. He'll get to you one day or another. He's chosen complaints, so don't complain.'

Julian had tried to listen round the door while pretending to pee. He got nothing out of the girl. The baby was Alex's. The visit was a flop.

But not for Jane. He certainly had stirred her up, made her feel dissatisfied and rejected. Increasingly she felt cut in half. She was a mother and a wife but she couldn't be who she really was. Alex would never let her go out and perform, because he'd never had anyone to himself before and he was happy. She did a lot of scrubbing floors. He noticed that. Once, she scrubbed the wall.

'Go on doing that and you'll be washing the bricks.'

'I want it clean for the baby.'

'You're going through to the plaster.' He took the brush away. 'You want to watch that. Joan Crawford used to do that, even in our house. She'd scrub everything, twice.'

'So what's so surprising? I was conceived during a Joan Crawford movie.'

'Veronica Lake – your mother told me.' He got the pram ready for the walk in Holland Park.

Of course she was OK. She was twenty-three, happily married with a baby. She just felt cut in half.

. . . Chapter 29 . . .

Before Kay left for her wedding, Robert Frey asked her over for lunch. Because he was number one she had to go, even though it meant an hour's drive to his estate in the country. It was September and the leaves were on the turn. He was powerful but even he couldn't control the weather or the seasons.

'I don't know much about nature,' he said. 'I was a town boy.'

His house was an extension of himself, the professional shell of an ambitious superstar. There was a well-equipped gym, a sauna, a Turkish bath, a jacuzzi. There were indoor and outdoor pools surrounded by fronds and ferns, white tables and chairs, with phones everywhere. Around the indoor pool he'd arranged jungle greenery filled with parrots and exotic birds. Frey didn't offer to show Kay round his house – she just took a look on her way to the lavatory. She was curious about his bedroom, but staff discreetly guarded the staircase to make sure guests knew the rules. Mozart filled the downstairs rooms; the sound quality was excellent although there were no visible speakers. As Marion had said, the house was chrome and glass and black ebony, hard brittle surfaces, low sofas, low glass tables. The social part of the house was Japanese in atmosphere. Frey controlled everything by an electric key carried casually in his trouser pocket. From a distance he could control even the fake gas logs: one press of a switch and within seconds there were wonderful living log fires.

One room, which was closed to strangers, was done in the style of a Marseilles café to remind him where he'd come from. It was called the 'never go back room' and it had a zinc bar, a cash till, a jukebox, a billiard table, a pinball machine, and sawdust on the floor. The jukebox contained the records from his youth. He also had some tapes of original bal musette music. He knew more about the bal musette dancehalls than he cared to mention.

Outside the house waited a Lamborghini, an Aston Martin, an E-type Jaguar and a Daimler saloon. To the left of the house the stables held a dozen horses for guests' use.

They lunched alone, which surprised Kay. Just one servant, nothing ostentatious. Frey wore a Cardin shirt, and a cashmere sweater over his shoulders, well-cut jeans and shoes with high Cuban heels – she hadn't realised he was short. He was deft and charming. There was no trace of his poor background in his table manners.

The point of the lunch, it transpired, was not Kay but Margery. Frey wanted to meet the biggest star of all time.

'Why?' Kay asked.

'Maybe I can find out why she is so fabulous and copy her. Then I will inherit her crown.'

Kay thought she should laugh, but coming from a man like Frey the request wasn't funny. She knew he was right-wing – felt it, didn't even need to check it.

She said, 'My father supported the Left so I don't think my mother could make you welcome. For instance, my mother was on the side of the students in the recent Paris riots. So was Jaspard. He's a regular visitor in our Cannes home. He could be the next French President.'

'*Could* is the operative word in that sentence.' Frey went on eating.

'My mother also has members of the Left –'

'That's all right, Kay, don't go down the guest list. I can get to her via another source. She's with Rick de Palma. They're seen around. They're hitched, aren't they? How is it kept so private? Is the CIA still looking after your mother? That must cost the US a lot of money.'

'Sure!' snapped Kay. 'But they didn't do such a good job looking after my father.' She was no longer the smiling, nicely mannered girl she was on the set.

'I want to meet her, so set it up, Kay. And there's something in it for you.'

'Why?'

He asked instead about Dino's death, wanting to know all the unprinted facts.

'We were all there. Mummy and the younger children and Nanny.'

'And a guy came close?'

'That's what I think, yes.'

'One, two?'

'I don't know. It was a professional killing.'

'Five bullets. That's the Organisation. It must have been someone he knew to get that close.'

She shrugged. 'It was all so quick. I just remember Daddy lying there.'

'Did you look at the guy?'

'I didn't even know he had a gun. I didn't expect it to happen. We were on our way down Jamaica Avenue from the airport. There was to be a ceremony for Mummy in New York, and then we were going to the Oscars in LA. It was her fourth. Katharine Hepburn accepted it for her because she was in mourning.'

'Didn't your mother want it avenged? His murder?'

'Look, they did everything. They couldn't find the killers or killer. It's closed. Why do you want to meet my mother?'

'Because I want to play your father in a movie. Get the rights for me, Kay, and you'll play Margery and you'll never stop working. I'll guarantee that.'

Kay was speechless. She didn't know if she could contain her laughter: these emotional outbursts were becoming a real problem.

'You're a nice little actress, Kay,' he went on. 'But I think you've delivered your goods and we've all seen them. You're going to need some help. I'm still in movies, your mother isn't. How long will she have pull? People forget even great stars.'

Kay made the request over Frey's telephone. It was what he wanted.

Margery said, 'Never!'

Frey said, 'She's making a mistake – because someone will do it. At least I'd have done it tastefully.'

The renowned Italian conductor Marcello Tallaforos and his wife attended Kay's wedding at the end of September '68. His charisma and marvellous physical presence made a great impression on Charlotte. Though he was a great man, he was not detached from life. He was considered a genius, yet his lifestyle was almost humble. He still liked to sit in the Italian countryside and eat bread and olives and listen to the sounds of nature. He did not like smart society but to honour Margery he attended Kay's wedding. He liked talking to Charlotte. His face, like that of an eagle, with piercing eyes, was sensual and dominating. When he came into a room everyone looked at him. Only Margery outdid him on an entrance. The wedding celebrations went on for three days, so Charlotte had enough time to fall in love. She was overwhelmed by the glorious swirling passion, and felt as if she was being swept by a hurricane up the side of a New York skyscraper. It wasn't what he said but what he was.

Margery, who missed nothing, said, 'Remember the wife.'

Charlotte pretended not to know what she meant.

'You think *you* worked with the low-lifes, that you were really dedicated – but believe me, that's nothing compared with *his* dedication. For him work is something else. It's his life, Charlotte. His music? It's a vocation. And the wife is part of it. She travels with him, helps him, advises him, and is knowledgeable about music so she's a good critic. Watch the wife. Also he does not and never has slept around.'

Charlotte said nothing, but she told herself that Marcello's burning glances would last her a lifetime. The way he held her hand would stay with her always. She'd caught him like she would a flu virus.

Before he left to conduct the Los Angeles Symphony Orchestra she said, 'I'd love to come to one of your concerts. I know you're very busy, but if we could have dinner afterwards?' She had a radiant smile. Marcello said of course – he would look forward to it. He kissed her hand. 'Shall I see you in Los Angeles then?' she asked.

'That is very difficult. I am there for only one week, then Boston, then Chicago. I am in New York for two days at the end of October.'

'Do you know New York?'

'A little.'

'I'll show you the part you don't know.'

His wife kissed her as well – not a good sign, Charlotte thought.

When they got outside, Marcello said to his wife, 'She is the human one in that family. She has done very good work for the homeless, and yet she doesn't draw attention to it. I like her.'

'Marcello, she's eighteen.'

'I was thinking that too. She'd be marvellous for Alessandro – we must get them together.'

Their son was a doctor in Rome. He had the same remarkable hands as his father, but instead of producing music he liked stroking them over blondes, the bigger their breasts the better. It didn't stop him being a good doctor.

Marcello's wife knew her husband had not been unfaithful, not once in thirty years of marriage: he simply had not had the time.

Margery flung her Yves Saint Laurent 'les smoking' jacket on the floor and dropped back on the bed. Rick was surprised. She usually performed a long night-time beauty ritual that he pretended not to notice. She would never come to bed gleaming with cream, but sometimes she laid cucumber pads on her eyes.

She let him pull off her grey suede skirt with inserts of silver lace, then she said, 'Charlotte is just getting normal, like having fun and shopping, and now she has to fall in love with the most impossible man in the world.'

'Why?' asked Rick.

'Why? Because he'll never do it. The wife turns the music sheets and the bed sheets, opens the letters, answers the phone. She absorbs the problems of his life and in return he gives her total fidelity. No, more than that – she sacrificed herself. She had quite a promising career as a violinist. They were Dino's friends. Still, Charlotte and Marcello were certainly a lot more sparky than the bride and groom. There's nothing going on there.'

'So why the marriage?'

'I think my daughter wants to give herself a framework in which to exist. Otherwise she'll start living – and that could be catastrophic.'

Rick ran his hands through the famous golden hair, his own, and looked in the mirror. Dissipated. Also his prick was sore. He didn't know whether to tell her or not. She might think he'd had a guy. 'Did you and Dino do it every night?' he asked suddenly.

'What's that got to do with you and me?'

'I just wondered.'

'Well, don't,' she said. 'Dino is my business, not yours.'

'But I've told you about my life.'

'Your choice. Kay is wild. If it doesn't find expression it can become degenerate and cruel.' Margery had talked to Guido and tried to shake the point of it all out of him. He said he wanted to make Kay happy. Margery assured him that was impossible: only Kay could make Kay happy. Was there a deal? she asked.

'She sleeps with who she likes, and you the same?'

He stayed with the happiness story.

'You wouldn't believe Kay's troubles,' Margery told Rick. 'At least she can talk to Guido about them and give me a break.' With that she rolled on to her side and fell asleep, still fully made up.

Rick didn't know what to do about the soreness. If he went to a local doctor Julian would find out – everybody told everybody every damn thing. Maybe he could get something over a chemist's counter and say it was for someone else.

Life with Margery had been like one big pop concert. Now he'd come offstage and wanted a rest.

Jane saw enough of the wedding on television to feel jealous and snubbed. All those directors, stars, celebrities – the rich and famous in droves. She was hurt. What had she ever done except make Alex Caversham happy? 'I should be there,' she said. 'I should be one of them. It's where I belong.'

'Then marry my brother Shane. Give him a couple of years and fuck him!' Alex retorted.

Kay's wedding dress alone cost what Jane lived on for a year. Her trousseau was photographed for the top glossy mags and supplements. The guests agreed that it was Kay's party and dressed down – with an effort.

Margery's wedding present to the daughter who'd done everything right was a villa in Cagnes-sur-Mer near Nice. Kay turned this into the symbol of her own stardom. She filled it with the Eileen Gray furniture she liked, a Steinway grand piano, the Dali chair from the Château. In one corner a waterfall trickled over a display of coloured rocks.

The bedroom was the fantasy room with carefully chosen erotic sculptures and Japanese pornographic paintings. The chairs had leather straps around their legs, and over the huge, old-fashioned, noisily sprung bed hung a jet black whip. A large collection of pornographic books filled one wall. There was a huge golden dildo on which to hang clothes. And that was the most sex the room ever saw: she and Guido did nothing. Guests, though, were intrigued. Who did what to whom and how many players? they wondered. They assumed that Kay had a definite sexual preference and gave it full rein. The walls of every room were painted the same colour as her skin; the lights had been chosen to show her to the best possible advantage. Guido's contribution was music, and it poured forth from his study and rolled over the surrounding countryside.

Jane blamed Alex for the fact that they weren't invited. Again she said she wanted a proper home. Julian was right: was she a third-class citizen or something?

'I haven't got money for a house, Jane,' Alex told her.

'Ask your mother.'

'Never. I would not ask her for a drop of her sweat if my life depended on it.'

'Alex, I need things. It's getting towards winter. I haven't any clothes. I've got no money.'

'Wait till I'm twenty-one – I get bread then.'

His allowance was adequate for one person on drugs. He was frugal in every way: didn't buy clothes, walked to his philosophy classes, didn't eat out any more. She got what was left. He saw there was going to be trouble because Julian had put some idea in her head about a glamorous house. Alex had spent his whole life getting away from all that. She wanted sofas and carpets; he hated comfort. He had liked her flat in the Finchley Road because it was bleak and totally without illusion. He was having other troubles too: every night he dreamed his zoo bird had died.

Kay was bride of the decade. Most of the papers ran the headlines, 'First Caversham wedding' and 'Smiling bride – Perfect love'. They listed the wedding presents. In the end Jane couldn't bear to watch the television or read a newspaper. A journalist waited at the door and asked what she thought of her sister-in-law's wedding.

'Piss off!'

The headlines next day read – 'Runaway bride pissed off at Kay'.

. . . Chapter 30 . . .

The second time Kay went to Frey's house he had guests: the racing driver Alessandro Giuletti, Violette the star of the twenties, and Princess Miranda's daughter Jacey. Frey wanted action on the Dino movie. He'd consulted with his lawyers: he could fictionalise the story or he could go to another member of the family – for example, Dino had a brother in Turin. 'I could do it from that angle. *Cinéma vérité*. And I'll use actual events and dialogue. Your uncle may do it.'

'*May* is the operative word in that sentence,' said Kay, mimicking him. She couldn't look at Jacey. The girl was looking at her, hard. Who in their right mind would stand up to Frey? Even the Doberman dogs were on alert.

'Use one sentence of dialogue from my mother's life and she'll break you.' Kay's voice was soft and yet hard as steel, like an iron fist in a velvet glove.

'We both want your father's life – your mother to keep it to herself, and me to immortalise it. I think, Kay, you should talk to your lawyers.'

'Do you admire my father? Empathise with him? Wish you were him? What? Perhaps you hate him?'

'He did in life what I can only do in movies.'

He got up and left the room with the racing driver. Kay talked to Violette. She still would not look at Jacey – the girl had starred in too many fantasies. Jacey couldn't be more than twenty-five but already she had lines in her face – one between the brows, two nose-to-mouth, deeply etched. Her hair was cropped, the blonde dye growing out leaving brown roots. Her voice was husky like a rough boy's. She didn't bother with herself much. She was beautiful enough and got by without care. The eyes were like bits of crystal, greenish blue, shining with a hard light. She wore an apple-green petticoat as a dress and scarlet sandals with very high heels.

Violette said, 'Jacey reminds me of a street urchin.'

'I'm sure she does better than that,' Kay replied.

Jacey told her, 'You're so immaculate, you're such a star. I should have put on some makeup, made an effort, to meet you. But sleeping with Frey is already an effort.'

Violette said, 'If you play the whore, keep quiet about it. The best whores are always discreet.' She turned to Kay. 'She was talking to you just now about the way you looked, this naughty girl here. Acknowledge her compliment or she'll sulk.'

'Thank you,' said Kay and made an effort to look at Jacey.

'You've got incredible hair,' said Jacey. 'I couldn't find a comb so I ran a carpenter's nail through mine.'

'Kay's got Margery's hair,' said Violette. 'I was in *Heart of the South* with her, you know.'

Kay said she remembered.

'Why doesn't she work? It's a crime to shut that beautiful talent away.'

'It's the only way she can get back at God. He took my father. She's killing herself by denying her talent.'

'But surely she's cheered up? She's got Rick de Palma,' said Jacey, who obviously lived only for the moment.

Violette said, 'Jacey, I think you should have been in movies. Frey said he'd star you in something.'

'He doesn't have to now. He's already starred me.' She pointed upstairs.

'What do you do?' asked Kay.

'I fuck.'

They looked at each other then. Kay felt embarrassed. 'Well, at least the fellas know where to come,' she said.

'And they do – come and come.' Jacey went over to the bar, her walk a slight swagger, and drank from a bottle. She had a vivid physical presence and was proud of her body. Hips swinging, shoulders back, it was all loose, all for enjoyment. Then she shimmied her hips very fast, like a belly dancer.

Violette said, 'I love it when she does that.'

Jacey's hips circled one way, then the other, stomach bumps, figure-of-eight swings; her body moved in all manner of ways. 'I'm double-jointed. Frey said I do it better than a vibrator.'

'Get something out of it,' said Violette.

'Oh, I do. I meet nice people.' Jacey indicated Kay and smiled.

When later they walked through the grounds, Frey had his

arm through Jacey's. She still wore the green petticoat, with nothing underneath. Kay thought she must be quite smart to be the mistress of Mr Number One Movie Star.

Violette said, 'He really only likes hookers. That's why she plays it up so much. Normally she talks very sensibly. She's clever. She does charity work, does her mother's charities, and she genuinely likes animals. She's just a show off,' she went on. 'Don't take her seriously.'

Jacey said to Frey, 'That Caversham girl's stuck up – won't even look at me.'

'She isn't half the woman you are,' he replied.

'What do you know about women?' said Jacey. 'You're just into technology.' She made a gesture to suggest a vibrator. He laughed, and slapped her playfully.

Kay was surprised that seeing them have fun could hurt her so much.

Jane told Alex she felt cut in half. Part of her was dying to go back to work – to do acting and movement classes, to get in front of a camera. Life was going by. It actually hurt her to see parts going to Gracie, Susannah York, Sarah Miles. 'I want to be someone,' she said. But she couldn't be that someone – not an acting, performing person – and live with him. He tried to get her to take up scriptwriting – she'd be involved with the business; she'd also be at home. She had no idea what a scriptwriter even looked like. She wanted something more obvious.

'But you can't do it, babe. It's what I've tried to tell you. I've lived with you constantly for a year. You're great, you give a feeling of life going on. You're visible. But the star is lonely, isolated, way out on her own. A star worries about her age, her looks, her stamina. She's in competition with her last performance. She makes sacrifices. If she was taken out of the limelight she'd close up and die like a flower being taken from the sun. Maybe in the future you will be a star. My mother predicts that television will produce the new stars. Well, maybe that'll be you. But now it's '68 and you're not it.'

'But Al Streep said –'

'He's an old man. He kissed arse back in the forties. They had the studio system then and he's never forgotten it.'

She felt such a sense of deprivation and loss that she could no longer speak.

Alex picked baby Kit out of his pram and changed him. He had begun to hate domestic life. How he hated regular meals, cleaning floors, washing clothes. How he missed the bikeboys, the drugs, the clubs, the danger. He didn't want to make love to Jane any more. They'd been put together for one glorious year and produced a child, and now they were strangers.

On his twenty-first birthday he received a note from Julian. 'Your mother sends best wishes on your twenty-first. You will not receive your money because you are on drugs, and your mother as executor of the trust has the power to stop payment until such time as you are in a fit mind. Incidentally, she can withdraw the release of your trust money for mental illness or criminal activity, as well as addiction. Happy Birthday.'

Alex did not tell Jane.

Jane said, 'We could have a house now you're twenty-one.'

'We could but, I genuinely dislike comfort. I like to feel I'm on the move.'

He went up the Fulham Road looking for Lucien. Someone must have told his mother he still used stuff. Lucien was the only one who knew – they shared the same dealer. He hoped he wouldn't kill Lucien: that would count as 'criminal activity' and he still wouldn't get his money.

Jane started going to an actors' rehearsal class in Leicester Square. She was plugged in again. She could breathe properly and her body felt light. The anonymity panic was over. She asked the teacher what sort of work she could expect to get.

'Come on, Jane. *You* ask *me*, with your family connections? Kay Caversham is doing a second Robert Frey film, and through Margery Caversham you could have the world.'

There was no point talking to him. He saw the world as it was supposed to be.

When she got home the flat was full of bikers who had come up from Southend. There was a strong smell of dope. Alex was feeding Kit. Rick de Palma's latest was on loud. The neighbours were calling in person to complain or banging anonymously.

'I wish they'd bang in time to the music,' said a biker.

'Rick's great. I don't hold it against him that he married my mother,' said Alex.

Jane said, 'Get rid of them, all of them. And I won't have dope smoked over my child.'

So he said he lived there too and they had their first big row. To comfort himself he went to the zoo, but his bird wasn't there: it had just died.

Lucien called again to see Jane. This time he wore a long leather coat trimmed with fur by Giorgio Armani and a swirling rainbow silk scarf designed especially for him by Bill Gibb. His ankle-high thonged Red Indian moccasins were genuine. He smelt of amber perfume.

Again he brought gifts and she wouldn't let him in. Standing on the stairs he said, 'Alex is in trouble, he's got a drug problem. We should talk.' She let him in then, and told him about the packets of white powder lying around openly.

'You can get busted,' said Lucien. He gathered up dope, grass, coke and some acid tabs and put them in a bag, then hid it behind the baby's nappies.

With his wonderful bone structure and remarkable colouring Lucien looked like something out of a fairytale.

'Don't look closely, but the writing's on the wall,' he said.

Jane looked, expecting to see some of Lucy's paranoid scrawls.

'He'll either get picked up with it on him and that's jail or he'll get sick and that's hospital.'

'Does he shoot up, then?'

'He freebases heroin.'

She didn't know what freebase meant.

'You don't use it too?' he asked.

'I don't like drugs. I didn't know he was taking them. He always seems the same. I have nothing more to say.'

Lucien said, 'We're on the same side, you just don't know it yet. I haven't time to talk to him. I'm off skiing. You don't understand, Jane, that I love him too. The drug thing is out of hand. There was always a chance it could be. A lot of people love him but he doesn't want love, only what he thinks he gives himself with drugs. His mother loves him. She would help.'

Jane considered phoning her, then she imagined Alex's

reaction. Letting Lucien in without his permission would be bad enough.

She didn't encourage him to stay so he left with the words, 'Alex. He needs to be saved.'

When Alex came in she asked how much stuff he used.

'A bit of that, a bit of this. Nothing I can't handle.'

So she told him Lucien had called and that she knew about the heroin. That was too much.

'And you listen to him. He's a liar, Jane. And a spy. He tells my mother everything I do.'

'Because he cares about you. Why do you use it?'

He said, 'It gives me the chemical feeling of being loved.'

. . . Chapter 31 . . .

In January 1969 Shane, now fifteen, ran away from school. The agency men brought him back and Margery sent him to a boarding school well known for its discipline. He left after a week. High fences and constant supervision were no deterrent to a boy who seriously needed freedom. Again he was brought back to Cannes. He'd slept rough on the road for three nights despite the cold. Margery could see, under her very eyes, her little boy turning into another Alex. Instead of beating him, which was her first impulse, she asked him what was wrong.

'I want to do hang-gliding – you say no. I hate those schools – you say stay. You're not in them.' He was clearly upset. 'Everyone gets shot: Papa, then Alex's friend Andy Warhol, both the Kennedys. And I bet the Greek gets shot and I liked him. Everyone always goes. They come here, I get to know them, they're gone.'

'That's showbiz,' said Kay, who was polishing her nails in the corner.

'Rick's still here,' said Margery. 'He was always your favourite.'

'No, he's gone,' said Shane angrily. 'He's not the same, not at all.'

Margery felt quite shocked. 'How d'you mean?'

'He's all quiet.'

'They always are off stage,' said Kay.

'But he's gloomy quiet,' said Shane, 'not anticlimactic.'

'Out of the mouth of babes,' said Kay.

'What do you want, then?' asked Margery.

The boy snivelled and she gave him her handkerchief. This time she'd get it right. In the past she'd tried to make her children do things her way; she admitted it hadn't been a success.

'I want to see the Greek. He said I could go on one of his boats.'

Margery turned and looked at Kay. Kay made a huge twisted shrug: how difficult did life have to get?'

'He's with the Japanese pianist and Princess Miranda and he sleeps with Lucia. In fact I think he'll marry Lucia,' said Kay.

'Kay, you take Shane to Greece.'

Kay said she would: Princess Miranda would be there and Jacey wouldn't miss an occasion like that.

Alex tracked Lucien down at the de Luces'. They were playing poker and Lucien refused to move. He'd sensed that the father was on a bummer and his friend Anton de Luce was on change. Loss was in the air but the de Luces didn't know it.

Alex said, 'Lucien, put your cards down. You're all through playing games.'

'Let me just see this round through.' He hardly dared speak. The change was there. Loss to gain. For him. He doubled. They all held their position. He doubled again. The de Luces took it. Others folded. He doubled and added an extra £500.

'Table stakes only.'

He had to lift up the £500.

'I'll see you,' said Anton and paid up. So did his father. No one spoke. Then Alex said, 'Get out here, Lucien, or I'll drag you out.'

'Pay to see,' said Lucien and laid down his cards. 'Full house beats anything you've got.'

It did, and they didn't have to show. Lucien gathered up the money. How had he known? He wasn't particularly lucky. A full house wasn't anything much but he knew he was better than them. It was as if a light had gone out around them. He was so enthralled by his experience he hardly noticed the karate chops and kicks Alex delivered. He ended up on the floor quicker than he need have done because he didn't want to get in trouble.

Alex said, 'You two-faced fuck!'

Lucien said, 'I love you, Alex – that's why I did it. Your mother does too. I'm not going to see you kill yourself.' He got up and put his arms around his beloved friend. 'I just realised I'm a clairvoyant. In Spain they used to call me La Savia, the one who sees. I thought it was because I had green eyes. You want to get on the payroll. Go and see your mother. She's eating her heart out over you.'

Alex had his bird cremated and its ashes put in an urn. He was going to take them to the bird's original home and scatter them over the earth.

'What if it's Central Africa?' said Jane.

'I'll still go.'

'You'll need shots – they're horrible. Why don't you give the ashes to the pilot of a plane going there?'

The bird came from Ecuador. Jane didn't even know where that was. 'Scatter them on the sea. It solves everything in the end,' she said.

'It took your father,' said Alex. 'Perhaps that's why you're such a mess.'

It was the first time he'd been deliberately cruel and she was determined it would be the last. She said, 'Thank God I once knew Del Grainger. At least I was valued.'

Alex was quite shocked. 'But I thought it was all fixed?' he said.

'Well, I would tell you that. How could I know what the interior of his cabin was like if I hadn't been there?'

He picked up the jar of bird ashes and went to the door.

'Where are you going?'

'Ecuador. I'm not sure it's far enough.'

Again Margery Caversham watched the newsreel clips of Dino throwing money to the street girl at Leicester Square. 'Is it her? Isn't it her?'

Rick de Palma said, 'Margery, you've seen that thirty times. Even with your glasses.'

'Kay said give her money. I think we already have.'

'What is it about her?'

Margery turned on him. 'About her? She took my son! I will never forgive her.'

'He went,' said Rick.

'She has taken him away from me. He won't even see me. He sends abusive letters.'

Guido and Kay had come into the room. Then Marcello and his wife, Mo Cohen, Marion. The evening was beginning.

'Shall I put the screen away, ma'am?' asked Jennifer.

'She put him on drugs, d'you understand?' shouted Margery. 'And he writes to me that her mother is better than me. A true loving woman in harmony with life. Drug talk. I'm going to break that bitch's fucking life.'

'Put him on drugs?' echoed Rick, irritated. 'She did not! The Cavershams have conveniently short memories when it comes to their own failings.'

'Fuck you too!' replied Margery. Then she realised there were guests in the room and she calmed down. She said politely, 'Marcello, Nestorin want a concert in aid of that tragic accident in Africa – was it two years ago? I thought I would sponsor the event here in Cannes. Or Paris if you prefer?'

Behind her soft words she saw Jane's face clearly, and then she knew how to punish her. Everything Jane wanted would be taken from her. She'd see, read and smell success then it would pass out of reach of those common, grabbing fingers. Involuntarily, and incongruously, she said, 'Let her come here. Then she'll know where she belongs.'

Alex padded in softly and tried to smile at Jane. 'I didn't get to Ecuador.'

'Your mother phoned. She actually spoke to me. She sounded very nice.'

'She isn't.'

'She asked if we'd take Kit over to Cannes. Just for a weekend.'

'Definitely not.' He put the coffee on. 'Lucien has taken up hang-gliding.' Alex seemed to be trying to contain his excitement. 'I went with him.'

'If you do it too, Alex, I'm going. You see, I can't go on being frightened and nagging. I'm losing me. I can't be brave around you, because I've got to be the careful one. I hate it. I don't even skate any more. Drugs kill – even your flying friend knows that.'

'Just a minute. Did you say you'd leave?' He waved a hot spoon at her. Kit started to cry.

'No, I won't leave. I should though, because the drugs you take are the real thing. You're hooked, aren't you?'

'I want to get hooked then observe myself, so I understand the state. Then I'm going to be in a position to help others get off.'

'Like a doctor, you mean?'

'Better, much better – because I've been there. I've written a lot of stuff on it. It's like Lucien going to the end of the night. His God is Céline: have every experience, experience every evil, ecstasy, good, pain.'

'So how are you going to get off?'

'Easy. I'm not an addict, I can stop tomorrow.'

She watched him drink his coffee. He looked quite normal. She had no idea what mixture of uppers and downers produced that effect. 'Stop now.'

He paused. She sounded tough and he didn't like it. 'But I've just told you what I'm doing.'

'Let someone else do it. You're the father of a child. It's bullshit, Alex. It's such a waste, your taking all those drugs. You've got so much. Don't you value yourself?'

'It's to do with feeling loved. I just get it from drugs. Some chemical feeling.'

'*I* love you.'

'Yeah, but it's not as good as smack. That little white powder makes up the love deficit.'

'Go for treatment, I'll come with you – my Mum can have Kit. You want perfection – that's dangerous. You'll just have to make do with everyday love.'

'How do you know that kind of thing?' He was amused and surprised.

'Let's say I knew a guy who wanted perfection and it turned out dangerous, but I didn't spot it at the time'. She was remembering Jay Stone. 'Now I do. Let's go on the programme.'

. . . Chapter 32 . . .

The Greek, wearing white slacks and a yachting blazer, embraced Shane, and the young boy felt as though he'd come home. For the first hour it was great, looking over the boat, learning about navigation, but then all the society people came on board and Shane was disappointed. It was just like being at Cannes. They took the boat out and lunched on one of the islands. Photographers and journalists were swarming round them, but the Greek didn't seem to mind. Kay had been shopping with Princess Miranda and had bought some diving equipment for Shane, and a new camera for herself.

'Mummy wouldn't stand for this,' said Shane.

'No,' said Kay. 'But he needs it.'

'Why?'

'Because he's a nobody who got rich.'

Kay stayed close to her brother during the lunch. They were family and clung together in adversity, and some of the guests were adverse. Before she left, Kay asked the Greek if Shane could be treated like a child.

The Greek said, 'These people are just here for you, Kay. Your brother is here for me. Tomorrow we go off alone.'

The Greek showed Shane to his cabin and waited while he got ready for bed. He liked this little kid with his hair that stuck up in spikes. He had a face just like an imp's when he was happy. 'We're going to be good friends,' said the Greek. 'I'm going to teach you things and you're going to ask me questions. That way we both learn. Chess, deep-sea diving, navigation –'

'Hang-gliding?' asked Shane.

'Sure. Whatever you want.'

'I'm so glad you're still here,' said Shane.

'Why shouldn't I be?'

'Alex's friend Andy Warhol got shot. It happens all the time.'

Kay found Jacey in Athens after searching for her for a day and a half. Princess Miranda thought her daughter had gone to see a Greek actress – she knew the face but couldn't recall the name. Kay finally ran into the girl at the airport. She was flying to Rome and was wearing the same apple-green short petticoat and no bra. A red rose, which matched her scarlet shoes, was pinned on one of the plain shoulderstraps. Again she wore no makeup and her breasts were as hard and firm as apples.

'I hate the Greeks,' Jacey said. 'They're so soft and corrupt. Liars. Get me out of here. Where are you going?'

'Rome,' said Kay.

On the way up the steps to the plane Kay saw that Jacey did not wear knickers. It was rumoured that this was so she could have a man at any time without obstruction.

Alex agreed to go on a drug programme but he wanted time. Jane thought that was part of the addiction. She said, 'Now.' He then said he couldn't afford it and explained about his mother withholding the money.

'The best thing I can do is come off it. I can. If I go into a clinic she'll know and I'll never get the money.'

How the hell was Jane going to trust him? She yanked the sheet off him. 'Now. Let's do it,' she said.

Lucy had got the name of a doctor. Alex could be admitted on a programme immediately. It would take at least six weeks, maybe three months. Jane had the baby bundled up under her arm. 'I'll take him to my Mum when I've taken you to the doctor.'

He pulled the sheet back. 'You're doing this because you feel guilty. You don't really give a shit, so you're pretending to.'

'Just get your frigging clothes on and let's go, Alex. Or I'm off with Kit. Choose.'

He said he wouldn't leave his baby solely in her care so he'd go on the programme if that would make her happy, but he'd never forgive her.

'People die of drugs,' she said, thinking of the latest popstar to end up dead.

'People die.' And Alex wouldn't speak again. She knew that the love he wanted he could never get from her. She didn't have it to give, not that intensity. It was back to the mother, the mother's milk – the warm cradling total love. Because she was an optimist she refused to see it as a bad time.

Rick de Palma went back to work. He did a concert tour of Europe and while he was away Margery had the Château redecorated. Instead of white, the main salon was now gold and yellow, all warm and sunny and filled with priceless vases containing sprays of red berries. On one gold wall was pinned a huge gold metal sun with enormous rays. The bedroom was now returned to its original state: ethnic fabrics, Provençal designs. She brought in the singing sunny colours of Van Gogh's Arles paintings. In the entrance hall she placed pots of plants, a nineteenth-century spinning wheel. The house gave the impression of health. You could almost smell the hay and the freshly churned milk. Margery's friends said the decorative turnaround had occurred after a visit to Kay's bedroom in the Cagnes villa. Margery's one comment had been, 'Why don't you get a snake in here? People might think you fuck that too.' But she was upset. She realised the bedroom represented a cry for help, for the satisfaction Kay never seemed to find in life. On a shopping trip to Paris Margery had said, 'Sex isn't everything, or even anything. It's like a lunch. It's nice sometimes then you forget it. I mean, what did you have for lunch two days ago?'

'Oh, Mummy, don't tell me you felt like that with Dino?'

'It's not such a big deal, Kay, I'm telling you. I've been without for years.'

Kay answered, surprisingly, 'I so want to do something worthwhile. I've even got the mental equipment, the willpower. It must be in me or I wouldn't feel the urge to do something. But I can't stop being the way I am and it's sad.'

Rick loved the refurbished Château, especially the Provençal chairs and tables. 'I really feel I'm in the South of France now and not old Hollywood.' His new song 'Children of Darkness' had shot to number one. Margery asked him to sing it for her.

'They were two kids in the darkness. Everyone else was in light.' He stopped.

'Go on, sing it,' she said.

'Margery, I wrote it for Alex and Jane. I dedicated it to them.'

'But you've never met them.'

'No. But I'm on the same side.'

'Are you my sweet boy? Not once you married me.' With one foot she kicked his hip so he fell forward across the bed.

'Do it,' she said.

He did it and she cried and sighed, but underneath she stayed nice and alert, wanting to make sure he'd saved it all for her. He never lost the urge to make it with Margery: she was a goddess, and if the gods had given him enough female hormones that's what he'd have been.

Margery had never known a man who understood women so well. Sometimes being with Rick was like having a sympathetic girlfriend who wouldn't take from you, only enhance.

Alex came out after half a day. He said the doctors agreed with him that he wasn't an addict. Where were the tracks? His arms were clear. He told them Jane was inclined to exaggerate, which made her furious. He also said she wanted him inside for her own reasons. She called him paranoid, and the doctors didn't like her using their terminology. They hadn't believed her! Alex's stable saneness went down a lot better than her anger. Alex got out because it was a free world and there was no law that said you had to be made well.

He was very excited by the addict he met who told him that a heroin user committed suicide by injecting a huge dose into his eyeball. It was worth the wasted morning to hear that. 'Like a Buñuel film,' said Alex.

When he got home he was not hostile. He just didn't sleep with her any more and he didn't eat with her and he wouldn't speak. Suspecting she was heading for a bad time she phoned her mother. She left out the drug stuff and just said he was moody.

Bette said, 'Let him work it out, Jane. Get on with your own life.'

'I can't, he won't let me. And I don't know if I'm good enough. I'm scared.'

'Well, dye your hair and get some dark contact lenses and come home.'

Home. The very word had the solitary, sad sound of a foghorn booming. Hastings. Jesus – how would she end up? Marry someone, bingo, cards, the pier.

'I've got to go forward not back, Mum. What should I say to him?'

'Nothing. People do what they want in the end. You'll see. He'll sort it out. He doesn't do what he doesn't want, that one. So don't forget what I told you when it's rough: don't look down, don't look back, just look forward.'

. . . Chapter 33 . . .

Jacey always stayed at the old hotel, the Hôtel de la Ville, at the top of the Spanish Steps. Kay had the use of Margery's apartment in the Piazza Navona but this time she took a room next to Jacey. They decided to dine with Jacey's cousin and friends, then take the evening from there.

'He's a terrible snob, being a minor prince – also not at all attractive but he knows everybody,' Jacey explained. 'Then we'll go to the clubs. I remember the early sixties – weren't they fun? Of course I was only a kid so they thought I didn't know anything. I knew enough to bribe the nanny and get out on the town. But of course, Kay, if there's someone you'd rather see? I mean, you have a reason for being in Rome.'

'Yes, I have a reason,' said Kay. And silently she implored the wayward girl, Don't disapppoint me. I'm desperate.

Jacey wore an almost transparent silver plastic raincoat, very short, with the collar up, tightly belted, and nothing underneath. When she moved, the wobble of her hips and breasts was just visible and there was a suggestion of pubic hair. She wore glass shoes with extremely high stiletto heels and a great deal of makeup. Her short ragged hair was gold-streaked. She was out to shock, and she succeeded before she'd even left the hotel.

Kay wore a 1918 black chemise frock by Paul Poiret. Its raised waistline emphasised her breasts and the calf-length skirt was full. Around it she wore a crêpe lamé shawl embroidered with beads. Her shoes, low black pumps, were studded with jet beads. She wore Amazone perfume which she'd originally discovered on Rick. Now she liked it so he'd had to switch to Pagan by Picot, which he thought no one else would copy.

As they walked along the Via Borghese arm in arm, Kay thought the key to her sexuality was to be found here with this girl. With her, she would find freedom.

They stopped off at Nino's in the via Borgognona for Jacey to reclaim five gold bangles from the owner. 'I lost them on a bet, but he very sweetly paid the money and got them back. I'll come and lunch here tomorrow and they can tip off the paparazzi if they want.' She believed in paying her way. If someone did her a good turn she felt she owed them one and didn't forget.

'But he's making a pile out of you already,' said Kay. 'The bangle story ups his clientele. You don't have to do the newspapers as well. That's being cheap.'

Jacey spun a bangle on her finger like a hoop. 'I'm just a princess. You're a Caversham.'

As they clicked along on their high-heeled expensive shoes, through the cobbled streets, to meet the cousin, Jacey talked only of ephemera: what was in front of her, the person across the street, cakes in a window, a drunk on a corner. She lived totally for the moment, and once gone it did not exist. I have no past, therefore I can truly know the present – that should be her motto, thought Kay. She didn't feel easy being with Jacey. It was as though she was in a scene from a movie and it might not go well. She felt she'd lowered herself, becoming part of this hoyden's life. And the transparent mac drew crowds of men behind them. No one had seen a girl without a bra before, not in public, and then there was the suggestive way she moved.

The dinner with Jacey's cousin was awkward. The prince kept saying it was amusing, but that was the last thing it was. He was surrounded by hangers-on and had a falcon on his wrist. He had a cruel face and an ignorant mind, and he gave her an inkling of how the old rulers of Rome had got their reputation. Nothing good could happen around this man. Jacey wasn't particularly exciting either. She ate a lot and said little. Where was the girl who walked into a restaurant and screwed every man in it within the hour? If Kay hadn't seen her lack of underwear she would have believed her reputation was founded on malicious rumour.

As they left the restaurant, the press bounded forward, flashbulbs on all sides like a firework display.

'I wanted my visit here to be quiet,' said Kay.

'I'm sorry,' said Jacey. 'Wherever my cousin goes things happen. A film extra was murdered trying to approach his table last week. Actually I'm feeling a little *piano* myself. I'd like to go to bed but it's obligatory I do all the clubs. I don't feel alive unless I stay up until after three.'

Jacey was *piano* because she'd recently had an abortion. The new birth pill didn't suit her, she wasn't keen on the coil, she loathed the whole menstrual business anyway. She didn't want children: her body was merely a vehicle for pleasure.

For the nightclub Jacey produced a minuscule transparent dress from her shoulderbag.

The glamorous nightspots were as Kay expected: dancing, drinking, a lot of attention. As soon as they were settled with escorts, Jacey's cousin and entourage left. 'He's paying for everything by the way,' said Jacey. 'It's all on his tab. He wonders if you've come slumming with me.'

Kay said she just wanted to do something different.

'But you're always two paces behind me,' she said provocatively.

'It's your night, Jacey.'

'Then we'll do something different, that even I haven't done. We'll go over to Trastevere to the artists' quarter. It's poor over there. We'll go and dance to their music.'

It was two o'clock and the second poor club. The music was loud but there was no dancing. The place was crammed with men. Suddenly Jacey's eyes lit up, like streetlamps coming on for the night. She was off, dancing through the men to the furthest exit. Several tried to grasp her as she passed. She opened the door, went through. A man followed, and another.

Kay stayed where she was, at the bar. The barman said, 'Has your friend gone to use the lavatory?'

Kay said yes.

'She should be careful. Always go two at a time. The men are dangerous here.'

Kay already had a circle of dangerous ones around her. She couldn't tell if they were going to rob her, molest her or murder her. She was on the way to being scared.

'Could you go?' she said to the barman. 'And see if she's all right?'

'And have the customers rob the till? Why do you girls cross over to this part? You cause trouble, you'll get trouble. We have our own girls.' And he pointed through the throng to a dozen tables where professional girls sat with men.

Kay pushed through to the exit door. Men grabbed at her

breasts, hands pulled at her skirt. She didn't like it. She called for Jacey. Finally she got through the door, her dress half pulled off her. Jacey was standing alone against the wall under the single lightbulb. A man stood opposite her, and behind him three others. 'Shut the fucking door,' said one of them.

'It's another girl. Where do they come from? Mars?'

The man in front said, 'I'm telling you, whore, get in the lavatory, because we're going to have you.'

Slowly, Jacey lifted up her skirt and opened her legs, spread them wide and thrust out her pelvis so her cunt was fully exposed. 'Come on then, fuck me. You keep saying you're going to do it.'

There was an almost reverent silence. Then the first guy approached her, pulling out his cock. Jacey reached out and pushed his pants right down.

'Go on. Stick it in. Make me like it.' She undid the top of her dress and put his hands on her breasts.

The men were transfixed. 'This must be a porn film in heaven,' said one of them.

The man fucked Jacey hard and she held her hand out for the others. 'Come on. Who wants a blow job? Why don't you all fuck me at once? God, I love the smell of unwashed men. I didn't know it smelt this good. Kay, you stay out of this. It's not your show.'

Kay couldn't sleep. Her hand was between her legs and she was dying to come. The bed was huge, big enough for three. It made her even more lonely. She needed to speak to Jacey. Finally as it was getting light she put on a silk robe and went to the girl's room. The door wasn't locked. Jacey was sitting up in bed, the lights still on. Her legs were open and she was looking at herself in the mirror.

'Are you all right?' Kay pretended to be solicitous.

'Of course I'm all right. My head's full of cocks. Seeing all those different ones – the lavatory was full of them.'

'You suddenly changed. You were one way, then you just sparked up. What causes that?'

Jacey almost laughed. 'Bennies. I took five. And a little of something else.'

'I've never seen people doing it before. Not an orgy. Not for real. Did you come?'

'Of course I did,' said Jacey. 'Why else would I do it?'

'Is it better with a lot of guys or one?'

'Yeah.' She sounded tired. 'It's a bigger bang. It's like you get to that point when you know you're going to come and you can keep there. A lot of guys delays it. And when you do finally get if off it's much more intense. And I can get two or three more after the first. And then I like it really kinky like –'

'Like what?'

'We shouldn't be having this conversation. I didn't want to get you into all that tonight. I'll do anything for oblivion. And I'm a good fuck. I'm sorry you didn't get any of the action. It was only just now I caught on. That's why she's hanging around me. If you'd said –'

'I didn't want any of the action.' But she couldn't stop looking at the girl's vagina. She asked Jacey what it felt like to come with a man. Jacey told her two or three versions. 'It's kind of nice to do it to yourself.' And Jacey's hand moved to her clitoris.

Kay felt overcome, hot, her throat tight. She looked away.

'Kay, play or go away.'

'Play?'

'Don't just sit there. Watch if you want. Is that what you want? But don't look – well – How do you look?' Jacey leaned forward and looked into Kay's face. She kissed her cheek, then lay back.

'Do you go with women too?' asked Kay.

Jacey shook her head. 'That's one thing that hasn't occurred to me. I don't think I've had time to fit that in.'

They looked at each other, both off their usual patch, unsure. Kay said quietly, 'If I tell you something can I trust you?'

'Well, that's a stupid question. Of course you can't. You take a risk or you don't.'

Kay fumbled around with the silk of her robe, feeling like a spinster schoolteacher who'd never had a sensual experience. She was suddenly desperate for it. She said abruptly, 'I've never had an orgasm with a man.'

'Really?' Jacey was interested. 'Do you get juiced up? You know, wet. When they touch you?'

'Yes, and sometimes no. No, I dry up. I know I do because it gets sore and boring like a gymnastic test. I fake orgasms.

Sometimes I have fantasies when they're having me and then I get aroused but the feeling goes away. What happens to you?'

Jacey laughed and swung her thighs

Kay looked away immediately. 'I don't know what to do.'

'But you have had a climax, haven't you?'

'Of course.'

'By yourself. What do you think about?'

Kay couldn't say, 'You,' so she didn't answer.

Jacey said, 'Lie beside me and tell me all about it and I'll make you come.'

'Oh no,' said Kay. 'I can't.

'Well, what do you want with me?' said the girl.

'I just wanted to know what it's like for you.'

'Get me that bottle of face lotion. No, forget that – it's too flat. Isn't there a candle? You know what I want.'

They looked around the room for something to use. Kay went into the bathroom and there was a long circular bottle of shampoo. She threw it to Jacey.

Jacey inserted it into her vagina and started to push it hard, in, out. 'Now I'm thinking about the men, their cocks, the way they smelt and the way they came and I'm wanting that.' She started to shake violently and the bottle slid in and out faster and she clawed at her breasts. Then she slithered onto her back to get as much penetration as she could and came, one long loud orgasm. She lay gasping, her face flushed. Kay put one hand tentatively on to her thigh.

'Are you all right?'

Jacey nodded, threw the bottle on to the floor and lay back on the bed, quite matter of fact. 'I liked it. Doing it in front of you.'

She rubbed Kay's arm, her hands very practised. 'I've got to sleep now.'

When Kay woke the next morning Jacey had gone. A note, under her door said, 'Don't worry about it. We'll work it out.'

Night after night Kay lay beside Guido, going through the taverna orgy and the scene in the hotel. What was it she still didn't understand? For God's sake, it was in her mind already. 'I'll have to see her again,' she said. 'For medical reasons.'

She went to Paris to loop some dialogue on the Frey movie.

On the third day Jacey showed up, hanging on Frey's arm. She wore a soft orange playsuit that looked conservative enough from the front. When she turned, however, it was backless and revealed half her buttocks. Around her waist, a Cartier gold chain was welded and padlocked. Kay knew it would be engraved with Frey's name. Jacey looked beautiful and used. For some reason Kay felt horrified when she saw them together. It gave her palpitations and she was unable to speak. The looping was held up until she felt better. She did her job but she couldn't bear to see Jacey and Frey together. If he'd touched her, Kay would have fainted.

Frey took them to lunch near the Etoile, and he noticed that Kay, in her mustard-yellow Ungaro coat like a triangle and long black wet-look pants, got more attention than he did. Ungaro's mathematical lines suited Kay. It was a celebration of symmetry; the triangular pockets over her breasts were two mathematical forms. He liked the precision of her clothes and decided to use it in the movie promotion. The live wet look should suit Jacey, he thought. He gave her a pile of money and told her to get some pants like Kay's and a shirt. 'You know the kind I like. Get it.' Then he rushed off to a meeting.

The girls sat silent, awkward. Then Jacey spoke, quite softly for her. 'I expect the Rome pictures didn't do your marriage any good.'

Kay, Jacey and her cousin had been on the front page of every Italian newspaper. It was implied that Kay, alone in Rome, was seeing Jacey's cousin.

'They just work up a story so I'll have to deny it. Then they get more of a story. I'm used to it.' Kay wanted the girl to come back to her hotel and was terrified of being refused. In the end she said, 'Jacey, help me.'

Jacey half laughed and looked at her provocatively. 'I bet they'd love this one, the press. It's a shame you're a girl.'

Kay turned scarlet and got up. She walked purposefully to the hotel off the Champs Elysées and assumed the girl would follow. She knew then why she hadn't stayed in her apartment: Guido could arrive at any moment. The hotel, anonymous, would encourage Jacey. A man shared the lift with them. Jacey eyed him and smiled. He half smiled and looked away. They all got out on the same floor and Jacey watched which corridor he took.

When they got to Kay's suite, Jacey made phone calls. She was fluent in several languages. 'We always moved around when I was a kid.' She turned on the television. 'I have to see a race. Frey put a load on. I'm sure it's fixed. He said not or where's the fun? How funny is it if he loses?'

Kay remembered she was supposed to be working on one of his films. She rang the studio and said she'd be late.

'How do you feel riding a horse?' said Jacey. 'Doesn't that give you a good feeling? All that hard power under you. So what do you want with me?' She held out her hand, feeling for Kay. Kay took the hand.

'Do that again. What you did,' she said.

'Don't you want to know what I've been doing since I last saw you? It's been plenty, let me tell you. But then I met a man who wouldn't play, and I really was intrigued. I did everything.'

'I know about the Greek.'

'Not the Greek. Marcello Tallaforos, the conductor. I went to a concert. I wanted him, tried to get him. It was like trying to bang the priest. He was –'

'Shocked?'

'No. Just definite. He said no very well. No moral hostility or looking down on me – just, I love my wife. Of course he may know of my reputation. I don't even know if he'd be any good. I just wanted him. I still do.'

Kay felt cold and sexless. 'I don't want to hear about a particular man. Not if you want him.'

'Oh my, you are bossy. Frey's right. Give you an inch and you take all of it.'

Kay slapped her hard and Jacey protected her face like a child.

'Are you going to stop? You're here for me. Take off your clothes.' She'd got the relationship worked out, Kay thought. 'Lie on the bed. Go on.' And she pushed Jacey towards the bedroom.

Jacey lay back across the bed. 'No rough stuff.'

'Don't you like it?'

'If Frey sees it –' She gestured trouble.

'Show me. Like you did in Rome.'

'Take off your clothes,' said Jacey.

'Please,' said Kay curtly.

'Please,' repeated Jacey, beginning to see the game.
'You take them off me.'
Jacey got up and undressed Kay. She was rough and fast. 'When the men do it to me they play with me so it takes longer.'
Kay didn't respond.
'I tell you what. We'll get a guy up here and I'll make it with him and you watch and I'll give you something. It's a present.' She got a small silk purse out of her bag. Inside were three silver balls. 'Now you put them up and move a bit so they roll around. Get a rhythm going and that will make you come. And if you watch me and the guy, then when you start to get it the guy can have you.'
'Jacey, we haven't got a guy.'
'Oh yes, I saw one on the way up.'
'No, Jacey. We can't take a stranger in here. He could blackmail us for the rest of our lives. No.'
'Then I'll call room service and get a waiter. Oh shit, Kay, I'll call up the guy I saw earlier in the lift. I caught his eye. He looks very appealing.'
Kay was far from sure but could see Jacey was excited.
'I'll go and get him. I'll go like this.' Still naked, she put on high-heeled black velvet shoes. Then she dialled Reception and asked for the name of the man in corridor 219 to 224. 'Medium height, well built, around forty. Looks like Kirk Douglas.' She listened to three names and said, 'That's it.' She hung up and dialled his suite. 'Are you a Canadian businessman I just saw in the lift? I had blonde short hair. Yeah, you looked as though you knew me too. That's right. We've met, obviously. Please come along to my suite right now. There's something I'd like you to do for me'
Kay just couldn't believe it.
As Jacey spoke she looked at herself in the mirror, stroking herself, her breasts, her buttocks. What she was doing was there in her voice.
Kay was excited and very scared. If he did know Jacey he'd also know her. 'I can't be seen,' she said when Jacey hung up.
'Then put on my dark glasses.' She got hold of Kay. 'Come on, you've got such a stacked body – your breasts are incredible. Join in. This time I promise you you'll get laid.'
The doorbell made Kay run into the bathroom. Jacey threw her the dark glasses, then, wearing only high-heeled shoes, opened the door.

Before he'd closed the door he was aroused. Then he expected a trap, Jacey said, 'No trap. Just two girls without anyone to have fun with.' She took his clothes off and got him into the bedroom. 'Don't use it all up. I've got a friend.'

'Come out, friend,' he said.

Kay appeared in the bathroom doorway.

'Can you do it to us both?' asked Jacey.

He said he could. He was certainly attractive. Kay had seen him before – something to do with her mother. Her mouth was dry and she felt nervous. Jacey and the guy got to work like a piece of machinery in action. Jacey kept saying, 'Do it to her.' Finally he wrestled out his penis and put it up Kay, who was kneeling on the bed.

'Now don't say that doesn't feel good,' said Jacey. 'That size. It's lovely.' To the guy she said, 'She doesn't take her glasses off.'

'No, and we don't call each other by name,' he murmured. He was controlled, could come when he wanted.

Kay took Jacey's hand. 'Stroke me,' she said.

And Jacey caressed Kay's clitoris, sucked it, then rubbed it as the man fucked Kay from behind. How Kay wanted to make it this time.

'Just let go,' said Jacey. 'Do what you want. Do it to yourself. Anything. You'll never see him again.'

The man, still caressing Kay's breasts, got back in Jacey, and Kay watched and that felt right, to watch. And then she realised it was Jacey she fancied, not a man. The discovery made her rather quiet as an orgy participant.

When he'd gone Jacey lay back and talked about him. She'd arranged to have dinner with him if Frey didn't need her. 'Now he's cool and erotic and magnetic and very, very good at it. And I bet he doesn't do it that much. Definitely married but more married to his business.'

'What's his name?'

'I don't know. Jaimie something. He's a Scorpio like me. Very good eyes. Mysterious.' Jacey pulled Kay down on to the bed and put her arms around her. 'You can take your shades off now. Tell me, go on. Whatever's in your head.'

'I used to watch. I used to see my mother and father do it. His cock used to come out of her still hard and steaming. Then I went into my bed and made myself come'.

'So you wanted him to give it to you?'

'No,' said Kay. 'I wanted what he had and do it to my mother.'

'Well, do it to me.' Jacey sounded very nice and warm.

'It's a funny thing to suddenly realise –'

'Do it to me.'

'I don't know how.'

'Make love to me as though you're a guy. Go on. Put your fingers up.'

Shaking and breathless, Kay started tentatively, kissing her breasts, caressing her. Then she rode her so their clitorises touched and rubbed together, and she knew this was what she wanted and hot sex flowed through her, effortless as a river, and the orgasms came, one after another. And Jacey said, 'I like it. I just wish you had a big hard cock.'

The next night a dark, beautiful boy with cropped hair and a lean tanned face arrived at Jacey's favourite bar in St Tropez. The boy wore a long dark cloak and tall leather boots. Jacey turned up late, even though she'd been told this boy had a message from Frey.

'What is it,' she asked, 'that can't be done over the telephone?' Then she looked at him and liked what she saw. He gestured for her to come to the stairs. 'Oh, not Frey. What now? Is he up there?' Wantonly she climbed ahead of him to the first floor. The boy pushed open the first door they came to and she went in. No one – just the bed.

She turned round and the boy gestured for her to lie back. Then he whipped back his black cloak and there was an enormous penis, thick, maybe twelve inches long. It was rigid with jewels and strapped around the woman's body so her pubic hairs were clustered over the top. Jacey reached up and stroked Kay's breasts and then lay back taking in as much of it as she could. 'I've never had one this big,' she said. When they came the dildo released a gush of semen-like fluid from its tip, but it stayed hard.

. . . Chapter 34 . . .

Guido sat in Margery's private sitting room and drank herb tea. His nerves were shot and he daren't drink any more alcohol. He had great admiration for Margery Caversham and wanted to make a favourable impression in spite of his humiliation.

'It's obvious she's having an affair with Prince Ornetti in Rome,' he said.

'He's a fag,' said Margery.

'They were photographed together. And now she spends all her time with Jacey. Obviously it's a cover – she's with Ornetti. All I want to know is what I should do.'

'But she sleeps with you, Guido?'

He shook his head. 'She hates me, I think.'

'I'm sure she doesn't,' said Margery, though she was far from sure.

'And she's so difficult.' He rubbed a hand over his forehead, a mild gesture considering what he was feeling. Margery was asking in what way. He couldn't tell her the stuff Kay had been getting up to. Measuring his penis, playing with it, asking how it felt. How did it feel when he started to come? How did it feel when the stuff splashed out? What was the height of pleasure? And did he feel the orgasm all the way along the penis or just at the head? And how long before he could do it again? Could he have it hard all day? How many spasms during one orgasm? Five, ten? Were some orgasms flat? How was his different from a woman's? The questions went on far into the night. She'd also made him ejaculate into a cup.

'She's going to drive me mad,' he said.

After what she'd learned, Kay had the dildo changed so that it gave both of them more pleasure. She had the ejaculation liquid made so it smelled of semen. The dildo could now swell and go down. Eventually it would, in full excitement, become huge. She now controlled Jacey with it, rubbing it over the girl's body, over her breasts, making her beg for it. Now Jacey had something so huge, so satisfying, she didn't go elsewhere. It also gave her an incredible turn-on that her lover had beautiful breasts and cropped hair. They started going out together as boy and girl, though that could only work in winter because in summer Kay's breasts would show.

Kay insisted that Jacey tone down her sexy style. No more transparent clothes: she wanted her mistress to look as ordinary as possible in public, so they weren't noticed. Now she was in love, she moved out all the erotic paraphernalia from her villa bedroom and ordered twin beds.

But instead of being happy Kay was more jealous, more upset, than ever. She'd found what she wanted: what happened if the love object decided she wanted to go back to men?

Margery called Kay to the Château and Kay did seem shaky and odd. She was worried the businessman had guessed who she was, had made the connection through Jacey. Margery asked why she spent so much time with the girl.

'I'm improving her. She's learning things. It's perfectly true.'

'I didn't say it wasn't. There's a photograph of her on a beach, topless. That caused quite a stir. I wouldn't run around with her, Kay.'

'Why not?'

'It's obvious she's an exhibitionist. Her clothes! They're notorious. I could tell you some stories! And you'll really upset Guido. There's not a lot of love in this world, Kay, and he really loves you. All that glitters is not gold.' Margery put on her tinted glasses. She felt queasy, unlike herself. Had the duck been fresh?

'What does all the gold-and-glitter speech mean?'

'Darling, there's obviously a man in this story somewhere. Jacey's the front. Guido's no fool. He also said something about you and he running an opera house together. I didn't know you were musical.'

'He shouldn't tell you things, Mummy. I resent that.'

'As you're musical come to Marcello's charity concert Saturday. It's in aid of the victims of Nestorin. And the following Saturday, being a dead weekend, I've invited your brother and his family. Be here.'

Before Alex flew to Cannes he phoned Marion in Los Angeles. She was amazed to hear from him but knew his voice instantly. She could almost feel his beauty, like a scent around her. She said, 'I'd love to see you, Alex. Why don't you come out here and lie in the sun? What else can you do in February?'

But it wasn't interest in her that had prompted the call. He said, 'Marion, I want you to speak to my mother. I don't care what you say, but I'm taking my wife and son there and she'd better be nice. I want my wife accepted. If anything goes wrong, Marion, I'm going to tell her about us.'

Marion was silent. She felt she'd been stabbed, literally. The Caversham family were ruthless, she thought. Dino had a point when he cursed the whole lot of them.

'Don't go quiet on me, Marion. Do it!' He hung up.

She said to the empty, noisy line, 'I'd still love to see you. I haven't got over you.'

Then Mo Cohen came in and enquired, 'What's up? Somebody die?'

. . . Chapter 35 . . .

Before he knocked on the main door, Alex said, 'I'm doing this for you, Jane. Because you want to belong to the beautiful people. Well, here they are.'

Carlo, the butler, embraced him, exclaiming, 'You look like your father – no, your mother. She's so emotional she can't come out of her room.'

Alex patted him on the back. 'It's OK, Carlo.' He introduced Jane. The butler had dreaded meeting her, and put a professional look on his face. He was more generous greeting the baby. Then Julian and Jennifer appeared and made a lot of noise and fuss. 'What is this? The host's day off? Why all the staff?' said Alex.

'Your mother is over-emotional,' said Carlo.

Jennifer showed them to the guest room at the back of the house, away from Kay's old apartment. 'No one's seeing you before your mother does. No, what I mean is your mother sees you first. When you're ready could you go along and speak with her, Alex?' She turned to Jane. 'Nanny will bring you anything you need for the baby.'

Alex sat on the bed and lit a ready rolled spliff. He had several already made: he knew what he was in for. He felt the radiators. Not even hot. 'We're in shantytown here. I want to be moved to the first floor.' He picked up the phone and pressed the bell for Carlo. 'Carlo, come and get our stuff and put us in the Spencer Tracy suite.'

Carlo said it was occupied.

'Throw 'em out. The prodigal son comes first. You've read the Bible.' He sat on the bed and waited, the room now full of dope fumes.

Jane knew now that coming here was a mistake. The hostility – you could cut it with a knife.

'Why worry about a lukewarm radiator? Have you forgotten the dump we come from?'

'I'm not in Earls Court now, honey, I'm in my home.'

There was a knock and the door opened. Margery Caversham, dressed all in black, stood there, quite still. She was a lot more solid than Jane imagined. Most stars were smaller in real life, but she was taller. Jane knew this was trouble, so she stayed half bent over the baby, wiping his face. Margery wore black because it was the only colour to do justice to her son's visit.

'Welcome home, Alex.' The voice was as always. It had everything in it that made her a legend. It was musical, low, tantalising, passionate and classless. It was slightly American, like Alex's. Her eyes were very dark as she looked at him. He was hers – hers for ever. And he looked back and knew it to be true, but that didn't mean he had to like it. Her eyes looked as though she was seeing for the first time in years. He gave her life. She ignored the smell of dope.

'And welcome, Jane.' She came into the room then and Jane didn't know what to do. Shake her hand? Kiss her? Curtsy? Margery kissed Jane on both cheeks, French-style, then looked down at the baby. Before she touched him she made sure it was her son's. It was a long look. 'He's a beautiful kid. How old?'

'Five months, nearly six.' Jane's voice shook. It was as though the Queen of England had suddenly walked into her mother's Hastings boarding house.

'We dine early, French-style, seven o'clock. I'm sorry about that.' She started to leave, then stopped. 'Alex, I believe you've got a problem with this suite.'

Alex looked at his hands as though they were guilty of murder. 'No, it's OK.'

Margery looked again at Jane, at her face, body, the way she held the child. She was a physical person, sensual. Afterwards Margery, when summing her up thought, she broke my heart but there was no remorse in her face.

Before they entered the dining room at 6.45, Alex got a bottle of Scotch from the butler's tray and took a gulp. Jane was wearing her white leather suit and Hollywood high heels. Alex wore his usual bike clothes – no concessions were going to be made here.

The number of things Jane had in her head. As soon as it was announced in the press that Alex was reunited with his mother, Jane was overwhelmed with scripts from agents, books from producers, letters from fans. 'Get them to Margery.' She knew that in this house none of this would be even mentioned: it had a solemn atmosphere, it was not a market place. She noticed Alex's hands were shaking.

'Are you nervous?' she asked him.

'I always shake before seeing my mother.'

She could hear voices in the room beyond the closed door. Elegant, confident people waited there. It was like going on stage. They went in and eight people stood up: Rick de Palma, Kay, Guido, Shane, Marcello Tallaforos and his wife, Charlotte and Margery.

Jane smiled warmly and greeted everybody as if she was in a repertory play. Alex said nothing, and head thrust forward padded to his seat. Margery's black Chanel dress was unadorned. Only Alex could get Mummy back into black, thought Kay.

Carlo served the soup. Everyone was nice enough without really saying anything to Jane. At first she tried to speak, to join in, but the subjects were not ones she was familiar with: a recently deceased opera singer's sale of art treasures, the stock market, the rigours of concert tour life, the trouble with spending too long in the Bahamas, the Manhattan would be 'in' crowd with too much money and ludicrous overdressing. Jane didn't know anything about the latest pop gossip either, so when Rick did his share, still nothing doing for her. They were polite but she got the impression she wasn't good enough. After a while she stopped trying and remained silent. Alex was silent anyway.

Fish was served with tiny potatoes, followed by salad, then cheese. Afterwards there was a huge icecream cake, the cook's speciality. It was a typical French meal, rather spare. Finally the fruit basket was passed around.

Jane couldn't exactly put her finger on what was wrong. It was as though she was sitting in a group of foreigners and straining to communicate. Her inner voice said, Don't even try.

Then Kay talked about filming with Frey and the promotional tour for the film in the States. Here was a chance for Jane to say something. She opened her mouth to ask, how many hours do you sleep if you do a city to city tour nonstop for a week? But Margery cut in with a more decisive question, then stopped and turned to Jane. 'Oh, I'm sorry. You were about to say something.' And all the attention was on Jane and she knew the question wasn't good enough. She couldn't speak. Alex sighed. Then she got angry with herself and the situation and asked the question.

'If you have to be in Baltimore one day and down in Florida the next and you do morning chat shows at 6 a.m. how do you get time to sleep?'

'Sleep?' Kay looked genuinely surprised.

'Sleep?' said Rick. 'Oh, Jane means going to sleep at night.'

'Stars on tour don't sleep,' said Kay. 'Nor do beauty queens. How much sleep did Miss World get a night on the big tour? Three hours? You don't even think about it.'

'It's certainly a different life, Jane,' said Margery. 'Hard to communicate to a – well –' She wanted to say 'outsider'. 'What shall I say? You have to be disciplined.' She looked at Jane and her look made it clear that Jane would never be disciplined enough. It wasn't much of a look but it hurt. The trivial subject good enough to concern the outsider was dismissed quickly. Back on to the in-stuff and there were no more gaps for Jane. She realised Margery did not like her. The woman doesn't even know me or anything about me and yet she dislikes me. It made Jane very uneasy.

Margery had planned her campaign against the girl quite deliberately. She would be thrown in with the superstar strangers who rarely saw outsiders except in an audience. She would be given no chance to get to know the people individually beforehand, nor they her. At that table Jane could see she came over as raw ambition, struggling for a position with no foot on any ladder, and they had made it and loathed hungry outsiders. No one had to deliberately put her down. She just had to sit there through five courses, unable to join in. And she saw how they all fussed over Kay. How warm Margery's eyes were when looking at her family. How Kay could discourse with Marcello Tallaforos because they had shared events, memories in common.

A little later Guido returned to the subject of sleep. He'd do anything, even lick the floor, for Margery, so getting the drift of the action at the table he turned to Jane and said, 'Sleep is for mothers and babies.' He implied that the famous didn't need it: they were fed and soothed by all the attention they received. She wanted to reply but Margery had cut in with a new subject, a witty remark. Everyone laughed. How Jane wished she was back in Earls Court. What should she do? Pretend to laugh? Pretend to be one of them?

Then Shane said loudly, 'Is she really a scarlet woman? But she's white. She doesn't look any different to other women.'

All conversation stopped. Jane was mortified. She looked at Alex – nothing doing there. Rick de Palma so wanted to help her. Words were there, dying to be said, but he didn't say one of them. Charlotte was the first to speak. 'D'you know in Harlem where I worked, the kids thought I was anaemic because I wasn't black.'

Everybody made a lot of that. Kit was brought in by Nanny but Kay had made sure he didn't get too much attention. She had Guido's year-old nephew staying and year-old kids were more fun than babies. And just to make sure, Kay had given Shane an Alsatian puppy. There was plenty of baby around that weekend.

Alex was looking at his mother, an assessing chilling look. Marion hadn't done a very good job.

The one thing about the evening that Jane did remember with pleasure was the conductor, Marcello. His hand as he held the glass was sensitive, exquisite. Being near him was a cool yet powerful experience like sitting near a splendid waterfall. He smoked continually. He had a gold signet ring on his little finger. His dark hair, streaked with grey, was long and elegant and he had a sensual mouth. How young his eyes were – how penetrating, commanding. In spite of her humiliation she wanted to stay near him; she could not be cut off from all that charisma. Yet he'd hardly acknowledged her existence.

After dinner Alex went straight to their guest room, which he knew was the worst in the house. Jane followed, her face burning as though stung.

He said, 'I'm sorry about that, Jane.'

She was suddenly furious. 'You didn't defend me. You didn't say one word.'

'Which word?' he shouted. 'Don't you see it's what they want? How could I defend you?'

'Your sister put him up to it.'

'No, babe, not Kay. It would have been much worse. I'm really sorry.'

'And now the conductor knows.'

'Knows what?'

'What they call me.' She closed her eyes against the horrible memory of their veiled hostility because she wasn't one of them. 'I'll tell you something,' she tore off the white leather clothes and threw them on the floor, 'I'm going to be a fucking star and show them!'

After a sleepless night Jane packed to leave. She was in worse shape than she thought. She'd always wanted stardom – and now she'd seen it close to, the very top rung, and nothing in her matched that. Panicking she thought of what she'd have to achieve just to sit at that table. A hit in a hit stage play. Get it to New York. A hit movie in Hollywood. Maybe two. Then she could talk about how much fucking sleep you needed on promotion tours.

The cook rang and asked if she'd be in for lunch. 'Absolutely not,' she said.

She felt chilled in the room and had to wear Alex's sweater. He came in without a sound. He always walked soft-footed, stealthily.

'I want to go,' she said.

'It's your party, Jane. You booked us in here. Let's go.' He went downstairs to negotiate a lift to the airport from the chauffeur or butler.

As Jane didn't want to see anyone she carried her bags to the front door herself. The group were in the Japanese salon having coffee, planning the day. She could see Marcello Tallaforos and her heart did something inappropriate – it missed a beat. She had nothing in her or about her that could match his world; so she picked up her baby and went towards the door. One more look at him, at his profile, the large Roman nose, the wonderful mercurial expressions designed to inflame, to encapture. How often did you see someone as marvellous as that? And she saw Charlotte watching him. The girl's eyes never left his face.

Jane lingered a moment too long, because as though affected

by her gaze the conductor turned and looked at her. 'Ah, the little mother.' And he strode towards her, his hands outstretched. 'Taking your baby for a walk? But it's too cold, no?' Everyone followed him, and they all saw her bags untidy by the door.

Margery's expression was colder than the day. She did not want an ugly scene in front of Marcello and his wife. Thinking fast Margery said, 'A walk. Let's all go and show Jane the garden. But put your coats on, it's really cold.' And she drew her family and Tallaforos and his wife off across the hall to get coats. Then Margery came straight back to Jane.

'In my house we have at least a modicum of manners. I don't expect thank you. But guests say goodbye before leaving. In fact –' She couldn't go on, she hated Jane so much. This girl dared to be pretty. She remembered that Tallaforos and his wife were pleased Alex was visiting and planned to show him a new species of bird since he liked them so much. The bird flew around Juan-les-Pins and they wanted to take him that afternoon. Madame Tallaforos knew exactly how long Alex was supposed to be visiting. 'You can't leave.' Margery's voice was a low hiss.

'Can't I?' said Jane, her voice soft and furious.

Margery tried to pull herself together. 'The car isn't here. Kay has gone into Cannes so there's no driver until she returns. That's what I meant.'

Silently Alex had arrived beside them. 'I'll call a cab,' he said.

'Alex, you and your wife are house guests until tomorrow evening. Marcello was invited by Charlotte and he is going to take you along the coast. There's a strain of wildlife he wants to show you.'

Alex stirred restlessly.

'He was, I may remind you, very close to your father. Don't insult him.'

'What about me?' said Jane. 'I suppose I wasn't insulted.' Her voice was too loud.

'If you choose to call yourself a scarlet woman then don't be offended if others do the same.'

'What do you know – you – about getting by?' Jane's voice was low, primitive, almost thrilling.

Alex touched her shoulder. 'Jane, come on, let's go.'

Kit started crying loudly.

'If I felt as reduced as you, Jane, I wouldn't go anywhere. I'd sit at home with all the lights out.' Margery's voice had risen with fury.

Charlotte, wearing a huge fur coat, appeared ready for the walk. She gave Jane a wide smile, prepared to be friendly. Jane ignored her. She hated them all equally.

'He's such a darling baby. I love his name. Did you choose it?' asked Charlotte.

'I'm off,' and Jane walked out with the crying child into the cold air. Margery watched her moving sullenly to the first security exit.

'This is ridiculous,' she said to Alex. 'Marcello and his wife want to spend time with you. We can't fall apart in front of them, the wife talks to everybody. Shane's remark was absolutely innocent but uncalled for.'

'And echoes the feelings of the entire family,' said Alex. 'Tell your important guest and his talkative wife we had to leave suddenly because I need a fix.' He picked up the bags and started to follow Jane. 'Tallaforos knows too much about you, Margery, so keep your act clean. I don't think he could take too many more surprises.'

Margery turned completely white. 'I'll never forgive you.'

'You're not alone. Over two hundred women have told me that. Did Marion ring you? She's one of them.'

Margery got the full drift of that, and felt even worse. Marcello and his wife had come to stand beside her, so instead of saying 'Bastard' she said, 'Goodbye, darling. See you soon.'

'Well, that all went OK,' said Rick. 'You dreaded seeing her and it was fine. She was a bit quiet.'

Margery made eyes indicating that Tallaforos could be listening. 'Yes, it went fine.' And she gave a lovely smile.

Inside her, in the place where she felt Dino's dying, words were made: I will see that girl in hell. She will never prosper. Certainly never work. She has ruined the only thing I've got. My son. And she carried on smiling as they walked into the winter sun.

Alex told Jane, 'It kind of blew my mother's plans having the conductor and his wife along. They draw water socially. Apparently my sister Charlotte invited them impulsively. She is impulsive because she's in love with him, but he's very married. I think she's even going to work for him. Like doing PA.' And after that speech he shut up for the rest of the journey home.

She thought: they ignored me. I didn't rate. I wasn't good enough. Alex was acceptable, wanted even, because he's her son. And she still affects him. He didn't complain to her about the cold room, just went quiet. He didn't have a go about the 'scarlet woman' insult. He's obviously still in her power. And he thinks more of her than he does of me.

... Chapter 36 ...

Back in Earls Court, the flat filled up immediately with bikeboys. They listened to sounds, used the phone constantly, openly smoked weed, took acid and were always in the lavatory. They made huge cheap messy meals and read the Beat poets aloud. They didn't hassle Jane or even speak to her – she was Alex's old lady. The crunch came when she saw one of their women on the Earls Court Road wearing a white leather suit with fur. How many of those were there around? She pursued the girl and asked whose suit she thought she was wearing. The girl was heavily painted up with streaked hair that made people stare. She looked tough. 'We share in our world. What's yours is mine and the other way round.' The girl's body was bigger than Jane's and the suit was well stretched.

'But you haven't got anything,' said Jane.

'Well, it's a fact,' said the girl. 'And as you see, that way you've got nothing to lose.'

'Get it off,' said Jane.

The girl was amused. 'Why don't you call a cop?'

'I don't need cops to sort out my troubles. Get the fucking thing off.' And Jane pulled at the jacket.

'What, you want me to stand here in my pants?'

'If you've got any on, yes.'

The suit represented Jane's hopes of stardom. It wasn't just an item of clothing. The bikegirl was amused because she wasn't going to lose or undress. She was bigger and much tougher than Jane.

'I think,' said Jane, 'I'll have a go with your bloke. He's

always trying to get me to bed. Well, he's got to have something to cheer him up. I'll see how he fits.' And she walked back to the flat, the bikegirl's insults reverberating down the street.

When she got in she turned off the sound system and said, 'You'll all have to get out. The smoke doesn't do my baby any good.'

The boys looked at Alex.

'I kind of like them around, Jane,' he said.

'Then be with them somewhere else.'

'That's cool.' He threw some money on to the bed and said to the chief biker, 'I'll ride on yours. Let's go to the coast.'

They departed like a gang of rampaging Vikings assaulting the area with their noise and anger.

Alex had left her thirty pounds.

She aired the flat, scrubbed it, took the baby out and got a friend of Lucy's to babysit while she went back to class. She refused to be down. Within three days she was picked for a part in a commercial TV series. The only problem – could she do an Essex accent? She said she'd get one. She could get anything. She also got a walk-on at the Royal Court. She took the TV deal to Al Streep. She owed him one because of his faith in her. He didn't look easy about it. 'You know, honey, I'd go and fix it yourself.'

'But I've told them you're my agent.'

'Look I went all out for you and raised your expectations. But I couldn't deliver. I failed. Come on – get going. Find someone else.'

His voice was low, but not low enough. Dinah stood in the doorway. 'Ah, there's the little girl who walks alone like the cat. What do you want from us? Well, you only come when you want something.'

'This time I brought something.' And she told Dinah about the deal. 'So I wanted Al to handle it for me. I do pay my way. It's my first real part.'

'Then, Al, you must handle it.' She looked at him meaningfully.

He didn't answer.

Dinah said, 'You run along, darling. You've got your baby to attend to. We'll sort you out.'

'It starts in ten days.' And she left, almost happy again.

Al didn't want anything to do with it, but Dinah said, 'You

know what you have to do. You phone Margery Caversham. You tell her about the deal.'

Al said he couldn't. Dinah could.

Margery said, 'Offer them someone else. Say she's a drug pusher. And Gracie gets the lead in Vito's next movie. He's here right now.'

Margery hung up and Al sat down slowly and said, 'I'm getting old, and glad I am.'

Dinah said, 'Al, you don't go up against a woman like Margery Caversham. She'd do it anyway. She owns shares in that company. She'd resist the director's choice at top level. Also I feel betrayed by the girl. I treated her like my child.'

Margery sent Al and Dinah a beautiful floral arrangement in the shape of an elephant. Gracie got international stardom. Jane got a phone call – the director didn't want her after all. She couldn't cry, it was far too bad for that. She tried phoning the director, couldn't reach him. She apologised to Al. 'I was so sure. He really wanted me. It was all fixed.'

'That's showbiz.' Al sounded tired. 'And babe, if you get anything else keep it close. Understand?'

She was beginning to – except she couldn't believe it. But there was his other client Gracie getting a sudden jerk up the ladder.

'So Margery Caversham's behind it?'

'Just keep everything to yourself.' He hung up.

She was beginning to see what it meant – going against Margery Caversham.

She tried phoning her but got Jennifer. Margery was always out. On her fifth try Jane said, 'I know about the change of cast.'

Jennifer said, 'Is that all? A short message.'

'She'll understand.' Jane hung up. She vowed then, on her life she would get even with Margery.

Jane got paid the Equity minimum for being an extra at the Royal Court. Then it was discovered that she wasn't a member of Equity, and she was replaced. The thirty pounds were gone and Alex not around. Jane applied for child support and social security benefits. The DHSS found the fact that a Caversham wanted money highly suspicious. It would be a long-drawn-out process getting six pounds a week.

She got credit at the chemist's for baby food and disposable nappies. No luck at the grocer's. Lucy brought over a box of tins from her father's house and gave Jane five pounds. 'Come on, you were always kind to me. Perhaps you should let the flat and move into a bedsit.'

Jane wanted things to get better not go backwards.

'Of course you could go to the press,' said Lucy.

Jane could, but could she prove Margery Caversham took away her job?

Lucien called. One afternoon he was at the door, once again with presents of fruit and cake. 'Can I speak to Alex?'

She said, 'No, go away.'

He handed her a pile of ten-pound notes. She looked at it, didn't like it, wanted it.

'Let me in.' His voice, like his eyes, could be hypnotic, and she let him in. 'Hard times. Well, it goes in cycles. The lean years, the fat years,' he said.

'What does Margery want now? My head on a plate? Well, you are her spy.'

'She and I talk,' said Lucien. 'I keep an eye on Alex. You'd be the first to admit someone should. Where is he now?'

'But you're his friend. Why spy?'

'I don't call it spying, I just see both sides of everything. Or even five sides. It makes life difficult, but it's the way I'm made.' He tickled Kit on the chest and smiled at him warmly. 'Alex is an addict, Jane. You're going to need money and support. They won't release his trust money. If I were you I'd go to court.'

All this was much worse than she'd thought. It implied an ending. All of a sudden she was scared: she was really alone with her baby to support.

'I think I'll wait for Alex to come back and talk to him.'

'Your marriage is over, Jane, and you know it. It's been over for months.'

'Did he tell you that?' She was crying silently, her face soaked with tears.

'No, he doesn't speak to anyone. He's totally paranoid. The drugs do that. I wouldn't like to be in his head. He ought to be on a treatment programme.'

So she said she'd tried that. And then she trusted Lucien because she had to trust someone. She told him about Margery getting her replaced in the TV show, about Alex going off with the bikers, about the fact he didn't speak. They never had sex any more.

'It's the drugs,' said Lucien. 'It kills the libido.' He put the money on the table and wrote his phone number on the wall. 'I'll be back.'

She lay on the bed, trying to comfort herself, and remembered Del Grainger. It was a strange choice of comfort but he had liked her, and approved of her. She remembered so clearly the scene on the boat when he couldn't lift her dress and she'd said no. How she wished she'd said yes. And the more she thought, the more real it was, that one night. The way he'd smiled, so warm and caressing. Of course he'd thought of her the day after. And maybe the one after that. He'd have taken her picture from the newspaper, maybe had it on him when he raced his last circuit. She'd make enquiries. She had a right to know.

Lucien used a call box to get Margery, reversing the charges. He didn't tell her everything the girl had said, but he made it clear that Alex was in trouble.

The masseur worked on Margery's body for an extra twenty minutes.

'He does reflexology. It's new – from the East,' she told Rick. 'You should let him try on you.'

'You've got an incredible build, Margery. Wonderful muscle tone.' Rick stroked the oiled body and the masseur thought it time to leave.

Ever since Jane had been insulted at the dinner table and Rick had done nothing, he'd felt ill at ease with himself. Somehow he was now on the side of the management, without even knowing it, but a silent partner, not allowed to vote. Whereas he really belonged on the other side with the ones who got it and did it and suffered and hungered for fame – like Jane Kirkland. So he should have said something when the spoilt boy insulted her. Because she was one of his lot, a receiver from the people who called the tune.

'I'd like to do something good,' he said to his wife.

'But you do,' she said. 'Your last concert – well, you read the reviews.'

'I don't read them. And that's not what I meant. I want to do something for the rest of the world.'

Margery sat up too fast and wished she hadn't. Her breasts were enlarged, the nipples bigger. She fought off a sickly feeling. 'Is there something about this house I don't know about? Charlotte does her Bac, with flying colours, ready for university, and then winds up in Harlem and the Bronx. And why? She wants to share what she's got with the rest of the world. Now you.'

'I want to get together a whole group of us, musicians, actors, singers, and get some money up for the hungry ones. Like a fund. Will you sponsor it? You could put in – well, a quarter of your money would feed a Third World country for –' He did sums on his fingers. 'While we get the rest of the money flowing in and the programmes started to get them self-sufficient. If we planted grain –'

'Rick, how do you know about my money, how much I have?'

'Margery, even your accountants call you a billionaire. And everytime one of your films is shown you get a cut. You own houses, apartments, a whole block in LA, a skyscraper in Manhattan. We call it property in South London. You say real estate.'

'I say shut up and mind your own business, Rick. If you want power – which you obviously do, because you'll need that to change the world – go into politics. You've got enough backup. You go and do what Dino died trying to do.' She took a deep breath and needed to be alone. In front of the mirror she did her creaming ritual, massaging her cheeks, her forehead, nose, chin, her fingers better than any beautician's, putting love into her face.

Rick said, 'I hate living in this superabundance. It tips the scales too far. Let's give some to those who need it and improve the world.'

'Why are you so guilty about money, Rick?'

'Because if you have too much it's dangerous.'

Kay lay along the garden swing and said to Charlotte, 'The incredible thing is he is still here. I thought Mummy would blow him out, after the honeymoon. I mean, he's boring. And now he's going to turn political. Well, Mummy could hardly do that with Alex.'

Charlotte said, 'All the performers want to be stars. Then they get rich. Then they get politics.'

'D'you remember when we were a happy family?'

'No,' said Charlotte honestly.

'Before he came?'

Charlotte shook her head.

'Well, we were. We were close, except for Alex. Mummy likes him, you know. Pretty boy. Shane calls him Beauty. He wears makeup. Even wears my perfume.'

'I'm glad she's found happiness,' said Charlotte.

'Oh, so am I,' said Kay. 'Don't get me wrong. It's just her choice is going to cause us unhappiness, because Julian overheard Beauty asking for a quarter of her money. He wants to plant beans in Africa.'

This made Charlotte quite thoughtful.

'And Mummy wants to please him – after all, she's getting older – and next he'll want half. And if he plants beans for blacks then my name isn't Caversham. He's out for one thing: Rick de Palma.'

'So Mummy gives the estate to Rick,' said Charlotte. 'And we get nothing. And he's Sam Spiegel, only richer. Or Elvis or whatever his dream is.'

'Just like all the fairy stories,' said Kay. 'So we have to bring along a Prince Charming and have him fall for Beauty and Mummy finds them banging on the bed and what have you got? A stable financial situation again, Charlotte.' She'd get Jacey's cousin, the warped prince from Rome, to do the deed.

Margery didn't tell Rick about her problem. She waited until she was alone with Kay.

'Lucien rang me and said Alex has left her. And she has the effrontery to say I manipulated some director so she didn't get some part.'

Kay laughed. 'Oh, Mummy, that's going too far.'

'What do I care what she does? But I don't like that sort of threat. It –'

'What?' asked Kay.

Margery had thought suddenly of Marcello, if the girl talked to him. Had he noticed her? Shane had certainly noticed her. He'd said, 'She dresses so odd. What kind of person is she?'

'A poor one,' Guido had said. 'That's how poor people dress.'

Shane had never seen any except on TV.

'I think she shouldn't get in too boastful a position,' Margery said to Kay. 'She's got those half-arsed ideas and she's fanciful. Obviously a drug user.'

'Then talk to a few people, Mummy. Get Mo Cohen to say something. It's these empty blondes that make the most noise. They want attention, can't get it, cause trouble. I think it's made you ill. You don't look good.'

'So you agree, Kay, the girl has to stop her insinuations.' Margery imagined her going from agency to casting call, knowing only rejection. She'd become a typist, her ego crushed, her heart broken. 'She ruined my son. For God's sake, she put him on drugs. I can't hate her enough.'

Kay knew Alex had been a user long before he fell into Jane Kirkland's company: but as Rick had discovered, the Cavershams had a short, convenient memory.

Rick sat around with a few guys from the old days, the old band, and talked about getting a move going to raise funds for the starving. They reckoned they could pull in Dylan and then the Stones, then all the stars would come. The Caversham family, one by one, quite insignificantly, left the room. Margery was upstairs in bed wearing a Dead Sea mudpack and huge eye pads. She was listening to Marcello Tallaforos' concert broadcast live from Germany. Rick poured some more drinks and put on some music, not too loud. He was the master of the house – but it wasn't his house. The portrait of Dino stared down on the room. Rick could never look at that face.

These days Rick wore plenty of eye makeup and foundation. His rich hippy clothes in purple or orange silk were heavily embroidered. He loved patterned silk kaftans and velvet jackets. He wore long paisley trousers flared at the bottom, with rings on his fingers, bells around his ankles. His long hair hung in ringlets over his high kaftan collar.

The boys reckoned Rick always went mad for colour. He had more clothes than a spoilt woman. Tonight he seemed a little more gay than just simply bi.

'How's your old lady?' asked one of the group.

Rick winced. He believed the room was bugged, the whole house under surveillance. He changed the subject.

'Not a friendly lot,' said another guy. 'I mean, they just went off. Aren't we good enough? We've gone gold. Tell 'em that.'

Rick again changed the subject and talked soothingly as though to the surveillance system, reassuring it. The laughter was too loud, and the voices, then the music was turned up. Then Rick thought, what the hell. I'm alive too. This is what I am. A spliff was rolled. Then another.

Kay crept into the kitchen, where Carlo was finishing his dinner. 'Carlo, Rick is in Daddy's room smoking pot.'

Carlo muttered an Italian curse and flew along the corridor to the main drawing room. He flung open the door, grabbed Rick by the neck, took him to the front door and threw him out on to the gravel. 'Don't you ever dare smoke that stuff in Dino de Stefano's house.' He slammed the door. It opened seconds later when single-handed he threw out the whole group.

Margery heard the sudden noise and assumed a party was in progress. At least there were no girls there. Wait a minute – boys were worse! She considered getting up and joining Rick, but she felt too sick. She was forty-six and three months pregnant. She hadn't had it confirmed by a doctor but she knew the signs. Her only problem, apart from telling her other children, was would the baby be all right? No, it wasn't her only problem. Dino wouldn't like it – that was the problem. She thought about him with love but these days her head, in return, filled with hateful thoughts. Dino staggering shot but alive into the bedroom watching her and Rick having intercourse. The day she made up Rick's face and let him wear her nightdress – Dino would have loved that one. Rick had got a hard-on in her nightdress and it had gone from there – a little more perverse than she'd known with Dino, but then there hadn't been any need for erotic extras. It had always worked with Dino. Dynamite. But then she'd loved him.

. . . Chapter 37 . . .

Alex came back after twenty-one days. He'd been to Morocco – that's all he said. He was unshaven and dirty, hair caked with mud, tired, pale but – she changed 'OK' for 'sane'. He didn't speak while he made a quick meal of baked beans, cold sausage and bread. He crunched an apple, then took a blanket off the bed. 'I'll sleep in here.' He went into the bathroom and shut the door.

The next day she asked, 'What have I done?'

He couldn't remember. He put on his jacket, torn ragged and dusty, fitting him like a skin, and wiped his hair out of his eyes. That was grooming out of the way. He rolled a spliff and didn't look at his baby. He fumbled about in the jacket pockets, checked he had money and lit the spliff. He started for the door.

'Whoa,' she said. 'Easy Rider. We aren't two hallucinations here. We need things. Money, food, love, attention.'

'I'll be back. I'm just going to see a guy.'

She washed the floors and Kit's clothes. It was spring again – she hadn't even noticed. She did her exercises: she had to keep going however lousy she felt. She said to Kit, 'I'm going to win. You'll be all right.'

'Win' – it was a tough word and reminded her of Del Grainger. She wasn't sure, absolutely clear now she came to remember it, that they hadn't had sex. She thought he'd had her against the cabin door. Or was that part of a fantasy because Del was now the main constituent of her sex life? He certainly had wanted her, the way his eyes searched hers when she walked on to the millionaire's boat. What he'd felt for her even made him sober. She got on to the press guy who'd printed the story in the Sunday paper. She said, yes, things were great. Yes, maybe she could get Margery to do an eight-part exposé of her life. She kept the 'maybe' small and the rest big. Then she asked about the cutting of her and Del in the car by the broken shed – yes, the photograph Del had had on him when he died – was it amongst his things? The editor said he'd call back.

'One thing,' she told Kit. 'Del wouldn't treat me like this. He'd love both of us. And he had sense. He knew how to make it work. He was bored because he was with the wrong set. He tried to play their game. Oh boy, is that a mistake!' She could never forget that disastrous evening at the Château.

The phone rang and the editor said yes, the press cutting was amongst Del's belongings. Maybe not on the body, but certainly in his case of racing accessories. And with that, a fantasy became reality. Sure he'd loved her. And she started to cry for her lost love. His face was so clear, the lines finely drawn Searching, clever eyes – she wasn't sure of the colour. She remembered his words as he'd tried to make love to her. He'd said, 'It's your choice. Our bodies really make it together. They're good together. I like high breasts.' No, it was a small waist he liked. He'd said, 'You're like nobody else. You're not one of the thousands wanting in.'

Del's approval – no, his love of her – gave Jane the strength to get the baby into the pram for a walk, to get more credit at the chemist's. She'd end up eating babyfood too, the way things were going. Then she sat in the crowded DHSS office for three hours while they shifted the homeless, the poor, and gave some of them money, others nothing. She got nothing. But she reread the two instalments of her love story with Del. They certainly cheered her up, for now she believed it.

'To think I had a guy like him.'

When she got back to the flat Alex was sitting cross-legged with a huge biker, the one whose girlfriend liked wearing other people's clothes. They were discussing the Irish question. She asked Alex if he was staying. She sounded buoyed up, confident.

'Well, it's my choice, babe,' he replied. His face was thin, its high cheekbones accentuated by the loss of weight.

'Perhaps she wants a lay,' suggested the biker.

'And who are you going to get to do that?' Jane demanded of Alex.

'Oh ho, family troubles.' The biker got up. 'I'm off. Never get domestic, Alex my friend. Just stay on the road.'

'Bugger off, you shitbag!' she shouted.

The biker winked at Alex. 'She don't talk like your sisters.' He left, laughing.

They stayed silent and sun filled the room. She wanted to make it right, to get him back. How could she do it? She tried to reach out, to touch him.

'I don't love you, Jane,' he said.

The pain was bad. She sank down into the Del legend. 'No, I'm sure you don't. After having had a real man like Del Grainger I know what love is.'

'So you did go with him?'

'Sure,' she said. 'He was the best fuck I ever had.'

'If he wasn't dead already I'd kill him.'

Her mouth felt dry, her throat tight, everything scared. She'd loved Alex. She couldn't lose him. She probably still loved him.

'That had better be mine.' He pointed to Kit.

'You know he is.' Her voice was small, solemn.

Alex got up in one smooth movement and left. She called after him. 'Where are you going?'

'That's my business.'

For two days she stayed safe in the glow of Del Grainger's love. She was in one boat, then another, then back in the car. She could simulate love enough to keep her going. It was like creating body heat when you were stranded on an iceberg. When she had to leave the cocoon and go into the chill of everyday she felt terrible, shaky, like Lucy. She kept saying, 'It's only temporary. Even good things end.'

The phone bill hadn't been paid so the phone was cut off. She used a call box to phone Lucien, and he said he'd come round. When he arrived he seemed so normal and safe she clung to him, crying, terrified, while he soothed her, held her. In spite of the rumours, he was not absolutely gay. She kissed him and the kiss got serious. He said, 'You need it. You certainly need it.'

At that moment the door opened and Alex crept in.

She would always remember the shock in his eyes. He seemed almost frightened. He looked at the two of them and his mind made decisions: keep him, I need him for drugs; she's out. Lucien said words that sounded OK then left. Jane didn't even hear them.

'It's not what you think,' she said as soon as he'd gone.

Alex said, 'Let's play the "let's" game. Let's go to London, let's go to Tinsel Town, let's get divorced.' And he took the key off his keyring and threw it on the bed.

He left with nothing. As he started down the road she screamed, 'Alex, I'm going to kill myself.'

He looked back up at her. 'Do it or don't do it. It's your problem.'

She crouched over, comforting herself, unable even to cry. And words got together deep inside her, where she said her prayers: 'I will survive.'

Kay stripped in the sun. She was wearing her second dildo, solid gold, ridged, enormous. The only trouble was it made Jacey come too fast. After they'd done it she was very gentle with the girl. 'I don't want to hurt you or stretch you. You're so beautiful and tight there. But I have to have it big. Bigger than a guy.'

'You don't come and see me much,' said Jacey.

They were lying on the deck of their boat, moored just outside Cannes. Kay had recently bought it for Jacey.

'It's my mother – I think she's pregnant.'

Jacey looked sulky. 'It's your husband. You sleep with him.'

'Oh, don't be a goose. I don't, I swear I don't. You know I don't.' She put the girl's fingers up her vagina. 'You could tell if he'd come in me.'

'I can't bear the thought of him touching you,' said Jacey.

'He doesn't, my darling.' And Kay caressed her, bruised her, bit her neck. She'd never felt so much love or been so happy.

'Get rid of him. He's so boring, Guido Cortese. And he knows about us. He came to my mother's party with some opera singers and was blatantly rude to me. He knows, Kay.'

'He thinks you're a front for someone else.'

'He stops us being together.'

'He doesn't.'

'Then he will. He's that sort of boring person.'

Kay stroked Jacey's breasts but the girl wasn't having it. 'Kay, tell me. Let me hear it.'

'OK, I'll get rid of him. But, Jacey, he is our front. Don't you see? Nothing can ever be said, because I'm married to Guido Cortese. I'm Mrs Straight Gay.'

Jacey laughed. 'Are you? Straight gay?'

'Are you?'

Jacey sat up so the sun got to her face. 'Surprisingly, I have to say yes. I just love the way your breasts bump against mine. I could come just from feeling that.'

'Let's do it.' And Kay got on top of her.

She noticed the sky was cloudless. She didn't like too much perfection, as far as weather was concerned. It was like that just before Daddy died.

. . . Chapter 38 . . .

Four months pregnant. Margery felt she'd been unfaithful to her family. Why did she need another child? They'd ask that. Not in words, but their eyes would demand answers. Because she loved Rick, so she was disloyal to Dino. Come on, life goes on. 'I'm entitled to go with it. I'm only forty. Forty-one.' She rehearsed the speech which she would deliver to them one by one. They all knew anyway but pretended to be shocked, then pleased when she said the baby was due in October.

Shane ran away from his boarding school and came home for once. Simply he said, 'I don't want to go to any school.'

'Then you'll have a tutor,' said Margery.

'Oh, Mom. All I want to do is hang-gliding and live on a boat.'

'The Greek is out,' said Margery. 'Your father – stepfather –is Rick.'

Shane was too polite to say what he thought of that arrangement. 'When I'm sixteen am I free?' he asked.

'No.'

'Well, when am I free?'

'Some people are never free,' and she left the room, thinking of Alex. He'd left too early, and what she'd gone through over that. He was living, so the agency said, in a boarding house in Hastings. The girl was alone with the baby.

Kay was offered a film in the States but kept making excuses not to do it. Finally she found the answer. Jacey would accompany her as her stand-in. She asked her agent to write it into all future contracts. Where she went, Jacey went.

Charlotte worked hard for Marcello and accompanied him and his wife around the world. She handled the press, wrote the programme notes, arranged his social life. His wife did the real stuff, listening to rehearsals and sleeping with him.

Rick, in honour of giving Margery a child, took down the portrait of Dino. As he said, he was now master of the house.

Kay divided her life between her love and her mother. She also guarded her material interests. The arrival of this new baby was so threatening she couldn't even visualise her future at the Château. Would Rick take down all their pictures? Were they out like an old dynasty, Chinese style? Would her apartment be used as a glorious nursery? And worse, would there be more of Rick's offspring?

Shortly after a press leak that Margery Caversham was married to pop star Rick de Palma – a rumour considered too incredible – Margery called a business meeting at the Château. Her bankers, lawyers, accountants, managers, dealers, brokers and a businessman called Jaimie Laurenson from Canada were there. Jaimie was clearly important because he stayed on for dinner. Because of the new baby Margery had reshuffled her business empire. There were two new mouths to feed: Rick's and the child's.

Guido was already at the table when Kay rushed in late. She hadn't bathed since making love with Jacey and the dust from the road was still in her hair. She apologised to her mother and sat down. Margery indicated discreetly that she looked a mess. Also she was wearing jodhpurs. Two men had stood up when she'd arrived: the banker and Jaimie. She hadn't really noticed either of them until Margery said, 'She drives far too fast. An Alfa Romeo – what else? – with the roof down. But she's very good. She broke the unofficial record from Cannes to the Italian border.'

'Do you ride horses?' asked the banker.

No, she did not. The jodhpurs were for Jacey's benefit. Then she looked at the second man, and choked. The oversize prawn stuck in her throat. Carlo came round the table and patted her back. So this man handled all her mother's film negotiations. Of course he wasn't just some agent. He had to be everything: real estate, owned a newspaper, was buying a record company. Did he recognise her?

He didn't say anything. Nor did she. Throughout the meal they were both silent. She was remembering the way he'd fucked Jacey and felt her breasts at the same time. And other things. He could ruin her, this man. A word to Guido and he'd tell Jacey's mother and that would be the end of love. It was no secret Jacey's mother wanted her daughter well married.

There was talk of a tie-up with a titled English family who owned half London. Kay looked with respect at Jaimie, this man who could with a light word topple her life like a house of cards.

Afterwards they played Monopoly with Shane. It was like the old days. Then Rick put on his new album and talked about feeding the world and saving it. The man was looking at Kay, his blue-grey eyes piercing. Worst of all was Mummy knowing. It had to come now when she Kay was so happy. She didn't know whether to leave or to stay. One thing, she'd have to get Guido upstairs for some real action. And if the guy said anything she'd deny it.

'Yes, my wife is often in Paris,' Guido was saying.

'Which hotel do you use?' Jaimie had a nice voice, clear. You wanted to hear more of it. It was like listening to music.

'We have an apartment near the Etoile,' said Guido. Then he talked about La Scala, and how he was opening his own opera house next year. He named the site, the sums, the seating, the artists he'd engage. The only thing he didn't mention was where the money was coming from and that its source was sitting right opposite him. But however it all came down, he'd never get that opera house. Kay wasn't like Jacey, she didn't pay her way. She despised him utterly because he'd been bought.

Discreetly she asked Carlo if the Canadian would be staying. Carlo nodded.

Questioned further Guido admitted to the Canadian that he was presently employed by his father in textile factory management.

The Canadian had fulfilled all his dreams. Now he was out for the big stuff. He was in Margery's league. Kay thought he was ruthless but attractive. She knew he was dynamite sexually, but she didn't think he was careless in normal life. He played a close hand.

Margery said later, 'Don't fall for Jaimie Laurenson whatever you do.'

'I haven't,' said Kay.

'You spent the entire evening ogling him. I've never seen you so quiet.'

'What's he like?'

'Dreadful.' Then she said she was tired and went to bed.

Guido wasn't in the apartment so Kay went looking for him, shouting his name. Jennifer appeared thinking something was wrong.

'It's always wrong, Jennifer. That's life – get used to it. What do you know about the Canadian guest?'

'Your mother did say two women had killed themselves because of him.'

'Let's hope there won't be a third.'

Kay searched the house for her husband. He was sitting outside with Jaimie enjoying the summer evening. She approached silently, and in the darkness the Canadian looked like Kirk Douglas. If only he was.

'Guido, I think we should go to bed. Mummy has to go to the clinic for a check-up tomorrow and I think we should go with her.'

Guido said goodnight to his new friend, who stayed sitting in the garden. Kay turned back. 'Mr Laurenson, the staff like to lock up early,' she said.

He nodded curtly. Then he looked at her as he had when he was screwing her – a deep, assessing look, examining her beauty, finding what pleased him. He was curious and intrusive. She felt a spasm of pleasure because he'd witnessed the biggest realisation of her life. She loved a woman. How she rejoiced in her passion for Jacey.

She waited for him to say, 'How's your friend?' or, 'It'll cost you a million dollars,' or, 'I need your influence with your mother,' or, 'Get rid of Rick.' He said nothing. She thought frantically that she could plead with him, seduce him, prosecute him for defamation, threaten him with Frey. He got up and walked with her to the side entrance. She said the garden was particularly lovely this year.

'Yes, it beats Paris in the winter. Goodnight.' And he walked off, silent and lethal.

Kay got on top of Guido and tried it again. It was like writing with your left hand when you were right-handed. She closed her eyes and imagined it was her penis and she was doing it to him, but he started to talk to her and direct the lovemaking. He got his hands all over her, even penetrated her arse. She really gave it everything she had, and it ended with her feeling sore and him limp.

'It's your fault,' she said.

'Don't bounce all over me, Kay, when you've been sleeping around for the past forty-eight hours. I've put detectives on to you: so you'd better stop.'

Her eyes closed in horror. 'Why did you do that, Guido?'

'To find out who you sleep with. I wanted to make you happy, have a child.'

'Make me happy – bend over the bed. Come on, let me tie you.' And she started to hit him with the belt. 'Oh, you want it, Guido. You keep coming back for it. I always said you were into it.'

She kept lashing him and talking erotically, all the dirty stuff she could think of. Her arm ached, but eventually he came, his penis pressed into the bed. She untied him and he lay humiliated, his face in the pillow. He was some sad stranger with whom she'd performed a ridiculous act. She was madly, passionately in love with a girl, and she was powerful and free enough to be with the girl and not go through all this.

'Guido, Mummy won't like the fact you've put detectives on to me. I mean the agency already have their people. It's gonna be a lot of people everywhere I go. And it all costs money.'

'You're a liar,' he said. 'I saved your face with this marriage. Where's the opera house?'

'Where is it?' she asked. 'In your mind.'

'You don't keep your promises.'

'Guido, I'm Kay Caversham. I'm sought after, a success story. I'm Margery's daughter. I'm wealthy. On one side my family are aristocrats, on the other the Vice-President of the United States. Come on, Guido. I don't have to buy guys opera houses just because they marry me. When I tell Mummy this you won't be welcome here.'

He turned and looked at her. She had eventually drawn blood. 'All right, Kay, you win.' She knew how much being a 'Caversham' meant to him. 'No detectives, no opera house, but you don't get a divorce.' He pointed a finger savagely. 'So whoever it is you like so much, screw you, you never marry him.' And he lay back exhausted, knowing he was a weak, spineless man who couldn't stand up to his father and would do anything to stay in Margery's world.

Kay dressed frantically and raced through the night back to Jacey's arms. It was only when they were rocking about on the bed that she remembered the Canadian was still in the house. She had to leave at first light and get back there before Guido became his friend again.

She made a coffee quietly, hoping not to wake Jacey. She loved watching her sleep – her face was so sensual. She picked a flower from the tub of geraniums and put it on her pillow. She left a note: 'I love you.' She drank the coffee.

Jacey woke and said, 'Why are you leaving?' She sounded quite frightened.

'Oh, darling, it's all right. I have to go back. It's Mummy. The baby.'

'Give me some coffee.' Jacey lit a cigarette. 'Oh, I feel awful. I must sleep. I can't do without enough sleep. What's up now?'

So Kay told her about Guido and the Canadian and the opera house. 'But I'll do anything to keep us together. You're coming on the film in July.'

'Kay, my mother keeps asking when I'm going to marry this young Englishman. He's very good-looking.'

'Well, is that what you want?' Kay enquired icily.

'No, but why should I give up my future if you stay with Guido Cortese?'

'I'll get rid of him. I really mean he's out.'

'I've got to think of my future, Kay. I've not exactly got a good reputation and I'm not a kid. They like them seventeen, eighteen these days.'

So Kay said she adored her and age made no difference. Even when she was old she'd still love her. 'I'll live with you if you like.' She paused. 'But Mummy would be difficult. The money thing. I mean, we all have our trusts, but she's got funny little moral controls over who gets it when. Alex found that out. And it'll kill my career. People don't go to watch lesbians. I have to have a cover. I'll just have to keep it sweet with Guido.'

'Marry the Greek,' said Jacey. 'He's got real money.'

'But he's thirty years older than me,' Kay objected.

'Yeah, and he'll let you do what you want.' She took a drink from Kay's cup. 'I tell you what – let's give him some action. Then he'll have to. You know. He'll get hooked on it.'

'But he's marrying the shoes heiress.'

'He always wanted a Caversham.'

. . . Chapter 39 . . .

Jaimie, wearing a Valentino suit and a roll-neck silver-grey sweater, sat with Margery Caversham going over the investments, the profits, the share-out. He had a quick agile mind that Margery liked. She didn't have to spell anything out until she got to Jane Kirkland.

'Now who's this girl Alex married?' Jaimie asked.

'Nobody,' said Margery. 'Well, yes, somebody. She took my son.'

'So they're out.' He crossed Kit's name off, and Jane's. 'What about Alex?'

'He's on hold.'

Instead of going on to the next share he sighed. 'Margery, who are Kit and Jane Kirkland?'

'Oh Christ, Jaimie, I've just told you.'

'Now I'll tell you. They're two people who are going to rise up and challenge Alex the minute he's worth a buck. They're going to be angry and vengeful. She'll turn into your worst fucking nightmare because she's got nothing.'

Margery didn't understand.

'If she married him for his money give her a little, then she'll go on her way a little satisfied. She can't come back at you. The courts will see Alex looked after her and his child.'

Margery felt burning hot. No one had ever challenged her, not about an enemy. 'Jaimie, she's cut off. She's nothing. She gets nothing.' He reminded her of the Greek suddenly. All this 'give a little'. 'Let her earn a little,' she snapped.

Jaimie didn't like it. 'I've got the press cuttings on her. If you want me to protect you, you'll have to meet me halfway. Let me send her a monthly allowance. Margery, your son is staying with her mother.'

Now Margery was surprised. This was turning into one lousy day.

'No one spotted it because the mother's name isn't Kirkland

but Jones. I've got a feeling about this girl. She means something to me. In other words, she's trouble.'

Margery got up and walked around fingering the antiques, Dino's guest book, the photographs of the children. 'After Dino died I thought I had nothing to lose.'

'She's a schemer, I've no doubt. Married him for his name.'

'*My* name,' said Margery. 'Somebody told me she's a street kid. She's got a street kid's eyes.' All of a sudden Margery had had enough. She shrieked, 'I brought them into the world. I gave them the best shot I know how. I loved them as much as I know how. I was never unfaithful to my husband. I never knowingly hurt my family. I gave them the fruits of my hard work. And what do they do?'

'They spit on the hand that feeds them.' Jaimie laughed, a quiet chuckling laugh.

'They bring me their problems. All of them, Jaimie. You don't know what I've gone through. But I keep thinking, yes, it'll get better. They'll become happy, do the right thing.'

'Thank God you're strong, Margery.

'And then I found someone I could love. And for five minutes I was happy. Then they intrude with their problems and addictions and –' She couldn't continue.

'Why don't you kick them all out?' he said.

'Not Shane. He's only fifteen.'

So Jaimie said he should be back at school and Margery should get on with her life with Rick.

'And Rick does nothing about them!' she shouted.

'Why should he? They're not his.'

He poured her a drink. She told him she was pregnant. He said he knew that, and a drink didn't hurt.

She said, 'Bringing children into this world is one big pain and it gets worse as they get older.'

'Just breathe easy,' he said. 'Deeply. Come on.' He held her diaphragm. For once, someone on her payroll wasn't scared of her. He rubbed Margery's back.

'It's just wind,' she said and laughed. 'And now Charlotte's besotted with Marcello Tallaforos. He knows far too much about us. About me. Just because he waves a baton around all his life doesn't mean he's blind.'

'Just breathe easy. Let the problems go. Just breathe them out.' His voice was very reassuring.

'You're good at this sort of thing. You must have had practice.'

He didn't reply. He let go of her and gathered up his papers. 'I'm glad you're strong,' he said.

When he had gone, Margery sat alone. Who would believe that she, the legend, had so many goddam problems with her kids? Dino's kids. Then she heard Rick come in whistling, his footsteps light and joyful. And she closed her eyes, feeling happy. He was still the golden sunrise in a dark day.

Jaimie called back with a news item. 'You won't want to see it. You've got to see it.' He placed a news page with a photograph of Jacey and Kay on a beach, both topless. 'I think we should sue.'

'Never,' said Margery. 'If Kay had ugly breasts, yes. Anyway topless is coming in.'

'You don't think you should discourage the journalists, then?'

Margery read the article quickly and found it harmless.

'Nothing about the picture worries you?' he asked.

'Tell me what should worry me. Two girls having fun.'

Jaimie made a neutral sort of gesture. All his movements were precise, flowing, meaningful. He'd spent a lot of time in the East. How she wished he would marry Kay. He wouldn't put up with the – She wanted to think it was tomfoolery. It was, of course, perversion.

'There is a great deal of speculation about who my daughter is seeing. Marion and Mo Cohen both say it must be Robert Frey. He's some kind of gangster, isn't he?'

Jaimie didn't answer. He went on looking at the picture hoping Margery would see the significance.

'What is Frey like?' asked Margery.

'Like you'd expect him to be, seeing he started out as a gangster. Big cars, big names, big house, *nouveau riche* manners.'

'Well, that's plenty to worry about,' she said.

It wasn't what she should have been worrying about. Jaimie decided to get heavy with the press, at least where Kay Caversham and her friend Jacey were concerned.

Alex went to the kind, life-loving woman in Hastings and she gave him a room, first floor back. And gradually, in her care, he got himself together. He hardly understood a word she said because of her accent and his drugs, but he loved her movements and atmosphere and the positive way she got on with life. She looked after him, fed him up as she said. When he started coming off smack he got sick. She said it was gastric and took care of that. He said no doctors, and she said she didn't believe in them. She made him herbal tisanes to calm his nerves and stop the shaking. 'He's very natural,' she told the neighbours. 'No airs and graces.'

When he got his head together he wrote to Jane. It was the kind of letter to make her put away her skates for good. He said he had loved her, he'd been completely happy, but for her hunger for fame. She was getting like his mother – Jesus, why did she think he'd left home? Because she'd turned into a tricky number, like his mother, he felt betrayed. He no longer loved her. He enclosed a cheque for fifty pounds.

He said to Jane's mother, 'I loved her because she was the first warm person I had ever met. But she became ambitious.'

Jane's mother said, 'She always was. She always wanted to be better than she was.'

He stayed in Hastings until he'd got his strength back. He walked for hours along the coast and knew he had to start again. He wrote to his mother and insisted his son Kit and his ex-wife be given a portion of his allowance. He played cards with Jane's mother, went dancing with her, played the horses, went to the fair. He left when the time was up. No problem about leaving: she understood. He didn't take anything from her by his leaving. She was the first woman who didn't scream and get upset and make him feel guilty. He said, 'I really love you, Bette.'

'I know you do. Drop us a line, duck.'

He took a boat from Dover to France then hitched through Spain down into Morocco. He was on the road for several months, and when he arrived in Andy Warhol's Factory he was a very different person. He'd understood that violating other people meant he was violating himself. Also by being a victim he was causing them to become what they weren't – gaolers, mothers, protectors. Immediately he met a Japanese girl practising Zen Buddhism. She didn't speak his language, nor he hers. He married her before he'd even taken her to bed. His divorce wasn't even final, but laws are for the meek. Andy let him work for a while, modelling for pictures, improvising movies. Then he took the girl to San Francisco and they did meditation together. She taught him harmony; he gave her sexual pleasure. He made only one condition – no children.

Jane had written to Alex at her mother's house and said she still loved him and wanted him back. The racing driver stuff was just to make him jealous, Kit needed him – it was that sort of letter. In the second one she had told him the story of her affair with Jay Stone and sent him the confessional letter she'd written the year before and hidden in her Bible. It was a letter he kept always. She asked him never to show it to anyone – she was always terrified of reprisals from Jay Stone. Because of her he'd lost his career, was in hiding, possibly even dead. If he was alive he'd hate her. It was because of that incident that she'd left Hastings, changed her name and would not go back.

She went through that, thought Alex. Well, she must have something. And he remembered how powerful she'd been getting him into the drug clinic. He told Warhol about the letter, leaving out the names. Warhol said it was a fantasy, but Alex doubted that. His sister Charlotte knew all about physical transformation – silicone implants and cosmetic surgery. She said you could have your whole face and body changed – wasn't she doing just that? She wanted to look like Marcello's wife when she was young.

When Jay's face had settled it was like a fire gone out: bits of bone, charred cosmetic flesh and skin, hanging veins. His eyes were the worst because they weren't properly supported. But he could speak. He was terrified of the story getting out. He said, 'I should have thrown cold water over my face immediately. They told me that, the doctors. But I wasn't in the sort of position to be at the sink.'

The film company was told he'd been taken ill and would have to stop filming. Insurance documents were filled in. Jay's man Jaimie Laurenson had looked after that and Jay got his money. For six weeks he lay in an isolated germ-free room until there was no longer any risk of infection.

Then they began the long process of rebuilding his face.

Jaimie Laurenson said, 'You'll never be Jay Stone again, but put it this way – you can be anyone. The world's your oyster.'

. . . Chapter 40 . . .

Each morning Jane said to Kit, 'It's just you and me now, baby,' and she tried to keep the icy spasm of panic to herself. The first day she went out, she saw her white leather suit hanging upside down from a lamppost. It was tied by a piece of rope and looked like someone hung upside down – the biker's revenge. She bought the necessities for Kit, then went back to the safety of her room, except it wasn't safe, so she escaped into the fantasies of Del Grainger. Because she was scared of what she might do she phoned Lucy and Lucy's friend, people from the acting class. She got as many around her as she could. She said, 'Yes, OK, my marriage failed. It's my fault. I just never got over the racing driver.'

She was cut off completely from Alex, his family, his friends, their mutual friends. There was no money and many lonely afternoons. Nights were torment. She was a victim and knew it. She was losing weight. After the first round of support from Lucy and her people Jane was left alone. She tried going out and talking to strangers; but when you're lonely no one wants to know: you put out a desperate signal and they run a mile. So she stopped talking to strangers.

One day late in June she knew she couldn't go on. She sank to the floor, terrified. 'Please don't kill yourself,' she said, as though to another person. 'Just hold on.' The room was weird and unfamiliar. She rushed out on to the street, fluttery and white. Sweat poured down her face and body. Without looking at the traffic she careered straight across into the pub opposite and got a double brandy. 'I'll pay you in a minute. I feel faint.'

The barman knew her and said it was OK. She followed up with a beer, a pint, then another, and she was in a happy safe world. What was all this shit about loneliness and being left? Another beer and she was ready for anything. 'Of course I'll do what I always said I would. I'll go to Hollywood.'

Back in the flat Kit was screaming in his cot. She found she'd left the flat door open and the gas on, but lit. The state of her little boy terrified her.

Her GP gave her some tranquillisers and suggested she go

into a home for unmarried mothers and babies. The welfare worker came round speedily and wanted to put Alex Caversham in court and Kit into care. He was liable for paternity payments. But Jane had found a comforter, a way out. She wasn't the first and she had plenty of company. Alcohol took away pain.

Everywhere she went people told Charlotte how much Marcello Tallaforos had loved his wife, how his love had been as bright and intense as the music he conducted. And she once asked him what sort of woman or girl he found attractive.

He said, 'I found her,' and he looked at his wife.

But she wasn't the person he'd fallen madly in love with – thirty years had changed that. Charlotte knew she was dumpy, the ugly duckling of the Cavershams. If she could be beautiful like Kay she'd be loved. She went on a strict diet and exercised, and the duckling looked healthier but still ugly. The main problem was her nose. The bridge at the top was too thick and wide. Also she wanted better cheekbones, a bigger bosom, a long slender neck. And her legs – well, bathing suits were out. She'd heard Lucia had had a lot done, so had others – so would she. She decided the nose and bosom were the most important and she checked into a New York clinic for two days. It was vital, she said, that her breasts felt natural. There was nothing worse than the Barbie Doll types that always stayed pointing in the same direction whichever position you were in. She wanted a soft padding. After the operation Marion looked after her and agreed to say nothing to the family.

Margery meanwhile was having her own medical attention. The doctors wanted to inject a needle into the fluid surrounding the baby and draw some off to ascertain whether there was any abnormality. Margery didn't like the idea.

'But at your age, madam, the baby could be a mongol. It could be deformed.' And the doctor listed the side effects of being the baby of a too old woman.

'But isn't it dangerous, injecting into the womb? Dangerous for the baby?'

'Very slightly. But –'

'Then I won't have it done.'

'But more dangerous if you produce a mongol child.'

Margery knew the answer would be a quick abortion, even at this late date. She said she'd have a normal delivery and take her chances. There was only one thing she asked. If the baby was unfit, her husband must not see it. She wouldn't have him at the delivery. The doctor said mongolism in children was not necessarily obvious at birth: it only became apparent in the weeks following. She didn't want to hear any more bad news.

Jaimie Laurenson drove her home. 'What did they say? Or don't you want to say?'

She laughed, a marvellous laugh like in the old days. 'Oh, Jaimie, you know how old I am.'

He smiled. 'It's my job to look after you.'

'Don't tell Rick.'

'Sometimes, Margery, you look like a thirteen-year-old kid. It must be genetic.'

Margery tried to ask if he'd had children, but he just didn't give away anything about himself at all. A direct question was answered by, 'You're paying me for my time. Don't waste it asking about me.'

The butler rushed out to open the car door. Guests were waiting for lunch. Jaimie said, 'You've a letter from Alex asking for his wife and child to receive money. I found it in the file.'

'You did not. I threw it away.'

'I have Jennifer keep copies of everything that comes in. It makes everyone's life easier. You should honour your son's wish, Margery.'

'She put my son on drugs and I'm supposed to give her money?'

'She's in need.'

'She's ruthless, ambitious, hard as nails. She'll do anything to push herself into the light of a streetlamp if nothing else. I saw through her. The answer's no.'

A man watched Jane as she crossed to the chemist's. She noticed him because he'd been there the day before. Was it Jay Stone with a new face? Jay Stone will get me for sure, now I'm down, she thought. She was still terrified of reprisals – not from his wife or his money people, but from him. How often did you kill off a fortune and a face? The thought of how disfigured he was sent her hurtling into the off-licence. She spent half a week's money on drink. In front of the salesman she uncorked the cheap wine and had a large untidy drink.

'Jay Stone finished horror films for me. I haven't seen one since,' she said taking another drink.

'Can't you wait till you get out of the shop?' asked the salesman.

Outside the shop she had another drink and by then she could have had twenty watching men – who cared? The welfare woman was waiting at the flat. She was surprised Jane hadn't locked the door. Then she smelt the drink on her breath. She asked how much she got through in a day.

'Look, I've been feeling down. I have a glass of wine.'

'How much wine? A day?'

'Half a bottle,' said Jane firmly.

'So when you've had half you put the cork on one of those litre bottles you're carrying?'

Jane said yes.

'So how long does a bottle last?'

Jane was already on the way to drunk. 'Not long enough.'

'I suggest you're becoming an alcoholic.'

'On this little?'

The woman nodded. 'You're dependent. Stop altogether or you'll lose your kid.'

She'd got Jane a social security book. She could draw rent and food money for her and Kit. In the meantime the social services would prosecute Alex Caversham.

'You've got to find him first,' said Jane.

Her face was drawn, and she looked like someone who was having a bad time. She still tried to get work: she joined the extras' union and every day went to an office in the Charing Cross Road. She got three films in two weeks. She got a job in a drinking club in the afternoons. Lucy and her friend looked after Kit. In September when Kit was one year old she could put him in a local nursery. Because she spent a lot of time in the pubs she got drinking friends and once again the flat filled up and the music was loud. Because she was a Caversham, a lot of out-of-work actors thought she could help them. And the gays from the Coleherne pub would cross over to her flat and bring presents for Kit and ask for photographs of Rick de Palma. For a month she was some extraordinary, broken, secretly drunk sort of PR person for the Caversham dynasty.

She got a call from a film director who said he had something he wanted to talk over. She made a big effort to dress up but was filled to the gills with cheap wine by the time she got to the Savoy. As it happened, he didn't mind her being pissed. All she had to do was get a script to Margery Caversham. It was one the superstar couldn't fail to accept.

Jane realised afterwards that she could have seized the opportunity to get money out of him for a supposed return ticket to Cannes, plus expenses. Instead she said, 'I don't go near that person.' Two drinks later she was telling him her troubles. After two more he went to the lavatory and didn't come back. As she fumbled her way out of the hotel, a couple of press guys rushed forward – but it was only a pissed blonde so they backed off. What a difference a year made. She could recall the time she'd left with Al Streep, and the press had treated her as though she was Jackie Kennedy or something. She walked to the Strand and realised she was completely alone.

'She put me here in this dark place. Margery Caversham. I'll get her. I swear it.' And because she hadn't eaten she staggered and fell. She told the people who picked her up she was OK, she just needed money.

'Don't give her anything, she's a drunk,' said a woman and they walked away in disgust.

Jane walked into the nearest pub.

Jane heard that Al Streep was ill in hospital and wanted to go and see him, but then she found out Dinah was by the bed day and night and she couldn't face it. It saddened Jane because she really wanted to talk to Al – he had believed in her. He died within the week and Jane was angry with herself. She wasn't enough of a person even to go and see a dying man she valued. She sent a small floral token. Margery Caversham sent a tribute the size of a flowerbed, which had pride of place at the funeral next to Dinah's wreath.

Now Jane started drinking as soon as she woke up. When the pub opened she'd go in with a large jug and get draught beer because she preferred it. It soothed away the hours in the flat. Once the publican looked at her as he filled the jug. 'You want to watch it,' he said. He didn't want to kill his sales, but he didn't want to kill her either.

For the afternoon walk with the baby she took a lemonade bottle filled with white wine. In the evening, her Earls Court drinking friends took care of her needs. One night she went to a party and afterwards she didn't remember what the hell she had done, or even what day it was. She lurched into the flat at dawn and Kit was screaming. Where was Alex? And then she remembered the past six weeks. She tried to sleep until the off-licence opened. She felt so terrible she didn't know how she made it to the Earls Court Road. She bought two bottles of wine and paid with a cheque which would bounce. They didn't speak to her any more in there: they knew what they were dealing with. It was a hot August day but she felt icy. The trees didn't look right – green heads kept popping out of the leaves. When she got into the flat the place looked busy out of the corner of her eye. She couldn't tell what it was busy with exactly. She felt apprehensive, sick, couldn't bear being in her body. It was hot, cold, the world was not right. She got on her knees and prayed. Then she dialled Alcoholics Anonymous, but the phone had been cut off. She lay in a foetal position, then threw cold water over her face. She was going fucking mad! She screamed, 'Get me out,' and Kit screamed too. It was all part of the busy, slithering hellish room.

'When the green creatures stop coming out of the walls I'll go to LA.' It was her voice, but she didn't recognise it. She was on the floor, and it was dark. Her first thought was a drink, so she half crawled into the street to find out the time – Earls Court was busy at all hours. Because it was long past closing time she burst into tears. She went back into the flat, wet with sweat and grief. She'd get the strength to go into a late restaurant and buy a bottle of wine. She still had the cheque book and her name was Caversham. Kit had given up sobbing and was lying exhausted in the corner of his playpen. Had she fed him? When had he last had a bottle? His nappy was soaked. Looking at him she hated herself. She said, 'That's it. That's as far as it goes.' She considered taking him to her mother. She got to her feet, made coffee, ate some bread, threw up, drank more coffee. This was as low as it got. At least the DTs had stopped. She was going to pull herself up. If you got out of this kind of low you could do anything. She asked herself aloud what she wanted most in the world. What she always had. Hollywood. 'I'll go!' she said. 'And I'll make it. And then I can say I did it. I did it all on my own.'

She never drank again. She sold the lease on the flat and a week later she and Kit were on a one-way trip to Los Angeles. Sometimes she thought that alcoholic descent into hell had been an atonement for losing Alex. She'd paid. Now she was free.

. . . Chapter 41 . . .

Rick and Margery liked to dine alone. Afterwards they'd sit in the garden and look down at the coast. Her maternity dresses were all brightly coloured because instinctively she felt that gorgeous primary colours gave energy and calm, all the good things, and she wore strings of coral and held lumps of pure crystal or moonstone because they too gave off generous harmonies and absorbed negative states. She wasn't into vibes at all, but she just spontaneously felt that absolute, unadulterated colour, yellow, red, blue, and the feel of the earth and grass under her bare feet, were doing her baby good. She listened to classical music, all of it soothing and joyous, nothing discordant. After all, music made plants flourish. And sometimes, in the garden in the evening, it seemed as though all the lovely things gathered around Margery.

Rick was deeply into his Byronic look – cream silk shirts with floppy sleeves and fine gold chains, lots of them. In the daytime he wore pale linen suits and long raincoats sweeping the floor. He looked good in the pale icecream colours – pistachio, ivory.

Margery adored gossip, and Rick was good with a story. She didn't have to be in the limelight any more: he brought it all to her – Janis Joplin, the Stones, Elvis, the Beatles, Dylan, and all the backstage stuff that made them stars. Margery would hold his hand and give her wonderful laugh. 'Stay with me, Rick.' He thought she meant until bedtime: she meant for ever. He slipped in, between anecdotes, his campaign to raise money. She told him he'd have to put it to her children. If she suddenly released to him a whole part of the estate they'd be left out, jealous. She was about to have a baby. She wanted things to be peaceful.

Charlotte came over from New York for Rick's money evening. Margery couldn't believe the change in her daughter. Kay said, 'She looks like a version of Barbra Streisand with a nose job.'

'Is this all for Marcello?'

'Well, he isn't sleeping with it,' said Kay. 'Any of it. And those boobs are ridiculous. She's too small.'

'Get her to get the silicone out, Kay.' Margery was almost breathless from the sudden violent kicking of her baby. Sometimes the foot banged so hard against her stomach she could feel its heel with her hand. 'He doesn't like it in there,' she said.

'Only six weeks to go, Mummy.'

Margery was waiting for Jaimie Laurenson to arrive then they could go in to dinner.

Jaimie had business in London, so he thought he'd call on Jane Kirkland. There was no answer at the flat, and as he was leaving the tenant below poked her head out and said, 'She's gone.'

'D'you know where?' he asked.

The woman came out of her flat deciding to trust him. 'She owes money to everyone. You too?'

'I came to give her some,' he said. So he paid the woman the thirty shillings Jane had borrowed for so-called launderette and baby food and a further fifteen shillings for milk. 'Of course she drinks,' said the woman. 'Oh, she's been shocking. Drunk and sick and that baby crying all hours. Twice my husband called the police. They wanted to take the baby and put him in care.'

Jaimie didn't want the story to get any worse. Hadn't he warned Margery to do something and help the girl? What if she'd died, the baby too? He asked who else was owed money. He wanted to close up the whole sorry business. As he followed Jane's path of debt from the chemists's to the off-licence to the pub he sensed her desperate life and it made him thoughtful and sad. The whole area for him was subdued. He no longer saw its quick energy, the transient people, the spontaneous relationships, the fun.

'D'you know where she could have gone?' he kept asking.

'The baby should be in care. Best for both of them,' said the publican. 'I don't think she knew what day it was. The baby was left screaming hours at a time.'

Jaimie paid them all and his money meant silence.

He arrived back at the Château an hour late. Margery had held dinner until he joined them, he was that important to her. He saw immediately that someone had been doing things to Charlotte. He hoped she'd gone to a proper surgeon – so much plastic surgery was unstable. Her family complimented her on the changes as though she'd done something worthwhile. Charlotte talked about it quite openly. 'When he did my nose he said he could slant my eyes slightly. So I thought why not?'

'They're wonderful,' said Kay.

'So I went out to celebrate and spent – well, far too much in Saks –'

Margery thought the girl looked ready for love. She hoped when Marcello let her down that a good lover would come along and pick up the pieces. Perhaps he already had. Jaimie Laurenson, she was sure, knew all about that pleasure.

After dinner, Rick, wearing a gold suit and a black shirt, took them into the home movie theatre and showed some footage of starving people. 'I need a million and a half to get it going,' he said.

'What exactly is your purpose?' asked Jaimie.

'To help the starving help themselves,' Rick replied.

'You know you've already got one on your doorstep. Alex's wife. Do something about her.' Jaimie looked at them one at a time and his expression was hard. No one wanted to argue with that look.

'That's personal,' said Kay.

'So are those,' and Jaimie flung an arm up at the screen.

'Rick isn't interested in one self-destructive girl. He wants to save the world,' said Margery.

'Save yourself, arsehole,' muttered Kay.

'Not our money,' said Charlotte.

Margery looked at Jaimie for help.

'So you want to invest in these countries so the itinerent population can save itself?' he asked.

'I think it's insulting just to give them money,' said Rick. 'Help them to make their own.'

'I'm in favour there,' said Jaimie. 'But I think, Rick, you've got yourself in a muddle. Your marriage has made you too rich and it's worrying you. But Margery does not feel guilty about her money, nor do the others. So why don't you go and tour and raise the money yourself? A three-month world tour will give you the initial investment you've just mentioned.'

'He can't,' said Margery. 'Because of the baby. It's due in October. I want him here.'
'Well, leave it for a while,' said Kay. 'The poor won't have gone just because you've had a baby.'
Rick bit his nails, a bad sign. 'I want to do this. It's a way of saying thank you that I've found happiness with Margery. I think Margery wants it too. She just wants to be sure you're happy about it.' He looked at Kay, then Charlotte.
'But we're not,' said Kay.
'Wait a year,' said Charlotte.
'Someone else will take the idea,' Rick said.
'Oh ho,' said Kay. 'Two people can't have the same saviour role – I get it. You have been wearing white a lot lately.' Then she shut up, remembering Jaimie Laurenson was present.
Jaimie signalled to Rick to put away the slides and stood up. 'If Margery really wanted you to save Africa she'd give you some money. She wouldn't need her daughters nodding their heads.'
Rick turned to Margery. For the first time he was angry. 'Is that true?' he asked.
'Oh, Rick, I don't want you to go to those places. You'll come back with hate in your heart. You'll see things that will change you forever. Don't do it. Of course I didn't need the girls' permission – but I can't just give money away –'
'But you're rich!' Rick shouted.
'But it doesn't work like that,' said Margery. 'It's all tied up. And I don't want you to go.'
'I'll never forgive you.' Rick walked swiftly from the room, his gold clothes flapping.
Margery looked at Jaimie and laughed. 'How often have I heard that?'

Jacey and Kay had been indiscreet on the American film, and there'd been talk. Kay had been recognised in downtown LA dressed in boyish clothes escorting a very feminine Jacey. They were lucky because it didn't make the *National Enquirer*, but it did make Guido's neck of the woods.
His father asked, 'No baby yet, Guido? What's the matter with that girl? And why has she cut her lovely hair? A boyish crop?'

Guido said he didn't know any of the answers.

'No, you wouldn't,' said his father. 'But I do. Lucia phoned me. Your wife plays lovegames with another woman.'

'Guido knows!' Kay was strained and nervous like an over-strung horse.

Jacey tried to soothe her. 'Then go to the Greek. Or better still get him here.'

But the Greek was in Washington and not due back till the following month.

They'd found many different ways to make love. Neither of them could bear too much repetition. One of their variations was doing it in public; another, making home movies. As Jacey lay with her head between Kay's raised thighs she said, 'I'd love a man to be here watching. Wanting it. God I would. I'd love him to get so aroused he'd jerk off all over us. Then we could get that on film.' She stopped kissing and sucking Kay's body and sat up. 'I need it.'

'So who can you trust? And does he fit in with what you want?'

Jacey said, 'That man we had before. You said he knows your mother. Jaimie.'

'Oh, don't be stupid, Jacey. Then Mummy would know and I'd be out.'

'So marry the Greek and you get even more money.'

What Jacey didn't realise was that it wasn't just money.

'Also it would shut him up, the Canadian, if we had him on celluloid. And we'd make him pay.'

Kay was thoughtful.

'He's very rich,' said Jacey.

'How do you know that?' Kay asked sharply.

'Frey told me.'

'But Frey doesn't know him, does he? And you don't see Frey, do you?'

'Kay, I hate this jealousy. I told Frey I'd met him. Months ago.'

The next night Jacey had a participant – a friend of her cousin in Rome. He was a surgeon, owned several clinics, was very attractive and considered a fabulous lover, but he was bored.

Jacey and Kay did their act and he paid $20,000 for the experience. They had him on tape.

Kay enjoyed the feeling of power she got from having the girl while he wanted her. The second time they did it, Kay was concerned in case the man should touch Jacey and perform with her. The third one wanted to join in – he wasn't happy with just coming over them. He pushed Kay off and got on to Jacey. Kay grabbed his belt and struck his buttocks as he moved. He didn't like it, but she didn't like the way Jacey looked. He was definitely giving her pleasure.

Afterwards Jacey said, 'It wouldn't go wrong if you got Jaimie Laurenson.'

'So you like him.' Kay felt chilled.

'You brought the subject up.'

'I said, Jacey, if he comes snooping around tell him nothing. Deny you were ever in that Paris hotel.'

But people were talking. Maybe Jacey was right and she should marry the Greek.

. . . Chapter 42 . . .

Kay took Charlotte to lunch at the Italian restaurant in the hills where she was sure of good food and no one staring at her. 'The trouble about being a star is you change the chemistry of a room,' she said. 'You look into a restaurant and all the people are eating and getting on with their lives. If you go in all that is altered because you are the focus of that room. Everyone knows you've come in.'

'You, yes,' said Charlotte. 'You're a star.'

'And that's what I was coming to, kid. I'd have all that taken out of your bosom. I mean, if Marcello likes you he likes you, little Charlotte, not a stand-in for Jayne Mansfield.'

'I told them not to put in too much. He said it would adapt. If it doesn't he'll adjust the shape next time.'

'Next time?'

'I'm going to have silicone in my lips, they're too thin. And my legs tapered, especially the ankles – that's a big job. And I want my chin pointed. When they handed out the Caversham looks Alex got the lot. And you, of course,' she added quickly.

Kay hastily changed the subject. 'Does Marcello like the boobs?'

Charlotte turned the same colour as the lobster.

'I mean, he has noticed, when you take your clothes off – surely?' And then Kay knew she was dealing with a virgin. 'Little sister, you have all this done which may or may not be harmful later on, to please a man I believe you haven't slept with. Now before you go and get jumbo lips you get him into bed. I mean it, Charlotte.'

Charlotte pushed away her food. She was about to run for it, but Kay took her hands and held them tight in a boyish grip. 'I really love you, Charlotte. You're the best of the lot – except Mummy. But don't keep changing yourself until you know he wants you. Has he made any –' she thought of a word to soothe her – 'overtures?'

'Yes, no. His eyes, they look at me. The expression changes when he sees me. He looks at me differently to anyone else in the world. But his mouth says, I'm married. I'm faithful to my wife.'

'Mixed messages,' said Kay. 'Fatal. He's a shit and he's confused.'

'He's not a shit,' said Charlotte.

'How long has this been going on?'

'Ever since I first saw him. Didn't he conduct at Margery's gala night in LA – oh, years ago.'

'Then it's time to ask him straight. Make a straight play. Life's too short.'

Charlotte released her hands. People were looking at them. 'You think I should? Confront him?'

'Seduce him. Get rid of the confusion. And if he's just playing with your feelings you'll save on surgery. Has he given you any real reason to think there's something between you?'

'I've reason to hope.'

Kay hated hope.

'Because his wife bleeds a lot. It might be the menopause. She doesn't want to sleep with him, so they haven't been doing it for a while. I overheard a conversation between Marcello and her doctor. They forgot I speak Italian. Also Marcello said to one of his friends how besotted he was by her when she was young, completely captivated by the way she looked and moved.'

Kay got the picture. 'You'll be operated on forever my sweet – she was sylph-like. Get a man who likes you the way you are, not one who wants you to become someone else.'

'I have. Their son. He's a doctor in Rome.'

Oh God, thought Kay, not the one who partied with her and Jacey. Would *he* be the next at the Château table? Luckily Charlotte's description made it clear he was too young.

'Marcello said to him, "Of course you like my darling Charlotte. Who wouldn't. She is not only charming but sweet with it."'

Oh no, thought Kay, this was not sexual. She said, 'Charlotte, you know what I think. Find out what he feels. Seduction's best – if he doesn't respond, then words.'

'You think so?' asked Charlotte. She was terrified of rejection.

'I do,' said Kay.

And then they got on to the subject of the impending birth. They both dreaded the new child.

'Rick's got thousands of his own,' said Kay. 'Julian told me. Why does he want Mummy's money? To put us down. And it makes saving the world more meaningful if it's Caversham cash. I hate him.'

The Greek liked Jacey's boat. It was a proper sailing craft, and skilfully he took it out to sea. And for an hour or two the girls had fun and didn't think about sex or problems. For once they felt free, even of themselves. The Greek certainly knew boats and got the best out of them.

They had dinner at a starry joint in Monte Carlo. Not Kay's idea, but the Greek liked the limelight and as far as he knew he had nothing to hide.

The girls dressed up for the occasion. Kay wore a black velvet 'les smoking' jacket cut like a man's dinner suit, with high-heeled black suede boots relieved only by diamond studs down her shirt front and in her ears. In contrast Jacey wore a dress made of perspex, like glass, completely transparent. Kay loved the dress, but only in private. She insisted that Jacey wear a slip underneath. Jacey refused and they had their first row. In the end Jacey covered the dress with Kay's black velvet cloak.

The Greek assumed Kay had wanted to speak to him about Shane.

'He's a nice kid but he needs a father. And he's lonely,' he said.

'He loves you,' said Kay. 'We all do. You know that.'

He didn't, but she'd put him on his guard and he talked briefly about the proposed marriage to the shoe heiress. She was stimulating because she supported the arts and he met everybody. He loved creative people, if they were famous. He talked about his Japanese pianist mistress. He didn't like the Japanese gay writer who was now getting a lot of attention. For some reason he felt compelled to go on and on about gays and how much he disliked them. Drag acts made him sick. 'If you're made one way why pretend to be another?'

Jacey's eyes crossed. The after-dinner entertainment would have to be changed.

When they got back to the boat Kay got the drink out and Jacey started dancing. Then she took her dress off and danced with the Greek. She asked Kay to join in, but Kay held back as though such a thought had never occurred to her.

'Come on,' said Jacey to the Greek. 'Let's get her clothes off. She's so stuck up.'

Kay let herself be stripped naked by the girl as though nothing like this had ever happened even in her fantasies. She put up the right amount of resistance, and then her suggestions seemed to come from a sudden desire to be bad. 'You fuck Jacey, then me,' she said to him. 'Then both of us together.'

The Greek got drawn into it by his own desire to conquer. He conquered Kay, but she'd already been ransacked hundreds of times. Jacey slept. Kay said, 'I've never felt like that. You're doing it to me is like taking drugs. I want it again. I've always wanted it with you. More and more of it.'

So he did it twice more, and she was turned on and receptive because Jacey was in there with her, stroking her.

The next day the Greek said, 'Don't be too innocent, ma chérie. A little is all right.' He'd seen her with Guido and knew her action. She explained that away by saying Guido was gay and had made her life hell – she hated being sadistic.

'Get rid of him,' were the Greek's words.

She said Guido put out rumours about her to cover his own play.

The Greek called her the next day and wanted a twosome. She didn't know how good she'd be without Jacey. She told him her problems, even cried. He stroked her cropped hair and told her not to worry. He was big enough for both of them. In the end it was his idea that they should marry. She raised plenty of objections, making sure they always ended with a bed scene. Margery dealt with the Guido divorce. It was so smoothly done that the Italian hardly had time to move his stuff from the Paris apartment and the villa in Cagnes. The locks were changed, the joint cheque book returned. Margery used only one argument: how dare Guido Cortese employ private detectives to follow her daughter? She didn't believe for a minute in the Greek marriage. That was just another attempt on Kay's part to find – her identity? But the Greek was certainly more capable of making Kay stable than the Italian. Margery accepted that the Greek did not love her daughter. On his part it was a business transaction to improve his social position. Kay would attract the unreachable. To Margery that was completely understandable. Kay was not being deceived. After all, she loved someone else. But who?

Guido limped back to Milan in disgrace having wasted five years of his life. He could never be the same after knowing such glamour. He couldn't return to the person he'd once been. He married an up-and-coming opera singer and devoted himself to her career. La Scala had changed but so had he. Even if he was allowed his old dream, to be administrator, it wasn't big enough. He'd tasted too much but absorbed so little nourishment.

When the doctor left the Maestro's wife Charlotte called in to see her.

'I have to have my womb and ovaries taken out. I'll have to rest at least two months after that. It's more than you think, that operation. You'll have to look after Marcello.'

With tears in her eyes Charlotte promised she would.

'Is it the sedative or do you look – well, different?'

Charlotte couldn't answer. These days she dressed fashionably in all the pale icecream colours and frills that would have suited Rick, but she hadn't yet found her style.

'I know you're growing up, losing your puppy fat. Look after him, Charlotte,' Madame Tallaforos said.

And the Caversham girl burst into tears of sheer joy.

She spent hours looking at herself naked from all angles. Was she perfect enough for this man who searched only for perfection? She'd had her lips injected and they were now a little odd-looking as though she'd just been to a dentist and they were swollen from the anaesthetic. She hoped that when he kissed her they wouldn't slide about. Pain – well she could take that from him.

When he came back from the hospital she made his supper. He liked it simple. He flopped back on Charlotte's couch and took off his shoes. He trusted her. He said he couldn't stay near his wife because the concert tour could not be cancelled. He wondered if Charlotte would stay so his wife had daily visits – they got on so well. Charlotte nearly bit through the new lips. She said music was now also her life. She'd realised watching him it meant sacrifice. 'So I'd rather go with you, Maestro. Even though it hurts me to leave her in the hospital. Of course we love each other. Her and me.' She dithered, wondering how Kay would handle this. She put down her knife and fork and went into the bedroom. When she didn't come out he called to her and asked if she was all right. No answer. He left the plate of pâté and knocked on the slightly open door. No answer. Had she fainted? It was running into a medical week.

Nothing could have prepared him for what was standing by the bed. Her enormous pale breasts looked waxy in the light. He saw the thick pubic hair. He tried to look at an unerotic area but the breasts and pubic hair seemed to fill the room. She was moving towards him.

He wanted to say he liked her as a daughter, but she got him in a tight hold, her lips clamped to his. The breasts felt cool against his shirt. The bottom half of her was burning hot. He felt an erection shoot up automatically. His mind told him it was just a muscular reaction, nothing more.

She offered him the gift of her virginity. 'I don't care how much it hurts. I want you to do it.' And she told him how long and how much she'd loved him.

Marcello realised how selfish he was. Why hadn't he noticed the girl's passion? He was so absorbed in music he saw little else. And now one fine night life had caught up with him. There was no concerto in the world that could get him out of this spot. How had he been so blind and foolish? It was like walking in the back streets of Naples at three in the morning and being surprised if you got mugged. If he hadn't got an erection it would all be easier – he blamed it on the long sexual abstinence. His vocation, as always, saved him. He said, 'I love you, Charlotte, but nothing can come between me and music. It's the way I am. If I became involved with you, which I could do so easily, the music would suffer. Please believe me.' He made it sound like a religion. He assured her that she was attractive. Hadn't she witnessed that by his reaction? He got his clothes straightened out and gently wrapped a robe around her. He would never forget how she'd offered him her pure body, they would always be friends, he said.

He had rejected her without once bringing his wife into it. He could so easily have had the girl and had his pleasure but it didn't compare with the joy he touched in the concert hall. And his wife was a partner in that joy. She made it possible. How could he be unfaithful?

Charlotte spent a night of torment. The musical excuse was bullshit. She remembered Dino explaining to her what bullshit was, how you could suss it out by the words they used. With Charlotte Dino was always right down there in the Naples streets. He taught her how to defend herself, to be streetwise. And now in her pain she could feel him beside her on the bed, his arms around her like when the kids said she was ugly at school.

'It's no good, Dino. I'm not as good as the wife and I never will be.'

And she could hear Dino in her mind answer, 'Don't shed one tear. The guy's a faggot.'

'Now that's bullshit,' she said aloud. And she laughed. She was almost cheered up because Dino felt so close.

The next day Charlotte left Marcello's employment. She took herself off to New York and had the silicone removed from her lips and reduced in her breasts. She confided in Kay, who said, 'D'you know, little sister, I think he does feel something for you. I think he loves you but his emotions are so suppressed, it all goes into the music. As Mummy says, she knows what work and dedication are, but it doesn't come near what he does.'

Charlotte longed for the wife to die so then she could take her place. In the meantime she accepted an invitation to dine with her mother's friend Jaspard, who was becoming politically powerful in France. She approved of him because he was left-wing. Once again she would have a cause to espouse.

. . . Chapter 43 . . .

Hollywood was lucky for Jane, starting at LA airport. Lydia Cobb said, 'I love your face. It's so lived, yet young. I'd love to paint you. I hope you don't mind my speaking out like that. I looked at you all the time on the plane. You've got such a sweet boy.'

Jane went to Lydia Cobb's apartment in West Hollywood. It was all new and bright and a good time was beginning. She posed for Lydia, a minor agent in one of the big theatrical corporations, four hours a day and got rent and food free. The rest of the time she spent looking at the city. The atmosphere was uplifting. This was where she should be.

She got a job serving tea in an old-world teashop where they were mad about her English voice. Another waitress did topless bar work at night. Jane said she'd do it too and soon she was earning enough to take movement, voice and acting classes. Lydia Cobb had friends at the university at UCLA, and students baby-sat. Jane learned to drive. She also learned to be happy without a man. Every day she told herself the past had gone, this day is new, a gift.

In January 1970 Lydia got her a small part as an English girl in a TV soap. She now had enough money to have her own place. She needed to be by the sea, so she took a small apartment in Venice, the city's arty sector. She went everywhere on roller skates, as did a lot of people in the neighbourhood, but she was so good she was nicknamed Skater. She started to incorporate her dance routines into her skating. A producer noticed her, and the next day she was the new symbol for an ad campaign against lead in petrol. Even the stars were beginning to know her – she was Skater. She was invited by the LA hostesses to functions to raise money for charity. She met all her heroes of the screen, except one. No one even mentioned Jay Stone. He'd disappeared. For a while, Lydia Cobb said, people were curious about his disappearance, but life went on and closed over the space Jay had left. And now it was as though he'd never existed.

And then she met Jaimie Laurenson.

Alex wrote to Lucien from San Francisco, 'Tell Jane to bring Kit out here. She could share my life. It's that kind of life.'

But Lucien didn't know where she'd gone. He went to Earls Court and made some enquiries but nobody said anything about her last, sick months. Jaimie Laurenson had cleared her debts and wanted one thing in return – silence. That way the press got nothing.

The Greek wanted the wedding to take place in Cannes before the film festival. Kay said she'd stay on afterwards because her new film was being entered in the competition. The producer planned to have a big showy boat and give parties and get plenty of publicity, Hollywood style. He wanted Kay around for that.

The Greek looked at her, his eyes wise. The face that so many women loved meant nothing to Kay. Sometimes she thought he looked like a clever lawyer or doctor, a professional man. 'Kay, I too have my business to attend to. I won't be with you all the time,' he said.

She nodded, trying not to look relieved.

'I'm sure you'll have your friend for company. Or Shane – he's always welcome.' He turned swiftly. 'I nearly forgot your birthday.' He opened a document case by the bed and gave her a flat box. Inside, a choker of rubies and diamonds lay coiled around a pair of matching earrings. She said how amazing they were and meant it.

'Let me put them on for you.' He fastened them around her neck and the unexpected touch of his hands made her shudder. As though he hadn't noticed, he fastened the earrings. If his very touch was starting to cause such a reaction, how was she going to handle the wedding night and all the nights that came after?

'They bring out your strong character, rubies – bold, fiery.'

'But I'm not at all. It's the last thing I am.' She tried very hard to be sweet. He came up behind her and said, 'Kay, what is it all about?'

She turned away from the mirror and gave him a lovely

smile. 'Is that a philosophical question? I can try and find out for you.'

'If it was, I wouldn't ask you. I have in mind, you and me.' He touched her chest, then his.

'If I've upset you in any way I'm extremely sorry. I think my experience with Guido has made me hesitant about men.'

'You don't love me. D'you think I don't know women? So why the marriage?'

'You asked me.'

'You worked it that way. I have to know, Kay. I'll still marry you.'

'All right, the truth. I'm afraid my career isn't going to work. So I need – well, a man. And I believe you want a Caversham in marriage. I'm better looking than my sister.'

He didn't like women putting things that bluntly, even if they were true. 'I'll look after you. But we have an agreement, Kay – no other man.'

She shrugged. That was no problem.

'You give all my parties and do the entertaining and arrange any introduction I may need. Paris, New York, occasionally London, Monte Carlo, here, but not Greece.'

She wondered what was in Greece.

'Also Sophia, my daughter, is put into the company of your brother.'

'Which brother? The older is out of the question. The other, too young.'

'And the only publicity we have is that which my advisors arrange. For example five pages in *Paris-Match*, the *Sunday Times* cover. You understand? And your career? Well, maybe I can make it a little brighter – we'll see.' He started to leave.

She was looking at the bed. 'What about that.'

'Oh, let's pretend,' he said. 'I have my pleasure in Greece with my own kind.'

And she thought, I have mine in Cannes with my own kind.

The baby was very late and they thought of inducing it. Margery stayed in her own bed in her own house and refused to be hospitalised. However, unknown to her, the doctor had brought in a whole staff and range of equipment from the clinic.

'The baby will come when it's ready,' she said. Her womb was so huge it pressed on her stomach and if she ate she threw up. Rick stayed by the bed calm and humorous.

'It's like me before a concert. But it can't stay in the dressing room for ever. The audience is waiting.' He tapped on her stomach. 'On stage. Last call.'

And her contractions began.

Rick held on to her hands. The nurse wiped her forehead. The pain was much worse than she remembered, but didn't they always say that? No, it was worse. She was getting into trouble. 'It's all right,' she said to Rick – she needed her hands free. She leant over the side of the bed, away from Rick, and was sick. She said to the nurse, 'Ask him to leave.' The doctor came in with a gas and air machine. He offered her a shot. She took the lot, mantras, shots, prayers. 'Dino!' she screamed and the baby started to come out. 'Dino!' The scream was huge; it filled the house. Margery clung to the doctor, groggy and confused.

'We've given you an epidural, Mrs de Palma, to stop the pain.' She didn't know who Mrs de Palma was. She asked again for Dino, her voice soft, pleading. Was this how he had felt lying on the pavement – shocked, numb, dying? She started to cry softly, and the baby plopped out.

They all looked quickly to see if it was normal. Its sex came later. Margery said immediately, 'If it's not all right don't show me. Let it die.'

'Why talk about death? You've had a beautiful, healthy, wonderful little girl.'

Jaimie was in LA for a couple of nights doing a deal on Margery's old movies. She'd decided to sell them off and so relinquish all control. Jaimie had located a very respectable offer. He stayed at the Beverly Hills Hotel as always and on the TV saw Jane Kirkland skating back into his life, introducing some cream. All he noticed was her face. He got her address from the ad production company and straight away took a cab to Venice. She was walking by the sea with Kit, who was now eighteen months old. The beach was crowded with men doing karate, running, skipping, and girls half naked selling paintings or home-made food. He crossed to Jane and spoke her name.

She turned, eyes blinking against the sun. She didn't know him but she liked what she saw. Stocky, a bit like Kirk Douglas, tough, attractive. Beautiful hands. No wedding ring. He shook hands and said he needed somewhere to talk.

'Here,' she said, and she sat on the sand and held the little boy close. He had Alex's eyes. She was wearing tight denim jeans embroidered across the front and down the legs in beautiful colourful inventive patterns that she'd done herself, white running shoes and a loose white string vest. She looked very clean. Jaimie was smart Hollywood, an Yves Saint Laurent sweatshirt and white trousers. A Boggi handknitted sweater was tied around his waist.

'Who are you exactly?' she asked.

'I'm handling the Caversham estate. I represent their interests abroad. Alex's mother would like to make you an allowance. After all, you have her grandchild. Alex too has made instructions to that effect.'

She didn't speak, just looked at him.

'So we could arrange for a regular payment every month for you and – I'm sorry, I don't know the little boy's name.'

'I don't want her money, thanks!' She got up, flushed with pride. She'd won – the first round.

'It's not so simple, Jane. You're owed this money, so you must take it.'

'Owed?'

'What bank are you with?' He had his pen out.

'Tell Margery Caversham I don't need her handouts.' Her voice was matter-of-fact. The emotional reaction was private – she kept it that way.

For some reason Jaimie felt insulted. 'All right, Miss Kirkland. But I want to agree one thing. You're fond of going to the press. If you go with one suggestion of a hard life, down on your luck, whatever, I will instruct the Caversham lawyers to come down on you hard. You've been offered the appropriate help and you've refused.'

'Prove it!'

'Sure.' He produced a tape recorder from his pocket. It was still running.

'Why d'you say a hard life?' She spoke clearly into the machine. 'I've done all right.'

And she walked off hating him.

Jaimie thought, doing all right as long as she kept a low profile. She'd be all right as long as she wasn't successful. If she touched Margery's world it would be over for her. It wasn't often he hoped people would fail.

He didn't tell Margery he'd seen her.

. . . Chapter 44 . . .

Kay was married for the second time in April 1970. Strings were pulled, money spent, so she got another church ceremony. It was a royal wedding again, attended by three thousand guests. It was one glide of pleasure and luxury. Kay remembered only one thing about her wedding – she was separated from Jacey. As she changed out of her wedding dress she wrote the girl a long desperate letter. Jacey was all she wanted and loved. They must run off together. She'd sell the wedding presents and jewels and they could live in a sultry land for the rest of their lives. She enclosed a pressed flower from her bouquet. 'The only real thing about this is you. I'm doing this for you.'

Kay cut the honeymoon short saying she had film commitments. The Greek asked if his being thirty years older than her put her off making love. She implied that had something to do with it. So they played cards, backgammon, chess, and sunbathed, and she got to know this man and even like him. He didn't have that sore desire that had made it impossible with Guido. The Greek had everything – she was just icing on his cake. After a tasteful Sunday-supplement spread she rushed back to Cannes.

At first Jacey's maid said she wasn't there. Kay thought she'd die, and the maid changed the story when she saw how ill the visitor looked. She got her a glass of water and said Jacey was playing tennis with an Englishman. This was the super-rich, super-smart choice of Jacey's mother. Jacey crossed to Kay, her racket twitching, face sulky. She was wearing orange hotpants, a minuscule black suntop and plimsolls.

'Get rid of him,' Kay said.

'Let me finish my game, please!' Jacey snapped, her mouth ugly with temper.

Kay grabbed her arm and shook her. 'Get rid of that person. I'll wait in your bedroom.'

Kay walked off, her legs shaking. Jacey took an hour to finish her game, shower and confront her lover. She chose to wear a completely transparent dress made of plastic that looked like glass. She'd painted her pubic hair gold and wore sequins around her nipples. 'The Glass Dress' had been made famous by the press and its shock value was everything that Jacey could desire. Kay tried to shatter it with one blow; the plastic remained unscathed. Jacey jumped over the bed, out of danger, and said, 'People in glass houses shouldn't throw stones. You marry, go round the world for weeks, and I'm supposed to drop my racket, leave a guest and jump into bed.'

'That's right.' Kay closed up on her, started taking off the offending dress. She'd learned a lot of new technique from her husband. 'I can't wait for you.' She laid the girl back over the bed. 'With it or without it. You choose.'

Jacey turned her head as though embarrassed. Kay, sensing trouble, sat beside her. 'What is it, darling?' she asked.

The girl didn't answer.

'I did it all for you – for us. Now we can really be together.' And she turned Jacey's face round and kissed her. She told her how she hated being with the Greek but had thought hotly of Jacey. Kay made love to her and at the climax of her sexual act she heard Jacey say coldly, 'If only you were a man.'

'What a thing to say at a time like that.' She turned and looked at Jacey, who hadn't even been aroused. Using her hand she made Jacey come but it was flat and mechanical. There was a definite coolness. 'What do you mean, Jacey – you wish I was a man?'

'Oh, don't go on. It slipped out.'

The truth was that Jacey was tired of the dyke scene. She liked variety, spice, and it was time to move on. She did know that Kay loved her and she had, for a while, genuinely been passionate in return. She did not want to hurt her.

'Look, I'm getting to the age where I've got to get it together. I'll be thirty before I know it. You're all right – you're married.'

'I'll look after you.'

'I don't get invited to your house. I'm not good enough.'

'Oh, Jacey, how can you come up there? Mummy would see through us in a minute.'

'So?'

Kay thought about it. Margery might accept it – she was

usually liberal about people unless they attached themselves to the family. But Kay couldn't imagine them sitting as a couple at dinner. Nor could Jacey.

'To be honest, Kay, I've thought about it. I don't like the dyke bit. What is our future? You in a suit and me in frills? We'd be pitied. I think there's something sad about lesbians. Not us, because we've had fun, but the serious ones. Until I fell for you it wasn't something that turned me on at all. It's the wickedness I've liked.'

'What you're saying, Jacey, is we can't go public.'

Jacey nodded.

'You're right. Because I want to be a movie actress and that sort of thing would kill me at the box office. The guys wouldn't pay to see me.' Then she told Jacey how much the Greek had settled on her, how much she had a month. 'When I'm not needed for his parties we can travel or make movies. I'll buy you a home.'

Jacey laughed. 'You sound just like the Greek.'

Kay's eyes closed. How she would love to be the Greek, to be a man with that kind of presence and power. 'But then I wouldn't be beautiful,' she said.

She returned to Jacey the next night wanting love, reassurance and support. Jacey wanted to be out on the town doing things. She was dressed in the apple-green petticoat and scarlet towering shoes. This outfit had become a symbol of Jacey's nights out. Kay tried to make her less sensational. She'd bought the girl a dozen exotic silk kimonos, which Jacey ruined by winding around the waist the ties of the men she'd had, dozens of them, like scalps on a totem pole.

'Why do you do it, Jacey?'

'Why not? Some people like to wear their medals.'

That night their relationship was definitely changed. It didn't have the usual mixture of harmony and excitement. Then Kay tried too hard, and Jacey hated lovers who became insecure, desperate. They ended up doing the sex act for a stranger, something Kay was always dead against. She made sure he had no camera or tape recorder His prick showed he was in for genuine action, but she didn't like the way Jacey played with it instead of with her – she even offered him a blow job. Kay struck her hard. The man said he'd like a rematch. He had a friend who'd love this – he implied royalty. It would have to be discreet. He'd offer a gift rather than money, if that was acceptable. He'd come back to Jacey with a date and time.

Kay distrusted it, but Jacey loved it.

'We play around and get more money than the world's best hookers. Come on, it's fantastic,' she enthused.

'Is it the money?' asked Kay.

'Of course not. It's the power,' said Jacey. And she promised when Prince Charming got his pants down they'd get that on celluloid.

As Kay didn't know who the royal personage was she couldn't check if he was one of her mother's friends. She did check that the original player was the person he said he was, a gambling aristocratic playboy. Kay insisted she wear a mask over her eyes. Jacey said they really needed a pimp to protect them. Kay knew it was wrong. A sudden compulsive sexual get-together was one thing; a sex show planned a week ahead, cold and deliberate, was dangerous. Jacey was insistent. She preferred a threesome which got her out of a twosome she no longer desired. The original man came in first and said the royal visitor, for reasons of security, would have to remain in shadow. A single light over the bed was sufficient.

'What about my security?' Kay put on her mask. 'I have to have a guarantee of his identity.'

The man showed her a ring with a crest which meant nothing to Kay. Then he showed her the payment, a gold cigarette case and lighter decorated with jewels. Before she could open it he took it away and the new visitor was in the room. He stood in the dark, wearing a scarf hiding his lower face, dark glasses and a hat pulled down low. He was slightly over medium height.

'Get on with it. You've been paid,' said the first man.

Jacey liked the touch of cruelty, it got her going. She asked him to spank her as she made it with Kay. For once she was on top.

The visitor saw that Jacey liked the man and Kay liked Jacey. He left before the show was over taking off his shoe lifts, which put him back at five foot seven. The first man pulled up his trousers and handed Kay the cigarette case and lighter.

'Where is he?' asked Jacey.

'He's seen enough.' The man signalled to Jacey, a kind of promise of return, and was gone.

Kay opened the cigarette case. Inside, engraved in diamonds, 'To Kay my Wife'. And the Greek had signed his name.

Although she went straight to his apartment in Monte Carlo she had to wait until the next day to see him. She was pale and overwrought when finally he summoned her in.

'So you do shows for men?'

'Yes.'

'Why?'

'It turns me on. Jacey likes it. It's kind of frightening, which makes it more exciting I suppose. Like Russian roulette. It's dangerous, I know.'

'And you've got them all filmed?'

She nodded.

'It is dangerous, Kay. Because some of your clients may not like being filmed. Does Jacey intend to blackmail them?'

'Heavens, no! They're just exciting to watch afterwards. We watch them quite a lot.'

He was surprised she was so honest, but more that he hadn't spotted it, which indicated some flaw in him. He didn't take the making love with her own sex seriously. It was just two girls having fun. The male audience worried him though. He wanted to protect Kay, and couldn't believe his luck that the aristocratic gambler they'd picked up had recognised Kay Caversham during the original orgy, but would say nothing because of his loyalty to the Greek. The gambler, when telling the Greek of the incident, suggested that Kay go to a shrink. But the Greek could not get over-worried about a woman he wasn't sleeping with indulging in gay sex.

'You'll grow out of it, Kay. Lots of girls play around with each other.'

'Darling, I'm twenty-six. I know I'm not in a very good position, but please can I ask one thing? Don't tell my mother.'

When she'd left, the Greek sat on his terrace and thought long sad thoughts. He was fifty-seven, in his prime, and he had a very sexy, insatiable wife who did it with another girl for strangers. She'd obviously married him for protection and a cover. His eldest son wanted to be a racing driver, but on the streets of Athens. Sophia couldn't get a husband or lover, in spite of the money. The other three were so-so, but nothing had gone right emotionally since his wife died. He thought of her with love, how they'd come from the same poor beginnings. Maybe if they'd stayed poor they'd have been luckier. He got up and poured a large drink. The day he turned on money he was licked.

Kay considered a sex change. She believed it was the only way she'd keep Jacey. She talked to a Parisian transvestite who worked the streets near Les Halles.

'I think you can only get it done in Morocco. Somewhere like that.' The boy said he'd get Kay an introduction. 'It's usually the other way round.' He giggled. 'Make sure they keep your boobs. I'll have them.'

Kay thought they might go together and swap. As long as he had a big penis – Jacey needed that.

Before she booked into the clinic in Marrakesh she wrote her will, leaving everything to her love. And she wrote a letter of explanation to her mother. She no longer cared about a career in movies. She just wanted the girl.

Discreet enquiries had been made. It was a long, difficult and hazardous operation. She'd have to stay in Morocco for several weeks. Then she went to see Jacey. She'd waited until her mind was made up before telling her. Of course she'd expect Jacey to come with her to Marrakesh.

Robert Frey sat on Jacey's bed as though he belonged there, quite casual, smoking a cigarette.

'Where's Jacey?'

'Jacey is your worst fucking nightmare. You know why?'

Shakily Kay sat down.

'Because she knows me. Now, Kay, I asked you for something and you haven't had the courtesy to reply. I want your mother's permission to film Dino's story. I want family photographs. I want to live inside all of you. In exchange you remain Kay Caversham, wife of the shipowner. If I don't get what I want I give your story and copies of you and Jacey on the videos go to the press. I've even got the one of your husband coming in as Prince Charming. Of course he was taller, he wore lifts. I'll break you, Kay. I'm not an artist, I'm a businessman. Someone, someday, will get that story and, its going to be me.'

'Did she tell you?'

'Of course – she tells me everything,' said Frey impatiently. 'I own her.'

Kay walked along the coast for hours. Night, day, then night again. She was recognised. Someone said she looked in bad shape and the chauffeur sped thirty-five kilometres to get her. She couldn't put up too much of a fight – she'd lost hours ago.

Margery's doctor sedated her but she still tried to get to Jacey. She phoned, but Jacey was never there.

She kept hearing the baby crying. She wasn't sure it wasn't her. For hours Margery sat by her bed. They gave her soup, and she spat it out. She wanted to die. So they injected her to soothe and give nourishment. She no longer cared about herself. She'd loved and lost because she'd been born in the wrong body. She'd never love again. But she did still adore her mother so she told her the whole story.

Margery nodded, and stroked her hand. Then she got up. 'Frey will never play Dino.' The power in her voice made Kay shiver. It belonged in a Greek tragedy.

Margery called Jaimie Laurenson in New York and spoke for nearly an hour. Two days later, Frey, surrounded by his usual bodyguards, walked on to the location outside Paris, and a man, believed to be an extra, threw acid in his face.

Frey, lying disfigured in a Paris clinic, would never work again. The attacker had got away. Some said it was the Left opposing Frey's backing of a politician on the far Right. Or a demented cinematic rival? A cast-off mistress?

The acid attack had been agonising and got part of his left eye, leaving it without vision. Even his hair had been burned. The only plus in the disaster was that the attacker, in his speed to get it over with and get away, had only reached Frey's left profile. The right side of his face was untouched. It would be months and many skin grafts later before he'd even be sure what he'd look like. It might be too much of a horror story to go out on the street.

Frey took it well. He'd lived a tough gang life before getting big in movies, and he knew all about vendettas and retaliation. But acid? For him this was a first. It suggested a woman's touch. His friends gathered around the bed writhing with sympathy. One said, 'Frey, what do you want?'

'Get me a dozen eye patches. All kinds – Yves Saint Laurent, Cardin.' He laughed. 'I could start a new fashion. And get me something pretty to look at. Bring me a photograph of Margery Caversham. Then I'll know I'm going to get well.'

Jacey got the hell out of France, afraid she'd be the next victim. She couldn't consider marrying an English aristocrat now. The revenge that might attract was too horrible to contemplate. She didn't know how to lie low – her sexual appetites made that difficult. She spun around the world for several months in out-of-the-way places, then ended up in a village near Malaga. At the local fiesta she'd danced with a young shepherd and had taken him to bed. He was a virgin. She liked it enough to stay in the village. She had plenty to teach him.

Margery found her daughter's farewell letters and will. She cancelled the clinic appointment in Marrakesh. For some reason Kay had chosen the name Jane Kirkland. Later, Kay said it was the only one she could think of that no one would ever know.

Margery promised her she'd get through this. It all came down to willpower and dedication. Work was the answer. And the bad experience would only add to her stature as an actress. Every day Margery fired her ambition. She exercised with her, walked in the grounds, swam, read plays with her, coached her in front of a camera.

Finally Margery chose a Clifford Odets script, *The Big Knife*. What's more, Kay would star with Rick de Palma – so she couldn't fail.

. . . Chapter 45 . . .

September 1970 and Jane got the big one, the part that made her name. In a small-budget film about street life she played Skater. Street life was something she'd experienced. She hated the poverty, exhaustion, uncertainty, but it had a strange kind of energy. It wasn't romantic, whatever people wanted to think. She was very pushy with the script, kept changing things. The writer got angry but she said, 'I just have to. I've been there.'

Jonny Citta, the Sicilian director, liked her input. He was now the hottest director in Hollywood. His first film *Terracina*, had picked up three Oscars and five nominations. He was very keen on using actual street characters to get the movie he wanted, which was how Jane came to get the part. Two recently reformed thieves – reformed since they'd got in the movie – were playing opposite her. Jonny Citta was mad about poker, and Jane kept him company in LA and Las Vegas. He lost. She won. She said it was because he had more money so got reckless, whereas she went on instinct and couldn't afford to lose. She always knew where she was in a group. If she felt like a loser she folded.

Jonny gave Kit a party on his second birthday. Her friend Lydia Cobb presented a portrait of Kit. Absurdly it reminded Jane of Alex's painting of the zoo bird, and for a moment she felt a surge of grief. She had been so happy – how had it gone wrong? Margery Caversham. In the Château Alex had felt belittled, in his mother's home. Margery had cut his balls off and blown away the marriage. Jane would get even. She looked at Jonny Citta – she was getting even already.

The next day Jaimie Laurenson came on to the set. For a moment she'd forgotten who he was. He looked like one of the money men around Jonny. Didn't they always wear Italian suits? But he'd come to see her skate.

'Of course I can't throw him off the lot,' said Jonny. 'He draws water in this town. He's our lawyer, for one. Or he owns the firm that has the lawyer. He's pals with my exec producer, Mo Cohen.'

Jaimie said to him, 'I want to take Skater out for lunch,' so Jonny told her she was through for the day.

Jane did not want to lunch with Mr Laurenson. 'I wish Margery Caversham would leave me alone. I don't want anything from her. Or her son.'

'I think that's unfinished business, but that's not why I'm here. I wanted to see you.'

He tried not to look at her shapely thighs, which were shown to full advantage by the denim hotpants. She wore a denim sleeveless backless top and nothing else. Because the clothes made her feel suddenly vulnerable she changed into her calf-length gypsy skirt of many colours and soft suede shirt, tied at the waist. She asked why he wanted to see her.

'To get to know you, I suppose.'

'There's lots of people I'd like to get to know. Marlon Brando, for example. But I can't just go up to Mulholland Drive and ask him out to lunch. I'm not going to the press with my hard luck stories or any personal revelations, so go and lunch with a starlet.'

He was smiling at her. His eyes were warm, flecked with gold lights when he was amused. 'I'm not going to hurt you, Jane.'

'No you're not,' she promised him.

They ate in an out-of-the-way fish place between Malibu and Zuma beach, where the sea had strong currents. He asked if she had an agent. She shrugged. She wasn't telling him anything.

'The last time I had an agent Margery Caversham got to him, or at least his wife, and I didn't have a job.'

'Margery loves her children.'

'Sure, I love my son,' she said quickly. She liked the way he ate. It was casual and graceful at the same time and made her feel relaxed. 'You could have been a movie actor,' she said.

'No, thanks. I like the background.'

'What exactly do you do?'

'Business. It has me running around the world. I'm here for five days then on to Sydney then off to Switzerland, then Cannes.'

'How does your wife deal with the jetlag, or doesn't she travel?'

'No wife.' It was final, the way he said it, so she let the subject drop.

After lunch they walked along the beach. In spite of everything, she liked the man – worse, fancied him. He held her hand and it was as though he'd made love to her completely. It had that sort of impact. She gasped and pulled away her hand.

'Mr Laurenson, I want to hang loose, as they say around here. I've had a very unusual time. I want the rest of my life to be at least bearable.'

'Perhaps you haven't got over Alex. But don't turn him into a fantasy like you did the racing driver. Jane, I could have shot that exposé down – it was so full of holes.'

'I loved that man. He died. I don't want to talk about it.'

'You knew him for twenty minutes and made twenty thousand pounds. You gave half to the ghost writer.'

She was amazed at the stuff he'd got hold of.

'Think what you like. I loved him. And I think it was reciprocal.'

'Tell me one thing to make me believe it.'

'He couldn't go on with his life as it was. Sometimes he didn't know how to get through the next five minutes.'

'OK, perhaps you could only tell that to a stranger. Did he have a nickname for you?'

'Why?'

'He did for his wife.'

'He called me Toots.'

'I could call you Toots.'

'He called me that because he drove a car and you toot a horn, honey. Also he called me Starry Eyes. I don't have to justify my relationship with Del Grainger. Margery Caversham can't hurt me there. The man's dead. Do you work for Del Grainger's wife too?' Of course he didn't – she wasn't fast lane.

She still almost believed in her Del Grainger affair. It had been fuelled by drink. When the drink was drained away, the fantasies remained stubborn, dry and hard like fossils.

'I want to help you, Jane.'

'Then stay out of my life,' she said promptly. She never expected to sound so hard. She realised that in her new life she had to be hard in order to handle the everyday routine, looking after Kit, the classes, the rejections. No one got one on her. But love took her away from her centre. She was no longer in control. Once again, by wanting joy, she would end up a victim.

He had hold of her hand again. He considered her a suitable sexual partner, the female submissive type he liked. But what he really liked about her was that she said no. By rejecting Margery Caversham she was rejecting him and that made him all the more determined to seduce her. But then he saw there was more to it than that. She was like him. They'd both been bitterly hurt, almost over the edge. They'd come back and got it right and would never be hurt again. And neither of them would ever reveal one glimpse of what they'd suffered. Yes, that was why he liked her. So he treated her as he would himself: no demands, no requests – the answer would be negative. The people who succeeded with him were the ones that got on with their lives and were just there, their mouths not hanging open all day with demands for love and company and constant reassurance. He decided not to ask her out to dinner. Again his hand was in hers. Plenty of electricity there, enough to light up the beach. He liked the way her fingers pulled away from his, and at the last minute just as she thought she was getting free, his held on tight. That's how the sex would be: intense, tight, a chase with no one doing any running.

'Who do you go out with now?' he asked.

'I go around with Jonny Citta.'

'Del Grainger, Alex Caversham, now Jonny. All big names. I wonder why? To get what they've got? Fame? You don't have to associate with famous people. You're good enough to get recognition for yourself.'

'Isn't that what I'm trying to do?' She took her shoes off and walked along the water's edge. Never think of the past – every thought positive. She was all right as long as she was centred. This man took her away from herself, made reality a little different. He watched her as though she gave him pleasure. But wasn't that the secret of all charming people? They made you feel fantastic then they were gone.

'I still think you should have some money invested for Kit. You're doing very well. But if you hit a hard patch you need to be independent. And then it's nice if you can choose what you do.'

'I don't want her money.'

'It's mine.'

She stopped and looked at him closely. 'Do you owe me?'

He shook his head. 'Jane, I never saw you until a few months ago here on the beach. I've never crossed you, but its a hard world.' He was thinking of Margery's reaction to Jane's Skater role in Jonny Citta's film.

She declined his offer and said she had to go.

'Better get the Del Grainger story straightened up.'

'Why?'

'Because if you start to make it big they'll ask you about it.' What he also meant was that if she started to make it, Margery would rake the story up and expose it as false. He had the urge to surround this girl with his protection. She was professionally vulnerable and worse, stubborn. He watched her walk along the seashore, in and out of the water.

She thought, if I get involved it will lead to pain. I'm fine alone. Every time I need sex I just think about fame. When I need love I think about success. Don't fuck me. Just make my name.

He thought, she won't take my money but I'll protect her. She won't know but I'll save her from the Cavershams. When Margery starts wanting her cut down I'll use what I've got on Kay.

. . . Chapter 46 . . .

Margery's baby girl was called Muriel after Margery's mother. Rick called her Frou Frou. She was the joy of their life. Rick thought it was perhaps the happiest time he'd ever known, and so unexpected. The only cloud was that Kay was home. She was getting over – well, he thought it was probably her life.

The day after Frou Frou's first birthday Jaimie Laurenson came to stay. Kay disliked the way Margery kept deferring to him. Didn't anyone else count? Couldn't she Kay give an opinion on the Irish troubles or the possibility of Concorde actually going ahead? Jaimie was very attractive. Jacey had thought so, and Kay thought her mother was not exactly indifferent to him. She treated him the exact opposite of the way she treated Julian.

Kay smiled at him, a long wolfy job. 'What are you into exactly, Jaimie? All we hear about is business. Had any threesomes?'

'Oh, Kay!' muttered Margery.

'I bet you like two at a time in an anonymous hotel.'

'No, I only like doing that at the Ritz – if it's Paris we're talking about.'

'So it's two at a time as long as they're anonymous?'

'As long as they're appealing.'

'Famous?'

'It helps.'

'Makes you feel good, does it?' She went on taunting him. She'd lost Jacey so who cared.

Margery tried to shut her up. No one else could. Kay said, 'Where were you just after the student riots in Paris?'

'Up you,' he said coldly.

Margery went rigid.

Jaimie said quite kindly, 'Your friend needed a proper man not a girl dressed up as one. She'd only have hurt you in the end.'

'You bastard! You still see her!' She got up from the table, her face scarlet.

'I don't see her. I haven't time.' He said it quickly before the plates went flying.

'All right, Mr Cool Guy, Margery's friend. If you're so smart find Jacey.'

He looked at her insolently. 'Why?'

'Yes, why?' asked Margery. 'You'd better think of that.'

'You don't think I'd let that slut slip away? She knows too much about me. I'm a Caversham, for heaven's sake. Find her, Jaimic, that's an order. And if anything happens to you, Mummy, I still take over. That' – and she pointed at Rick – 'does not mean a thing. Just remember, Daddy wouldn't like it. So no changing any wills.' And Kay left the room.

Margery said, 'She's not been well. But she's in preproduction with Rick. Mo Cohen will put up the budget. The Clifford Odets play. You know, *The Big Knife*.'

Jaimie laughed softly. 'Well named.' Rick overheard and crossed his eyes, indicating horror.

'I'd like George to direct her.'

'But I've said I'd like the new hot one, Jonny Citta, to direct me. OK?' said Rick sharply .

Jaimie wiped a hand across his face. Exhausted, needing a holiday, needing a rebirth almost, he would still have to get the next plane back to LA. Jonny Citta would have to be tied up good from now till Rick de Palma went back to singing. Jaimie owed it to the girl.

They did some street shooting in San Francisco. Jane, wearing white suede hotpants, and a silk scarf tied around her breasts, skated into a bar for a Coke and found Alex sitting at the counter. His hair was almost to his waist and he had a beard. He didn't quite have bells around his neck but he should have.

'So you've come,' he said, by way of greeting. 'Where's my kid?'

She wondered what drug he was on that had so transformed things.

'I wrote to Lucien. I told him to send you and Kit out here. It's great.'

'Just one of the problems, honey – I hate to be logical, but there was no money. You remember when you left –'

'But I instructed them to give you a third of my allowance –'

'Since when did they listen to your instructions?'

He couldn't remember when he'd last seen her. Was it two Mays ago?

'Come and meet my wife. She doesn't speak English and I'm going to keep it that way. She's a very harmonious person.'

'Wife?'

'Well, life goes on.'

Just then Jonny Citta came into the bar. 'Hey, Skater, guess who's on the line for you? Jaimie Laurenson calling from LA.'

'Jaimie Laurenson,' said Alex. 'He looks after my mother's investments. You want to be careful. He used to look after Jay Stone.'

Jaimie was waiting in her apartment when she got back to LA. He was playing with Kit, showing him how to put together a miniature bicycle made of Lego. Kit only wanted to bash him over the head with the pieces. The nanny, a young director just finishing film school, hung around till Jane got back. The Canadian had told her she could go. He seemed to know Kit but that didn't mean he couldn't kidnap him. Jane said she was right to stay.

Jane felt the Canadian's appearance in her flat was an intrusion. She didn't mind people dropping by, in fact it was full of friends non-stop, and music and phone calls from earliest morning until ten at night – Hollywood went to bed early. But she did mind the Canadian. It was a functional apartment with a sofa that could turn into a guest bed, floor cushions, an exercise bike and gym equipment, a good sound system, a juice extractor, James Dean posters on the wall. Her bed was indisputably single. Jane's place was good for parties or to just relax in. People felt they could be themselves there: you weren't self-conscious, there was nothing to protect – it was just somewhere to be easy. Really it was a hotchpotch of objects necessary for her advancement and Kit's playtime. Her life wasn't led indoors but out on the boardwalk or beach.

She didn't want to be alone with Jaimie in the apartment so took him down on to the beach. Everyone in the neighbourhood knew her and Kit. She was wanted, part of it.

'You like it here, don't you?' asked Jaimie.

'It's the very best time. It must stay that way.'

Jaimie asked how much Jane would be used to promote the film. She didn't know. What was Jonny doing next? What was all this? She was sure Jaimie had enough pull to ask himself.

'He said he wants to work with McQueen. He's got a script about a poker game. He's mad about poker. He wants me for that. Sort of a street pusher to get people into the game – I wear a scarlet dress, a lot of glamour.'

'No skates there.'

'Just high heels. When I put those on I usually get into trouble.'

'I think you should do theatre,' said Jaimie. 'You could become typecast working with Jonny, and who knows when he's going to burn out? He has a very compelling coke habit.'

'Isn't there anything you don't know?'

He turned to her quickly. 'Whether you like me.'

'I'm better off alone.'

'Don't you have anybody?'

'No, I haven't. Not since Alex.'

'You haven't had any sex? That's a long time.'

'Not for losers. I haven't found anybody. And frankly if I'm busy my mind stays off it. If I feel like it I just wait for the feeling to go. It always does. It's a hell of a lot better than getting into wanting someone and they let you down. Fame is a wonderful replacement.'

He was looking at her, unsure whether to believe what he was hearing. 'I'd like to sleep with you.'

She thought that was quite a brave thing to say seeing he must know he'd get rejected. 'It's nice to know,' she said.

'You already know. As I know you want me. We may or may not act on it. In the meantime go to the Neighbourhood Playhouse. I've talked to them about you. You'd get a lot of range there, Jane.' It would also keep her off Margery's patch.

She went back inside and realised she didn't want to sleep with anyone again. That belonged to the time before the dark terrible months alone in Earls Court. She couldn't allow herself to enjoy the act of love, not all the time the Cavershams were standing strong and powerful.

When Jaimie got back to Cannes he told Margery he'd seen Jonny Citta. He considered him a bad business proposition because he had a coke habit.

'As long as he keeps it to himself,' said Margery.

'Oh, come on,' said Jaimie irritated. 'He'll make a coke movie and they're obvious a mile off. He keeps his coke inside an inflatable sex doll.'

Margery laughed raucously. 'Rick wants him, so get him. Or I'll use my agent Susie Landor. She still represents me if I ever decide to go back. That's ten per cent of a lot of bucks, Jaimie. On the other hand if you get Jonny Citta you do the deal. And say I did go back, you get that deal.'

'Why?'

'Because you're my idea of a man. There's not a lot around. You're the old pioneer type. I wish you'd sink the Greek and all his goddam boats and marry Kay.'

He was quite amazed by Margery because usually she was very astute. Apart from being a pioneer type he only married for love.

Margery had a little girl, and a young superstar who loved her. The house should be happy, but it wasn't. Dino kept coming into her mind – sometimes as she and Rick made love. She would become chilled as though he were there at the end of the bed watching, sapping her energy to support his earthly appearance, and the lovemaking would stop as abruptly and as finally as if chopped by a guillotine. She thought secretly of Alex, of the wrong he'd done her. How she wanted his love and approval. She'd wring her hands and murmur, 'We used to be a happy family.'

And then she saw a photograph of Skater in a film magazine. The improbable person had married her son, insulted her and was now roller skating her way into Margery's world. She phoned Mo Cohen in LA.

'Yes, she's around,' he said. 'At parties and benefits. A street kid. Thin. Nice tits. She's quite popular with the underground lot. Jonny Citta likes her. She sets clothes trends with the street kids – in fact all the kids.'

Margery hung up. 'Do one thing, you tart, and I'll get you. Step over my line. I'm waiting,' she said.

How come Jaimie Laurenson was so subdued on the subject? Margery went to talk to her daughter. Kay seemed steady. She did her dinner parties and galas for the Greek, she wore amazing clothes and hung on to his arm, and they went to premières and benefits and parties and clubs. But underneath the polite façade, he was remote and she was seething. He had his mistress in Greece and she was desperately looking for Jacey. Laurenson had finally put a team on to it. For once he'd not been successful. No one could find her.

The house seemed empty. Shane was away with the Greek, and Charlotte was a permanent house guest of Jaspard. He was now head of the Opposition party and had a tough wife. Charlotte was always suffering in someone else's marriage. Margery hoped that at least the Frenchman would give her some pleasure.

At the end of the corridor Margery saw Dino. Her heart leapt and she tried to cry out for Julian. Icy cold, she could go neither back or forward. Then she managed a scream. Jennifer opened the office door.

'Go and see who that is.' Margery pointed. 'That figure.'

Jennifer started along the corridor, then stopped. 'Ma'am, it's no one. It's a roll of carpet with a box at a funny angle.'

'Get it out of the corridor!' Margery shouted.

'We're having this whole wing redone, don't you remember? It's always too cold here.'

Margery nearly strangled her, she'd had such a fright. She made herself approach the box and the roll. No, this wasn't what she'd seen. He, the shade of Dino, was in front of these objects. 'Come here, Jennifer. Why is it so cold here?'

'Ma'am, it always is.'

'But it's not a cold day.' Whenever Dino was present in her bedroom the temperature dropped.

Jennifer put a soft hand to her mouth. 'Oh, Ma'am. It's not a ghost, is it?'

It was that day that Margery noticed Frou Frou's eyes. They didn't look normal.

The doctors said children, as they developed, looked quite terrifying sometimes. She was a perfectly normal little girl.

'But she doesn't walk,' said Margery.

'Worry about that at eighteen months.'

Margery rang Mo Cohen again and asked how much he knew about Jaimie Laurenson.

'Margery, you know more than any of us. If there's a difficult job to be done he's the man. Dynamite. Very good business know-how. Uses it to his own advantage. He does a lot in a day. No steady woman. A loner. You know his track record's impeccable – you checked it yourself.'

Margery wanted it fixed so that when Jaimie went to LA he was under surveillance.

Mo laughed, 'But that's the job he does.'

'Do it!' She hung up, angry at the thought that Jaimie could betray her. Next using Jaspard's influence she got the Minister for Home Affairs. She wanted Jacey found quietly. It was a small private matter.

When Jaimie visited the next week she asked how the Jacey search was progressing.

'She's dropped out of sight.'

'If I was looking for her I'd start with her mother. That's her money source.'

Jaimie asked how much money he should spend on this.

'Don't even count. Find her.'

He was surprised because Margery was usually frugal. Her staff were adequate, but she liked a close watch kept on household bills. She spent plenty on clothes but that was considered professional. Her indulgence was food. She liked people to eat well. Even the staff didn't complain.

'You've not done very well at finding Jacey,' she said. 'Being such an attractive man I thought you'd enjoy it. I mean, you like the bad girls.' And she laid out the picture of skater Jane Kirkland. It was in a tat magazine, not one he'd thought she'd see. 'Don't tell me you saw Jonny Citta sniffing all this coke yet you didn't see her?'

'Margery, I didn't think you wanted to know about her. I was not under the impression I was meant to find her.'

'But she's doing OK.'

He was on the spot. How much did Margery know? He must never visit the girl in LA again.

'I gather she's functioning, just about. Nothing big.'

'Who does she see? Come on, Jaimie. We know Alex is in the next big town, which is no doubt why she's living where she is.'

So he came clean and told Margery he'd offered the girl an allowance and had given her a warning about going to the press. He'd done a lot of warning her.

And Margery realised this man was all right after all. Maybe hate made you suspicious.

'And as for Jacey,' he said, 'finding her won't do your daughter any good. She's no threat. The Frey incident took the steam out of her.'

And then he noticed Frou Frou's expression. He hoped, how he hoped, it was just a baby simper combined with his jetlag.

'She's dribbling a lot,' said Margery.

'She's teething,' he said. But he felt cold.

To cheer herself up Margery went shopping with Kay in London. Kay bought half a dozen Zandra Rhodes fantastic embroidered beaded shirts. She'd seen them on Rick and liked them. Now he'd have to find something else to suit him. She, like Mummy, had style privilege in the Château. Margery found a simple black jersey dress by Jean Muir and had a dozen of them made.

'Is someone going to die?' asked Kay.

'He already did.'

'Oh, come on, Mummy. You've got Rick now.'

'Kay, I married Rick to get over your father.' She chose yet more black. She hadn't got over anything. She bought Rick a full-length wolfskin coat worked in horizontal bands. It was the only one in existence. These days both women ordered Maud Frizon shoes, always a dozen pairs at a time. Bags and baggage by Gucci: Margery disliked the celebrated Vuitton because there were too many imitations. All the preferred perfumes were out – Je Reviens, Ma Griffe, Caborchard – people like Jane Kirkland wore those. Kay discovered a honey-sweet musk. It made her feel nostalgic and Margery sick.

They had facials and saunas, a vegetarian lunch. Three furriers sent a collection of furs to the London house. Each furrier offered Margery one free as a token of esteem. Kay chose a grey cashmere and wool ankle-length coat with fur around the sleeves and collar. She liked the Russian look. Then before returning to Cannes they spent another obligatory hour at Jean Muir. Margery adored the simple classic slices of silk jersey and jersey trousers, sensuous and flowing. Normally she wore structured Chanel suits.

They both spent over a thousand pounds on Janet Reger super-glamorous lingerie. Finally Margery had her hair re-modelled. To fit the new image she had the crown raised up with added false pieces. She had a fringe and in the evening an elaborate piled style twirled and knotted. Kay simply back-combed her hair at the crown to give it the desired effect.

On the plane back Kay said, 'Mummy, why give the wolfskin coat to Rick when you know I want it?'

Margery didn't answer. She looked odd, unusual, with the new hairstyle. The fringe made her look old-fashioned and otherworldly. Her eyes were haunted. She was thinking she'd forgotten all about Frou Frou. She hadn't bought her one damn thing.

. . . Chapter 47 . . .

Jacey did shepherds. She had the whole mountainside and in the winter of '71 the village threw her out. They said her morals would bring them bad luck and their livestock disease. She fled to Malaga, and Jaimie Laurenson was waiting. All he had to do was follow the money. She was paid by her family estate monthly into a Malaga bank. Naturally she'd changed her name. He didn't want to find her, but if he brought her back he could shut up about Jane.

'It's like leading a lamb to the slaughter, Jacey, but you've got to come back to France.'

'For what reason?'

'Police reasons. It seems you've absconded with personal belongings of Miss Caversham.'

'That's so sick. Untrue too.'

'I'm sure it is. But they can get you back. It's easier with me. You get a first-class seat and my company.'

So Jacey tried to do a deal. She'd sleep with him if he failed to find her. She'd take a boat over to Africa and just never come back.

'You can say Robert Frey set you up, that you never intended hurting Kay. I'll back you there – I know Frey's past.'

The girl wanted to know what would happen to her. He thought Kay would get emotional and sadistic. He hoped that was all it would be.

Jaimie kept the girl in a room over the Italian restaurant outside Grasse until Kay arrived. The colour was back in her cheeks. She was alive again. It was amazing what love could do.

Very calmly he told Kay what he'd promised the girl. 'Blame Robert Frey. Not her. I know him.' Kay pushed past, eager to get to her betrayer. 'And Kay, go easy in there. She is Princess Miranda's daughter.'

She turned and looked at him, her eyes large and wild. Then she slammed the door in his face. He had a drink downstairs but there were no screams. Then he returned to the Château.

Kay beat Jacey, then she cried, then she tried to make love to her. Jacey wasn't having any.

She sat up, one cheek swollen, and said, 'What do you think I am? I am a free person, not your slave.'

'Really?' said Kay icily. 'I'm not a gambling type but let's see how free you are. I wouldn't lay a buck on freedom right now.' She forced Jacey back on the bed and tied her wrists to the bedhead. With difficulty, she wrestled the girl's legs into a strange garment. It laced up and locked. Jacey could pee and crap through two small holes but nothing else. It was called a chastity belt. Kay had added special touches. She put a gag across Jacey's mouth and pulled her into a deep clothes cupboard. She fixed a rope from the girl's tied hands to the clothes rail, then shut the door and locked it. She had considered getting her into a diving suit and submerging her in cold water for hours on end but this seemed more appropriate. She stood by the cupboard waiting for the so longed for release of vengeance. None came.

When she returned six hours later, she led the girl to the bathroom. She let her go to the lavatory then took off her gag and let her drink.

'I'll prosecute you, Kay Caversham.'

'Of course you will, my darling. But let me remind you you're now my cupboard guest and in not much of a position to do anything.'

Again, she locked her away. This time she felt frightened. Would she, then, be obliged to kill her, as she had done so often in her fantasies?

When she returned the next morning the Italian owner looked perplexed. He'd heard banging from the room Kay had recently rented. What should he do? The door was locked.

Kay said she'd look into it.

Jacey had peed herself and hated the dark. She'd been banging on the wall with her feet. Kay put her into a warm bath and removed the gag. 'Scream and I'll drown you.'

'I feel terrible,' said Jacey.

'I know the feeling.'

'How long does this go on?'

Kay didn't know. Jacey thought sleeping with her captor was infinitely better than being locked up but Kay didn't believe her entreaties. She knew the girl's eyes. There was no desire today. Back into the cupboard.

Kay told the owner she had an animal in there. It was to be a present for her baby sister.

'Ah, a donkey!'

They didn't believe her, and when she'd gone the owner's wife said they should call Margery Caversham. 'It's a girl up there. If she dies what happens to us?'

The owner didn't know what to do. Miss Caversham was like Margery Caversham. He'd confront Kay when she returned.

However, the Canadian brought some friends for lunch. Discreetly the proprietor told him about the banging in the night, the locked door, a tale of a donkey. Jaimie said he'd sort it out. He caught Kay as she came down the stairs having given the girl some soup.

'What does she get for exercise? A whipping? A dildo fuck?'

'Where's she been, Jaimie?'

'You can't keep people tied up. Nasty things get into them. Like death. And you've got the owner rattled. Why don't you keep the donkey at home?'

'My mother would never allow it.'

'The Greek's home.'

'I can handle this.'

She deliberately stayed away a whole night. She didn't sleep but it gave her such pleasure to think of the wanton girl captive and suffering.

The Italians phoned Kay at 6 a.m. and said animals were not allowed on their premises. They said the police had called.

So Kay drove over, gave them a huge sum of money and a satisfactory tale. 'Yes, it's a girl up there. She's on drugs. We're trying to cure her. OK? You've done your part, believe me. She owes us her life.'

Jacey seemed to be sleeping. Kay kicked her awake.

'I'd rather die,' said Jacey. Her mouth was dry, she felt ill. Kay cut the rope.

'Ready for work now?' She motioned to Jacey to sit on the bed, but she couldn't move. Her circulation was wrecked.

'All right, tell me where you've been. All of it.'

Jacey told her about the Spanish village – just one shepherd.

'I'd like it more if there were others.'

'Yes. Other shepherds.'

'What about a bullfighter.'

'No bullfighter.'

'I'd like it better.'

Jacey couldn't help it. There were no bullfights up there. Frey was right – Kay Caversham had a certain mad streak.

Kay washed her face, gave her some water. Then she put her clothes on. The chastity belt stayed. 'Your problem, Jacey, is you've had it too soft. So what I'm going to do is take pity on you and give you a job. You work for me. I need a new personal maid. And that' – she indicated the chastity belt – 'stays on.'

'It's ludicrous.'

'Well, go back in the cupboard,' and Kay pushed her towards it. When angry she had a man's strength. 'Personally, I'd be a maid any day. It's a good idea. It has to be because it came from Jaimie Laurenson. But I'm not going to push you. I'll give you another twenty-four hours to think it over.'

Jacey begged to be the maid. She was now a sweating wreck. Before they left, Kay made her sign a document. She'd be maid for Kay Caversham for a period of three years, by which time her looks would have gone.

. . . Chapter 48 . . .

Alex showed up a month after Jane finished filming in San Francisco. He casually walked up the wooden steps into her small apartment. Kit said, 'Are you from the studio?'

'You could say that,' said Alex. He sat on the bed and held out his hands to his son. Jane came out of the bathroom. She wanted to throw him out, to scream. Having him there put her back in a bad place. She almost needed a drink. His hair was streaked, the beard gone. He wore glamorous Italian-style clothes and looked sensational.

'What are you doing exactly?' she asked.

'I've got a job. I run a set of machines. They tell the future. You put your hand in a slot along with five bucks and you get your fortune on a card. I stand them in supermarkets, airports, fairgrounds. They've made me rich.'

Jane had seen them: big fairground-type machines with winking lights and music, and sometimes a TV screen on the top showing a speeded-up journey over canyons, up into the sky, swooping down into the ocean, into cities, along dark narrow roads, back into the desert. Jonny Citta said it was good footage. Alex said Lucien had filmed it. 'It's the journey from purity to death.'

'When I asked what you were doing I didn't mean career details. I meant sitting here.'

'I've come to see my son.' He picked Kit up and sat him on his knee. 'I wanna take him over to Mexico, see some sights.'

'Absolutely not. Please don't ruin it for me, Alex.'

'But, babe, this kid is mine too. I have a right.'

'Go and get it in a court of law.'

He got up, very cool, and for a moment she thought he would take Kit. She grabbed the child's legs. 'Alex, I'll scream this town down.'

'I'll get it, Jane, and I'll remember how cooperative you are.'

He disappeared into the crowd on the boardwalk. She'd keep her door locked from now on.

She called the number the Canadian had given her for any bad moments and got a secretary. Within an hour he phoned her and she told him about Alex.

'But he's the father,' said Jaimie. 'He has a right to see his boy. And face it, the boy needs a father.'

Jane was terrified. 'He'll ruin him. Please, please help me,' she pleaded.

He wouldn't see her in LA. She was welcome to fly to New York.

Margery had total artistic control over *The Big Knife*. Rick didn't like that, because it meant Kay would get the advantage. Margery said, 'Rick, it's your first movie. You need help as much as my daughter. We'll see how hot Jonny Citta is after this street film.'

'It'll be too late then,' said Rick. 'Everyone will want him.'

'Darling, I already have him. He's under contract to Mo Cohen's studio.'

'But he doesn't work out of a major studio.'

'Oh, he does. Now he's after McQueen. It's as they say in Tinsel Town, who's got the juice. Now if we don't like him we use George.'

'But he's a ladies' director.'

'So?' Margery's eyes widened playfully.

'Come on, Margery, that's all over. I just wanted to play the piano with both hands. Guys are out. My career though – another story. I must use my own people.'

'Not where Kay is concerned. She gets the best.' To Rick, Margery sounded totally unlike herself, ruthless. Then, behind his back, they changed the movie altogether. Kay wanted to remake one of Mummy's classics. Rick responded unexpectedly. He fired the first person he saw, who happened to be Julian.

Later Rick explained to his wife that he was sick of being surrounded by old people. Their energy was all wrong – it drained him. She was horrified. Did he mean her? For God's sake, she and Julian were the same age. 'He's too old, Margery. I want new young faces.' And he meant it. He'd had his charity programme stopped and that had really meant something to him. Now the film was changed. He was determined to keep control of the staff change.

It wasn't a disaster for Margery, because she'd never liked Julian. She explained quite openly that her husband was young and wanted new blood. She'd give Julian an impeccable reference – and that's all she gave him. He reeled from the emptiness of his pocket as he left the Château. Over thirty years, gone, unacknowledged. Hardly a thank you. Not even a lift to the station. And he looked at his hands and somehow he saw them writing. He'd go out of the exclusion zone. South America was what Margery always feared as she had no control there. He'd go to Ecuador and write a book – Margery Caversham's secret life. He'd start the story the day Nestorin got found out, when their African factory blew up. Margery did the decent thing and sold her shares. Then she instructed her daughter Kay to do the indecent thing and go and buy the lot. Now she almost owned Nestorin Babyfoods Europe and it was flourishing. Which was more than he could say for her baby.

Jane, on roller skates and wearing hotpants, appeared on the posters of *Street*. Jonny Citta was hot. Everyone wanted to deal with him. Margery read about it in the *LA Times*. 'The bitch has made it.' Not in Margery's terms, of course, but in popular cinema. She phoned Mo Cohen and said to cancel Jonny Citta's new movie. 'Tell him he'd get busted for coke if he did one reel. Give him a fright. Then a way out; he is to fly to Cannes immediately and make Kay Caversham's new film.'

... Chapter 49 ...

Jane flew overnight to New York and met Jaimie Laurenson in a hotel off Lexington and fifty-seventh. 'I had to bring Kit. You never know – Alex always knew some wrong people.'

There was no problem. Jaimie was pleased to see Kit.

She was wearing her skin-tight blue denim jeans embroidered over the hips and down the legs with astrological signs and mystic symbols. The jeans fitted so well it was as though her body had been poured into them. Her towering perspex sandals like glass skyscrapers made her two inches taller. She'd already set a style with her button-through midi-skirts and now the embroidered jeans were starting a trend. Her crimson toe- and fingernails were decorated with green palm trees. Over her makeup she'd sprayed gold and silver glitter. She did look fabulous, he had to admit that.

Before she'd got up to the suite she was telling Jaimie the news. He already knew it. 'She's done it, stopped my film. They say, the studio, how Jonny has decided he needs the stimulating influence of Cannes. I know that guy. He hates those hard kind of people. We were about to make our movie.'

'I know it looks that way.'

'It is that way.'

'But Rick de Palma always wanted him. Originally they were going to make one kind of film and now Kay's changed it.

So to recreate a balance they've given him his choice of director.'

It was a lot of words. It made sense to the guy who'd created them. She, however, knew Margery. 'It was the same speedy knife in the back that she pulled on me in London. Got Al Streep to do it. Gracie got the role, I got the door.'

'Jonny Citta gets quite a lot of money,' said Jaimie.

'He didn't even say goodbye.'

'No, well, that's film business. Friendships are for ever until the camera stops. Then you hardly remember the person's name.'

She told him she'd be broke again. She got nothing on the Skater film: it was all deferred payments until they were in pure profit. So he told her again to go to the Neighbourhood Playhouse.

Jaimie ordered up a good breakfast from the deli across the street, then he was taking the day off to show Jane and Kit New York. Already she loved its pulsing dynamic beat that took her along with it. She'd not slept since hearing the bad news, but she no longer felt tired. Before they started their day of enjoyment she asked him if he'd help with Alex.

'He's quite capable of stealing Kit. He's ignored him for two years. Why suddenly want him now? I want to fight this.'

Jaimie had given it a lot of thought. 'If he wants to see his son, no court will stop that. You can't prove anything against Alex – that he'll harm the boy. My advice is agree to visiting rights under supervision.'

'What's that exactly?'

'He spends time with the boy but you have someone on your side along too.'

'Alex will never agree to that.'

'Oh, I think he will. You see I'll be the one on your side.'

It was one lovely day. They went from the top to the bottom of Manhattan Island and then across. They took the Staten Island ferry. They ate in Chinatown, went to St Patrick's, then to the park. He took her back to the hotel and helped put Kit to bed. While she took a bath he read the boy a story. Kit wasn't sure about it. TV was his story. What were all these words suddenly?

'Are you my Dad?' Kit asked.

'No,' said Jaimie. 'But I love you. So you can treat me like a dad.'

'You don't know me.' And Kit went to sleep. How like his mother he was. She came out of the bathroom wearing a short transparent dress. Her hair was wet.

'You shouldn't wear pants with that kind of dress,' he said.

'I don't normally. But you're here.' She laughed. 'You've been really all right. But why are you doing it?'

'Because I have to do something good for someone. I feel the urge to be nice now and then and there's nobody there.'

'No women?'

'Of course there are women. I'm really married to my business.'

'It's nice to have a friend,' said Jane.

'I'll drink to that.' He went to the minibar. 'Shall we celebrate our friendship with champagne?'

'I don't drink. Give me Perrier.'

'Haven't you ever drunk?'

'No.'

'You cut a lot out.' He gave her the mineral water and looked into her eyes, challenging her.

'That's right.' She toasted him with her water glass, almost insolently.

He opened the champagne.

'What do you do, Jaimie? Ride round on a lightbeam? You seem to be everywhere at once, knowing everything, snooping into the dustbins.'

'Oh, Earls Court wasn't difficult to fathom, Jane. You left a lot of creditors.'

'If you're on my side how come you're on Margery Caversham's side?'

'I look after Margery. I like you. I didn't plan it. I liked the way you walked along the sea that day, the way your hips move. You're solid. You're solid about your child. I like that.'

'You like a lot of things but Margery rules OK.'

'I respect her. She's strong. She's got a lot of problems but she doesn't go on about them. I really admire her. Yes.'

'It's so funny because I wanted to be like her. Years ago when I first started. Who didn't? And then I met Alex and he was such a beautiful person. He really was. But he never forgave me and now his heart has turned to stone. That's why I don't want him to have Kit.'

'What is there to forgive, Jane?'

'I made him go back to his mother's life, because I wanted to be famous. He said I craved fame. That's when it went wrong. Marcello Tallaforos was there. He was so marvellous, mesmerising almost. I couldn't believe I was at the same table. Everyone was a star. And I saw I hadn't enough on board to mingle with those people and I was glad to get back to Earls Court with Alex and Kit. At least there I wasn't threatened by fame. You can feel more anonymous amongst the famous than the anonymous. But it was too late. They hadn't accepted me or my child and that really humiliated Alex. Yet he couldn't go up against them. It showed him he was weak and he hated me for it.'

Jaimie said, 'The funny thing is, Margery would sympathise with that. She's really a liberal person. She becomes difficult if you try and stand on her space.'

'What do you do?'

So he told her about his business, his past. He was working-class from Montreal. He'd got himself into university, a good degree, a law practice. Then into the money business – he was good on speculation.

'How old are you?' she asked.

'Forty-three.'

Then he did something totally out of character. He told her about his wife, about whom he never spoke.

'I knew she was ill long before they diagnosed cancer. I can always tell. My grandmother had a corner shop that sold everything. But the people really went there to have their cards done. She could tell a person's life. I just have a sense of chemical change. I can tell, for instance, that you're well, just as I could tell my wife was sick. But the doctors couldn't, because it was too early for clinical diagnosis. When she was dying, I think it was her last walk outside, we took the children, a girl of three, a boy of five. And a car took the corner too fast and came on to the sidewalk and got both the children but not her. Ironic, because she was nearly dead anyway. The boy was DOA and the girl – well, that took longer. I buried them, and my wife died of a broken heart more than cancer. I mourned her for a day then I went after the hit-and-run car and I found the driver and I killed him.'

Jane couldn't find any words to do justice to that. It was so immense, his suffering, and it was still there. She wanted to hold his hand but decided that was wrong.

'Was it a long time ago?' she asked.

'Fourteen years.'

'So that's why you work so hard.'

'Life goes on, Jane. I get by.'

'I suppose that makes a link with Margery Caversham. After all, she lost her husband through a violent act.'

'No, I never told Margery or anyone so –'

'I won't say anything. You can trust me.'

'I'm sure I can.'

He stroked her thigh and it was like being struck by lightning again and again. She pulled away. Her body ached with a terrible desire that she would have to assuage this time. She hadn't had it for so long. He felt her face burning, and kissed it.

'I don't want sex, please. I don't want anything from anyone.'

'Well, don't wear that dress' – he put his hand between her legs – 'or you'll give a false impression. I'd say you wanted it in spite of yourself.' And he started to push her back on the second bed away from Kit.

'No,' she said. 'I mean what I say.'

'You want it, you need it.' He pulled the dress up and her bikini briefs down. 'Let's just do it. Pretend it's just for me. We don't have to talk about it. Come on, it's good for you. Just do it, whatever you like.'

Christ, hadn't she said that to Jay Stone? She was stuck between intense, agonising desire and fear. She said she didn't use any contraceptive.

'I'll take care of that,' he said.

'How?' These days she liked to know the how, the why of everything. She lost fun that way but she stayed secure

'I'll pull out or use a rubber. Whatever you prefer.'

'Not in front of Kit. Definitely not.'

He took her hand and pulled her into the bathroom. He owned more companies than she could count, he was worth more in stocks than she could imagine, he ran lives, saved them and took them, and she was not all he thought about or all he wanted. She still shut the bathroom door and gave herself completely, just gave in to it. And during that time she was all that mattered to him. When he'd done it straight he liked it a little violent, not too much, just spiced up. Then he liked a lot of play and caressing and then a long satisfying blow job.

When it was over he said, 'You like it that much. So what have you been doing with yourself? Come on, tell me. You do it to yourself?'

'I told you. I don't think about it.' After what she'd been through she thought she could do without anything.

He looked younger, happy even. 'I really did like it, Jane. You keep doing it with me and I'll keep you and Kit.'

She felt so right with him. How she'd longed for a man. Perhaps she only really felt right when she was part of a man's life, when she felt near to him and loved. But it also brought pain. Would it this time? She thought, like Jonny Citta, that relationships were down to luck or karma. Was there really anything you could do to make them work? Only be yourself and the other person would either stick with that or not. Jane refused to see herself as unlucky.

Jane's face was everywhere in America: on posters, newspapers, even on the cover of two big magazines. She went on chat shows, pop shows, and she got offered movies, TV movies of the week, porn movies. They were all just offers. Two newspapers wanted to publish her life story nationwide. Then she got what she wanted – no, Jaimie wanted it. He said, 'Take that one.' It was a new TV series being made in oil country. Filming would begin in early '72. Most of the actors were unknown outside the States.

'In this series you could be a frontrunner,' said Jaimie.

'Why?'

'Because I smell a hit.'

When Margery read about it she thought it would kill her.

... Chapter 50 ...

Kay walked to the outskirts of Monte Carlo. The Greek was anchored for two nights because he wanted to take a party gambling. Kay's hands were clenched in her Yves Saint Laurent trouser pockets, but otherwise she looked serene.

'I've got to be a star,' she said, over and over. How could she do her next movie with Rick? They hated each other. She suspected that she wasn't a movie actress after all, just a beautiful Caversham girl who succeeded best by simply appearing. She was always the same – a version of Mummy. It would last as long as her youth. She wanted to take the acting business seriously because she liked doing things well. More, she needed to be the best. She was considering going on the stage. That was a real test – no bullshitters telling her she was wonderful because of her name. She kept it a secret and added ideas to the stage plan every day. It was like a baby growing inside her. She'd already instructed a theatrical agent in Paris to find her some plays. After the Rick movie she was scheduled to do three pictures back to back. Her agent had suggested she do them – who knew how long she'd be in demand? How she envied Lucia – her femaleness, beauty and talent. It didn't matter that she'd fucked her way in, she delivered the goods. She thought about Lucia too much. She was scared she might be getting a thing about her. And with a smile, Lucia would destroy her and tell half Europe.

Always Kay pretended to be happy with the Greek. She certainly did a good job with the social stuff, but then she'd learned that from her mother. She'd get the Greek to invite Lucia the following night. If she told him anything in advance he'd worry for a month what present to give her. The last time, Kay had laughed. 'A present for Lucia? Give her me.'

'Don't you think she would prefer me?' He wasn't joking: it had become a habit in private to quarrel over the attractive female guests and who'd made the most impact. Of course Kay still loved Jacey. The girl served Kay breakfast, made her bed, attended to her clothes, took her phone calls, ran her bath. The chastity belt was locked in such a way it was impossible to get off without medical help. It was like a plaster cast and should be kept on only for a certain number of weeks, no longer. She could wash herself but even so the Greek said she stank. Jacey was totally reduced and full of hate. Every chance she got she recounted to Kay how each and every shepherd on the hillside had screwed her, what she'd done, how it felt. Kay would reply coldly, 'And look at you now. You look so down no one even recognises you.'

The Greek sensed some of this. 'She is unhappy, Kay. Why don't you tell her to go?'

'But I want her here.'

'Are you keeping her here against her wishes?'

'No. She just stays. She knows it's best.'

'Well, I hope so because her mother draws water –'

'Not nearly as much as mine. Just tell Princess Miranda her daughter's your guest.'

'How can I let her see the girl like that?'

'It's none of your business. She tried to do something terrible to my mother.'

'Oh,' he said. 'Oh.' And that was all he said.

He could see the pressure on his wife was enormous. She smiled far too much, especially in the company of his children. She behaved beautifully, impeccably, her lovely voice a pleasure to hear. She played the piano, was courteous and so eager to help. People felt comfortable with her, which was strange because to begin with they hadn't liked her. He had to admit her social technique was marvellous.

He couldn't even remember the deal he'd done with her about marital rights. He didn't want to claim them anyway. She wasn't a full-blown passionate creature like her mother, but because he was kind sometimes, he thought a little loving would soothe her. He suggested she come to his bed when she felt like it.

'What's this now?' She was irritated. 'We've fixed all that.'

'It will relax you. It's good for the nerves.'

'We agreed you leave me alone. Come on. You had a deal with my mother. Don't look so surprised.'

'I was only trying to help you.'

The second time she walked through the back streets of Monte Carlo, her mind was again wandering. The locals stared. She was someone particular – they couldn't think who. Her corduroy rust trousers were beautifully cut. She was so deep in thought it didn't occur to her she was in a bad area. The Château was no longer home. Rick had his people in: flash modern types who livened the place up. Margery was prepared to move with the times to keep Rick, who never seemed to age. And it was fun for Frou Frou.

Rick and Margery liked to be exclusive. When you dined with them now they made it clear you were an outsider. Kay had tried to get Jacey's cousin, the homosexual prince from Rome, to screw Rick and let Margery catch him at it.

'And lose my head or, worse, my balls? Kay, you should go to the Mafia. I mean, your father –' He stopped. He thought it was time to get the hell out back to the safe violence of Rome.

Rick and Margery had taken Frou Frou off for a cruise. The house was really Kay's until they returned the next week to welcome Jonny Citta. She also knew they were planning to go away alone for Christmas. It would be the first one she'd spent away from her mother.

So she walked, not caring, too far away from her sort of people. The car with the four men in it followed slowly. She was aware of it but she didn't run. A part of her knew that the trouble that was coming would get Mummy back.

At first the men wanted to rape and rob her. Then when they recognised her they reacted with a lot of religious oaths and curses. Finally they decided to kidnap her. They sent a ransom note to the Greek and another to the Château.

Kay said, 'You could send one to the Royal Family in England. Why not? Mummy's an aristocrat, you know.'

. . . Chapter 51 . . .

Charlotte spent every weekend with Jaspard and his wife. Her love of helping people came back and they admired her for what she'd done in New York and never tired of listening to her stories. Jaspard said that when he became President, as he certainly would by '75, he would give her a position in his government: Social Service Department in charge of welfare for the poor. 'We want a well world, don't we, Charlotte?'

During the week she stayed in her mother's Paris apartment and studied piano at the Conservatoire. She wanted to impress Marcello because she was still, in spite of everything, his. Twice she'd sent long, impassioned letters. He'd replied by telephone. He said he wasn't worthy of such love.

Marcello was used to women adoring him – it came with the job. He enjoyed it as long as no one got hurt, but serious, long-term, inflamed passion from a young girl upset him. He wasn't in the business of hurting people. He did her one favour. He kept his lecherous son away. She was too good for Alessandro, the doctor who liked a lot of playtime. Marcello cancelled a concert tour to be with his wife while she recovered from another major operation. He put all his energy and gift for life into making her well.

Charlotte, now over twenty-one, was stuck. The music, like her body, was only for another person who, unfortunately, belonged to someone else. As an act of defiance against her very nature and her love, she allowed Jaspard to take her virginity. It all happened so fast. So that was what they were all so mad about. She couldn't blame Jaspard or herself as she had nothing to compare it with. She would have to discuss this with Kay. Jaspard remained for some time after the act, caressing her breasts. 'They're so big and strong. I'm crazy about them.' At last the plastic surgeon had got it right. 'We mustn't tell anyone, Charlotte. My wife must not know.'

Charlotte decided this was a wonderful way to arouse Marcello. She would have every surgical improvement done to her, dress incredibly, wear jewels, establish a salon and swan around as Jaspard's mistress. She'd get him then. And for a while the poor of the world went out of the window.

Whenever Jane went out on the town she met Margery Caversham's kind of people. She was now in that league. The 'Street' film had done it for her. She worked out at the gym, worked on her voice, went to the Actors' Studio. She was getting ready for the TV series. It was nicknamed 'Oil'. A lot of Hollywood people tried to use Jane to get to Margery. She was offered a sum of money to get scripts and books into the legend's hands. She was even offered a huge sum from a publishing house to write a book about the family. Everyone wanted to know about Margery. She, Jane, wanted to know about Jay Stone. Had he survived? How did he look? How did he feel towards her? The one man she could ask, her lover, she couldn't trust. Business came first and Jay Stone had been real money in the sixties.

Jaimie flew to LA and stayed at the Beverly Hills Hotel whenever he could. Otherwise she'd fly to New York or Chicago and they'd spend a day or two together, never more. There was a lot of love and a lot of travelling. When he was in LA he liked seeing Kit and really enjoyed playing with him.

One day as Kit came running towards them across the sand Jane's eyes filled with tears. 'Oh, the pain,' she said.

Jaimie held her, thinking she was ill.

'He's so perfect. He will never be this good again.' And she burst into tears.

'It will be different,' said Jaimie. 'He'll be beautiful in a different way. He'll change, and you'll like what he changes into. There'll be other things in him to be very pleased about.'

Jaimie didn't understand. Jane knew the child would never be as perfect as he was in that moment running towards them, his back to the sea. And whenever she thought of it afterwards her heart almost broke inside her.

Alex's desire to see his son had to fit in with Jaimie Laurenson's availability, and Alex did not like it. Jaimie explained his intervention to Margery. 'He's your grandchild, your only grandchild. Alex lives in a low-security area. I worry about the child being kidnapped, Margery.'

This was a new one. 'Couldn't they kidnap him just as well from that girl?'

'Actually she does look after him. He's never left alone and she has good people.'

'You sound as though you quite like her.'

'She's a good mother. I know that surprises you.'

'I will never change my view of her.'

'If they snatch the child from Jane they won't get a buck. From Alex, another story. Kit has to be chaperoned. It's business, Margery.'

And then the day came when she got the call about Kay. Jaimie Laurenson did get things right.

Jane started to want him too much. The sexual pleasure was so intense as to be almost unbearable.

He was knocked out by it too. 'We should try and do it more often. Coming with you just about takes my head off,' he said.

She was getting possessive and thought about him too much – in fact all the time. She decided she was no good with a man because she was so needful. She was jealous of everyone he saw.

He tried to help her. 'Why would I waste all that pleasure on someone I don't really value? You must know I'm not like that? I only want the best.'

So she started worrying about all the amazingly beautiful women he came into contact with professionally.

'They were there before you.'

'So?' she said. 'I bet you slept with them.'

'Not in a meaningful way. And only when I had the urge to do so.'

'You used them.'

'If they let me.'

She even got jealous of that. She said, 'I'm better alone.'

He felt upset. It was the first time a woman had got to him since the death of his wife. For a mad moment he considered marrying her, but then he'd lose Margery and she'd make sure he lost a lot of other business. He said, 'Let's go on as we are.'

'When I was alone I used to think only of my work, of the future, of the success I'd make. It was all hope. Now I've got something, I've got something to lose.'

'Find a play and I'll put it on for you. We'll start small then move it over to say the Huntington Hertford. You'll love theatre – it's very alive.'

'You mean something I really care about and want to work on?'

'Exactly.' She loved it when he spoke softly. It was so sexy. He was the epitome of a real male film star from the fifties. Apart from Kirk Douglas, he also looked like Robert Stack – Margery used to tell him that. The trouble was, he was too physically endowed and too tragic. Business healed. Time was just a clock making him older. It didn't do a thing about his dead wife and kids. And that's why Margery and he got on together: they'd had the same tragedy and couldn't get over it. They never spoke about it, they'd had different lives, but they'd arrived at the same place.

Edie Sedgewick, Warhol's society superstar, had recently died from a drug overdose. Margery was all stirred up. What if Alex met the same end? He was still under Warhol's influence. Jaimie was of the opinion that Alex handled his own road to hell and didn't need any help from Andy Warhol.

. . . Chapter 52 . . .

The kidnappers took Kay to a political activist. She was too big for them to handle. It was like watching the changing of the guard at Buckingham Palace and walking off with Prince Charles – you didn't do that sort of operation. Snatching her had been an impulsive mistake. They sold her to the extreme Left, associated with German and Arab terrorists. The one in charge, Bruno Lanz, looked like a movie version of Che Guevara, but any likeness ended there. He was powerful, clever, in fact he'd excelled at university, and was committed to putting the world right. The only way to do it these days was by acts of violence. People were so saturated with horror that they would only notice super-horror. Bruno said he'd cut Kay's ear off and send it to Margery if the money didn't arrive within twenty-four hours. The Greek was given twelve because quite soon in the conversation Bruno realised who cared about the heiress most.

Kay said she'd like a shower and a change of clothes. She'd never been unwashed in her life and didn't like it. Also she hated to be idle and was hungry. She suggested she cook a meal.

'Look, we both know the situation. Let's make the best of it,' she said.

He said, 'People like you will have to die. Your ex-husband's father is next. The fascist industrialist.'

Kay thought at last Guido would get his opera house.

She felt very attracted to Bruno. He was a bandit, however he wrapped it up politically. Given the chance, she'd have been one too. His eyes were piercing and clever. The others respected him.

'I don't care much whether I live or die,' she said. 'I've not had a particularly happy life.'

'Happy!' said Bruno. 'I'm talking about people who don't live because they don't eat or get medicine. Happiness is a luxury.'

'But I'm sure you remember my father. He did care – and died for it.'

'He didn't take it far enough. Controversial words from a safe seat. Don't use him as a bargaining piece. He cuts no ice here.'

'Can I take a shower?'

He paused for a while. 'You know, Kay, you could have been something. You were just born into the wrong house.'

'Because I like to be clean?'

'Because you have a capacity for passionate involvement. Of course you're scared, because whatever you say you don't want to die. And you want your earlobes so you can go on hanging the Greek's pretty presents. You know right from wrong. You just play society's game.'

'Why?'

'Because they stunted your development. You should hate them, your class. Putting you in a fairytale when you could have been real.'

She thought he was flattering her. She cast her mind back down her teenage years. She'd been outraged by her father's killing but she didn't remember any passionate involvement – unless she counted Jacey, and he couldn't know about that. It was hardly espousing a cause. Kay's rule was 'me first'. She tried to explain herself.

Bruno said, 'You don't like deceit. You don't like people screwing you around.'

'No, I don't.'

'Nor does anyone else. You want a fair chance. I mean, you're saying you want a shower. You're asserting yourself. A shower before dying.' His voice changed, became soft and furious. 'If that money doesn't come I'm going to kill you. The ear goes first. Then you. Because I can't risk them finding me. They're already looking for you.'

She thought: Your luck runs out, terrorist, once Jaimie gets here.

She felt panicky. It was odd, but all she could think about was Jacey's chastity belt, how if it wasn't removed in time it would stick to her skin.

Bruno said, 'Go and take your shower. I still tell you you're better than you know.'

'Well, my father's blood must be good for something.'

Bruno told the men to leave her alone, not to ridicule or insult her. She was after all Dino de Stefano's daughter.

She stood under the trickle of water and used a nameless soap. She had no idea where she was – Italy probably. Was she better than she knew? She was well educated and intelligent. She cared deeply about her mother and disliked the pop star taking over their lives. She'd felt passionate about Jacey and was affirmative enough to go around as a guy, and even consider having the operation. She found things in herself which corresponded with what he'd just said. But no, she'd never felt passionately about the state of the world. For crissake, she'd even bought up Nestorin when it was very dubious. Over five hundred dead because of the company's lack of care. And she'd bought the shares. Also she could be cruel.

Bruno thought, She doesn't irritate me, because she's not a victim.

Jaimie Laurenson had been snatched from between the thighs of his mistress by the news of Kay's kidnap.

'It's always the Cavershams.' Jane was furious.

Jamie still had a hard-on when he got to the airport. How he wished there was a fast plane. When the hell was Concorde getting off the ground? The military were waiting at Paris and took him by special plane to Cannes. He'd said, 'Don't do anything until I get there.'

The police were pawing the ground ready to kill people. Jaspard seemed to be running the operation. Margery, Rick and Frou Frou had been flown in by helicopter from the middle of the ocean. There was little to go on: only a ransome note to Margery and the Greek.

'Pay it,' said Jaimie. If it was the terrorist group he thought it was they'd kill her and use it as an example. The money and her killing were about equal for them. Jaimie said he'd be the negotiator. The Greek got the first call. His instructions were simple. He was to walk with the bag of money to a café near his boat. Someone would tell him the time in Greek and take the bag. He'd go back to the boat and forget about it. Naturally there would be no police, army, private marksman, personal bodyguards, or the Greek would forgo his old age. If he chose not to pay he'd get her ear with one of his baubles still attached.

After her shower Kay ate with Bruno, a plate of tinned ham and tinned rice, cold. He sent one of the men out for bread and wine. He increased his strength by denying his appetites. He'd eat horseshit if he had to and get something positive out of the experience. He had one quality she remembered in Dino: he was absolute. His no was for ever; compromise, unthinkable. She used to watch her father as he dealt with the unhappy ones, in Italy or New York. The queue for his wisdom would begin at dawn and not end at sundown. There was always a queue. Kay said, 'Daddy, you work fifteen hours a day solving people's problems. What happens when you can't find an answer?'

He said, 'I tell them the reason I can't find an answer.'

She told Bruno Lanz about her father. 'But he'd never do a criminal act like you. The end certainly does not justify the means.'

'I told you, Kay Caversham. He didn't take it far enough. But he's all we've got. The Italians have made him a martyr. Even the men here, some of them, allow him respect. Still he cursed you as he lay dying. That's not very moral.'

'How do you know that?' Her voice was slight, like a little girl's.

'It's a handed down story – everyone knows it. Why did he do that?'

She sat thinking, her face pained.

'Was it because you didn't get a paramedic van and try and save him? Or did he mistake you for someone else?'

'Yes, I expect so. Yes, that's it,' she agreed.

'I don't expect so.' He laughed drily.

'To be honest it's not something I've gone into, because it hurts Mummy – my mother. He cursed us all, not by name but we were all there. He cursed his family, his blood. It was terrible. He just put out a hand into the pool forming beside him, as though he had all the time in the world, and lifted it a little. "I curse my blood." And then he was gone.' Kay looked pale, her face pinched. She wore no makeup. '"I curse you all, my blood".' Then she tried to brighten up. 'You must have a very exciting life.'

'Kay Caversham, I'm not some dinner party guest you can patronise. I'd better get that money.' His eyes seemed to look right through her.

'You'll get it. They hate funerals.' She made coffee and he spent the next hours on the telephone. Kay sat, she stood, she lay down, but she couldn't get comfortable. It was clear he was going to abscond with old man Cortese. The phone conversations concerned the outcome. A live Cortese or a corpse? Bruno wanted him dead.

'What exactly has he done?' she asked.

'He breathes.'

'I know he disapproves of the poor. Is that it?'

'No,' said Bruno coldly. 'He fucks up the rich so they start thinking they can do what they like. They take liberties – even with the natural law of things. If you want to know what God thinks of money look who he gives it to.'

'Why kill him?'

'They're so corrupt they're sick, and they should be put down. Until they've gone the real judges, the real politicians, can't even breathe.' He stopped speaking suddenly. There were moments when he resented her being there.

'I know you're right.' She thought of the cruel way the old man had stopped Guido's musical career. 'He doesn't give people their freedom.'

'Give! Who is he to give anything? He should never have had control in the first place.'

'My father said you should always allow a person free will. To take that away is a crime. I should join you, Bruno.'

'Money first. Until then anything else is hypothetical.' He wondered why she wanted to join him. It wasn't that uncommon in kidnap cases but this was quick. Often he'd seen a victim fervently espouse the point of view of the kidnapper. He thought it was to do with tension and fear. Get linked to your aggressor and so live. The cause didn't matter.

A little later Kay said, 'Look, I'll help you. You won't appreciate what I say but think about it. I'll go and collect the money from the Greek. They daren't touch me. And I'll get it from Mummy – my mother.'

'Why?'

'Maybe I've some scores to settle. Also they'll get you – you must know that – I'm too big to snatch. They'll never get off your back whether I'm alive or not. The American agency won't. So I collect the money.'

'Why?' he asked again. 'Why help me?'

'There's so much corruption about. I'm used to the stink, you're not. If you clean it up and something gets better, that's fine. I don't believe it will be better, but I'm on your side. I think I owe it to my father. Also I like you and I don't like Guido's father. Also I believe you've spent a lot of time thinking things out. I remember seeing your face in the newsreels of the Paris student riots in '68. If I recognise you, so will they. Let me collect the money.'

'You must hate them very much.'

She wore Bruno's clothes and dark glasses and was sitting at the empty bar when the Greek walked in with the money.

'But Kay? Is this a joke? You're free?'

She got off the bar stool and asked him for the time in Greek.

'I'll divorce you!' he shouted as she walked away with half a million. The vicious revengeful chick.

When Kay went to the railway station Rick wasn't there as Bruno had requested. Instead, Jaimie Laurenson sat on the platform bench nonchalantly smoking a cigarette. That didn't fool her – she knew he was armed to the teeth. The bag with the million rested on his lap. She was barefoot, wearing a fisherman's sweater and ill-fitting trousers. She looked like a beggar except for the sunglasses.

'Give it to me, Jaimie.'

'Fuck you, Kay.'

'They'll kill me. Don't start doing any clever thinking.' She made a grab at the bag.

'Is it something against your mother?'

'You know it isn't.'

'If it's Bruno Lanz you're in with, you must have done something. Because you're running around large as life.'

'Are you going to give me the money? Mummy won't like it if –'

'So what have you done, Kay?' he said quietly. 'Joined them?'

'I was always one of them. I just didn't realise it. So give me the goddam money.'

'You stay away from your mother. I mean it. Don't give her any more pain.'

Kay snatched the bag. 'As you're so in with the family, Jaimie, get the Greek off my back. I'm marrying my captor.'

And with that she melted away, like a shade, before his eyes.

. . . Chapter 53 . . .

Jaimie was the only one who could comfort Margery. Frou Frou couldn't speak, she made sounds and her walking was clumsy. The eyes were not right. 'There's a lot they can do,' he said. 'They're doing research non-stop on this – this –'

'Subnormal. She's subnormal,' said Margery calmly.

'They work around the clock. We have to find the best

treatment. I'm going to get in touch with Professor Knole in Paris. He's an expert on chromosomes and the genetic structure and –'

'She's not properly mongol,' said Margery. Her voice shook, but she remained calm.

'No, it's slight,' he said. 'And reversible.'

'I love her so much, Jaimie. But I was too old.'

'Oh, come on, Margery. It could equally be Rick. Or it could just be the luck of the draw.' And to take her mind off that problem he said, 'By the way, your daughter Kay is living with a certain Bruno Lanz. It's rumoured they're married. For once she was cheap. She didn't get a church wedding.'

'I hope to God she'll be happy at last.'

'Margery, for heaven's sake, the guy's a terrorist.'

Without looking at him Margery had reached for his hand and held it. 'You give me strength, Jaimie.'

He was in one tough spot. Margery was a woman in trouble and she needed him. There were a lot of big-mouthed hangers-on around Margery but no one effective. The effective ones were all married and had lives of their own. He, Jaimie, was free but he was missing Jane Kirkland. He wanted her in bed. And she was worse in Margery's book than the terrorist who'd abducted Kay.

Whenever Jaimie tried to leave the Château, Margery always handed him another proposition. Last time it was 'Sell off my movies. Take a percentage, Jaimie, on top of your fee.' This time it was 'Go and get her back so Jonny Citta can start filming. You're on as exec producer. You decide your fee.'

He squeezed her hand. 'Margery, you don't have to buy me.'

'You're a businessman. Do business. You don't have to be my nanny. Life's got tough for me but I can handle it. I just need some things done. You do them. You'll get paid.'

'Margery,' he tried to get her to look at him. 'I like you. Don't buy me.'

She didn't think anyone had ever said 'like' to her before. She'd heard everything else.

Jonny Citta waited around in Cannes for nearly a month. He was spectacular because of his huge black and white checked handkerchief with which he constantly mopped his cocaine-inflamed nostrils. Whenever anyone saw Jonny they saw the handkerchief flapping. His shades were huge and covered half his face. He wore the same leather jacket, scarlet string vest and red espadrilles, whatever the weather. His cord trousers were battered, torn and patched. He wasn't used to old places and Cannes, compared with LA, was ancient. Jaimie gave him money on a daily rate and kept him in a hotel, but Kay's kidnap, then her disappearance made it unlikely they'd be filming. Shooting of another style was going on in Italy. It made downtown LA seem very safe. Also the dramas were too big and he was just an onlooker and didn't like it. Rick said it was a shame, but they'd get together another time on another gig. Rick saw him off at the airport and for a moment wished he was going with him.

The house had a terrible atmosphere even apart from the horror of Kay's kidnap and Frou Frou's oddness. There was a certain corridor in the inferior guest wing which seemed chilly at all times. Rick dreaded going there – he felt something bad would happen. And the bedroom worried him too. It had a mournful atmosphere as though someone was dying in there. Nothing in it really seemed to belong to him. He felt unwanted. By the house, not Margery. She was always smiling and lovely – to him.

When Jacey heard about Kay's kidnapping she got one of the Greek's guards to contact Frey in Paris. She needed to be saved. Her abdomen burned and seemed swollen. She went to the Greek and asked for a doctor. He had his head in his hands. She thought the ransom, rather than the lost wife, caused that. She had no reason to love Kay and said, 'I bet she's done it herself.'

'No,' said the Greek. 'It's the fanatics from the Italian Left. The world isn't safe any more.'

But when he came back from the café delivery, he called Jacey into his cabin. 'Why did you say she was behind it?' he asked.

'Because she hates everybody.'

'Really?' He was surprised. 'Why?'

'Because she can't get what she wants from them. We don't stand still like figures on a Greek urn forever in love with Kay Caversham. That's what she wants: stop the world, love me.'

'But I am not on the vase. I don't love her. Never have.'

'Then you're OK because you haven't let her down. The ones she's after are me and her mother.'

She lifted up her skirt and he was amazed by the strange corset prison with its lock and necessary holes. 'Please get it taken off me before she comes back. And please, I want to go. I must be free.'

'And where are you going to find that, Jacey? Free?'

He arranged for a doctor to cut off the chastity belt and Jacey soaked in a salted bath. 'You're lucky,' said the Greek. 'You could have had a skin infection. You can't be free, my dear, because she wants you here. And I want a divorce. I'm old. I'm entitled to some happiness. You may be the coinage to use in this negotiation. I'm sorry about this. You sunbathe and rest. Like my guest. The day I get my freedom, you get yours.'

And Jacey realised there wasn't too much choice. He'd placed a dozen armed guards around his boat. As he said, the world was a frightening place. For the rich.

Jane was well into the oil series when Jaimie Laurenson came back. It was June 1972. She said she was better off not seeing him. 'I'm working and I want to give it my best shot.'

'Not with that voice, I hope. You've lost your English accent.'

She now spoke with an approximation of an American accent.

'I had to stay with Margery,' he explained.

'Really? All those months? Well, you obviously know what you want. I'm sure you'll both be happy.' The jealousy in her voice appalled even her.

'You know it's not like that.' He was irritated.

'I don't. I understand she was a goddess. They seem to get what they want. If they can't, who can?'

'Oddly I'm the only one she can trust.'

Jane was sarcastic and hostile. 'Yeah, and she pays you for it. Let's face it, Jaimie, she makes you rich.'

'I do my work. I get paid. I've always been the same. I don't overcharge and I get results.' He couldn't tell her about Kay's problems, her rumoured marriage to the terrorist, Margery's daughter's illness, Rick's depression. It had nothing to do with

Jane. At least he valued Margery that much. So he invented a dozen business deals, and Jane said fine, keep doing them. She only pretended to be offhand. He knew her too well. She wanted him as much as he did her. 'I'm due a vacation. Let's go to the Bahamas,' he said.

'I'm due one too. So leave me alone.'

He wanted to see Kit but she said Alex handled the visits now. 'The Japanese wife isn't allowed any kids so has to make do with mine.'

She was furious because, against her better instincts, she'd become involved again. Although he gave her ecstatic sexual pleasure, he also caused the pain of separation. He called the shots. When it suited him he turned up in her life. Well, she'd change all that. She'd gone without love and sex before, she'd do it again. She asked him to leave. For a while he waited around as she marked up her 'Oil' scripts. He was trying to decide how to make it up to her. The trouble was he couldn't think of one thing he could give her that she'd want. Not money. Not company. Not love. Not his needs. Was it his imagination or had her hard life made her invincible?

Three months later Jane sat on the boardwalk in Venice and the tourists looked at her, knowing her face. 'That's Miss Oil,' said the locals, even though the series would not be shown until early '73. The promotion was already underway and she was being coached to handle the chat shows. She was twenty-seven, alone, had a son she loved. Wearing a beige knitted bikini, she walked across the littered sand to the water's edge. She always loved the sea. It never let her down. It seemed to offer hope. Was it bringing her someone back? Or someone new? Did it offer adventure or maybe oblivion? Jaimie came and sat beside her. 'I always know where to find you. Jonny Citta's making a movie, *La Vamp*. I suggested he think about you for the lead.' She hadn't seen or heard from Jaimie for months. He spoke as though there'd been no gap.

'But I'm not free.' Her contract wasn't up until February '74.

'I could get the series to fit in around you. They can shoot around your character. You'd only be off six weeks.' He suggested going out for dinner and to the latest movie. She shook her head. She still couldn't take horror movies. She'd never be able to forget the boarding house afternoon of love with Jay Stone.

'Well, you choose.' He stroked her leg and she turned and looked at him. His eyes were hot, wanting her. She could see he was getting a hard-on. She needed him, but she couldn't divide herself up – when she was with him and when he was away. She was either too up or fearful, then jealous. She really was better alone. So far, although she'd looked, she'd found no one with whom to share the sexual act. She'd supposed it was because she was still in love with Jaimie. She moved her leg hoping he'd remove his hand. He didn't.

'Is this my punishment for staying with Margery? I told you I had things to do there. I did not abandon you. I wrote and I phoned. So why do you have to feel abandoned?' He got up and stood in front of her. 'I have my work and you have yours. And I have to do some abroad. I work better, faster alone.' That was the only good thing to come out of his wife's death. 'So why can't you accept that?'

'Because I'm putting my heart in the wrong place. I'm twenty-seven. I need to be married.'

He took hold of her hand and her blood sang. It was that good. He pulled her to him. 'Why don't we just allow each other what we like best? And in return I'll help your career. I can do a lot for that.'

And she saw he wouldn't marry her. He had all those glamorous society girls to pick and choose from. She still wasn't good enough. 'How famous do I have to get?' She turned away so he wouldn't see the tears.

He got her to bed and fucked her slowly, making it last. He kept telling her what he'd been thinking about her, wanting her, what he'd fantasised about her. He made Jane feel special and warm but that was his talent. Her mind said, take what he offers. He's talking movies. One up from theatre. But her wise heart said, he'll burn you. In comparison what Alex did would look like a match being lit.

She decided to ask him for a lot of money since she was once again his mistress, but before he left she was too happy and forgot.

Jaimie had pull. She got the starring role in *La Vamp* and also stayed in the TV series.

Kay traipsed across Italy twenty times a week with Bruno and his group. Usually they travelled separately. It was obvious Bruno was on the lookout for something but he didn't include her in his schemes. After two days of sexual intimacy he discovered she was not a passive lay. So he said, 'You do it to me' – he indicated a jerk-off – 'and I'll do it to you.' It took her ages to come and she had to rely on varied fantasies. She told him some of them and he got aroused again. That became their lovemaking: fantasies and masturbation. The getting married was a rumour, put out by Kay to upset Jacey and her family. Bruno would never get married: that sort of hypocrisy was for the bourgeoisie.

They lived in third-class hotels and looked nondescript. Her one absolute need, always to be clean and wash her hair, he agreed to. He actually went in search of clean water so she could brush her teeth. 'What about your prayers?' he said.

She didn't have any.

'Well, I have. People in our line of business might need them suddenly. You might all at once arrive in a better place. Better know the language.' And he mimed a bomb going off.

Bruno was born in the workers' town of Strasbourg in north-east France. His mother was a lawyer, his father a factory worker. He'd been educated at the Sorbonne. He'd read law, Marx, Trotsky and spoke several languages. He liked fast revolutionary conversation, he didn't go in for small talk. He told her what he thought. She could absorb what she could about the ways of his world.

His second-in-command had the mind of a rat and hated Kay. The other men thought she was a rich fool. She belonged to the other side. They didn't respect her for joining the anarchist Left. They nicknamed her La Caisse – the cash till. She gave Bruno whatever he needed. She was amazed at the number of activists he knew, the groups he met with. The Germans, the Palestinians. He wouldn't deal with the IRA. In general, apart from the lunatics, it was all one fight.

After the thirtieth train ride south she got the point of the operation. They were going to plant a bomb on one station between Milan and Genoa. If their demands were not met it would go off. Dozens of people would be injured, killed. Kay could not bear it and made the mistake of saying so.

'This is real,' said Bruno, 'not a film.'

She thought she had enough pull with him to state her point of view. He was furious.

'You Italians are all the same. Well, you're half Italian. Your father came from Naples. What a dump he came from. Don't tell me he didn't know about being born on the wrong side of the tracks. Why do you think he hated fascism. Yet you step up into cloud-cuckoo-land with a bunch of money. And you're all bourgeois and you're on the wrong fucking side. Have you no integrity? Can't you see you keep switching? You come from Castle Caversham down to me. Originally you came from a crawling infested suburb in Naples. So what are you?'

'I'm a lesbian.' She admitted it with difficulty.

'Oh shit, I don't care about sex. You! Are you rich? Poor? Left? Right? I tell you, Kay, you can never love anybody or anything, because as soon as you're involved you have to switch and hurt the thing you love. Why?'

'Because I can't trust that my mother loves me.'

'She betrayed you?'

Kay nodded. She seemed very young suddenly. She whispered, 'I think she betrayed me.'

'Well, you'd better stay with me, because they won't have you back. And I can't let you leave, can I? You know too much.'

'Don't do the railway station. It's a terrible thing to do. They're innocent.'

'No one's innocent. Ignorant not innocent.'

'Bruno, if you point out an enemy of progress I'll shoot him myself. That's fair. But I won't be part of that bomb.'

He gave her a gun. 'Go and kill your ex-father-in-law, Cortese. Through the head. Two bullets. No, five. Come on, Kay. A Mafia killing. Don't tell me you don't know about that. Make your bones. That's what it's called. Your father did.'

She wouldn't have her father's name mentioned in such a discussion with these killers.

They escorted her back along the railway line to Milan, Bruno and his first lieutenant. They knew the way to Cortese's house. Before she went in she said, 'That station bomb will lose you all support. You'll have no political credibility. You'll become violent thugs. Do it another way'.

Bruno said, 'The world wants it this way. Violence is

credible. The bigger the outrage the more they'll listen. So go and get on with this one-to-one business you say you approve of.'

She rang the bell and the maid had trouble recognising her. The master of the house was ill. Kay said she'd go into his bedroom. No problem. Bruno and the rat-faced thug were about to follow her into the hall. The armed policeman in the entrance stirred as he saw them. 'My brother and a friend,' she said in Italian. The policeman didn't look impressed. She didn't look like a Caversham either.

Bruno and Ratface hung back. 'We'll wait outside. No problem, sister.' Bruno pretended to kiss her and whispered, 'The place is crawling with alarms. Do the old man and I'll take care of –' He indicated the policeman.

The maid returned and said the old man was getting dressed in Kay's honour. She was to wait in a salon.

As she sat in the cool civilised room surrounded by books and works of art she thought of Margery. She was suddenly pulled back as though out of a bad dream, into her mother's world. She was her mother's daughter again. The Bruno escapade had been nothing but revenge because her mother had shut herself away with her husband and the preferred child and she, Kay, was kept out. But the escape was no light matter. Outside, her supposed third husband and Ratface were waiting for her to kill a man. There wasn't a chance that she could evade them by some other exit. They would still murder the old man. Everything she'd done since being with Jacey had been against life, anti-establishment, to punish her mother for not loving her enough. It was all clear in her head. She went to the phone and dialled a number. When the old man came in she said, 'Hello, Papa. Sit down. The police are on their way.'

Ratface was surprised that Bruno walked to the very end of the Cortese property, more surprised when he continued walking on to the main street.

'What's this?'

'Let's catch a train.'

'What about her?' He jerked his head towards the Cortese house.

'Cracking up.'

Ratface was baffled. 'Why?'

'Because she doesn't know who she is.'

That didn't seem like a problem to Ratface.

'Because what she is – really is – has been rejected. So she has to keep switching about. So let her do it in there and crack up.'

'Will she do the job on him?'

'No,' said Bruno.' 'But on everyone else. I liked her, but she was falling apart. It's better this way. I'd only have had to kill her.'

The Greek wasn't too pleased to see Kay. She was shaking and wet and desperate-looking. She started the conversation by saying, 'I have no one else to come to.'

'Not to me.'

'You've always been kind. If you don't help me I'll kill myself.'

She'd spent half the night looking for his boat. His security people had given her the wrong location, and the boat was different, disguised. And so, come to think of it, was he. His powers of turning off were greater than her mother's. It was as though they'd never met.

She sat on the soft leather couch and he flung himself at her to put newspapers under her sodden, dirty clothes.

'I'm old. I'm owed some happpiness.' He hated squalor.

'Why should the old get it?' said Jacey, who sat in the corner on a cushion. 'The young don't seem to get much.'

At first sight Jacey was looking modest, for her. She wore a pale lavender Bill Gibb knitted coat hanging open and thigh-length black wet-look boots, thonged with leather ropes all the way up. Kay felt an unwelcome surge of sickening jealousy. But when Jacey passed by to pour the Greek a Scotch she was reassured to see that the outfit had more to it. A minuscule bikini bottom covered her pubic hair, and her breasts were encased in a green plastic bra. No jewellery. No bedtimes with the Greek.

The boat was so calm. It had the feeling of being cared for – all highly polished wood and brass, the luxury of everything hidden away. Ancient parchment maps were protected by glass and silver frames. All the onyx ornaments were functional. They held pens, matches, Scotch or letters.

'How's the new marriage working out?' asked the Greek.

Kay shook her head. 'That was a lie.' She was still in shock. She'd not eaten or drunk for twenty hours. The police had surrounded Cortese's house setting a watch and picked up everyone loitering or just walking a dog, but they didn't get the ones she wanted them to. Kay had a good story as it went. She said she was visiting her ex-father-in-law because he was ill. Three burglars had tried to enter a window. They were armed. Because the seventies were becoming very dangerous in Italy she carried a gun. She'd produced the gun and the men had disappeared. Then she called the police. She didn't alert the guard standing in the hallway, because he was too far away and she didn't want to put his life at risk. The police didn't believe her story for an instant, but Old Man Cortese was grateful to her for saving his life. He'd always liked her and he had enough power to see she got across the border into France. Once there, the journey had to be devious and undercover. She hitched lifts, walked through the mountains. Bruno might or might not track her down. She hoped desperately that he and Ratface were blown up in the station bomb which had killed twenty that morning.

Kay needed security for her mother, brothers and sisters. But first she needed a hot bath, a hot drink, something to eat, sleep. Jacey got up and started to leave the room. The Greek stopped her.

'Oh, come on, I'm in the way. Well, you were married once,' said Jacey.

The Greek said he'd allow Kay to stay on his boat for one night. First she had to contact her mother and warn her there might be reprisals from Bruno Lanz. Then she and Jacey must do a sex show for a man he loathed and wanted to trap.

Kay closed her eyes. 'Does it never stop?'

'I send his wife the video. You get the idea? Of course you do. You've done it dozens of times.'

. . . Chapter 54 . . .

Margery took Kay back. She even moved Rick's people out of the house. She offered Rick an apartment in Juan-les-Pins from which to run his pop concerts, but the truth was he didn't sing any more. There was nothing to sing about. All the money, all the power, all the connections in the world couldn't make his daughter well. Christmas '72 was a quiet occasion. The little girl was three, didn't speak, had trouble standing up. She laughed a lot, dribbled too much. He tried not to think about it.

Margery had all the rooms Frou Frou used painted a beautiful royal blue with gold-stencilled borders. Blue, she believed, healed. All objects of value or potential danger were removed. The carpets were thick so when the child fell she was unharmed. Margery asked the child to choose the colours she liked for her frocks. It was a coincidence but she always chose a particular pink that had been Dino's favourite. How many shirts had he worn in that colour?

Rick was blamed. Those who adored Margery blamed him because he was not a proper man. His genetic structure was uncertain, faulty. He should never have gone in for fatherhood. He'd heard Kay say, 'What can you expect from a gay? Of course he still is. There's no such thing as a bisexual. And I know for a fact he's had male lovers since being with Mummy.' Coming from her, Rick thought that was a bit strong. Even Charlotte, who was normally gentle, said unkind things behind his back. 'He's drugged too much. It's not Mummy. She's had four to prove it.' Whatever happened it couldn't be Margery. No one mentioned the fact that she might have been too old to conceive a child, except the doctors. The butler blamed Rick's onetime diet. 'Nothing but olives. That's what did it. He was deficient.' The butler put the portrait of Dino back on the wall.

More and more Rick kept to his room. He was thirty and it was over for him. He no longer cared about his appearance. Clothes were just something he threw on. He just about got into the shower.

The pain Margery suffered was beyond measure. She consulted doctors, surgeons, professors. The drug companies were involved, their latest research examined for the slightest chance of improvement. Margery spent many hours with the little girl trying to get her to stand, walk, respond. Margery was very patient. Social life was now over at the Château. Neither Margery or Rick wanted the state of their child to be known. They didn't even discuss it with the family.

Rick so wanted to leave, but he didn't go, because he still felt entranced by Margery, her beauty and grace, her laughter. She aged, but the qualities stayed, especially gaiety. All those years of discipline were not for nothing.

Margery lay on her bed waiting for the Belgian doctor to give his opinion. She closed her eyes and thought she must have slept. Dino was lying beside her. He was so sweet and loving. He said, 'It won't be long now.' And she opened her eyes and her face was flooded with tears. She felt for the pearls around her neck. They gave her comfort. Then she got up and went to the mirror. For the first time the pearls were more beautiful than her. This was Dino's room. She'd dishonoured it by sleeping with two other men, the Greek and Rick de Palma. She'd dared to conceive a child and hope for a new life, when she was still his.

Kay came in without knocking. She often did that, as though hoping to find Margery with Rick. 'Mummy, I don't want to bother you at a time like this but I don't feel well either. I went through a very terrible time. You think, I know you do, that I deliberately set it up to get attention. Doesn't it occur to you that I was terrified and had to comply with that man's orders?'

'Kay, I'm –'

'No, listen. It's always the little girl. She's always the centre. Everyone running around her. I know she's a problem but frankly Rick is – well – I need help. Why can't I have some attention?'

'Kay, you're twenty-nine years of age. Grow up!'

Kay shook as though stung. 'You don't love me. You still pine for Alex. Yet I've been faithful to you, Mummy. If you don't love me you shouldn't have had me.'

'Call me Margery, not Mummy. Kay, get back to work. I told you it's the answer. You're an actress. Go and act. Get Mo Cohen to find you a movie. Do it.'

'After what I've been through?'

Margery stood up, tall and proud. 'I've not told you my troubles. Believe me, life with your father was not the yellow brick road. I've gone through what you have and worse, and I still got in front of that camera and did my job. You don't let fear eat your soul.' And with that she swept from the room.

Kay sat feeling very ordinary. In a minute she'd have to go and fuss over the little girl, pretending everything was all right. Pretending, she was good at.

In February 1973 Kay went shopping in Paris, had her hair coloured red, bought herself a good fur and some modest diamonds that enhanced her but wouldn't get ripped off her in the street. Two people she knew had been mugged recently. Even Paris was a dangerous place. Her resolve: look good but don't incite envy. She did the social round, parties, openings, restaurants, theatres. She was out for a good time. The agency people were now back in force. After her kidnap she agreed it was sensible. These days she had nothing to hide. No one in Paris knew of her liaison with the notorious Bruno Lanz. Her divorce from the Greek had been quick, quiet and expensive.

She knew, she didn't have to be told, that he was hanging out with Jacey. That was clear on that terrible evening she'd asked for refuge on his boat. How little he cared once there was nothing in it for him. Margery had promised to remove Shane from his influence. Shane, however, did what he wanted, and only what he wanted. He was polite and nicely turned out but he was impossible.

As Jacey was so much in her mind it didn't surprise Kay to see her and the Greek shopping in the Rue Faubourg St Honoré. The girl was too small for so much fur. She was literally weighed down by the stuff. Kay enjoyed catching them together. The Greek was surprised Kay looked so good.

'Everything all right now? Ça va?'

'Of course.' She gave the famous Caversham smile. 'I start filming in March.'

'Well, let's not stand on the street. Come back to my apartment and we'll have a drink.'

What he wanted was for Kay to arrange a meeting with Jaspard, who was now looking like serious competition in the forthcoming elections. He knew, as did half Europe, that Charlotte was his mistress.

The Greek's apartment near Trocadéro was stuffed with antiques and paintings. 'Excuse the chaos. I'm having it all shipped to Greece. I will spend my last days there.'

'Oh, come on,' said Jacey. 'What are you? Fifty-nine?'

His phone rang – his eldest son wanting advice. He'd slowed down and was now married with a family.

Kay looked closely at Jacey. What a change. Where was the girl she'd loved so much? 'What are you up to these days?' she asked.

'I do what you did,' said Jacey. 'Hostess for him. I bring him a worse clientèle but they're more fun.'

Kay wanted to ask if she slept with him but it was no longer her concern. 'Well, it's a short position that.' Kay looked at the Greek. 'He'll cram as much in as he can, then kick you out. He always thinks he's dying. The shoe heiress might even get a turn.'

'So what?' said Jacey. 'There are plenty of fish in his sea.'

'But Jacey! You're old!'

Jacey gasped.

The Greek joined them. 'You see, it all comes out right in the end. My son kept me awake at nights. Always in the fast car. But the wildness has sped out of him and he's a nice, serious good man.'

'And he'll get it all,' said Jacey.

'Of course. He was always my heir. It's all for him and his children. I always think the sea is a very clean business.' He asked about Margery, then his phone rang again.

'Not everyone thinks so,' said Jacey as though there'd been no interruption. 'That I've aged.'

She can still get at me, thought Kay. She sits there with a face that's never had a moment's care, but she's well over thirty. Her eyes are baggy. Every debauch has left a reminder. It was the dried-up face of someone who never saw daylight. A nighttime indoors face in smoky rooms, pressed against many men.

'Go on, Jacey. Break my heart.'

And Jacey smiled straight into her eyes with familiarity remembering all the different hotels in different countries.

Kay closed her eyes. 'Well, who?'

'Oh, you wouldn't know her.'

'Her!'

The Greek put a hand over the phone and told them to quieten it.

'You're with a woman? Come outside.'

'Don't be silly,' said Jacey, laughing. 'Come outside! I love it.' She tried to look dignified. 'I'm with the Greek, remember?'

Kay's mind sped through the women in New York, London, Rome. 'Is she gay?'

'I'm getting her that way,' said Jacey. 'I have a lot to thank you for because you put me on the road. Otherwise I'd never have found her.'

'You're too old,' said Kay standing up. 'So I wouldn't want you back.'

'She's an English girl called Jane Kirkland.'

. . . Chapter 55 . . .

Everywhere Charlotte went she hoped she'd see Marcello, but he wasn't a social figure. Occasionally he attended a reception for a charity or a musical event or to please the concert orchestra's backers, but he was mostly on the podium or with his wife near the Italian lakes. She saw him twice. She looked good and she had power. The first time he nodded, kissed her hand, then looked straight at Jaspard as though acknowledging the younger man's right to the girl. Jaspard said, 'It's not often the Maestro goes across the room to a woman to kiss her hand. And I always thought he was a very married man.'

'He always treats me with respect,' said Charlotte.

'So do I,' and he squeezed her hand, the one Marcello had kissed.

When she was pregnant by Jaspard she dreaded seeing Marcello. He was conducting at the Paris Opera in honour of visiting royalty. And afterwards at the reception Charlotte hid away in an adjoining salon. Jaspard congratulated Marcello on the concert. Marcello was always so effortlessly elegant he made everyone else feel overdressed, including Jaspard.

Marcello had asked Jaspard how Charlotte was.

'She's having my baby,' said the politician.

'Oh, I am so pleased. I'd love to see her.'

And Jaspard brought the love of her life into the side salon. Marcello took both of her hands and smiled so beautifully, that she responded. He could make anyone smile.

'Charlotte, you look lovelier than ever.' She was wearing a pale chiffon gown by Givenchy. And for a brief moment his eyes were drawn to her breasts. How he remembered those. He'd never imagined anything like that. 'How many months?' Just thinking about them could give him an erection. The breasts had become the centrepiece of his sexual fantasies.

'Seven.' And she added softly, 'I wish it was yours.'

He didn't know how to reply. He said, 'So do I.' He meant because it would have made her happy. The remark inflamed Charlotte and her love surged back, twice as strong. She wouldn't let go of his hands. 'Will you be the godfather?'

'Of course.' He tried to extricate himself. The future

President of France was standing behind him. How much could he hear or sense?

'I am so happy for you both. It would be my honour. Let's compose something for the baby's baptism.'

Still she didn't let go. 'Then come to see me. At my mother's house. Come next week.'

He wished he could excuse himself because of engagements but she knew his schedule. In February he did not conduct.

'Yes, all right.' He finally extricated himself and turned round. All the worry for nothing. The politician was talking with the Queen.

Charlotte watched him go. 'You are mine, have always been. We've known other lives and been together. I'll die with you,' she said to herself.

She remembered his words, 'So do I,' and she cried with happiness.

Charlotte was called to the Château the following day. Kay had had a breakdown. It was disconcerting because she was a woman of twenty-nine yet she behaved like a child of four. One look at her stricken eyes and Charlotte knew the visit from Marcello would have to be cancelled.

Margery said, 'You'll have to help me. Bad luck is beginning to be a pattern in this place.'

Charlotte mentioned Marcello's proposed visit.

'Jesus!' said Margery. 'Who's happy? Cancel it. The doctor wants Kay on Valium and some other thing but she won't take it. I can't have Marcello seeing all this.'

Jaimie Laurenson came in carrying Frou Frou. Carlo brought in the drinks. Jaimie said, 'Your sister tangled up with a very wrong guy, the left-wing activist Bruno Lanz. He blows up trains, torches embassies, shoots industrialists. I want you to get Jaspard to intervene. I want him caught. I'll write a letter explaining what information has been given to me. And I don't care how the arrest is made. If he's shot dead resisting arrest it's easier all round. We don't want Kay in it.'

'Why can't you get him yourself?' said Charlotte. 'You were very good knocking Frey out the ring.'

'Oh, Charlotte!' said Margery. 'What had Jaimie to do with a loony fan? It could happen to any one of us. The man was a lunatic.'

'I believe it,' said Charlotte. 'Except he was never caught.'

'I was in New York at the time,' said Jaimie coldly. 'Twenty people saw me. Now I need Jaspard in this because the train assassin admires him. He'll want him to take on some of his proposals at the next election. Jaspard must trap him, otherwise this family is never really safe.'

Charlotte wouldn't answer.

Jaimie said, 'I think the politician owes you, Charlotte. You're having his child and he hasn't even considered marrying you.'

Charlotte got up holding her stomach. 'I'll talk to him. But don't pressurise me, Jaimie Laurenson. I'm not part of what Kay does.' She left the room.

Margery was looking at him, and for the first time the strain showed in her face.

'He'll do it, Margery. He will if he wants to win an election. Otherwise I'll go to the rival press and blow his love child.'

'Would you?' she asked.

'No, because it's Charlotte. But he doesn't know I won't.'

Margery fumbled for his hand. 'Don't ever get married. Please. Don't let a woman take you away. I need you.'

Frou Frou made noises like a bird.

'The only thing I think about is they don't live long,' said Margery softly.

They sat watching the fire. Then Jaimie said, 'Jaspard could have caught up with Bruno Lanz. He hasn't really tried. The students admire Lanz, that's why.'

'Do you?' asked Margery.

'I think,' said Jaimie, 'he's not what he seems. He could be from the Right, posing as the Left, discrediting the Left. He's infiltrated the Left – I'm sure of it – because blowing up people is never the answer. It loses you votes.' He took hold of Margery's hand, caressed it, by his touch assuring her everything would all be all right.

'As it's problem day d'you want another one?' asked Margery. 'Dino used to say if the bullfighter's in the ring let all the bulls come out. Kay's lesbian friend told her she's with – wait for it – Jane Kirkland!'

It wasn't often Jaimie was so taken aback that he allowed a reaction to show.

The next day he assured Margery that Jacey was back with Frey and doing parties for the Greek.

'You found that out fast,' said Margery caustically.

'Jacey was just winding your daughter up.'

Margery took Kay her hot drink laced with Valium. 'I don't want you to worry about Bruno Lanz. It's being taken care of. Jaimie's doing it.'

'He was so like Daddy. He was absolute. His "no" was eternal, absolute.'

'I don't think that was such a good thing,' said Margery. She sounded sharp in spite of herself.

'You don't?' Kay was alert.

'I don't think Dino being so categorically absolute about every goddam thing was right. No!'

Kay was shocked, and Margery's face became careful. The outburst had come from nowhere. Dino was not a safe subject for her at this time.

Margery tried to explain what Jaimie had said about Jacey's lovelife, but Kay didn't want to listen. So Margery said, 'If you want to see Jacey we can arrange it.'

'I just want you to hold me, Mummy. Don't leave me again.'

And Margery held her and thought, in one room the child doesn't speak and in this room the twenty-nine-year-old is asking what the three-year-old should. Alex tells people's futures by vending machines. Charlotte is having a child illegitimately but something says she's not in love with the father. And Shane keeps out of sight. Maybe he's got a point. And then she remembered her husband Rick who stayed out of it altogether. She said to herself, 'I want Kay working and Rick goes into politics.'

. . . Chapter 56 . . .

'Oil' greased its way on to the TV screens nationwide but after episode three the ratings were poor. It was too slick. The status quo in Jane's relationship with Jaimie Laurenson remained the same. He'd sleep with her, she'd desperately want him again but he'd be off to Hawaii or places she'd never even heard of. She'd spend weeks distressed, jealous, needing him but keeping it to herself. Then he'd come back and give her more sex and the pent-up emotion made it even better. The sex was getting a million miles away from the missionary position. Neither of them had ever dreamed there could be so many variations. They'd do it for hours and she'd never had anything like it. And the next morning he'd be gone. She consoled herself by looking actively for someone else. She went to all the parties, accepted every date, but no one came near Jaimie Laurenson so she didn't even get as far as a first kiss. Her second consolation was his power. He was wonderful for her work. Her career could only rise astronomically. If only she didn't love him.

She also worked with Jonny Citta cutting *La Vamp*. Most of the time he was coked up and everything was sheer energy. It sounded all right but had little meaning when you got away from him and thought it over. He was like a sane madman. He reminded Jane of Lucy and her rabbit in London in the old days. Jane was no editor but at least she could think. She believed that even in this day and age a film should have a beginning and an end. If you got a middle too you were winning. Jonny snorted coke straight off the back of his hand. 'I want to make a movie that no one's seen before. Let's throw it up in the air and run it the way it lies. Like a huge accident.'

As it was Jane's starring role she did not look pleased.

'We'll call it, *Slaughter of a Vamp*. Like *The Naked Lunch*. Burroughs didn't bother with A, B and C.'

'Jonny, we're trying to get from one to two. D'you think we'll do it? Reel one, remember. Reel two follows.'

'What's one and two got to do with it?' And he walked off in disgust.

Jane heard his weekly coke bills ran into thousands. His eyes were fiery bright, his skin pulled back, his face like a white wolf's. And this girl from France kept hanging around. They said she was a princess. She remembered a ravishing girl called Jacey from the gossip columns but this one was all washed up. It couldn't be the same girl. She wore dark glasses and a dark green gaberdine raincoat – no makeup. She certainly didn't look LA, but as though she'd walked off a French movie.

Jacey kept saying, 'Frey wants to see you. He's got something for you.'

'I thought he'd had a terrible accident?'

'People get better from those,' said the French girl. 'I can get you to Frey.'

Jane sighed. She wished the girl could get her a good editor. In the end she called Jaimie. He said he had to go to Paris.

Important business. He'd sort out the editor problem – give him a week. And she knew she didn't have a week. Jonny Citta was blowing so much white powder up his nose he wasn't going to last. He'd go out of the studio on to the street looking as though he'd had his head in a flour bin. He'd party all night. He didn't eat. He wanted out. He said, 'I wanna go like a white rain firework. Everything shoot up out the top of my head like a huge brilliant white firework.'

She tried to get him to a doctor, but he only liked doctors if they pushed coke. She went to the producer. He wasn't doing anything – he was on coke himself. What was she fussing about? A couple of days later she came home and Jonny Citta was in her apartment sitting at the table, his head slumped forward in a gigantic mound of white powder. He'd died trying to snort the lot. Scrawled on the mirror, in her lipstick, were the words 'See you in the next place. So don't be too good.' Kit was running round and round thinking it was a game. He kept putting his finger in Uncle Jonny's castor sugar. The nanny had run out to get a doctor who lived along the boardwalk.

Jaimie said, 'You shouldn't have got the paramedics. What good could they do? He was dead. You should have got me.'

'How do I know where you are?'

'There's always someone on call, Jane. An assistant would have been here within the hour and cleaned up the mess. And you shouldn't have let it be known that Kit witnessed the incident – the paramedics say he was playing with the stuff.'

Every paper in the States carried the story. The Conservative Midwest was very hostile. This little-known street star from England was implicated as Jonny's pusher. Why else did he die in her flat?'

Jaimie said, 'You might be suspended or written out of the series. You could come up for trial. We'll get an editor on that movie and put it out quick. Jonny Citta's last shot.' God, was he tired. If he slept now he'd not get up for a week. He moved Jane out of her Venice apartment to a rented house near Zuma beach. 'It's only temporary,' he said. Her driving was lousy and Zuma was a long way from the studio. She wanted to go back to her apartment. She'd been happy there.

'But whenever you go in you'll see that small suicidal dope lying slumped in a mountain of coke. Why did he do it?'

She didn't think it was suicide. She was certain he'd planned a party but who knew the guest list? They were unlikely to come forward. Jonny knew he could die at any time. He didn't have to do any more towards taking his life than he already was.

'He couldn't take it, success,' said Jaimie. 'Or life. Only his art was real for him. A world he could control. He couldn't have relationships. He couldn't take fame so he wanted a coke mountain. He couldn't even make it with a girl in the end.'

'Well,' said Jane,' 'I haven't made it with a man for weeks, and I'm not on coke.'

He said he'd make it up to her. Their happiness was in the bank, interest growing. He had a few Caversham scrapes to sort out, then he'd ease off and give himself some life. 'By the way, Jane. What gives with this French chick hanging around?'

'Gives?'

'She's hanging around your action, so I hear. Her name's Jacey. Someone said you sleep with her.'

'Oh, bullshit! I don't even know her.'

Jane Kirkland was one of the few women he knew who wouldn't lie. He told her to watch her back, watch the French chick, stay away from reporters, keep Kit out of sight, stay low – it was a dangerous world.

So she went out immediately and talked to the press, went on TV nationwide. She told people about Jonny Citta, her friend, a wonderful talented guy who'd died from drug abuse. She explained how it began so insiduously. You took a snort, a snort took a snort, a snort takes you. She appealed to the kids. 'It's not pretty. Coke kills.'

People believed her and they liked her. She was beginning to find out how to save herself. What was more, it didn't do the show's ratings any harm. The producer said, 'Write that lively English girl in more.'

Margery held three different US newspapers. She said, 'What do you mean, Jaimie, you didn't tell her to do it?'

'It was her idea, her words and her success. I told her to keep out of sight.'

'It's monstrous,' said Margery. 'She gets off on a corpse. Is there no stopping her?'

Jaimie tried to get Margery's mind on a possible party for Frou Frou's next birthday.

'You see that Kirkland girl, Jaimie? Mo Cohen told me.'

'So you've got me watching your enemies, and your friends watching me.' He didn't like it.

'And you slept with my daughter. You slept with her in a Paris hotel in '68 or '69. A threesome. It won't do. I thought you were better than that.'

'Come on, Margery, you don't want to hear the story. You know it's not going to be a boy meets girl affair.'

'The trouble is, Jaimie, I don't know if I can trust you, but you're all I've got. You've got balls, which means you go your own way. You're like Dino. People say I took Rick's balls off. I didn't. Eunuchs are no fun.' She stopped feeling sorry for herself and thought of Jane Kirkland. 'That girl's done a picture. *La Vamp*. You kept that hidden. It's coming to the festival here in May. But she doesn't come with it, not to Cannes. For crissake, she's taking over the old places, making them common. She's a shock. It's like going into Harrods and finding you're in Woolworths.'

'She's invited.'

'This is my town. I'm going to make you an offer. You have complete control of the Caversham estate. You run all my business on percentage. We get rid of the gang, and –'

She'd just offered him life security.

'– you won't get all that jetlag.'

He said he'd think about it. The price would be high. No freedom. No Jane Kirkland.

. . . Chapter 57 . . .

When Margery got back from the Swiss hospital with Frou Frou she was stripped of illusions and all hope. She could spend all the money she had, but no doctor could change the course of the little girl's deterioration. The Swiss consultants were adamant. 'Anyone who says they can help is a fake. So you're wasting money. Your best plan of action is to put her into a home where she'll be properly looked after.'

But the child loved Margery. She knew her smiling face, the smell of her, her touch, her hair. All her best noises were made for Margery.

On the drive back Rick kept saying, 'Put her away and forget about it, Marge. Then do a film. Start again. It's what you keep telling Kay. I'll be there for you.'

The child wanted constant attention: nappies changed, feeding, consoling, holding. She couldn't be alone for a moment. Then she said one word: 'Mama.' And Margery's fate was sealed. She'd never let her go.

Margery tried to get Alex back. She needed him beside her. In her letter she wrote, 'This is a time for the family to be together.'

He wrote back, 'Too far to come. Why d'you think I'm in Mexico?'

His next letter said, 'Isn't Mexico far enough? I don't live in the sticks for nothing. I wasn't any part of it, Margery.'

Charlotte had a girl, and called her Margery. She continued living in Paris so Jaspard could visit daily. He didn't talk about divorce and she didn't suggest he get one. It wasn't as though she loved him. Because of Kay's breakdown Marcello had not been able to visit the Château. She now invited him to dinner in Paris to discuss the baby's christening. She said he was one person who must see her baby.

Marcello's wife was constantly ill and certainly not in the mood for physical love. But he still loved her. Infidelity was impossible for him. He put all his energy and frustration into his music. He sent Charlotte flowers and a promise to call when his busy schedule ended. Excuses were perhaps not the best way to deal with a passionate woman, but he did not want to hurt her. And some people, because of their name or powerful allies, could not be ignored. His wife said, 'I think you like her.'

Marcello gave a casual shrug.

'She's young, healthy. I'm no good to you.'

He assured his wife that love did not depend on scintillating encounters in bed, though they'd had enough of those to remember. But secretly he did want a young woman, that was true. But not Charlotte. For one thing she reminded him of his wife.

Jonny's last film *La Vamp* was predicted to be a winner at

Cannes and of course the now famous street star would appear in person.

Kay said, 'She's going to make it. I don't believe it. What are we going to do?'

'She'll never come here,' said Margery. 'It's always drugs with her, isn't it? She ruined my son, now she's killed a gifted director.' And then Margery used a big word. 'Evil, that's her.'

And on the strength of her conviction she called Mo Cohen and told him to buy up the film. 'Get it, Mo. Whatever it costs. Then shelve it. That's one picture that never sees the light of day.'

'Why d'you hate her so much?' asked Mo.

Margery didn't know any more. Lately the hate had changed. It took her some time to give a name to the new emotion. It wasn't one she experienced often. It was fear. They'd all done too much to the girl.

Mo Cohen wasn't happy. He made stars, not smothered them. He felt insulted. It was like asking a doctor to kill off a patient. He said he'd have a look at the movie and let Margery know.

Then Marion reminded him he couldn't buy it anyway. Margery already owned it. She'd taken the option on Jonny Citta after *Street*. Marion said, 'He was supposed to work with Kay and Rick. She's forgotten. She must be in a bad way to forget that.'

Mo remembered and told Margery himself. At least the deed was out of his hands. Margery called her lawyers and checked out a few contractual details. Then she called Jaimie in New York and told him, 'I'm blocking Jonny Citta's last film.'

'Why?' asked Jaimie.

'It's mine. He was under contract to me. I was to have his next film. He walked out so this one's mine. I've got the deal letter. So don't get difficult, Jaimie, because I own enough of Mo Cohen's studio. No unions, no lawyers, no publicity.'

'Jonny Citta left Cannes because Kay was – indisposed.'

'If that's polite for fucking her kidnapper, sure. But who's going to say so? Jonny Citta's dead.'

'What is it you've got against the English girl?'

'Read the deal letter and the contract, Jaimie.' Margery sounded very smooth. 'I have the option rights. I have chosen to shelve this picture because of its drug connection.'

He knew he couldn't object on legal grounds. It would have to be big guns. Like he knew too much about the Cavershams. She'd fire him before he got to the end of it and he'd lose the comfortable life-security job. How strongly did he feel about Jane? He'd recently seen Guido Cortese in Milan, third-rate, wrecked. It frightened him. This was a young man who once upon a time had everything going for him. Get off the fast lane and you were in a cul-de-sac. The sight of Guido had made him very thoughtful.

'I'll go and look at the footage, Margery.'

'You'll find Mo Cohen also looking.'

She thought a lot of frightened men were going to the cinema.

Margery told Kay a dozen times a day the answer was to go to work. The new obsession in the Château was thinking up a film for Kay. They read newspapers, books, watched old movies. Writing Kay's movie became a parlour game. Even Carlo the butler joined in.

'Of course your best story is your marriage to Bruno Lanz,' said Margery. 'That is box office. But Jaimie isn't sure he is a left-wing hero.'

'And I was never married to him. D'you want me assassinated?' said Kay.

'You were married. Why not? You do everything else.' And Margery waited daily for news of the son-in-law she'd never seen. Jaspard agreed to have him dealt with. He was an embarrassment with his extreme views and violence.

Less than a week later Jaimie called the Château. Bruno had been blown up in a car carrying explosives near the Italian border. That was the official story.

Kay lay on the floor at her mother's feet in one of the blue rooms. They were alone as Rick was upstairs with yet another so-called virus. Watching the fire, enjoying its warmth and abundance, she thought of Jacey, of the early days. She was always reliving the seduction, the exploration, the wildness of the affair. Nothing in her life had matched that. And now Jacey had got old-looking all of a sudden, dried up like a prune.

'Baron Kurtz asked me to marry him,' said Kay. He was a wealthy art collector with health problems. 'He's worth three hundred million dollars.'

'But a person is worth more than money.' And Marcello was suddenly in the room. It was such a simple statement, yet so logical, that Margery wondered why the hell she hadn't thought of it. Frou Frou appeared beside him and he held her hand. She was dressed up as Columbine. 'We've had such fun finding the right costume. And now we have it we are going to celebrate. Aren't we?' The little girl looked at him, her mouth hanging open. 'We are going to play some music and dance.' He looked at Margery. 'Music would be marvellous for her. This house is so silent, so sad.'

'Do you wonder?' said Margery.

'But it doesn't help her. And you surprise me, Margery. Come on, turn all your lights on full. Let's celebrate life.' And he took Frou Frou off to the social part of the house.

Margery sighed deeply.

'Rick isn't ill, Mummy. He's just sulking.'

'Oh, quit, Kay. He's sad. Leave him alone.'

'Why don't you get rid of him and marry Jaimie Laurenson?' Kay loved that choice because Jaimie was always away and she'd have Mummy to herself. 'Don't you fancy Jaimie? Just a little bit?'

'Kay, he likes young women. I know the type he goes for. I am not that type. Nor that young.'

'Rick doesn't do anything for you any more. We've all noticed that.'

Margery didn't answer.

'All these so-called blue flues. He certainly cheers up when a male pop star comes into the room. If there's anything worse than a gay it's an old gay.'

'Funny, he said the same thing about you,' said Margery maliciously. Rick had said nothing. He was beyond speech. 'Are you going to marry Kurtz?'

'Of course not,' said Kay.

'Do another film.'

But Kay wasn't sure that was what she wanted. Her own face wasn't exactly young.

Margery let out a long, exhausted breath. 'Then do something because you've got money and choice. You can do anything. Open a boutique.'

Kay pulled a face.

'It could be very chic and original. You adore clothes. Or run a theatre.'

'Oh, I don't know. You have to be so committed.'

'Then get married.'

Kay couldn't think of one person she wanted to share her life with. And there was nothing she wanted to do. She just wanted Jacey back, the way she once was.

'Put it this way,' said Margery. 'I want you off your arse and doing something.' She spoke in the sharp tone she used on the maid from Dover. Kay did not like it.

'How about if I stay here and look after you? Because he's off.' She pointed upstairs to where Rick was sulking.

Margery doubted it. You had to have somewhere to go. And the sixties were over.

... Chapter 58 ...

Jane marched into Mo Cohen's office and the secretaries fell over themselves trying to stop her. 'What shit is this?' she demanded. '*La Vamp* isn't going to Cannes? It's been entered and accepted.'

'Darling,' said Mo. 'It's not coming out this year, that's all.'

'What?' Jane grabbed his heavy silver lighter. For a moment he thought she was going to hit him with it.

'Darling, the board have decided to shelve Jonny's film till late '74 maybe '75. Let the notoriety die down. No one likes drugs.'

'But it's my goddam picture.'

'Sure and you're good. Let's find you another one. Trust us, Jane. That coke OD doesn't do a movie any good.'

'You talk about coke as though Jonny Citta invented it. People do take it out here, you know. It's one of the city's major profit transactions.'

'Oh, please don't give me figures and facts, darling. Just trust me.'

She remembered Dinah, Al Streep's wife saying that – and how trustworthy that turned out to be.

Jane realised she'd got hold of the lighter. She wanted to light it, hold it in front of his face and say, 'You've got just as long as this flame flickers to get the movie back on.' And then she'd snap it off. That's what Margery would do. But she didn't have the clout.

Jaimie spent a sleepless night in the Beverly Hills Hotel. He'd seen her face as she'd left Mo Cohen's office, the pain, and he couldn't bear it. He decided to go up against the Cavershams and get the film released. When it was light he went straight to her apartment in Venice. These days she kept the door locked and she had to get up to let him in.

'Go back to bed,' he said.

But she made some coffee. She'd spent an entirely sleepless night too.

He said, 'I don't know why I'm in awe of Margery, but I am, that's the truth. You've always been right about that. I guess it's my working-class beginnings. Why don't I go up against her? What can she do to me? What have I to lose? There's nothing more to die.'

'Yes, I feel joyless myself.' She took his nothing-more-to-lose speech to mean he did not love her. 'Mo Cohen's not releasing the film.'

Jaimie thought fast – he'd nearly walked into that one. He assumed she knew Margery was behind Mo Cohen's move. Oddly, she didn't. And now she just thought he had problems with Margery and was sharing them. At least his feelings.

He got up and held her, kissed her. And it was all lovely and sexy, but as he did it to her, her mind was off on its own. This man will not live with you or marry you. He's still married to the dead wife and can't get over it. He uses you for sex. And now and then for warmth. His life is made bearable by fast business and the fact he controls it himself. Have an orgasm but don't lose your heart.

Alex came by in the afternoon and she made the mistake of telling him the bad news about the film. He didn't want to hear about her career. He'd come for Kit. He hadn't driven all this way up from Mexico to hear a lot of movie gloom. Kit said he didn't want to go with Alex. He wanted to stay with his Mum because she was sad. Jane tried to encourage Kit to go with his father. She promised she'd be OK.

Kit pulled her off to one side, his eyes big and scared. 'Alex never talks to me. Nor does the slant-eyed lady.'

'Come on. He's your Dad.'

Alex went outside and sat on the step patiently. She thought he only wanted the kid when she didn't want him to have him. Now the kid was a drag. So she said, 'Alex, are you sure you want to take Kit.'

Alex turned and looked at her. 'Yeah.'

'I mean, he can stay here,' she said.

Alex didn't answer.

So she whispered to Kit that Dad did want him. 'You can take your skates.'

Kit ran down the wooden stairs to the boardwalk. He shouted up, 'I don't want to go with him. He doesn't want me. I want to stay with you, Mum, because you're all sad.' And he ran off.

Alex shouted, 'Get your arse in the truck, Kit. We're off to Mexico. No shit.'

Kit stopped and turned. 'I like the other one better than you.' And he ran around the corner.

'Which out of the dozens of other ones could that be?' asked Alex.

'Only one,' said Jane.

'Playing with fire. My mother's got Jaimie Laurenson like this.' And he held out a hand flat and closed it and mangled air. 'You're not smart. She wants him to marry Kay. Now go and look for the kid. He needs some discipline, Jane.'

'Yeah,' she said, going down the steps. 'And who are you going to get to do that?'

Then she heard the screams. The screaming of her child. The screams of the passers-by. The shouts of those trying to save him. Kit, aged five, died after being impaled on some railings. He'd tried to get over because he was running away.

'Oh shit!' said Kay. 'They'll make her into a martyr.'

Margery was staring at the Modigliani painting. 'It always reminds me of my son – Modigliani's story. And this woman was his model, had a child by him. When Modigliani died of drink and drugs she was so obsessed she went to the top of the house and threw herself off. She and her soon-to-be-born second child were killed.'

How often Margery had longed for Jane Kirkland to do just that. 'I hate her more than any other being alive. More than words can say. I have to descend to the mundane to get it across to you.'

'What, that model?' asked Kay looking at the painting.
'That girl. She's killed my son's child.'

Margery was so upset she'd had to take to her bed. Underneath her anger she felt something, not exactly pity, for Jane. It was never Alex's child, not in her mind, but Jane's. But whatever the feeling was it made her weep.

'The kid's probably better off dead.' She slammed a fist into her pillow. 'Why grow up to be a drug addict?' And she refused to admit she was crying. But the thought of the child impaled on the railings devastated her.

Kay told Charlotte that Mummy was taking it very well.

Charlotte said, 'We must do something for Jane.'

'Jaimie Laurenson's trying to reach her but she's gone away. No one knows where.'

Charlotte looked at the masses of floral tributes. 'It's odd. People from all over the world sent them. To Dino's grandchild.'

'Yes, it's funny,' agreed Kay. 'I always thought of the boy as Mummy's grandchild. But these people are right. He was Dino's.'

'We should bury him here,' said Charlotte. The house felt very cold suddenly. 'Is there no heating?'

'Of course the house is heated,' said Kay. 'But Mummy won't hear of him coming to rest here. He wasn't one of us.'

'I think he should.' Charlotte was quite imperious. 'In fact I insist. And I think we should take some care of that poor woman. And where is Alex? Out denying life on a drug binge?'

Kay had never heard Charlotte so challenging.

Jane rejected Mo Cohen's offer to arrange the funeral. She said, 'I bury my own.' Kit was cremated and she alone scattered his ashes at sea. After the ashes she threw some white flowers, then his skates, then hers. 'I'll never skate again, or be happy, Kit. That was all for you.'

And she signalled for the boatman to take her back. As usual in the bad times she was alone. But when the boat pulled in a man held out his hand. She thought it was Alex, but as she got nearer she saw it was Jaimie. He puts his arms around her tight and then they walked up to the apartment, not speaking. She still had the candles lit. She watched them burn down and said, 'I think it's time I moved from here.'

'You've got me. All the way. I'm with you.' Then he said, 'I've been there, don't forget.'

... Chapter 59 ...

As soon as the memory of Kit's dying came into her mind she shut it out and thought about something else – anything. She kept busy. She read scripts, books, made meals that she couldn't eat, watched movies. She refused to talk about it. Then his face as he struggled to free himself would come into her mind and stayed there. His solemn eyes implored her to help. And she would scream, all the horrors of hell in her cry, and she'd run from whatever room she was in, out into the street, beach or country. When she'd seen him impaled, at first she hadn't dared approach. Then she'd run and held him and the full horror, the ghastly gaping horror of his injury became clear. His small body was writhing with agony, and she cried for someone in the crowd to give him a shot, to take away his pain. And she cried to God. And she knew but dare not accept it that he would die. And she said to Alex, 'Move him off the spike. Let's do it.' Alex said, 'Leave him, Jane. Don't move him.' And it was so bad, that death, that no one dared approach. Just she and Alex and the dying boy together. And the paramedic van took an eternity to come. And two onlookers had to be taken off in it for treatment for shock. It was too late for Kit. He was covered with blankets and she given a shot for trauma, her bloodied clothes taken from her. She too was covered with blankets. And for days afterwards neighbours laid flowers in front of the place where Kit had died. It was never without flowers.

As she ran screaming through the countryside the sky seemed to be as red as his blood. And she stopped and shouted up, 'Fuck you! Take me too. Do it to me! Bastard!' And then she crouched in the grass and took the tranquillisers, enough to shut everything out. And everything went out – except Kit's dying.

Alex came then – she didn't know how he'd found her – and he said, 'Don't take so many pills, Jane. It just makes you more vulnerable because you lose control of your mind.' And he tried to get her to take some morphine, which he'd been on steadily since the death. She thought he had a lot of courage, the way he stayed by Kit and was calm. He'd turned very pale but he did a lot better than the passers-by.

'D'you want to talk to me?' he asked. 'Maybe we should talk to each other.'

'You should have got him off the railings.'

'No, Jane. I checked. Pulling him free would have been much much worse. Too much was pierced and –' He couldn't go on. 'I think you should have a good cry. Get it out of your system.'

She'd be surprised if a good cry would get that out of her mind. She'd die with that one. How she hated life! Her best means of survival was to attack – attack life which so relentlessly punished her. She got up from the grass. 'I have to phone my Mum. The newspapers and TV will upset her. I'm going to tell her it was very quick.'

'Yeah,' said Alex. 'I'd like to talk to her too.'

After they'd made the phone call to Hastings they sat in the garden of a house which Jane didn't even know. It was in fact Jaimie Laurenson's Connecticut home, used mainly by his business associates. Jaimie was in the study, not working, just waiting to see what she'd do next. He left her alone with Alex.

For a long while they sat in silence. Then Alex said, 'Lucien would like to come and see you. He's a very healing guy. I think we should stay together through this one.'

She said, 'I'd rather be by myself.'

She didn't blame Alex. Just life.

Alex said, 'It'll all get better, Jane. No one gets it all bad.'

Jane decided to go back to work on the series. It took all her strength to push through the first days. Her other idea had been to run away and hide. She knew that if she did that she'd go back on the drink, so to save herself she kept on the set in the company of people she knew. Everyone admired her courage. The story hit the press. Soon the whole of America took the bereaved mother to their hearts. The show's ratings soared. For the last quarter of '73 and the beginning of '74 it was in the top ten worldwide. Disaster had made her a star.

In London, her onetime agent Al Streep's widow said, 'I always knew she'd make it. From the first moment. She came in with nothing, off the streets, and my husband Al and I looked after her.'

Reading that, Jane almost laughed. Dinah rewriting her life.

Marcello Tallaforos sent her a beautiful and compassionate letter from New York. He said how well he remembered her and the baby from their brief meeting a few years ago. He had never forgotten the good impression she made on him. Her warmth and her strength would see her through the grief. She kept that letter.

Alex couldn't get the horror of Kit's death out of his mind. He genuinely thought he should go to the desert and stay there and wait to die. Because the more actions you did, the more shit you got. Life wasn't at all what it seemed. You think it's one birdsong sunrise after another. He knew different. He had to admit, if only to himself, that Jane had guts. She got on that set in front of a camera. He'd loved Kit. He felt bad that his dislike of Jane had soured it. But it all came down from Margery, so really the desert was the best place. Margery couldn't get at him there.

It was a year after Kit died that Robert Frey made his move. Wearing a patch over his left eye, he stood beside her on the set of 'Oil' and said, 'I tried to reach you. I sent Jacey to see you. You never replied. So I waited for my face to be healed and I came to you.' It was autumn 1974.

His face was not bad, considering what it had gone through. The scarring on the left cheek and brow did not stop him being attractive. The more she looked at him, the more she saw that the violation of his face would not stop him being what he was. And France, the French public, had certainly agreed with her. After one film he was back at the top.

She apologised for not contacting him but she'd been through a few bad spots herself. He made a short delicate speech of condolence.

'My film was pulled too. *La Vamp*.'

'But of course.' He laughed bitterly.

'Of course?'

'Why do you think? You were getting somewhere.'

'But the studio shelved it because of Jonny and the coke and –'

'Margery Caversham killed your film because you were getting too big.'

Jane sat down shocked.

'So I know when I offer you my little help – I wish it were more – you will not say no. I am going to direct and star in the movie of Dino de Stefano's life. And you will play Margery Caversham.'

Jane's mouth fell open.

'Why not? You're English. So is she.'

Jane was amazed, absolutely knocked out. Then she saw it was impossible. 'They'll never let you. They've got lawyers and Jaspard and other politicians and –'

'And I've got a little book written in South America by a little forgotten retainer called Julian. And there's not one fucking thing they can do about it.'

'It's me or her.' Margery looked very young. Jaimie suspected she'd had her face remodelled. Even her dress was girlish. The Dior dress was made up of layers of transparent fabric like rose petals, out of which her shoulders and bosom rose triumphant. The flesh was good and firm. A hibiscus flower was tucked behind one ear. Long gloves of lime-green satin reached all the way up her arms, fastened with tiny buttons of real jet. For a moment Jaimie felt uneasy. He'd seen the movies about the movie stars going nuts in middle age and behaving like young kids. As though reading his thoughts Margery laughed. 'Not *Sunset Boulevard*, sweet. I'm just posing for some shots. They want to know how I looked as a deb. You know, in London when I was a girl.'

He just about knew. 'Who wants to know?'

'The White House. They're doing a retrospective of our lives. Mine and Dino's.'

Why hadn't he heard about it?

'So I'm just putting on the old clothes through the ages. Letting them see how I evolved. And letting them have the photographs of Dino.'

'Don't put too many frocks on, Margery, until I check it out.' He felt very uneasy about this one. The usual chemical feeling of uneasiness.

He was wearing Cerutti clothes these days and Margery

thought he looked divine. 'Come in and say hello to the girls,' she said.

'Way back there, Margery, before we started admiring each other, you said something that sounded unfriendly.'

'You heard it. I don't have to repeat it. Make up your mind. If it's La Kirkland, please go. If it's me, come in to lunch. Marcello Tallaforos and his adoring opera singers are coming, and Jaspard and Charlotte, and Prince William whom they're trying to put with Kay. It's about the only thing she hasn't had, a prince. And the philosopher Erhart.'

Erhart, the Nobel prizewinner, Jaimie would have loved to meet. To talk to such a man would be something he'd cherish for life. He had to admit the social life in his Manhattan apartment with Jane couldn't match this. It was usually just him and Jane. She'd have brought over actors from 'Oil' but he was sick of the entertainment world by the time the weekend came.

There wasn't a choice though. 'She's been through something terrible. I have to be there,' he said.

Margery turned on him, 'Haven't I?'

'Margery, you have people around you. She doesn't. I don't see where the problem lies. I do business with you. I have an intimate relationship with her.'

'And you're fired.' Quite simply Margery ended fifteen years of their friendship. They were conspirators more than friends.

'Block her career again, Margery, and it's your biggest mistake. I've got enough on you.'

She lifted two fingers at him insolently. 'Snap!'

He left. He got back into the Ferrari but felt too shaky to drive. Had he done the right thing?

Margery smiled gaily and welcomed her first guests. She was into happiness and pleasure again. So the world was a sad place – that didn't stop her being a life-loving person.

'Sometimes we have to celebrate. Just the fact of having life,' she said. Five-year-old Frou Frou was not included in these social events. She made people sad.

Jane met Jacey and Frey at Grand Central Station. He was nervous and wanted the meeting somewhere with a lot of exits. It was ironic because all around were magazine covers of Kay

Caversham. Kay wearing a Spanish outfit by Karl Lagerfeld, tight black and red matador pants and a high cummerbund of scarlet. A short bolero jacket embroidered with gold and rhinestones and flashing ruby red. The hat, a matador shape of black velvet lined with scarlet silk under the brim to match the scarlet slash of her lipstick. Earrings, big gold hoops from Cartier. Jane, while waiting for Frey, had read all about the outfit inside the magazine. It was a very famous ensemble.

Frey said, 'Kay's clothes are all you read about these days. That's all she does, magazine covers. To keep her face in.'

Frey wore Ray-Ban glasses. In the early days before they became too fashionable he favoured Porsche. After several eye operations he'd partially regained his sight in the damaged eye. The process had been painful but he didn't talk about pain. He wore bell-bottom jeans and a leather fur-trimmed jacket. Jacey wore orange hotpants and six-inch-heeled orange sandals showered with diamanté. Her Yves Saint Laurent blazer was studded with jewellery in geometrical shapes. She wore geometrical earrings. Her hair was tousled. Dark glasses hid the ravages of the afternoon's sins.

Jane wore a wrap-around skirt and a ruffled blouse in black and mauve crêpe with black canvas shoes.

'The completely amazing thing,' said Frey, 'is that Margery has fallen for the White House crap and has sent a million photographs of herself through the ages to my contact there. So we know exactly how she looked. We'll go into preproduction early '76. Your series terminates then. And it gives me time.' He'd learned how to wait – had he ever! Waiting for his injuries to heal. Waiting to get Dino's brother. Trying to get him to talk. Patience was rewarded in the end because although Dino's brother didn't talk, there was this little book-keeper in South America knocking out a paperback goldmine. He just hadn't believed it when Jacey told him. But she knew some people – some guys she saw whom Julian had approached to do the deal for him in New York. Frey showed Jane the book. 'Cost me half the money I've made and I've had a long career. But I own the book, the film, even the fucking T-shirts. The mildest thing in it is good old left-wing Kay Caversham, daughter of Dino, buying up Nestorin stock after that explosion. Everyone else sold their shares as a protest, but sly Kay bought more. Her mother doing the seen thing with one hand and Kay busy being bad with the other. All you can do for now, Jane, is study the role. Be patient. Say nothing.'

The depression hit as Jaimie expected it would. Jane couldn't get away so easily from her son's death. Between one take and another she was different. She felt solid with sadness. She just couldn't believe she'd never see Kit again. And she remembered the afternoon he'd come running to her, the sun shining in his face. Running, smiling, perfect, beautiful. And she had known he'd never be that good again. Perfection being taken away had made her cry. Was there nothing you could hang on to? Everything was transitory, except hate. She'd done her crying then.

The director said, 'Take the day, Jane.'

Catch me doing that, she thought. Take the day and someone takes my scenes. It was just a soap, but it was big. It was melodrama but it was making her rich.

Jaimie found her lying by the bed unable to get into it. She'd taken pills, a medical dose to blot out the pain. He wanted to negotiate her contract when it terminated in '76. He couldn't understand why she wanted it to lapse.

'Maybe I'll do theatre,' she said. 'That's what you've always wanted me to do. I'm going to see about something off Broadway.'

'I can get you a lot of money.' He helped her into the bed. 'It just means sticking in there till spring of '77.'

'Jaimie, being in "Oil" is exactly that. You can't fly. It's like being a dummy in a window with other dummies. We move our arms, our mouths. We're beautifully made up. Costumes are great, but dummies aren't alive.'

He sat with his arm around her on the bed and kept flicking the channels for a movie to watch. She took another Valium.

'Watch those pills,' he said.

'You think it's delayed shock?'

'Of course I do,' he said. 'It may be two days or twenty, but you see a doctor.'

In the end he watched the news. Jaspard was now President of France.

Jane had chosen the flat in Manhattan because that way they both flew in from wherever they were, for the weekends. It was off Central Park West and convenient for the airport. Jane was no homemaker so Jaimie got his assistant in to dress the place up a bit. They didn't bother to cook or entertain and got food sent in from the deli.

The flat was very clean, ultrahygienic because he was a professional man. Modern black and white paintings on ice-white walls. The light was bright, the air fresh at all times. Several ionisers in each room kept it mountain-clear. The sofas were black leather with silver rims. There were a few low glass tables, a glass vase with bronze flowers. Dramatic spotlights brought out the essence of the room. It was, of course, a hotel room.

The ultramodern kitchen contained every gadget but was never used for proper cooking. The bathroom was large with double washbasins, and movie star bulbs around the huge mirror. There were fluffy piles of towels in many sizes and colours, all warm and fresh.

Two more full-length mirrors were ruthlessly lighted. If he had any flaws, Jaimie saw them first. The shower had glass doors. There was an ultraviolet and infrared sunlamp in the ceiling, a sauna, a steam cabinet, a huge bath and a jacuzzi.

He kept his gym equipment and exercise bike in his dressing room, which was surrounded by cupboards filled with clothes. As he had been the only one around Margery allowed to wear black, one rail contained Valentino suits in blue-black, black and white check, black streaked with grey, black overcoats. Then came the navy section: two Burberry raincoats, suits by Balmain, Lanvin, Cardin. Then three-piece suits in all colours except brown, which he loathed.

His blue shirts were made of the finest sea island cotton emphasising the blue of his eyes. Bags, luggage, ties from Fendi in Rome. The country weekend rail covered all climates and cultures. There were plenty of Scotch cashmere jackets and black and grey check jackets, dinner jackets. Nothing in velvet. Nothing obvious that would draw attention. He relied on his good looks, charm and the good cut of a suit. He liked the feel of cool heavy wool and had sweaters in all styles, always single colours. He was a very tactile person, and feeling thick, cool smooth wool actually gave him pleasure. The LA rail and the beach stuff were all white or pale blue. There was a new pile of Aran sweaters which he'd bought while fishing in Scotland.

The exercise weights took up too much space so his rowing machine was kept in the bedroom. The room held a low king-size bed with a cotton duvet in black and white stripes, dimmer lights, two TV's because they watched different channels. He hated clutter and she had to keep all her stuff in the bedroom cupboards, and makeup under the sink in the bathroom. His products were lined neatly above the sink so he could get at them quickly. He wore Vétiver by Yves Saint Laurent. He liked clean lemony non-cloying scents. He had several ranges of male beauty treatments. Part of his business depended on his looking his best.

On Sundays they drove to his house on the coast. That stretch of beach, the Hamptons, was becoming fashionable and he considered selling and making a profit. Jane didn't seem to identify with the house any more than she did with the apartment. The truth was that Jane hardly knew what her lover looked like any more. She was so obsessed with work, with getting up that ladder to the Oscars, that his face had become a blob. It was only when he was away that he came back into focus. They were familiar to the point of overlap. Where did he begin and she end? They didn't even bother with sex now.

Finally he said, 'You have to work at it.'

'Jaimie, I work all the week. Do I have to work at being at home too?'

'You have to put new things in. Recharge it. A rebirth. Don't take me for granted.'

'Do I?' She didn't know.

'You come in, you take off the paint, you slop around for the rest of the weekend waiting to go back on that set.'

The trouble was that Jane had explored him, he was hers. It was like a part. You learned it, you took it for granted. What excited her was the next part. She'd been offered a remake of *The Postman Always Rings Twice*, but it meant going back to LA. Could she face it?

Jaimie found her a doctor and he said she was going through a reactive depression and needed treatment.

'I'll be all right when I've made it,' she said.

The doctor replied, 'Ninety-nine per cent of the people that come through my door have made it.'

So the top of the mountain was no answer. She said she'd find out and let him know. She threw the anti-depressants down the lavatory and for a moment wished she hadn't. The sea would heal her – if she could get to it.

She was quite surprised how ordinary Jaimie Laurenson was to live with. Like the racing driver he'd come from a working-class background. She found those men much more interesting. They'd had to get there, unlike those who were just born there. She liked muscle in people. She just hoped that Jaimie, unlike Del, was not so bored he couldn't get through the next five minutes.

She said, 'I'll try to be more *allegre*. I think in 1976 I might be quite interesting. Wait and see. My secret.'

'You shouldn't have to try.' And he kissed her, a long one on the mouth. The more he was with her, the more he thought about his wife. Comparisons had set in. He'd have gone off with other girls months ago but he felt that was not the answer. It was electric and exciting to begin with, then the new person became too familiar so you moved on to the next electric and exciting stranger. He was told that a lot of married people had that problem – stagnation. Thank God he hadn't actually married Jane Kirkland.

Because Jane was the star of 'Oil' she did most of the promotion. On screen she played a glamorous survivor with guts, dressed very feminine in the big labels – Missoni, Yves Saint Laurent, Jap. Off screen she felt her way towards a new image. A Janice Wainwright clean-cut velvet jacket spotted and dotted with black, and impeccable grey flannel trousers from Yves Saint Laurent. Sometimes she added a white felt or a cloche hat. The shoes always had thick high heels. The outfit made her look as though she meant business. She wanted to be taken seriously. On the street, where she still did her real living, she wore ethnic gear – Cossack boots and capes and swirling cloaks and long skirts with lots of layers. The outfits amused Jaimie, who, waiting by the latest New York 'in' place or the Russian Tea Room, would say, 'Here she comes, dragging her feathers through the gutters.'

At home she wore tracksuits, his white towel robes and curlers.

On one of the chat shows when asked how it felt to be a Caversham she replied swiftly, 'But I'm not. My name's Kirkland.'

'So you didn't use the Cavershams to get where you are?'

'I got where I am by my own efforts.'

Did she regret the dissolving of her marriage to Alex Caversham?

'Oh, that was years ago. You need binoculars for that one. The thing about a dynasty like the Cavershams – no, I'll put it this way. People are misguided. The children of a great person can inherit the name, the money, even the fame – but never the greatness. That original, glorious unique way of taking life and making it immortal is not passed on with the bankroll, unfortunately for them.'

'So who is great, in your opinion?'

Jane couldn't think of anyone. 'Oh, just a minute. Marcello Tallaforos. Now he is a great man.'

Margery read the interview in the *New York Times* and whispered hungrily, 'Now I've got her!'

She rang her New York business people and said 'Find out who owns the company that produce "Oil". Then buy me share majority. Put it in the usual several names. It doesn't matter what it costs. This time it doesn't matter.'

Normally she said, 'Don't spend more than you have to.'

A week later Jane walked on to the set and was fired. She didn't have to wait long to find who was behind it because the following day Kay Caversham took over her role.

. . . Chapter 60 . . .

Frey was loyal to his friends – everyone said that. Maybe it was because he'd been through a bad time himself, but once you were his friend he never let you down. It was unusual in a star, the darling of European directors, one so good-looking with a charisma as big and obvious as a blast of cheap scent. Audiences imagined him gambling, travelling in luxury, making love to the beauties of the film industry, eating in the best restaurants. And he kept it that way. As long as he lived their dreams for them they paid to see him. In fact he stayed in his country house guarded by security men and Doberman dogs.

Those in the film industry were in awe of him. He had a chilling authority. But his friends always knew where to turn. Jacey said, 'I've been on the skids a long time, Robert. I'm nearly thirty-two. My looks have had it. Maybe youth was my real asset. I'm bored with screwing. I've done it all. There's nothing left. In the old days I'd be made a madam and put out to pasture.'

'And you're truthful, quite often entertaining, reliable and I like you. So what do you want to do?'

She didn't know. She'd been so desperate lately. She'd considered taking up religion. There had to be a point to it all. She blamed Kay Caversham for the failure of her dissolute life but she didn't hate her. Jacey didn't hate or want revenge. She just felt bad when at a party the men went with the young girls and she was left for the unlucky or went home alone.

'I've got a very bad reputation,' she said.

'Oh, Jacey. *I've* got a very bad reputation. It doesn't do me any harm. I tell you what I'm going to do for you. I'm going to open a club on the Seine. It will be very chic, just for the "in" crowd. You run it. OK? It's my present to you.'

She felt good again. Someone cared.

'And I want you dressing up and colouring your hair. Get it streaked green. Let's start some trends, be sensational.'

He'd been watching the Cavershams, the ones he could actually get to. Charlotte now was a real mother. The way she held the little girl, played with her, gave her all her time. Her smile was genuine and he found her moving. He'd never had a mother, that he remembered. Every day Charlotte walked with the child in the Bois de Boulogne, and Frey watched her eagerly. She wore lovely womanly wrap-around skirts in soft materials and silk shirts or matching jackets and ankle-length skirts in pale lavender organza flecked with white. Sometimes she arrived in a lovely wild silk dress with an elasticated waist. Its spring-green colour matched his car. Her Titian hair was full and radiant. To him she was the epitome of woman. He realised she didn't dress like her mother or sister. In fact she dressed down. So did the child. She was obviously concerned about the possibility of kidnap. He spotted only one security man, never closer than fifty yards, mostly a hundred. Did he have X-ray eyes? And what kind of weapon was going to protect Charlotte and her child at that distance? What was she doing with a Commie prick like Jaspard?

Frey had never had a religious moment in his life, but this woman and her baby were his Madonna and Child, to be worshipped. For the first time in his life – and he was now forty-three – Frey was running after a woman.

A direct move would be a mistake. He decided the Caver-shams jumped the best when there was a little chaos in the air. He found out through Jacey's political friend that Jaspard's wife wasn't exactly having a good time. She didn't mind about her husband's affair with a Caversham or the child. She did mind that he was such a lousy fuck. Frey loved to go to work on a bored woman. Everyone wanted to meet him. They dis-approved that he was right-wing, disliked his gangster past, there were colourful rumours about his sex life – but whatever he did he couldn't kill the charisma. They saw it on the screen, they wanted to meet it in real life.

It was so easy to meet the President's wife. He almost put the guest list together himself. Wearing a white Cardin suit, he sat away from her and gave all his attention to an Italian starlet. He ignored the President's wife completely but let her have a good view of how he looked in seductive mood. She was put out, especially during coffee when he kept to his group and made no move towards her. Antagonised, she was already thinking of ways to repay him when he suddenly turned and looked her full in the eyes. His eyes smouldered. His smile was like the first spring day. Her bored body changed. He made a direct gesture. She should approach – and she did. She blamed it later on faulty hormones and sexual longing, but there she was in front of him aching for it.

He was masterful, a little cruel, a marvellous erotic lover. He gave it to her from all positions and plenty of it. She got in one night what she'd been missing for fifteen years. His secretary, hidden behind the drapes, took the photographs. Jaspard got the photographs in the morning.

The head of security told him to wait. Frey would make his demands. No one else must know. Just the top security, Jaspard and the participants. And the photographer. Jaspard at first believed Frey would put it in the press. Did he need publicity? OK, he wanted political advantage. Jaspard's sources said that although political, Frey had nothing orga-nised himself. It was incomprehensible to Jaspard that Frey could want his wife.

Frey called. The message was short. 'Give me the keys to Charlotte Caversham's apartment and the photos won't make my holiday album.'

Jaspard said he'd think about it.

'I thought about it,' said Frey. 'She keeps the child. You have no visiting rights. You didn't even marry her.' He hung up.

So Margery Caversham was behind it. Why had she waited so long? Jaspard had always thought Margery was truthful, had courage and dignity. She'd seemed a person of principle. Was he blind, or did that sort of thing no longer exist?

Six weeks later when he found out his mistress was now Frey's mistress he saw he could lose control of the country. There'd be a referendum. 'She knows nothing of importance,' he kept saying to the chief of security. 'I have naturally persuaded her round to my way of thinking. She can give Frey no political information or advantage. The government is not threatened.'

For a while it looked as though Jaspard would have to resign. But the French people liked him. So what he'd had a mistress? Didn't every Frenchman? And why not lose her to Frey? Frey was good-looking, a national hero. It was a love story, not a question of politics.

When he was safe again he told his ministers he was going to crack down on the rich. Margery Caversham, for example, had been given every aid to help her subnormal daughter. Jaspard had made sure that the best doctors in the world were aware of the child's case. He said stop the courtesy. Then he reflected on her suffering and said keep on helping the child. Margery's taxes would rocket instead. Also if one of the Cavershams committed any unlawful act in his country or while passing through they should be apprehended and given the maximum punishment. They'd be used as an example. He was thinking of Alex's drug use.

Also he got Charlotte's phone bugged. He'd have bugged Frey's house too, but the film star's security was too efficient.

The physical act with Rick had changed. It was as though neither of them had their minds on it. They seemed to be listening for something. Finally Rick said, 'Margery, I feel I'm being watched.' He collapsed on top of her unable to go on. She assured him that no one was allowed near the bedroom and the door was locked.

'I know there's no one there, but I feel as though I'm being watched.' And he told her all about the coldness of the corridor. The house was becoming like a tomb. Everything about it harked back to the past, to the glorious time, to Dino.

She too believed in Dino's presence in the bedroom. It made sex difficult for her. She was sure Dino's dying curse had deformed her little girl. An umbrella of darkness was beginning to cover the whole family. Margery sent everyone to Paris for a fun weekend and had the house exorcised. She told the priest about her recurring horror, experiencing her husband's murder.

'Can curses work?'

The priest said, 'Only if the person cursed believes it. It's like voodoo. You send an enemy a black hex on a piece of paper and the information that he'll soon die. And it preys on the victim's mind and he blames everything that happens on this curse. He gets into a low state of mind and anything can befall him. If he hadn't received the note, his misfortunes would have just been part of life.'

'So you have to know?' She was intrigued by that.

'You alone affect your mind, Margery. The thoughts of others, even black ones, can't harm you.'

Then the priest asked why Dino had cursed his family.

'Sicilian blood,' she said quickly. 'You never get away from it, however high you rise. He was struck down in the prime of life. He died in a rage.'

'But surely it was a political killing?'

Margery got up, impatient. 'Oh, does it matter? It was years ago. If I sell the house will the curse follow me to the next one?'

'The curse doesn't exist,' said the priest.

Margery, alone for once, went back to bed. It was quite evident that now she was alone, the room had a lighter, even happy atmosphere. The room wanted her this way, solitary, because it was Dino's room.

She fingered the pearls over and over like worry beads. 'But what should I do, Dino?'

Of course he was there. In her mind she could hear his voice quite clearly. 'Cut the crap, Margery. The guy's a fag hanger-on. Get rid of him.'

When Rick returned from Paris with Frou Frou and Shane and the nanny, Margery said, 'You really must go into politics. You want to influence things. You had a huge public – you still have. You've got the style, Rick. Get in on Jaspard's ticket.'

'I'll try.'

'Not try, do it. Succeed. You could be an incredible voice for the young. There's an idea around that the eighties are not going to be a lot of fun. There's going to be unemployment, recession. The philosopher Erhart talked about it, and he predicts everything. He said even the weather will change.'

So Rick asked how he should start. He'd do anything to get away from the Château.

'Act. Let's see you in a movie. You don't want to sing any more. Be a cult figure.'

He wanted to know what kind of movie. God, if he could just get to South London he'd know what to do. He'd been wearing silk shirts and Italian suits for just too long.

'It's a wild one, but why not do *The Oresteia*.'

He didn't even know what that was until she told him. He thought it was ludicrous, but the audience didn't.

He did it first as a stage production which was then filmed for television in America. Next he did *The Tempest*. He couldn't believe it: he was at home in the heavy stuff. Living in the Château for years had given him a good start.

. . . Chapter 61 . . .

Jaimie spent hours a day fighting with the 'Oil' lawyers over Jane's sudden replacement. There wasn't a lot to be done. The company had been purchased by a major concern which wanted Jane out and Kay in. The 'Oil' lawyers did agree that Jane should be paid the salary which would have been due to her until contract renewal in '76. Jaimie phoned Margery and reminded her of his earlier threat. 'I know revenge is a high priority in your life and you use powerful interference to shape careers and ruin them. I know Rick de Palma's doing well and that's a lot to do with you. But you misfired with "Oil". You'll not get the revenge you're looking for. Kay's too cold.'

And he was right. To add to Margery's chagrin Kay was certainly not loved by the American audience as Jane had been. A month later Margery got in touch with Jaimie and asked, 'What shall I do about Kay?'

'Take her out – you put her in. It's not doing her any good. And the cast are giving her a bad time.'

'She can handle that,' said Margery.

Jaimie wasn't so sure. 'D'you want another breakdown on your hands? I thought you found twenty-nine acting four kind of disconcerting? Now she's over thirty. The public want to see a Caversham in glimpses. They don't want her shoved down their throat in an inappropriate role. And Margery, there's no reason why I owe you anything, but there's a rumour around. You remember your longtime business manager? He's taken to remembering things and writing about them.'

'Oh shit! Where?'

Jaimie didn't know. It was just something he'd heard.

'I miss you,' she said.

'Snap!' And he hung up.

When Jane lost the 'Oil' role she panicked. Her first thought was, don't lose Jaimie. I can't have him walk out now. I'll have to get back what we originally had. It's not just a question of a see-through dress and putting on perfume. What shall I do? He doesn't speak to me about us. But it's not to do with talk. It's maybe chemistry. And has our Bunsen burner gone out! She thought they hadn't screwed for maybe three months. It was longer. She did try to get it back – nothing doing. His penis expressed the relationship – limp.

Depressed but fighting it, she walked along the edge of Central Park from the Metropolitan Museum of Art towards the Plaza Hotel. She decided to keep walking and go right down into SoHo and maybe Chinatown. Go into the Buddhist temple there – it always gave her peace. Then for a Chinese meal. That would take care of the rest of the day. As she passed the chic Pierre Hotel she noticed an excited commotion at the entrance. TV cameras were being hurriedly set up. And then out came Miss Kay Caversham. Jane hung back in the crowd.

Kay was wearing another of the Spanish outfits she was now making famous. This time by Yves Saint Laurent. A tight figure-hugging sheath of velvet lime-green, purple and orange bursting at knee level into a froth of exuberant flounces and ruffles like a flamenco dancer's outfit. Net and lace layers of vivid electric colours, blues, greens, violets, a black mantilla pinned to her hair. It was now fashionable to have pierced ears and Kay had a rare collection of amber, silver, jade and coral earrings brought back by her friends after visiting Afghanistan and Tibet, jewels captured from the Dalai Lama. Today she wore exquisite long jade ones in the shape of temple bells. They almost touched her shoulders.

Jane, wearing a ragged patched pre-punk-style T-shirt with a replica of a David Hockney on the back, well-worn sneakers and flared jeans, hung back in the crowd. It was unlikely that Kay would recognise her, or that she'd speak if she did.

The press wanted to know if Kay was wearing Spanish gear because of her much-flaunted friendship with L'Estrella, the celebrated young bullfighter. She denied that he influenced her wardrobe. She was in fact about to marry Prince William de Hautenbourg – so she said. The press had trouble with that one. How did she say his name exactly?

Jane thought, is there nothing this woman doesn't get? Maybe if you wore Spanish stuff long enough you got lucky.

Jane flew to Paris to talk to Frey and he took her to the nightspot Jacey was running with such success. She told him about how she'd been replaced by Kay.

'It doesn't matter. The more the Empress does, the better you do that film. Let her boil your blood.'

'I don't trust Jacey,' she whispered to Frey.

'Around that kind of money you don't trust anyone,' he said.

They danced together and she could see why the women went mad. He had a definite sexuality that was irresistible. And he looked curiously young. He had a marvellous body and did he work on it. 'I'm going to enjoy filming with you,' he said.

She wanted to ask if he'd got all the money, but she felt shy. He was a much bigger star than her. Compared with him she was still in the chorus line. Once again she thought, you feel more of a failure with stars than with ordinary people.

When the club shut Frey took Jane and Jacey to a brasserie for choucroute. 'Sometimes I crave food from Alsace so I phone them and they stay open until I come.' He went behind the bar and put on some French bal musette music. 'The bal musette. That's where I did my growing up – the working-class dance halls. The chicks paid me to dance with them.'

Jacey wore a leather coat by Beged'or over a dress designed from the original green silk petticoat with a slit to her thigh and a red rose on one shoulder. Her hair, less lustrous because of constant indoor life, was streaked green. Around her ankle she wore a gold chain with a lock. Inside the lock was an engraved message or warning – MINE. It was signed Robert Frey. A lot of work had gone into her face to put moisture in and get rid of the crow's-feet and lines. She looked better in France. America hadn't suited her.

Frey was dressed in Cerutti and looked elegant, like a cat. He no longer needed dark glasses to hide the damage to his eye. It looked nearly normal but the sight had not fully returned.

'How's Jaimie Laurenson these days?' asked Jacey.

Jane said fine. By the end of the meal she was getting on with the woman. There was something receptive about her – you could get close. She was very sexy without making a point of it. During the coffee and liqueurs she was telling Jacey her problems. Frey was occupied flirting with the owner's young daughter.

'It's like the fire's gone out and I can't even get a spark going. I feel stranded. It's like we're too familiar. I see him in the morning. I know everything about him. I see him at night. We're two old pets all comfortable together. Sex seems like an affront on our closeness. What could get it going?'

'Jealousy,' said Jacey.

'But I haven't got anyone.'

'He has.'

Jane was amazed.

'His dead wife. Compete with her.'

'How do you know?'

'Honey, he's one of the best lays around. I know, I've had him – so there you are. A live one, a dead one. Get jealous. Don't be so damned confident. He's not yours. Go and get him.'

Frey said, 'About some things you really can trust Jacey.'

When she got in from the airport Jaimie, in shirtsleeves, was sitting behind his desk looking over contracts, making calls, writing notes, answering phones. A pile of film scripts waited for his approval. Without even looking up he said, 'Kay's out. You're in if you want.'

'No. It'll stop me getting other parts. Isn't that what happens? Stuck in a long-running soap, that's all you're in. You said that.' And she was back talking about her work.

'They are not going to use you for *Postman* but you've been offered something I like. There was a French murderess in the seventeenth century. She used poison – wiped out rather a lot of family and rivals. She liked sex. Then she had a religious conversion before her execution. You should read the script. And they want you to go to Cannes to publicise it and help raise finance.'

'Cannes,' she said, her voice almost ghostly. 'I'll do it.'

'But you haven't read the script yet.'

'Who's producing it?'

'Oddly enough, Jack Fogg, who was executive producer on some of the best cowboy movies. He says he wants to do something different. He calls you "Our Lady of Sorrows". Think about it.'

'Are the Cavershams still there?'

'Where else?' And he signed some more documents. Only then did she remember that she was supposed to give him the works. Jacey had told her the one to ten of instant seduction. But that was Jacey – she, Jane, had difficulty beyond number three.

'I wish you'd put that pen down and come and fuck me.'

He looked up at her, the pen hovered. 'Let me just finish these.'

'Fuck these. I want it now.'

'I can't come to bed now. The phone –'

'Then do it on the desk.' And she lifted her skirt and sat on his lap. Jacey's words, 'He's the best lay around,' stayed in her mind and certainly helped. She valued him again.

He said afterwards, 'We can really get it on. Why don't we do it more? It's always work work. We're obsessed, Jane, and we don't make time for us.'

She made sure they did it again before going to sleep. He lay back across the bed, his feet on the floor and she sat on him and it was a rediscovery, as exciting as a new love. He was glad he hadn't gone off with all the temptations on offer. As she was going to sleep she said, 'It reminds me of an actor, Jay Stone, who didn't do much sex because he put everything into his image and –'

Then she realised who she was talking to.

He was wide awake. 'So you knew Jay?'

'I didn't know him. I was a fan years ago. What happened to him?'

'I don't know. Perhaps he joined the hippy movement. A lot of people disappeared into all that sharing and love.'

'Is that what you really think?'

Jay's description of the girl fitted exactly, he thought: big breasts, lovely high-coloured skin, liked the sea. Jay had fucked her and fucked his career. And she did come from Hastings. How he'd love to know what happened, how she got him at it. The women and men that had tried.

'Did he join the hippy set?' she asked.

'No.'

'So where is he?'

He turned and looked at her almost admiringly. 'We swap. You played a close hand on that one, lady.'

So she told him and he told her. Of course for months after it happened Jaimie had sent investigators to Hastings. They'd watched the mother's boarding house. Jaimie had even stayed there himself once.

'So you see we could have met then. We were obviously meant to.'

'What were you going to do to me?'

'Make sure you kept quiet.'

She asked how.

'Money, threats, whatever it took. But you stayed quiet, didn't you?'

'Does he hold it against me?'

'No,' said Jaimie. 'But we did. He was big money.' He decided not to go on about the business aspects of his lost star. They'd promised to keep business out of their lives and put sex in.

'So where was he?' she asked.

'Bad for a long time. Depressed.'

'And now?'

'A new start. A new face. A new name.'

She didn't dare ask who or where. He was going to be someone who knew her – she was that sort of person. And he wouldn't be that sanguine either. He loved his body and looks. 'You won't let me get into anything dangerous?'

'Jane, he runs a gym in Florida. It's very successful. He produced all those male health books. Guys with beautiful bodies. He initiated that exercise system. He's made a pile. I go and work out with Jay when I'm in Florida.'

She tried to imagine him speeding round on the exercise bikes. 'So he still works out.'

'Not him. He's seventy at least.'

'What?' So when she'd slept with him on that never-to-be-forgotten afternoon he wasn't forty but nearly sixty.

. . . Chapter 62 . . .

Charlotte had her first child with Frey in 1975. It was a boy and he was ecstatic – his first kid, that he knew of. He didn't want to watch her have it. Some things women did better alone. He was proud and as much in love with her as he could be with anyone. Then she started fussing the child, giving it constant attention. He didn't understand that babies took up time. He wanted her for himself.

'Get a nanny. They do all that,' he said.

She refused and they had their first row.

Charlotte was exactly how he imagined a society prima donna to be. She was fairly good at a lot of things, played the piano occasionally, filled flower vases and handled a lot of people at once. She had a nice voice and manner and made him comfortable. It would have stopped there if it wasn't for the love which he so craved. He loved to lie his head in her breasts which, now the silicone had been removed so that she could breastfeed the baby, were not exactly successful. They hung down and were too soft but he wanted their warmth and nourishment. He drank her milk. He lay with his head between her legs. He wanted to be inside her. This girl took all of him and it wasn't sexual.

Charlotte was always inclined to be lazy and too passive, but he didn't realise that. You didn't criticise mothers. She was happy with him because there was no real sexual interference. He did a quick, rather prim job and there she was with his baby. He wanted to be cuddled and soothed and she still wanted Marcello – ached, burned for him. She kept her fantasies to herself.

After Kay's divorce from the Greek, Shane had been

removed from his company and sent to a college. Now he was staying with Frey. He was always on the lookout for a father figure amongst his sisters' men. Shane was now twenty-one and good-looking. He too had pleasant manners, but Frey could see this was a kid who did only what he wanted, when he wanted to. He was selfish, liked going to clubs, being looked at, didn't do too much. But he did need a father, so Frey taught him to shoot and gamble and to fuck well. He gave him too much money.

While driving to Milan to meet an old schoolfriend, Charlotte saw Marcello Tallaforos eating in a simple taverna near the Italian lakes. She'd stopped because her daughter wanted a drink. Marcello was alone. He wore simple dark cord trousers and a polo-neck sweater.

He seemed pleased to see her. He got the owner to make her a lunch of pasta and clam sauce and a soup for the little girl. Frey's baby she fed herself.

'I never see you,' he said. 'It's been too long.'

'I can't come backstage, Marcello, I'm not a groupie. But I do go to all your concerts, at least in Europe: Rome, London, Paris, Geneva, Munich. It's my one joy in life.'

'Oh, you make me feel terrible. I didn't know. We are friends. I would gladly have given you tickets.'

Unlike the rest of the world, he didn't look any different. He was filled with a positive energy and the possibilities of joy. He was well fitted to receive perfection. He was like a stained-glass window through which only the best and highest states could pass. He made ordinary light holy. Marcello enhanced that which was already wondrous. Charlotte watched his hands holding her little girl. Divine hands.

He apologised for not having made the time to be a godfather. But his wife – he shrugged. 'Many problems.'

She told him again how she felt, how her love for him never ceased. She knew that by doing so she'd ruin the friendship he was offering but she'd spent so many lonely nights lost in fantasies. With this man she'd done everything, all that Jacey and Kay and Jaimie Laurenson could think up, and more. 'So you see, Marcello, it isn't the crush of an adolescent girl.'

Marcello felt moved by her story, but what could he do? Her love was not requited. He said, 'Your story is the stuff of music. Opera especially. It is the longings of the soul to find perfection. I think, although I do not know, that such resolution only happens in a higher realm. Human people are trapped with passion and unresolved longings.'

'Trapped?' She didn't like that word. 'But you have a proper –' She disliked the word 'sex' when talking to him – 'a proper lovelife, surely?'

'Charlotte, it all goes into music. I told you before. That's where I touch happiness.'

'So your wife –'

'Is my friend.'

She noticed he still wore a ring. 'But you have a marriage?'

'But of course. But not as you imagine it.' And he put one of his hands on hers. She felt blessed.

'So, Marcello, you are implying you don't have a physical love with anyone.'

'Well, my dear, look at you. You tell me you're feeling love for me, yet I see you have two beautiful children by two different men. Please, I am not criticising. But by the look of the thing you seem well provided for in the sexual sense.'

'I've just told you I love you.' She was near to tears. 'I don't expect you to do anything about it. But love is selfish.'

He asked if he'd ever done anything to give her reason to feel so strongly.

'Just by being you. Do you sleep with your wife? Tell me.' she asked greedily.

'I am not going to leave her, Charlotte. We stay together – that's it.'

'But one of these days, Marcello, you will reach out for your share. You'll want a girl to love you. You're too passionate a man to go without. If you don't choose me I'll die.'

He'd had many avowals and requests from women but usually backstage. So far the country taverna had been a place of peace. He needed solitude as he did indeed need food and music and sex. It was all harmonious for him. No one thing took precedence. The passion belonged in the concert hall.

'I don't think I will take a girl, so you won't die on my account. You have your children and I will see them if you ask me. I want us to be loving friends.' Again he held her hand. Once again she was filled with hope. Then he said, 'Do you remember that other girl with a baby? Your coming in just now reminded me of her. She was your sister, or your brother's wife.'

'Why?' Charlotte felt a sudden chill.

'You know she lost the child. It was something terrible. What happened to her?'

Charlotte shrugged. 'Can you remember her so well?'

'I thought she had something about her. I remember being surprised she wasn't at the Château more often.'

Again Charlotte asked why.

'Because she was so *allegra*. She came into the room and it was as though something lovely had come in.'

'She disappeared,' said Charlotte. People who disappeared seemed to hack out a good life for themselves.

Charlotte found Kay in a beauty shop having her eyelashes dyed and her skin whitened. A pack around her eyes kept the lines away. She'd just had her red hair cut shoulder-length. The roots were black. 'Just streak them. I don't want this red colour again.' She was in a lousy mood and couldn't decide whether to marry the handsome young prince from a good family who was penniless, or the sick old art collector who'd leave her a billion if he didn't live till ninety. A creaking door lasts longest – that's what Mummy had said. After leaving 'Oil' she'd gone to London to lick her wounds in the clothes shops. She now favoured Browns in South Molton Street and liked La Squadra knitting. She'd bought several velvet 'les smoking' – still her favourite outfit, cut like a man's dinner suit but these days with flares. She'd wear high-heeled black suede boots, the severity relieved only by diamond studs down her shirt front and in her ears. She bought a whole season's range of Missoni and a dozen simple black cashmere coats by Jean Muir.

She thought Charlotte's ankle-length skirt and waisted jacket made her look dumpy and said so. 'Like us all, darling, you'll have to go into black. For some reason the Caversham women suit black.'

Charlotte shuddered. 'Robert asked me about Daddy's cursing us. An awful lot of people know about it.'

Kay shrugged. 'Nothing has more clout than a legend.'

'He thinks it comes from the Italians. They know. Talking of which, I saw Marcello.'

Kay wondered why the Caversham women all seemed to

suit, apart from black, never-ending, never to be resolved love affairs that brought only pain. Her mother could never get over Dino, nor she Jacey.

'He didn't say he didn't want to see me', said Charlotte. 'On the other hand I don't like the good friends angle. But he's not having sex with his wife. Why would he tell me that? That's a message.'

Kay was very good about other people's affairs. It was clear that this was one-sided. If someone wanted to sleep with you it had an urgency about it and you definitely arranged to meet. This had not happened with Marcello. Kay said, 'I wouldn't say too much to Mummy about Frey.'

'But it's been in all the papers. She knows I live with him.'

'And I wouldn't say too much to Frey about Mummy. In fact, nothing. Because, little sister, I think Mummy was behind the acid-throwing attack that put him out of business for three years.'

Charlotte decided not to see Mummy at all. Tired of driving she took her children back to Paris by train. She had them – that was reality. Marcello had spent years being out of reach. She was twenty-six. She wasn't getting any younger. The children needed a father.

The next week she married Frey in a simple church service in his village. She wore white. He promised her the best and she'd get it. For openers he gave her another child. She was spoilt, petted and adored. There were two kinds of women in Frey's opinion. The hookers got his action but nothing else. Charlotte, the mother, got him. She was one of the elite, the princes and princesses of society. They all mixed at the top level except Alex, who couldn't go low enough. Frey liked the way Jane Kirkland had slammed into them in the press. He saw, though they couldn't, that she was the natural inheritor of Margery Caversham's mantle. She had all the qualities, except luck. She'd had to claw her way to fame and there was Margery in a Gucci boot stamping on her fingers if she got too high up the ladder.

Yet were Margery's children happy? Kay constantly felt unloved and betrayed by her mother. She'd do anything to get her attention away from the others. Shane was star of the discotheques but not so good in daylight. Charlotte had superstar men but couldn't have the one she wanted and, worse, couldn't forget him. And Alex, with his Japanese wife, lived on the edge of a desert. There wasn't too much future there, just sand and amazing sky patterns. His mind still had to think. It chose the past and he was sad.

Then Jane arrived in Cannes in May '77. Margery said, 'I did everything I knew, and believe me that's a lot. Yet the girl ends up here.'

. . . Chapter 63 . . .

Mr Fogg, the producer of the French poisoner picture, hired the biggest boat and got all the press. Jane sunbathed and with hair streaked gold was stunning. At thirty-two she could still look young. She wore a white suede dress slit at the sides. Fogg wanted her to roller skate for the journalists, but she said that was over – personal reasons. She made a lot of sense talking about the French poisoner, but then she had a lot of hate. Her sudden flashing smile hid her thoughts.

Frey took her to dinner and the press pounced. 'It's OK,' he said, 'because we're ready to start.'

'Do we announce it?'

'Why should we? We just make it. I've got all the money now. You're not political, are you?'

'I expect so. Don't tell me where you got it.'

'A lot of it comes from the Right, a lot of it is hate money. We just make the film. I've got a final fantastic script.' He slipped it to her after dinner. 'Study Margery's movies. Read the books on her. There are seven and she's in every film bio. How long to do your poisoner movie?'

They needed her for six weeks, then two for dubbing. He could have stopped her making that film but he was professional. He liked movies being made. She'd waited for him. He'd wait for her.

She didn't read the books or see the movies, which obviously she had done dozens of times. Instead she went to see the legend herself. After all, she was right there at the top of the hill.

The Greek was calling when she arrived. The Greek and Margery had had so many rows he couldn't remember whether they were speaking or not. But he'd brought a boat into harbour for Shane and some lobsters for Margery. The Greek said, 'I'm over sixty-three. I'm dying, Margery, so I want to be friends with everybody.'

'Oh shit, you fraud. You've been dying of the same hangover for the last ten years.'

'But I can still make it in bed. Twice, sometimes three times.'

'That's luckier than most. What are you complaining about?'

She thought he looked in good shape. His body was always good and he still had his own teeth. His navy and white clothes were impeccable.

'I'm worried about dying because I don't know what its like,' he said.

'Everyone who becomes too rich immediately starts worrying about death. I've seen it so often. Maybe if you're poor you don't mind so much, because you're glad to get out of it. But I don't recommend it, poor.'

What he wanted to ask was if she would be with him when he died. Out of all the women she was the best, the most fabulous. He didn't want to sound pathetic so he left presents for Charlotte's children. 'I don't do it three times a night, Margery.'

'Only in your head.' And she laughed. 'Don't worry, my love. Nor do I.'

He was so frightened to die he had to be honest. It could make him a laughing stock because he might hang on to a hundred. 'Do you worry about it, dying?'

'Never.' And she let out a long breath as though it were her last.

Margery said the girl should be allowed in. The wolf was no longer at the door, it was in the house. Margery in her new fashion discovery, Ralph Lauren, was the epitome of grace and good breeding. Her welcome alone made Jane feel like a shopgirl in a supermarket, a mongrel at Crufts. She took Jane on to the terrace overlooking Cannes.

'How nice of you to call, Jane. I did hear you were at the festival.'

And Jane murmured a few words about the poisoner film.

'You're doing very well. A lead in a Jack Fogg movie. He knows how to make them. He's never had a flop.'

Jane made another murmur belittling the years of struggle and hard work.

Margery's eyes watched her, hostile and dark, and Jane knew she still hated her.

'So really,' said Jane, 'it's good luck.'

'Oh no, you're not lucky.' And Margery gave a sudden laugh. Not wishing her remark to be interpreted correctly she said, 'What I mean is you've worked as you've just been telling me. Luck has nothing to do with it. Surely Alex could see you had potential?'

'I wasn't a star in Alex's way. Anything I've got has come from countless rehearsals and watching others.'

'You came from nothing and clicked. Alex couldn't have forseen that.'

There was a short silence. Carlo the butler brought Madam her fruit juice. He asked if Jane wanted to take something. She didn't. In Margery's company she felt very reduced and very young. That hadn't changed in ten years. Margery was thinking that Alex wouldn't know about someone coming from nothing because he never saw nothing, not in her house.

If you belittle yourself you're killing everything you've ever achieved, thought Jane. She'll belittle you afterwards. You don't have to do it. Then Kit came into her mind as he used to skate along the boardwalk.

'I came up here because I know that you have a terrible problem with your little girl. I know a doctor in London who uses homeopathy. He's done amazing things reversing the mongol effects in children. He works on the genetic structure. I'm not a scientist so I can't explain the process but here is his number and address.' She couldn't give anything to Margery. She put the card on the table between them and her hands were shaking. She cleared her throat again. 'I know another case where the child was really helped. So I thought you should know.'

'Do you know him? This doctor?' Margery picked up the card.

'No, I don't. But Jaimie went to him for exhaustion and depression. And he had a great effect on Jaimie. He is nearly fifty – he's getting old, you know.' Then Jane realised she was talking to someone possibly older than Jaimie. She cleared her throat again.

Margery thought, why the hell didn't Jaimie tell me.

As though reading her mind, Jane said, 'Jaimie would have told you, obviously, but he knows you don't go for unorthodox medicine.'

'I go for what works. Same as him.'

'And through Jaimie's visits I heard about this woman with the subnormal child. I expect you wonder why I'm intruding like this. I guess it's because I feel very sad for your child. Children are special, neutral. And I feel for your suffering. I've been through it all, after all.'

'Oh, look,' said Margery. 'I was sorry to hear about that. And I told Alex to give you our greatest sympathy and anything we could do – well, I told Alex.' It was one of Margery's few lies and she hated telling it. 'I'll look into the doctor. Thank you for coming here.' She rang the bell and Carlo came and took away the intruder.

She's young, thought Jane. Her hands are young. Not a line on her face. Yet she's well into her fifties. Kay's thirty-three.

Margery did not ask her to call again, but before she did leave, she said, 'Jane, a moment. How's Jaimie Laurenson?'

Jane made a positive face. Margery thought, he's not here. Didn't dare show up in Cannes with her. That means he still cares about me. He should marry Kay.

Margery went to the house phone and asked Jennifer to check out the doctor, but she still wasn't buying it. 'She comes up here proffering charity like a door-to-door brush salesman when underneath she's – Buying? Selling?'

Rick's two critically acclaimed performances in serious plays had given him a new lease of life. He was now writing new-wave songs which were taken up by other pop stars in the US and England. They reached the charts and stayed there. His songs were beautifully constructed reflections of the time. Rick had turned punk, at least in his dress style. Although he was well over thirty he didn't look it. In 1976 he cut off his ringlets and in an attempt to brutalise his rather feminine features dyed his hair black and painted Red Indian lines across his face. He went to Vivienne Westwood for his clothes. He found old leather jackets, tore them, stuck safety pins in the tears, put safety pins through his pierced ears, wore heavy chain metal vests. He looked grim.

Margery had been very generous about his long absences from the Château. She'd always attended his theatrical first nights no matter what town or country – with one exception. She would not visit America. The opening nights were always packed with huge crowds at every entrance. They'd come to see, not the spectacle on the stage, but a glimpse of the truly fabulous, one of her kind, Margery Caversham. She liked to sit in the centre stalls, six rows back.

After the first night of *The Tempest* in Frankfurt she did not go backstage. Bad news about Frou Frou caused her to return to the hotel and phone the Château. Rick, thinking she'd left for Cannes, came in, all punk, hair black. It was the first time she'd seen it.

'A mistake!'

He smiled, thinking he hadn't heard correctly.

'Change it back. You look hard.'

'But, Marge, everyone's doing it.'

'Everyone's not thirty-three.' And she made him see feature by feature why it didn't work. So he let his hair return to its original golden Pre-Raphaelite ringlets and turned in contrast to the proper English gentleman style of dressing. His suits were made in Savile Row, not by Tommy Nutter but by Huntsman. His shoes were made for him by Lobb. His old hippy tendencies still broke out in beautiful hand-embroidered waistcoats and braces by Blades. He chose grey flannels and cream linen for summer and plenty of riding gear, although he'd never got on a horse in his life. Lots of Liberty's scarves – always red. And in the Portobello Road market Bill Gibb found some thirties scarves for him which he redesigned. In the evening Rick wore classical suits and swathes of Liberty silk and French chiffon in Missoni colours. His new image was grown up, elegant, with sex appeal, and the fans liked it. He was almost ready to start singing again, but first he had to consult Margery. Was it fair that she had all the responsibility of Frou Frou while he basked in fame?

He arrived unexpectedly for a rare weekend. Jane Kirkland was on her way to make a second visit. She had a gap in her shooting schedule on the poisoner film in Paris. Rick, driving his white Lamborghini, saw her leaving the railway station at Cannes. He almost stopped, then decided his arrival had better be unencumbered by enemies. He had things to discuss and must be at his best.

He was in good shape, in fact optimistic, until he saw Kay. He'd hardly stepped into the hall when she said, 'You really don't draw water here, slick Rick. So in future behave like a guest and telephone and ask me or Jennifer for an appointment to see my mother.'

'Don't waste it on me. You've got another guest arriving.'

Rick's dog rushed down the stairs and leapt up, overjoyed to see him. He patted the dog. 'Where's Marge?'

'Margery,' snapped Kay.

Rick could hear Frou Frou screaming and he started towards the drawing room. With each step a ton of confidence fell off him. There was nothing like life at the Château to kill off a career.

Kay blocked his way. 'You leave my mother to do everything while you swan around Europe. It's your kid too.'

As he tried to get past her, she slammed him one on the face. Instinctively he hit her back. Margery chose that moment to open the door. 'How dare you touch my daughter?'

Kay made a song and dance far surpassing the effect of the slap. Rick saw a disquieting possessiveness in his wife's eyes. Of course he'd laid a hand on Dino's child.

'She hit me first.' He didn't dare call her Marge. He went swiftly up the stairs, his dog nuzzling his hand.

'It comes to something,' said Charlotte, 'when the only one that loves him is his dog. Was he always so boring?'

'He used to be young,' muttered Kay. 'So we didn't notice.'

Frou Frou, left alone, had got the scissors Mummy used to cut flowers. She'd been helping put them in vases. She lifted the scissors to cut air. Then she cut herself.

Jane chose that moment to walk through the open front door. Because she coincided with a crisis no one handled her entrance correctly. In calmer times the instruction would have been 'Throw her out!' Everyone was gathered in the drawing room. The blood was alarming. The head security guy had rushed into Cannes to get the doctor. Jane pushed through the daughters and grabbed the child's arm. She lifted it and said to Margery, 'Lift it above her head. It stops the bleeding. Wrap her in a blanket.'

'I've already done that,' said Margery coldly.

'Another,' said Jane. 'She's cold.'

And she looked into the eight-year-old girl's face. So Margery Caversham had had to live with this.

They were all of them at the Italian restaurant near Grasse. Jane had to be included. Margery wasn't sure what she'd seen. She'd have to increase the goddam security again. Apparently the girl just swanned past the guard, calling herself Mrs Caversham. And the guard knew her face because he went to the movies and was an 'Oil' fan.

For Jane's benefit Margery listed some of the companies she held, her control in the entertainment complex. She could, believe it or not, influence Mr Fogg's career however big he thought he was. Margery was always bigger. Jane knew she was hearing bad news.

'What do you think of punk?' Rick kept trying to change the subject.

'It won't last,' said Margery. 'It's not identifiable with. People need to copy their idols.' She looked at Jane. Nothing to copy there, not now the skates were off. But she had strength. She was like a kind of female Clint Eastwood. Because of the accident she'd not enquired why Jane was once again visiting unasked. Then she described a film actress and made her sound like Jane. Physically, even her speech. 'They all wanted to lay her but she bored them to death.'

'What with?' asked Rick.

'Her good intentions. She was worthy. Kennedy dreaded her. She put him to sleep. With her around who needed a sedative? She asked Dino to come to the première of one of her movies, and he couldn't refuse. You see, when she was ill, she was alone, as movie actresses often are when they need something. Dino had stayed with her, taken care of her. So out of obligation he felt he should attend her opening. He got to the airport but could not get on to the plane. That was how boring she was. So he made a fantastic excuse. He said the thought of her beauty, and all that LA light and sunshine overwhelmed him. He wasn't worthy of such largesse and felt obliged instead to go to some dark and awful place. Her beauty and splendour had inspired him to go to the lowest depths and do some good. Instead of being at the première he'd gone to the insane asylum and sat with an unknown committed patient. And she believed it because it was incredible enough. And then he found out that the actress had hauled in as her latest lover a pretty effective politician. He might find Dino's absence insulting. So Dino damn well had to be seen doing what he'd said he was doing. He spent four hours in the local bin talking with the – well, the opposite of a movie star. And he said it was worth it, every second, because at least he wasn't bored to death.'

Jane shook as though stung, and her face flamed up. The story was a parable about Jaimie and her. Jaimie must have told Margery she was boring. He was bored. And Del Grainger had been bored to death. Jane had allowed that to appear as the mainstay of her Sunday tabloid exposé. Rick had been married to Margery for about nine years. He didn't seem bored with her.

Jane forced herself to speak. 'Did he check up on your husband, this powerful lover? To find out if he was sitting in an asylum?'

Margery laughed darkly. 'The actress wanted to do good where it wasn't wanted. Have you had that experience? A religious person approaches doing good. You don't want it. Why do they force themselves on you? Your eyes glaze over and you don't hear a word. Whereas someone not boring could make the whole thing have a point.'

Rick said, 'Give them money. Then they go away.'

Margery laughed again – not the nicest sound in the world. 'I doubt it. Not the dogooders, the worthy ones.'

'Mummy, you are awful,' laughed Kay. 'You made the whole thing up about the movie actress and Daddy.'

'Did I?' asked Margery innocently. 'Then it needed to be told. What's the difference?'

And then she talked about Alex, cutting Jane out completely. 'Jaimie always liked this place. I'm sure he mentioned it.' Margery knew he hadn't.

For a while no one spoke. Margery was deep in thought, not pleasant, judging by the look on her face. Jane felt her throat constrict. She couldn't eat a thing. There was not one person who could help her. Rick? He wasn't going to rock his boat. It had enough holes already. Nothing had changed in ten years. Just the cast.

On the way back Charlotte said, 'What is this with Margery and Jane Kirkland. It's the second time she's been over.'

'I don't know,' said Kay. 'Watch her.'

When they arrived back at the Château Margery suddenly

became very sweet to Jane. She would never give a bad impression. Feelings of dislike had got the better of her at the dinner table, and she didn't want that getting back to Jaimie Laurenson. She talked about current movies, fashion, the opera. What a marvellous profile Tallaforos had – he never palled. She refused to talk about acting to this nobody, or anything personal or meaningful.

Jane asked if she'd called the doctor in London.

'We had him flown over a couple of times. He's quite helpful.' Margery minimised his work. He had in fact worked a beneficial effect on the child's chromosomes and one result was that Frou Frou was more accessible. Margery, however, did not want to talk about her family. She asked instead about Jaimie Laurenson.

Kay and Charlotte exchanged apprehensive glances. What the hell was happening? Was Margery having some kind of menopause that made her embrace enemies?

And Margery smiled and chatted, all small talk, at the same time thinking, you took my son. You allowed his son to die. And you have the effrontery to come to me, to sit in Dino's house. Extraordinarily bad things will come to you, Jane Kirkland. Horror movies are in their infancy compared with what I wish you.

Aloud she said, 'Well, I look forward to seeing your film. I'm sure it's just wonderful.' And swiftly she took Jane to the door. 'I have to ask you to leave because I have friends coming over. I'm sorry I can't have you driven into town. Of course you're welcome to call a taxi.' She knew she was being irrational. There were five cars parked in the courtyard and the chauffeur was kicking his heels in the driveway smoking a cigarette.

Jane said she'd walk and thanked her for dinner. She'd never seen such total black hatred before. It was there, indisputably, in Margery Caversham's eyes.

And Jane skipped down into Cannes, free because the woman hated her so now she could do the film.

. . . Chapter 64 . . .

Frey had to put the film back again. He was sorry but Jaspard was giving him more hassle than he would have thought possible. The left-wing French President didn't mind his ex-mistress marrying Frey, but her views becoming right-wing was unforgivable. Did he have so little effect on those he cared about? What the hell would happen to the rest of the populace if Frey went to bed with them? He knew the film actor financed his worst rival, extreme right-wing Armand de Croix.

The change of men Charlotte had been able to handle, but the change of politics had confused her. Frey had been so jealous of Jaspard's influence that every time he appeared on television Frey rushed into the room and switched it off. And when he found the literature that Jaspard had sent her and was still sending her, he burnt it in the garden. Jaspard's surveillance had managed to capture that act of sabotage, and he was outraged. He'd get Frey. The actor naturally thought that when a man said 'get' he meant kill. It didn't occur to him that Jaspard was referring to everyday traps like money and tax. Frey didn't dare go up against the French government directly, so for a while he lay low. He didn't even collect his latest film award in person. He had big things to do. He must stay alive.

It didn't do Jaspard any good with his government. Why get so incensed because a Fascist like Frey burnt left-wing political matter? Jaspard was as jumpy as a neurotic woman and it wasn't admirable. It seemed to his ministers that he was still stuck on Charlotte Caversham.

Jaspard said to his wife, 'I send her the books because she has my daughter in her care. It's not her mind I care about but my child's.'

His wife promised him Frey would come to a very bad end. Jaspard doubted it. The man, like an alley cat, had nine lives.

So after her French poisoner movie, Jane was left to kick her heels in New York until Frey felt it opportune to make the film of a lifetime. Sometimes she longed to confide in Jaimie. What would be the long-term consequences? She couldn't see beyond the actual production. That would be challenging enough. The script was dynamite.

She disliked leisure, it made her depressed. So she did classes in Manhattan, went swimming, built up her stamina by exercises created by the onetime Jay Stone. She ran round Central Park, did meditation. She liked talking to people, just anyone in the streets. Then Frey rang. 'We're on.'

Jaimie felt betrayed when he heard the news. He said, 'Didn't you trust me enough for that?'

'Of course not. I know you're on her side. It's me you screw but it's her you live with.' She couldn't tell him any of the details he needed, like where Julian was hiding, where Frey was shooting. Jaimie insisted on reading the script, then said, 'That's not what you'll be shooting. That's not the definitive script. He's played that one close.'

That surprised her. When she admitted the deal had been in the air for over two years he shook her hard. She kicked him and he hit her. She screamed but no neighbours came running. This was New York.

'You're two-faced!' he shouted. They hadn't had so much physical action in weeks.

'Better than boring.'

'What does that mean?'

'You said I'm boring.'

He shook his head.

'Not to me. To the Empress.'

'Oh, Jane, I never discussed you.'

'Am I boring?'

What could he say? She didn't turn him on any more, but that was most probably his fault. 'I don't think I'm good at maintaining long-term relationships,' he said. 'I'm all geared up to deal with crises and murders. I don't like it too quiet. But I certainly did love you, Jane, and I've got a feeling that when I leave I'll realise I still do. But you're no great shakes in the home. You put all your life into your work and you slop around the place in jumpsuits. You don't make an effort for me. And you're no Margery Caversham.'

'For crissakes, Jaimie, you spend all your time doing her deals, her takeovers. I bet you sort out her kids. I know you do. You –'

'Not any more. You see, I'm not like you. I don't have a big thing on the side with a motherfucker like Frey. Not if it's going to terminate my real-life relationship. So I blew Margery out. For you.'

'Well, you can go back and get her again.'

He probably would. He eyed this chick who could look like a million dollars on screen and quite an eyeful in the street in her street-cred gear. But here in the house what did he see? A towelling robe hanging shapelessly around her body. Odd socks. No makeup. A thick pack on the open pores on her nose.

AA tape between her brows to keep lines out. Her hair was sticking up, not punk, just hair conditioner. What was he, a neutered masseur or something? Why should he have to look at all this? Worse, her body didn't respond any more. It didn't go tense and vibrant when he drew near. Their bodies didn't love each other.

'At least Margery keeps the mystery going.' He got up and stacked his work into one pile. 'You don't see her curlers.'

'I have to work, babe.'

'So does she. But she's a star, Jane. That's the difference.'

'You bastard! You love her. You just daren't admit it.'

It was all clear to her now – that's why he never divulged any of Margery's little secrets. He never made her vulnerable. And Margery? She couldn't stop talking about Jaimie.

He moved out so fast it was like one of his everyday trips to the airport. As a final present he starred her in a play in a little theatre off Broadway.

Jane got mixed reviews but the play, by an English writer, ran for six months. At the same time she prepared for the movie. She suggested its title, *Even the Rich Cry*. Frey got the significance of that. She didn't have time to move from the apartment, and now Jaimie was gone she really missed him. He didn't believe in amputation, he wasn't a cruel man, and he telephoned her several times. He promised that Margery had had no part in their breakup. He wasn't going back to work for her either. He had never said Jane was boring. He admitted that sometimes he'd felt less than alive with her but they were both obsessed by their careers. He told Jane that in his experience Margery could pick out the weak spot in a stranger. She could expose an underlying doubt or flaw and use it. So if Margery had given the boredom topic too much play it was because she must have sensed it was Jane's private worry and wanted to make her feel bad.

'Am I boring?'

Jaimie had to think about it. 'Not to me. But you don't know how to keep a relationship going. But then you like the new, a challenge. I'm the same.'

'Am I a dogooder? A boring one?'

He laughed. 'Only if you go running to Margery on pretexts like offering medical help.'

So he must have spoken to Margery about that. How could he pretend he was cut off from the woman?

'If Margery ever causes you trouble call me,' he said.

'I take care of myself.' And she hung up.

Jaimie went down to Florida to get himself some new ideas. He spent time chatting with Jay Stone. Jay gave him a personal massage and watched over his exercise programme. After all, Jaimie had saved his life and his face.

Frey found an old friend of Margery's who'd known her in England. 'Be quick,' he said to Jane. 'He's going to JFK now, on his way back to London. His name's Michael Rosen and he can tell us things.'

Jane arranged to meet Frey at the airport and rushed out to get a taxi.

Michael was in his early sixties, shabby, inconspicuous. He had grizzled grey hair and a kind gentle face. Once he'd been Margery Caversham's lover. They sat in the airport bar and drank coffee whilst he reminisced about her.

'I first saw her sitting in a café in the King's Road Chelsea, just after the war. I thought she was the most exquisite girl I'd ever seen. I went up to her and said, "I'm making a film and I want you to be in it." I was made quite foolish by her beauty and composure. She had a marvellous laugh. To understand Margery you must know her background. She is from the English aristocracy. Her father was an equerry to King George V. The mother was from one of the old families too – a dominating woman, and looking back I know the mother lived through Margery. Margery could have been the star of the London social set. But she disliked all that sort of thing. In fact she worked for the Labour party. She always did the opposite of what you'd expect. She was rebellious, trying to get away from her background, I suppose. Really she was trying to get away from her mother, but she never did. Years later she said, "I got away from my family as fast as I could." I said, "Margery. Get away? You're still in it." She broke away from people geographically but she had to replace those very dominating people with others. For her first lover she chose a GI, who was also black. She could have had anybody. There were princes, dukes, millionaires after her. The GI made her pregnant. In some ways Margery was naive. She was twenty-one but a virgin. It was during the war. She knew about sex, of course: she'd gone to one of those public schools, and you can't go there and not know about sex. Her mother was sifting through the men finding rich eligible ones and Margery wouldn't have anything to do with any of them and went to bed with the GI. When she became pregnant she was terrified and had a horrifying abortion on the GI's floor. I remember her saying the floor was filthy. They covered it with newspaper. The abortion was done by his friend with a knitting needle as the bombs were dropping.'

Frey shuddered and said he couldn't hear all that.

'She was four, maybe five month's pregnant. She got blood poisoning and nearly died. She was in hospital a long time. When she came out she was depressed. That's about the time I met her. Now I realise there was something dead in her face. She'd had a lonely childhood: nannies, governesses, the mother. Her father died when she was nineteen. I think film work was a way out. I'd seen her first in a wartime movie. She was a featured extra. My God, she was incredible. After her first proper English film she was acclaimed a star overnight. Then the Italian director Della Prima took over. He really made her. Signed her with Deluxe studios. He turned her into an enchantress, which I'm not sure was what she wanted then. She did later, of course, because she'd met Dino. And now I come to what I said earlier about how she could never break with her mother. They lived in Chelsea and Margery had a flat at the top of the house. To all appearances it was self-contained. I used to go upstairs with her but I was never allowed to stay the night, because her mother would not go to bed if there was anyone up there with Margery. I would sometimes leave at five or six in the morning, which was completely mad. And going down the stairs past her mother's room I would hear the woman moving about in the silence as she heard our footsteps. She was listening to make sure I was going. Margery would insist on creeping and whispering but it was a game because the minute I'd gone she'd have to go into her mother's room and account to her before going to sleep. It was a terrible relationship but she didn't care.'

'Didn't care?' said Frey.

'It was Margery's attitude really which was terrible. The way she'd give in to her mother. Men would have to leave. Ostensibly I was the only one but I'm sure there were others.

We were supposed to be making a film but Della Prima arrived in her life and snatched her away from me.'

'What do you mean, account to her mother?' asked Frey.

'She would have to confess to her mother all she'd done sexually upstairs. But she did not care. When I asked her about this she'd say almost gaily, "Oh, well, it doesn't matter." So I'd say, "You make out she mustn't know I'm with you and we do all that creeping and whispering and yet you tell her everything. It's a game, Margery." Of course her mother enjoyed by proxy her daughter's sex life. It was from Margery that the mother first knew of a blow job. And the old woman would creep up and listen to us like a conspirator in sin. It was a terrible house. There was never a feeling of nighttime there. She was always up.'

'What was the mother like?' Frey looked at his watch. Not much time.

'Awake all night. I didn't see her until almost the end. We kept the film idea away from her. Margery said it wouldn't go down well – another little game. The mother knew all about that. So I didn't see her. I crept in, I crept out. I could feel her atmosphere all over the house. I couldn't bear it. Especially when it started getting late. I imagined those skeletal hands and thin clinging body but she was fat and enormous like a huge pear with popping eyes. She was a tremendous snob and compulsive eater. And then while filming in Rome, Margery met Dino. She had this amazing, what shall I say, gaiety? In spite of everything she had that. And he wanted her. And he was the opposite of everything her mother would have wished for her. He was a businessman from the slums. He was small, dark, Sicilian. He too, was a controller, but her life as a film star he did not control. Della Prima saw him off there. So Margery went home to Chelsea and fed her mother little titbits of love with a Sicilian. And worse, she said she couldn't live without it. Margery was lascivious, and if she couldn't keep him any other way she'd marry him. It was a wonderful revenge on the mother. Instead of a lord it was a Sicilian hardboy. The mother died very suddenly. The doctor said it was overeating, but it was the thought of losing her lifeline to a slum boy. Margery said she didn't really care, her mother had kept her in a cage. And Dino said the mother was a monster. She hadn't taken care of this exquisite girl but had allowed her to run loose to feed her own obscene fantasies. He was furious about the abortion. The doctors said her insides were a mess and she couldn't have children. The first thing Dino did was get her attended to. Then he took her away for some good food and air. He gave her love. She had children all right.'

'Did she fear losing him?' said Frey.

'Of course not.'

'Isn't she afraid of anything?' said Jane.

'Of course. These beautiful women fear age. That's the enemy.'

And he was called to the plane.

Frey said, 'He left a lot out. I'm disappointed. But why did I think a shabby man would be more honest than anyone else?'

And Jane said, 'I can't play her.'

'I told you not to go near her. What the hell were you doing? Pretending to help her. How they sneered over that! Of course you feel inferior. Make up your own picture of her and play that.'

'She's got a coldness and power. A wildness. She's like the north wind. She's not a person but a force.'

Frey got Jane's mind off superlatives and back to every day. 'She fucked you. You fuck her. You hate her, remember? Never mind the winds.'

. . . Chapter 65 . . .

Rick said he wouldn't stay another night in the Château. Why didn't they move, just he, Marge and Frou Frou, to their house in the Swiss Alps.

Margery told him to go back to his world. There was no need for him to retire. Like lovers they'd meet from time to time. And that's what they were. When she was alone she knew she was still married to Dino. He liked her to be alone. She sensed his presence and approval. In whispers she spoke to him. Her recollection of their love took care of her sexual needs. She'd stay beautiful for him and pass into his world as ravishing as when he'd first entered hers in Rome.

Rick said, 'I can't take the hostility.'

'Oh, the girls are always jealous of something.'

'In this bedroom. Let's go to the mountains. I'll be political. How's that? I'll be mayor of the local village.'

'God!' said Margery. How the small-time depressed her. 'Get yourself back at Wembley Arena then go to Jaspard. He needs stars. The other side's got Frey.'

But Rick wanted Margery. Being with her was a thousand volts of ecstasy. What audience could give him that?

Margery sensed quite correctly that she was at the crossroads. Of course she'd been cursed. As Dino was powerful in life so he was in death. But how could she fight back? He was dead. She couldn't bear to leave the Château but she wasn't sure she could handle losing Rick. She said, 'I'll compromise. I'll stay here while you do your concerts. Then we'll meet.'

'On one condition, Marge. It's got to be New York. Because it's alive. I need that buzz. I've been shut away too long. So have you. Get over your prejudice about America and let's live. There's nowhere like it.'

She said, 'You get to Wembley, Rick.'

She had no confidence in his plans for a comeback. He was too old to be a pop star. Who else around her was successful? Certainly not Kay, who was now desperate because she hadn't had a child and it was getting late. She wouldn't, however, have liked to go through a pregnancy, the birth process and definitely not the conception. She couldn't go forward or backward. Prince William and the art collector were still hanging around. She was more involved with her body and face and being photographed. She wanted, needed, the cover of every magazine worldwide. She dreaded getting old. She thought she should marry a plastic surgeon then he could spot any flaw before she did and do something about it. Margery had discovered Ralph Lauren in New York before anyone had heard of him and now Kay took him up and went in for the quintessential English country house look, riding jodhpurs, boots, silk shirts, suede waistcoats, cashmere jackets, long ankle-length riding skirts which split to reveal the high polished black leather riding boots. Her only adornment was a small gold brooch in the shape of a riding crop that she wore pinned at her neck. She bought several items of jewellery from Van Cleef and Arpels but still found it vulgar to do real shopping in LA. Her shoes were by Maud Frizon, Kurt Geiger or Gucci, lingerie by Janet Reger. Kay was offered fantastic sums of money just to wear a new design or gown but she only put on what she approved. Putting on clothes was her real life.

Margery's last hope was the youngest, Shane, good-looking, tantalising, impish. How she liked him – not the deep love she'd felt for Alex but enough to be hopeful for. He'd shown her some writing he'd been doing. She said, 'Shane, I'm going to start believing in you. You know what that means? You've got to be the best.'

And she sent the writings off to a publishing house in Paris. Shane was Margery's last hope.

Jane was into the last week of the play and working long hours on preparation for *Even the Rich Cry*. Frey coached her and he was good. She was surprised he didn't let her see Charlotte but he liked to keep family away from business. Jane was now thirty-three, independent, famous, but her heart was empty, full to bursting with emptiness. Apparently a lot of the female stars had empty beds. There weren't any men, just plenty of hangers-on. Did fame and fortune put men off?

Frey said, 'A lot of guys are weak these days and they don't like the threat of being dominated by a powerful woman. Also you're in a high-stress job. That's a put-off for Mr Right. Make do with a toyboy. They've got energy and stars in their eyes. If you go looking for the big stuff you'll find nothing,' said the Frenchman. 'Real love is a meant thing. It will come along without you digging about for it.'

When the play ended the producer hosted a small party for the cast at the Plaza Hotel near the park. As Jane was going through the side entrance, Marcello Tallaforos was coming out. He noticed her, was about to pass by. She told him her name.

'Of course I know you. You are Jane.' He wore a grey suede jacket and a black roll-neck sweater, as always. His cashmere trousers were an example of precision. His elegance was simple and unchallenged.

'So you remember me? I'm surprised.' She laughed.

'Of course I remember you.'

'It's ten years ago. At least.'

He was looking into her eyes and she forgot what she was about to say.

'I was very sorry about your loss, Jane. I hope you received my letter of sympathy.'

They stood together, not sure of the next move or if there was one. He said, 'I have to go now for a rehearsal. I am giving some concerts at the Met.' She'd seen the posters.

'I am surprised you remember me, Maestro.'

'Of course, why should I not?' He gave a smile – not a flash of charm across his face but a real one from him to her. He gripped her hand firmly. 'I know you will do very well. Believe me.' He didn't want to let go – she could see that. 'I wish I had more time.' And with that he was gone.

She sat on a spindly golden chair in the lobby. How shaken up she felt. One smile from him and she was ready to take on the world.

Margery brought Shane to New York to help furnish her superb penthouse opposite the Plaza Hotel which she'd not personally used since Dino's death. The children and their friends stayed there occasionally, but otherwise it was unoccupied. Rick had not been a success at Wembley and needed cheering up. She'd overcome her prejudice about America to help him. Wembley had been her idea. Because stardom would never die in her it didn't mean it wouldn't in others. Rick was over, washed up – 100,000 kids said so.

She spent days with Shane choosing furniture and collecting antiques. She even managed to acquire a bowl from the T'ang dynasty. Of all the figures in history, the one she understood best was the Empress Wu. How she'd have loved to play her.

When Dino was alive the penthouse had pale blue wall-to-wall carpets, flowers everywhere, big drapes, swags over curtains, deep comfortable sofas, massive armchairs, a happy atmosphere. There were hundreds of books, family photographs, small tables crammed with silver-framed photos of the kids' first smiles and Dino shaking hands with Khrushchev. There was a chess set laid out to teach Alex, who could never learn, and a piano for Kay, two Renoirs, a Degas, and in Margery's bedroom Cezanne's view of the Provence hills in which their Château was situated. The rooms off the kitchen were small and had housed the maids, Jennifer, two nannies and Dino's secretary.

Later when Charlotte was in residence she occasionally let in a 'client' dosser so the maids moved the art treasures. Now

Margery had everything stripped out and the rooms were bare shells. She wanted to get rid of the feeling of family. She was also getting rid of the lingering presence of Dino. When she'd finished she felt she'd scraped off her very skin. The designer exposed the pipes and bricks. Rick said he wanted to see pipes snaking through walls. OK, he'd have it. She'd give him the bare bones of the building. Everything was monochrome – black, white, grey.

In the living room a waterfall slipped musically over glamorous rocks and gleaming moss. She arranged a mass of plants around its small pond. The terrace was turned into a Japanese garden, beautifully lit. The old comfortable sofas were replaced by Japanese futons. The Renoirs and the Cézanne were sent back to France, and a dozen Hockneys took their place. Rick needed amazing light-effects – they cheered him up. He liked water and glass and plants and she got Mo Cohen's Oscar-winning set designer to arrange Rick's room. He felt Mr de Palma would like yellow silk screens against dark green bay trees. 'OK,' said Margery and took another upper.

She felt lower than the lowest futon. She put sticky tape between her eyebrows to keep away the frown lines which would surely appear in battalions now she was so unhappy. Under the sticky tape she applied thick anti-ageing cream and some gauze. She dressed exclusively in Calvin Klein: a plain simple white silk blouse with beautifully cut wide grey flannel trousers. She took refuge in the simplicity and plainness of their lines. Her hair was often worn up in a chignon with a fringe, which made her look haunted and remote. Her sombre eyes saw beyond what she was looking at. Age increased her sensuality and inner strength. Even those who didn't recognise her said, 'That person really has something.'

Shane hung around and watched the workmen. Like Charlotte he wasn't overendowed with drive. The French publisher had accepted Shane's book but all the boy said was, 'God!'

Did the exclamation indicate pleasure? Margery booked a table at Orsons for dinner. Dino had always liked it.

'Margery, was Dino Mafia?' Shane asked.

'Oh, come on!' she replied. 'Where did you get that foul slander?'

'From Kay,' he said.

She thought things couldn't get worse, then the private phone rang and Nanny said Frou Frou was impossible. When Margery wasn't there the girl cried, became violent, wouldn't eat. The list was endless. It all meant one thing: Margery must return to Cannes.

Shane said, 'You should put her in a home. It's not fair to you or us. I can't take it, nor can Kay – she's not one of us.'

Margery had never heard him so outspoken about anything.

She went to the panoramic window and pointed. 'Look, you can see the Staten Island ferry.'

Shane said, 'Marcello's conducting in town. That means Charlotte will be over. For sure.'

Margery looked down the thirty floors to the strip of street, and she saw Jane Kirkland. There she was outside the apartment.

'Is there nowhere that girl doesn't get?'

Shane knew immediately who 'that girl' was. 'Don't be silly, Mom. You can't see anything down there. They're just insects.'

'And she's one of them!'

Shane leaned over the balcony. Desperately Margery pulled him back. 'Don't!' She was sweating and shaking. She'd remembered the Modigliani picture. 'You could fall. Don't go near that balcony.' And she backed off and poured herself a large drink, then another.

Shane said, 'You don't wear your pearls any more, Mom.'

She said, 'You'll do the promotion for the book. All right? The television, the press.'

'Oh, I can't, Mom.'

And she started to scream at him so he left. He thought she'd said, 'You're my only chance now.'

Shane ran into Jane Kirkland leaving the pharmacy at the top of the road, so his mother might have been right. He remembered her because of her photographs in the film mags and 'Oil'. She remembered him because he looked like Alex. They were pleased to see each other. It was quite incongruous, two enemies getting on so well. She sensed he was lonely and said she'd show him New York.

She was wearing clothes by Kenzo, the Japanese designer

who first started in Paris in the mid-seventies. She wasn't entirely sure they were right for her. Her usual street clothes were heavy-knit sweaters and gypsy skirts, ragged and colourful, and Red Indian moccasins. If she wanted to dress up these days she chose long culottes split up the front and designer T-shirts and transparent sandals.

Shane wore cords and a denim jacket and didn't look as though clothes bothered him. He wasn't outrageous the way Alex had been and he didn't belong on the streets.

'It's like being in *Romeo and Juliet*, you and me going down the street,' he said.

She thought he was beautiful, sinuous and, like his brother, old beyond his years. He had the same wise eyes.

'The Greek told me I'm an old soul,' he said.

She took him to the theatre, where they were wrapping her play. 'You must feel kind of down,' he said.

'I've felt a lot more down, believe me.'

He liked her attitude. She wasn't moaning like his sisters or getting him to do things. He felt easy with her. After she'd showed him the theatre, which had become her home, he told her about his book. 'I'm scared and so are they, the family. Can they take it if I'm a success? But worse, can they take a failure?'

'So what do you want to do?'

'Run.' Then he remembered his mother, sad and alone in the apartment. 'Margery thought she saw you in the street. I said thirty floors down?'

Jane said she'd been walking around dazed after meeting Tallaforos in the Plaza. So Margery was just up the street and might have seen her.

'Is the move to New York for good?' she asked the boy.

'It's for Rick. Rick's a very modern type of guy. You have to keep up with the times. So I guess she'll stay.'

Before they parted he said, 'I'm really sorry, Jane, that you've been humiliated by my family. If I'd been older I'd have put a stop to it.'

She just smiled. She was the one who put a stop to it.

Charlotte always wore white to Marcello's concerts. She'd sit in the stalls, six rows back, and throw him flowers so he'd notice her. It was her one act of emotional exuberance. The white symbolised purity. Whatever her life, she was spiritually intact for him. The dramatic white gowns were a complete contrast from her everyday style. She was constantly occupied with her three children and usually wore practical sweaters and jeans.

She leaned over her mother, who was splayed out on a futon. At first Margery thought she was some kind of bird of paradise, then Charlotte lifted her arms, and the white material fanned out like wings and Margery was sure. 'Am I dead?' she murmured.

Charlotte tried to get the pill bottle away from her mother.

'If you're an angel, then take me to Dino.'

Shane said, 'Let her stick with the pills. Then she'll pass out and I can get her to bed. She's been like this for hours.'

'What, out of it because she saw Jane Kirkland in the street?' Charlotte could see her evening was in jeopardy. She'd come all this way on Concorde to watch Marcello conduct *Il Trovatore*. 'It's much more likely to be the news from London. Rick wasn't exactly Elvis. He did all right, but all right isn't what Mummy likes. She hates failure.'

Margery laughed mercilessly. 'Failure is in the eye of the beholder. Your father said it was a human invention to put people down.' Her voice was slurred.

'Mummy, I think you should eat something and get it together!' Charlotte, for all her practice on the street, could not deal with a 'client' in her own family.

'I want to stay with Dino.' And Margery closed her eyes.

Charlotte opened her mother's clenched hand to get the pill bottle. Just a gold cross and chain.

'It's Daddy's,' said Shane. 'It's the first cross she ever saw him wear. At a train station.'

'Rome.' Margery smiled, and suddenly looked very young. 'September 29th, 2.20 from Naples.'

'How many has she taken?' Charlotte took her mother's pulse. Her vital signs were good. Good enough to let Charlotte out for the concert. 'Has she been drinking too?' she asked.

Shane had never seen his mother helpless before. She'd never even been ill. Did this happen when people got old?

'Now get her some soup, Shane. Send out for it if there's nothing here. I've got to go. Why aren't there any staff?'

'Mom told them to go. She didn't want them to see her

feeling blue about Dad. You know how she is.' Then he said he was going to a party so Charlotte would have to deal with it. 'Jack Nicholson's going to be there. He's my favourite actor.' He started towards the door.

Charlotte called him back. 'And you're her favourite child. Get on with it.' She let go of her mother and left for the concert. Shane waited until Margery passed out, then he left too. He thought his mother was right: New York didn't suit her.

Frey, wanting to keep out of his wife's way, stayed with Jane. As they were crossing over to the deli she saw a poster of Marcello Tallaforos, and his face was such that she stayed on the kerb, forgetting everything.

'Impossible to get seats.' Frey waited beside her.

'Do you know him?'

'I've said hello. He's the hottest conductor in the world. His fee for one concert is higher than what I pay my actors for an entire movie.'

'Is he still married?'

'Very much so.' He now understood her interest and went on, 'Straight up and down. Never a touch of scandal. The same woman, thirty years. You won't get action there. Out of your league. Please let's eat.' And he pushed her towards the deli. In France he couldn't walk down a road without being recognised. In New York his films didn't mean a thing.

As she ate lentil soup Jane reflected that Tallaforos was a true star, charismatic yet modest, humane, respected. How she wanted to see him. But how could she ever attract such a man? Nothing in her character could possibly match the perfection of the Maestro. But his approval of her at that brief meeting had given her confidence: she was ready for anything.

Frey outlined the shooting schedule. He wasn't keen on London, nor was she. She never wanted to go back and be reminded of Kit. They decided to film the scenes set in the King's Road Chelsea, late forties, in Amsterdam. Jane would have the best makeup, lighting and cameraman in the world. The rest was up to her.

Frey flung on his leather jacket. 'Let's go and have some fun.'

He took her to a party in the Village, crammed with stars,

and Shane was amongst the crowd talking to Jack Nicholson. Shane saw her and smiled. The smile said he was on her side. It was almost a replica of her meeting with Alex. Shane spent the rest of the evening with her because he needed someone strong in his life. He was much more terrified about his book publication than even he realised.

'If it succeeds people will say it's because of the family. If it fails they'll say I couldn't make it even with the family.'

Jane offered to read it. Gratefully he took her back to get his only copy from the penthouse.

She hesitated about going in.

'Of course you can come in. You're my guest, and I'm the young prince.' He sounded cynical.

Margery was awake and bewildered. Where the fuck was Cannes? Why was she alone?

'You're in New York, Mom,' Shane told her.

Then she saw Jane Kirkland and knew she must be in hell. Between the temptress and her son there was an undeniable intimacy in spite of the age difference.

Margery rose up out of the chaos of depression and pills and said, 'D'you know what I wish you? Obscurity. But you won't get that. You've got hell coming. You break lives as easily as a starlet breaks contracts. You cling to my family like a leech.' And then she really started. Shane could do nothing about the savage attack on the English girl. In the end he pulled her out of the apartment and they ran down the staff stairs.

Jane was shaking. She noticed he was strong and lithe, and agile as Alex had been. He held her hand. It felt so familiar. 'Don't mind her – she's a pillhead. She dreads getting old. Let me take you home.'

She didn't want him to meet Frey, so she suggested they go to a bar. She was disturbed by the intimacy between them. This boy who had always been so favoured, so remote. He was nice – no, he was nicely calculating. Maybe he didn't even realise it.

'Let's go up to Lucia's house on the coast,' he said.

'Let's run away,' she said.

'Let's get married.' And his eyes heated up, just as Alex's had. It was the 'Let's' game all over again.

They took the first train out of Grand Central and the next morning booked into a hotel room near Niagara Falls. Jane's opportunity for revenge had come about in an unexpected way. She could seduce him now and run off with him as she had with Alex. What better punishment for Margery? Shane was not as innocent as he appeared. He was more than willing to run off with her. A lot of his interest in Jane Kirkland was fired by the fact that his sisters and mother hated her. He was disappointed in his mother because she had feet of clay after all, especially when the pills were around. When the little girl got too much she took an upper. When Rick blew Wembley she took a downer. In New York she'd needed quite a lot of uppers and downers. She said it was because of Dino. She couldn't bear the city because it reminded her of a time she'd been loved – more, she'd been blessed.

And Shane's sisters competed with him. He didn't get a look in. At twenty-four he was still Little Brother. And Rick was weak. Shane had so many points to score of his own.

They decided not to sleep together. They'd got into bed quite prepared for a sexual dalliance, but before the preliminary moves were over they realised the runaway was not about that sort of gratification. They were conspirators, not lovers.

At midday they were ready for revenge. Jane phoned Margery. Her voice taunting she said, 'History repeats itself. Here's your son.'

. . . Chapter 66 . . .

Jaimie was standing at Frey's bar in Paris. Jacey was having a quiet drink on one side and Kay was noisy on the other. A lot of drinking had gone on. Kay said she could marry anyone. He'd asked why.

'Because everyone's for sale. You've got your price.'

'I wouldn't marry you,' said Jaimie. 'Whatever the price. Stay single, Kay. Do everyone a favour.'

'You don't just get me, you get Mummy and the estate, Dino's estate, and probably a cut of Rick's investments because he can't even wipe his nose these days.'

'What does this one' – Jacey pointed at Jaimie – 'Get for a simple bang?'

'It wouldn't be simple.' Jaimie ordered more drinks. 'I'd stay with Jacey. At least you know her.'

'Know? What's *know* got to do with it?' shouted Kay.

'Men are just things in trousers. You don't know me. You didn't even know who you ran off with the last time. You said he was a left-wing hero: he was a killer from the Right. Stay with what you know.'

'And what are you, Mr Laurenson?' asked Jacey.

'A bounty hunter. At least, I was when I worked for Margery.'

Jacey looked feminine and calm. She wore a silver beaded coat over a plain black classic dress, a beaded helmet and long earrings. Kay had peeped at her ankle chain and seen Frey's message, MINE. She shuddered.

Kay wore Gianfranco Ferre. The shawl alone cost £900. She wore designer labels night and day – Ralph Lauren, Calvin Klein, Georgio Armani, Ungaro – and now she was hearing about Bill Blass. Kay changed her clothes on average five times a day. Her black hair with its red streaks hung in coils around her face. Her skin was chalk white.

Kay was still involved with Jacey, as her insults and orders showed. Jacey had changed beyond comprehension. Kay considered this a crime, an insult to those who'd loved her. There'd never been anyone else; but it wasn't enough to build a life on and, Kay, now in her mid-thirties, was getting desperate. Marriage was the obvious solution – but to whom? She'd hoped he was standing beside her at the bar, but he was single-minded and selfish.

She turned to him helplessly. 'Jaimie, what am I?'

He said, 'Washed up.'

They took the Amtrack to and fro across North America for the next two days. Shane had never really known his brother Alex. He'd seen him maybe a dozen times in all, and he wanted to know what he was like. Shane didn't have much to tell. His life had been a round of parties, girls, a search for a father. They looked out at passing America and ate well and slept a little and, for the first time in a long while, they both felt free. They got on so well that it seemed an imposition even to mention marriage. The didn't discuss the future. Without putting it into words, they both knew that the future in this instance would be made for them. Jane barely thought of Margery, she was having such a good time. When she'd heard down the phone the woman's appalled cry she'd said, yes, this was revenge. It was unsatisfactory when what she really needed was love. As the train sped north, it took her further and further away from Marcello. Some people had the talent of making you feel special and then you were hooked for life. Unfortunately it worked on others as well. For the enchanter it meant nothing. He was often amazed to find this following made idiotic by love. How had it happened? He was innocent.

Shane laughed. 'Well, Marcello has to have someone. He may be Mr Fix but he's still human.'

'What's he like?' She wanted to hear something crude, ordinary, low, so she could stop loving him.

'Very Italian and knows how to play it. When he's in Italy or New York he's one of them. He doesn't forget where he came from. He doesn't judge them. My father, you see, did.'

'Were they friends, Marcello and your father?'

'Oh yes. He respected my father. Especially because he – well, he got out of Naples. The other brothers, my uncles, didn't. I mean, they're in New York, but they're still in Naples, mentally speaking. But Marcello knows Dino's brothers and eats with them. And he also eats with royalty. He goes into a room and is so sure of himself that nothing can faze him. High, low, he stays what he is.'

'Do you see Dino's brothers?'

Shane shook his head, then changed the subject. 'I think Marcello liked you because I heard Kay tell Mom that Charlotte was rattled he'd remembered you. And he'd only seen you once.'

And then she asked the big one. 'Does your sister go with him?'

He'd forgotten Jane was not part of the family. Of course she was an outsider, always had been – but so was he, now. He replied honestly, 'She'd like to, but she never has. That's why she wears a lot of white when she sees him. Like a virgin. If she changes her colour I'll let you know.' He laughed.

Jaimie, wearing a sheepskin coat, met them as they pulled into Cleveland, Ohio. 'Welcome to my part of the world,' he said as he helped Jane down on to the platform and wrapped his coat around her. She was never suitably dressed for the cold. Perhaps she didn't feel it. Shane followed. It was all very polite. Jaimie had simply followed the credit card trail: it had all been too easy for him to feel any pride about the capture. He bought them breakfast at a diner he liked near the station.

'What's it gonna cost?' He looked at both of them. 'Come on. You're stuck. You're not Bonnie and Clyde and you're not in love. You can't ride trains for ever. And it takes more than you two dumbos to finish off Margery.'

'Can't you find us one day later?' asked Shane. 'I'm just thinking about my sister Kay's face. It'll cost a lot.'

Jaimie didn't take out his cheque book. He knew it wasn't that kind of 'lot'.

'Get Mom to cancel the book. I want my own life. I actually like the Greek and I resent the fact I'm not allowed to stay with him.'

Jaimie said, 'The book might do well.'

'I'll settle for not knowing.' Shane turned to Jane. 'What about you?' Because he really liked her he said, 'Ask for a real lot. You deserve it. Take my mother to the cleaners.'

She laughed and Jaimie remembered why he'd loved her. And she thought, I used to sleep with this man. Now we're apart I can see him clearly again.

'I've already had mine.' She recalled Margery's cry. As she walked on to the street she thought she was having hallucinations. Had she never left New York? There was Tallaforos on a poster opposite. He'd come to Cleveland for a three-day appearance.

Jaimie took the young prince back to New York and she stayed in Cleveland. Not much light got through the hotel blinds: all requirements like lights, change of air, heat were mechanically produced. Jane longed for a rich sensual atmosphere – Italy or Spain. The hotel room seemed to hold on to everything – Jaimie's cigarette smoke, her perfume, depression. Jane reached a new low in that atmosphere. The only way up out of it was to hold the exquisite hand of Marcello Tallaforos. But what if he rejected her? Could she feel worse?

The conductor answered the phone immediately. Once again being in contact with him was a cool yet powerful experience like sitting near a splendid waterfall. He was intrigued that she was in Cleveland, and arranged to meet her in the hotel coffee shop. He was there before her, drinking black coffee and smoking brown cigarettes. He wore a gold signet ring. His dark hair, well-streaked with grey, was long and elegant. Dark glasses hid his eyes. He had a well-defined, sensual mouth. He was all Jane had ever wanted in a man so he had to be out of reach. She accepted that and sat down. He'd risen to register her arrival into his life.

People looked at him because he had an inner elegance, not because they recognised him. His aristocratic nose was less noticeable than on the posters. When he started speaking about his life he took off his glasses and she was surprised how young his eyes were. His voice was low and well-modulated and he still had an Italian accent.

She started to speak and his eyes glowed. She stopped speaking. She was going to tell him about the ride around North America with Shane. Their eyes met, and the experience was more sexual than any caress. The moment had taken him by surprise. His face hot, he looked away and took a quivering breath. Next he'd have an erection. He looked at something else until he'd got himself under control. But when he looked at her again he saw her breasts. They were very evident and naked under the silk top. He hadn't had sexual release for weeks. He couldn't take his eyes off her breasts, and then when he looked up at her face it was as though they were in bed together. She licked her lips, involuntarily. His erection was now total, almost painful. All he had to do was look away and think about the concert he was going to conduct, his wife. He'd even use his past, the early days of his marriage, to block this girl.

She could feel his heat but couldn't read his thoughts. She was telling him about the film Frey was making against Margery – she was that out of control.

'I would not do it, Jane. You can't go up against these people. We can't. They are too rich. Wait until she's dead.' He took a deep breath. His body was back in his control.

'I might be dead first.' And she told him some of the moves Margery had made against her.

'But that's just show business.' He made it seem quite insignificant, and for the first time since her childhood she was at peace. She no longer wanted to be someone – just his.

He said he had to give a performance and got the bill. He

liked being with her, and it both surprised and alarmed him. He helped her into her coat, picked up her bag, all his movements gentle and caring. When he held open the door for her it was more like an embrace. They walked through the winter sunlight to the concert hall. She felt strangely light and unrecognisable as though she'd changed from a mollusc into a moth. Then he was holding her hand. Almost fainting with happiness she tried to think of a plan for the future. She said, 'I'd love to go to the sea with you.'

She remembered she'd made that offer to Alex in 1967. Now when she said it she had time to do it justice. There was no ambition any more.

He said, 'I would like that.'

'Let's do it now.'

'Be patient. You see, my life is going to be different too. I won't forget you.'

He called a cab. 'Do you need some money?' His voice was caring, like his movements. She shook her head. There was still a chance he'd get in with her and come to the hotel. She knew it was a possibility that he'd considered. He opened the cab door and kissed her gently, then he was gone.

Back in the empty hotel room she couldn't rest. He was so caring, something she hadn't experienced for a long time – and now he was gone. She burst into tears.

Before she left for New York she phoned to see if he had time to see her. He didn't.

Jane said recklessly, 'I just want to say I really like you.'

'I really like you too, but my wife is very ill. Light a candle for us, please. I cannot have a relationship with another woman, Jane. Not all the time she lives. Be patient.'

Jane took the first train to New York. She knew she was on the brink of something delirious, marvellous, beyond even her imagination.

Frey said, 'Of course you'll do the movie. We're ready to go in Amsterdam.'

She didn't want to leave America, in case Tallaforos might call her. Frey was irritated. 'Maybe he did get a buzz off you in a coffee shop, but he meets thirty exciting people a week. He's not short of excitement.'

'I know his wife is dying. I should comfort him. He's desperate.'

'He showed no signs of desperation when I saw him. I went backstage with Charlotte. A lot of people think they're dying – look at the Greek. Did he say he wanted you to stay?'

'He didn't say he didn't.'

'Trust me, Jane, we're on the same side. I don't know how you feel personally because I have never been in love like that. But you and me, we weren't born with silver spoons in our mouths – more like old tin cans. We've had to fight to get even. Please don't throw it away now. It's so beautiful. The same woman fucked us both, and now she's going to make us into stars as big as she was and she doesn't even know it. Isn't that beautiful?'

She hesitated.

Frey said, 'If it's meant, you'll get him. Right now you've got the film. It's your next life move.'

'Frey, I want to be happy. I know I can be with him. What if she dies and I'm in Europe? And someone else gets him?' Her eyes were suddenly large and childish.

'If you stay in New York you'll get impatient, then pushy, and he'll blow you out. I'm sure he's tough, for all his magnetism. All the women fantasise about him. You're worth more than frigging fantasies. Get to work.'

In May 1980 Jane arrived in Cannes in triumph. *Even the Rich Cry* was the big success of the year, and she and Frey got every award going. Now she was a fame person herself, yet she felt no different. She waited for success to make some golden chemical change inside her. The only change was that she could never again be anonymous. And she felt the stirring of competition. She was thirty-five, said she was thirty. There were girls of twenty and they wanted what she had.

It was during the final gala day that she heard the news about Marcello's wife. She'd died recently of a stroke. Jane hired a car and went straight to his home in Northern Italy. Even Frey approved of that move. 'Be quick or there'll be fifty comforting chicks ahead of you.'

Marcello was in mourning and at first his son Alessandro would not let Jane into the house.

'I've come to pay my respects,' she said. She was wearing a sea-green sheer Bill Blass costume – she hadn't had time to change into black.

Alessandro went into the darkened house to get his father. Jane thought, I've been patient, it's not a quality I come in contact with often. I've been chaste – that's rare too. I have a right to claim him.

He looked thinner and much older. She realised with a shock that he was in his sixties. He'd not changed over the years then suddenly he'd slipped into his actual age. He did not want her in the house and suggested they sit in the sun. He offered her food and drink. He was always courteous to others however dreadful he felt himself.

'I promised to take you to the sea,' she said. 'You must come. It's a very healing thing to do.'

'Oh, Jane, I am old.'

'I'm not.'

Jane didn't sleep with him until the period of mourning for his wife was over. His only regret was that he wasn't a younger man to do justice to what he felt. Because of his wife's last illness he'd been absent from the concert hall for over a year. He wanted to get back as soon as possible and he'd take the first offer. She knew before he even told her it would be London. She said she'd go with him.

'But what about your career?'

'I just want to be with you.'

He was sixty-two but he had more going for him than any man she'd known.

. . . Chapter 67 . . .

Margery massaged her face and body with La Prairie products. Her beauty routine took longer these days. She was still on hormone replacement therapy and the ravages of time had been surgically lifted from her face. She was fifty-nine and some days looked seventy.

Rick was waiting in their house in the Swiss Alps with Frou Frou, who was now thirteen. Rick, perhaps because he had energy and didn't do pills or drink, had taken control. He'd designed a new life for them. Margery wouldn't live in New York although he needed the dynamics of Manhattan. She now hated social life. Her ideal was a life of solitude. But Rick would not return to the mausoleum in Cannes. Margery could take it or leave it. He and Frou Frou stayed in Switzerland. Because of her daughter's condition she would never have any friends, certainly no lover. Rick had decided to devote the rest of his life to looking after her.

The Château was too silent. The children had all gone, the servants had all gone. There was no one left except the Greek, who waited downstairs to complain about age. 'I'm an old man, Margery, waiting for death. I can't please a woman any more. I might as well be dead.'

Margery sat on the bed and looked at the Modigliani painting. There was something to be said for drugging yourself to death in your twenties. She took two painkillers and assorted anti-depressants.

The girl had won. Cannes would never be the same now her sort had arrived.

Margery could have stopped her. She could have made a film of her own life story and killed off Frey's movie. But Margery had vowed at Dino's grave that she'd never act again. And there'd be a remake of *Even the Rich Cry*, and in the nineties yet another. Jane Kirkland had got nowhere near the truth. The film was clever but it wasn't about Margery.

People always lived through me, even dead ones. And Margery thought of her mother, and all the stars and fans who'd tried to copy her. She lay back on the bed and looked over to the river, the woods, the vines, all hers. She was far better where she was, alone, with the memory of Dino. All the glorious hours they'd shared. She knew that Dino did not want her to leave the Château. She'd spent the spring making him an Italian garden on the south slope and she was sure he'd directed her in the choice of flowers and shrubs.

She could leave Frou Frou to Rick – he had a mother's heart – but could she herself stay in solitude? What happened when she got old? And dependent? Then strangers would take care of her.

'But I don't want to die alone,' she said. Could Dino hear her? His presence seemed to be there to suit him, not her needs. 'I can't die alone.'

She sat up decisively and started brushing her hair. A new perm had given it body. More and more it needed false pieces. Today it needed everything. It was like a tired orange weed.

It took an effort to get under the needle point shower. She remembered how Dino never took baths. He'd never seen a bathroom until he stayed with her in Rome. She laughed bitterly. 'And now we have six bathrooms.' He did get in the shower, though – he considered it a luxury.

Unaccountably she put on her shocking-pink Schiaparelli suit, which still fitted her. Schiaparelli had invented the colour and Margery had worn the suit in her first Italian film. She guessed her exit from the Château would be best in the costume that had made her famous. She wore the Schiaparelli shoes, specially made twists of gold and pink leather with heels like icecream cones. At the last minute she pulled her hair back, right off her face, giving her minimum trouble and her bone structure maximum advantage. As she left the room she said, 'I'm sorry,' instead of goodbye. She went down the stairs a little unsteadily.

The Greek said, 'I can't fuck. I might as well be dead.'

'I know the feeling.' And Margery laughed. The laugh hadn't changed: it was still full of gaiety.

'But you're twelve years younger than me,' said the Greek.

'Perhaps.'

'Why leave? It's your house.'

'Cowardice.'

'Margery don't go. I'll stay with you. You're still the most fantastic one of all.' And he took her hands.

'I won't fight any more,' she said. 'Let the others get on with it. Come with me if you want. You know you're welcome.'

Her bags were still by the door to be packed or unpacked.

'Who will buy this house?' he asked.

'Who cares? It's all changed now. Cannes is nothing. They even let that girl in. If that's a star give me obscurity.'

And she called to the chauffeur, 'Switzerland. Let's go.'

As she got into the silver Rolls the chauffeur heard her say, 'Dino, don't leave me.'

Marcello's wife had attended every rehearsal, and Jane did too. His life was hers. On their first night together he'd said, 'You're not a star. You were just looking for love.'

She didn't have to try with Marcello. She respected him and that was something marvellous and new. They both remembered their first meeting at the Château. It was then that the seed had been sown. It had grown unseen inside both of them. They had to find each other – there was no choice. He said, 'When you came into the room in your white suit I had never seen you before. But it was like meeting an old friend.'

Jane didn't go near the King's Road or Earls Court. She couldn't bear to be reminded of Kit. *Even the Rich Cry* was still playing in the West End, and she was surprised to see a newspaper article by a person called Jack Goddard, who ran a drama school in North London. He said he'd taught the Caversham children and Jane Kirkland. Their success was due to him. She reckoned that put his prices up some.

The phone never stopped and she began to understand Margery Caversham's life. Endorsements, parties, money, interviews, movie roles. Then Jack Goddard rang and she took that call. His inventions had obviously become part of reality. 'Jane, could you come to the school and give a talk? I've told all the students all about you,' he said.

'I hope not.' She laughed. She wouldn't see him but she wanted to know what he'd been doing.

'I dropped out. It's so easy to drop out. Everything just closes over you as though you'd never been. What happened to Alex?'

'The same.'

The next person she heard about was Lucien. An opera singer told her that while she was in London she must go to the fabulous 'in' clairvoyant. He lived not far from the Savoy, and the way the woman described him it could only be Lucien. 'All the movie people go to him. Everyone. He's amazing. Sees everything. He's got these green eyes.'

Would he remember her; this man who saw everything? Jane had a score to settle and she called to see him. She was disappointed because the eyes were too green to be Lucien's. Then she realised they were too green because they were false. He wore bright emerald contact lenses so unnatural that people assumed his eyes must be another colour altogether. She remembered he'd had eyes of an original, rather innocent green. The lenses were a disguise, like his hair, which had been straightened, and his skin, which was bleached. The voice he couldn't change. He pretended not to know her.

She said, 'I didn't come here for a reading.'

'Why not?'

'Because now I'm happy. I very much wanted you to know.'

'Why?'

'Because you fucked up a lot for me. Tell Alex I'm happy.'

The look he gave her as she walked out was disconcerting. Was she happy?

How glad she was to leave London and go back to Italy. These days she wore Armani designs, restrained, ladylike. She chose the understated subtle clothes designed for the woman who didn't have to try any more, and delicate high-heeled Maud Frizon shoes. Marcello still wore decisive beautifully cut suits in dark grey or black and a long camel coat. His shoes were all hand-made from Ferragamo. He always wore his trademark, the traditional polo-neck sweater.

She was surprised he wore nothing in bed. He never had. She'd arrived at the bedside in a super-glamorous La Perla nightdress but he'd made her take it off. For his recitals she wore silk shirts and suede skirts, Ralph Lauren, Calvin Klein. The days of street cred were over.

Their wedding in 1983 was musical and light-hearted, and it took place by the sea in Italy. She wore a calf-length simple eau-de-nil dress and a short veil held by orange blossom. Before they walked across the field to the church, Marcello sprinkled a handful of rose petals over her head. The day was full of laughter, its happiness shared by everyone. The music world came to pay respects to the Maestro. There were no stars that day, just people.

Then she heard, through Guido Cortese, that the Château was coming up for sale in Cannes.

'Get it!' She sounded ruthless and, Guido thought, not unlike Margery.

They moved in in late spring '84. Decorators had transformed the house. Jane wanted every vestige of Margery's taste to be destroyed. She filled the rooms with every movie star's face except Margery's. To please Marcello she tried to make everything Italian. She brought in carved chests with Florentine paintings and had the ground floor designed in the style of an old palazzo. She bought a huge outsize Italian bed with a canopy. The seventeenth-century candelabra were from Sienese churches. Then she started hanging tapestries and religious paintings. She insisted they sleep in Margery's bedroom. After all, it was the best.

Marcello kept saying he didn't like it. He would shiver dramatically as he entered the room. Lying in her huge bed, Jane looked out at the river, the trees, the vines. She was now lady of the Château, owner of all she beheld. She'd truly made it. She would dearly have liked to see Margery's face and Kay's when they heard about the sale.

One evening when she thought she was alone she went racing through the corridors screaming, 'Mine! Mine! All mine!' And she just wished she had her skates so she could go faster, wilder.

Marcello appeared from the music room and watched her. At first he'd thought something was wrong. She saw him and was immediately ashamed.

'Come here, Jane.' He turned off the Beethoven recording. Firmly he took her hand and led her into the garden. He motioned her to sit down. He remained standing.

'Do you like this house?'

'Of course.'

'I don't. It's full of atmospheres that are not mine. And you, well, you're dancing on top of a grave.'

She apologised again for behaving so boisterously in the corridor.

'It does not bring out the best in you, Jane. And what are you doing? All these religious tapestries and lamps. And the incense. It's like a tomb.'

She was stunned. 'You don't like it?'

'I hate it.' His words sounded stark.

'But I did it for you.'

'It's always so chilly.'

'Marcello, I've tried to make it warm for you. We've got new heating –'

'It's not a home, it's a catacomb. And I will not have it photographed for these magazines. You're doing this to hurt Margery. The Italian tomb.'

He looked at her. She didn't answer. Her attempt at grandeur had obviously not worked.

'Do you know this house is supposed to be cursed?'

'Do you believe it?' she asked him.

'I? I don't believe in curses. And if it does exist, this hatred from beyond the grave, I am sure human love can shut it out.' He sounded quite contemptuous. 'But Margery believed Dino visited her in the bedroom.'

Jane was surprised. 'She didn't seem that kind of woman.'

'That's why they all left – because Dino cursed them and they said they felt his presence here. Frey's film was not at all correct. Dino's death? All Frey got on the screen was a fairytale for a gangster. Do you know anything about the Mafia?'

She said she did.

'Dino was born into a Mafia family in Naples. Seven children, very poor. He'd certainly done his share of minor crimes before he got to the US. He began as a lawyer then a businessman, and the Mafia certainly used him in New York. But Dino grew wiser and he hated their brutality and criminal connections. He dreaded their power. I think he became a public figure in order to fight against them. But behind his back Margery had let them help her win one of the four Oscars. I am sure she had no idea what she was getting in to. She liked competition but only if she could win, and that year she had strong competition. The Mafia approached her saying they were on her side – Sicilian solidarity. Her children were half-Sicilian. The Mafia said they wanted her to win. She was married to a Sicilian, after all. And they got her Oscar number three. Afterwards she was ashamed and said nothing, certainly not to Dino. The Mafia, of course, expected Dino to repay them for their help. How could he? He knew nothing about it. Margery was very strong-willed about her career. I think to be such a star you have to have great arrogance. She believed she'd repaid them sufficiently by winning. A lovely smile, a laugh full of gaiety. Let them go back to Little Italy. And Dino often took second or even third place. I'm quite sure in his prayers at night he said, "God let her fail. Let her just be here for me." But she wanted success and would do anything to keep it. When he became Vice-President he said he'd indict the Mafia and name names. He was now a marked man. I'm sure they got to Margery and tried to persuade her to change his mind. She certainly told Dino then what she'd done to get the Oscar. But he wouldn't back down. He had a strong moral side

– in fact he was incorruptible. He arranged for maximum security but he didn't expect death to come from the direction it did. He cursed the blood of his family when he died, in the gutter. Sicilian blood, bad blood. Because his own brother killed him. Who else could have got that close?'

'How do you know all this, Marcello?'

'How? I know his brother.'

'Dino must have hated her,' said Jane. 'To be shot down for vanity – that's why he cursed her children and their children to come.'

'I think he still loved her. He understood, I'm sure, that a lot of things are done through ignorance and vanity.'

How often she'd thought of that lately, now she was happy. How ignorant she'd been when she'd conceived Kit. He was born out of her vanity. No thought had been given to the moment of his conception. It was just a blind selfish sexual act. Alex may have called it love.

Some nights Marcello slept downstairs. He had health problems he didn't want Jane to know about. She went to bed early and got up at six. They'd always go for a walk together at sunrise. They'd been in the Château nearly a year when she was awakened by the bedroom door opening. The man was too muscular for Marcello. She didn't put on the light. How she wished she had a gun by the bed.

'Hi, babe, remember me?'

She knew the voice.

'Sure you do. Jay Stone. Remember Hastings?'

She sat up, appalled.

He put on a light, a low one by the window

'Don't scream.' He came towards her. 'Just don't scream.' The face was average, just a stranger in her bedroom. Then he ripped off the face. It was some kind of mask that came off without trouble, revealing a horrific blackened disfigured hard thing with eyes and a gleam of teeth. And she knew Jaimie had been wrong. Of course she'd never be safe. Of course the man would never forgive her. Why had she believed Jaimie? Her instincts always told her what to fear. How could a Florida gym compare with stardom?

'Let's burn up some now. It's your show this time. Let's see what happens to your face.' And he tugged her by the legs so she slid down the silken bed.

When he heard her screams Marcello came running breathless into the room.

'For God's sake help me. Get him,' she cried.

Marcello turned on the lights. 'But Jane, there's no one here.'

Jaimie Laurenson confirmed that Jay Stone had been dead for years. She'd had a nightmare. Marcello said there was no light on by the window. The room had been dark and empty.

Jane said, 'Sell the Château, Jaimie.'

And she moved with Marcello to a village near his birthplace in Southern Italy. She lived inconspicuously and happily, a part of the village, the countryside. She was so much herself now she was in his life. And she felt valued. He told her that no one else could have replaced his first wife and she, Jane, had been worth waiting for. She learned Italian and he taught her about music, and more, how to please a man. At last she'd accepted that owning the Château was a revenge, and how could revenge compare with being in the company of such a great man? To be loved by him was, to her, a never-ending miracle. No Oscar could give her that joy.

Also available from Mandarin Paperbacks

JOAN JULIET BUCK

The Daughter of the Swan

Florence's world is elegant and claustrophobic. Her life in Paris, with her antique-dealer father, is regularly punctuated with trips to London, to her charismatic Aunt Julia. But when Julia is killed, Florence is devastated. In her anguish, she consults a clairvoyant, who tells her she is soon to encounter the love of her life. And then she meets Felix.

Flawlessly handsome yet enigmatic, Felix may indeed be Florence's romantic destiny. But their relationship is only the beginning of a dark, haunting, sensual journey, a fairy-tale spell of transcendent longing and frozen passion from which Florence must ultimately be released.

'Totally absorbing on all levels. Buck is a fantastic story-teller.' *Gail Godwin*

'Erotic, painful, funny and brilliantly constructed.'
Edmund White

'A wonderful voice for a wonderful story.'
Shirley Conran

'A moody, atmospheric tale of a woman's obsessive love – it's good and it gets better.'
New York Times

'A genuinely sophisticated entertainment.'
Vogue

AXEL AYLWEN

The Falcon of Siam

Siam – the Venice of the East, land of lavish courts and dazzling wealth, a worldly Eden where innocent sensuality and exquisite power games have long co-existed in ancient harmony.

Into this fabulous world of intrigue strides Constantine Phaulkon, trader, smuggler, cavalier and rogue. Ostensibly in the employ of the British East India Company, Phaulkon is in reality pursuing his own sense of purpose – his destined link with Siam and its all-powerful monarch, King Narai.

Here is a tale of seventeenth-century piracy and war, of history and opportunity, and of one man's love for two women. Set against a background of unrivalled beauty and fascination, *The Falcon of Siam* is a novel in the grand tradition and one which will entrance its many readers.

CONSTANCE HEAVEN

Larksghyll

Larksghyll, an ancestral home. The scene of a turbulent love affair. And a dramatic story of passion and tragedy set amidst the lowering Victorian splendour of the Yorkshire Moors, from one of our best-loved romantic novelists.

Delphine Craven's gambler father is deported to Botany Bay for a murder he did not commit. Alone and destitute, she must flee the scandal, and takes a position as teacher in a remote Yorkshire moorland village.

From the very start Castlebridge seems a disaster. Della faces the hostility of the local people, classroom battles and the disdain of the local mill-owner's spoilt and beautiful wife. Worse, Della's growing attraction to the mill-owner himself, Tom Clifford, confuses and disturbs her. Only pride and the fierce resolve to clear her father's name make her stay.

Then unrest at the mill, stirred by a brutal trouble-maker, flares into violence. Tom and Della are brought together in the turmoil but, before they may acknowledge their love, Della must confront the dark family secret lying hidden in the Clifford family home of Larksghyll. . . .